On The Back Foot
To Hell

by Roland Ladley

The fifth of the Sam Green novels

First edition prepared for publication with CreateSpace August 2019

ISBN 9781082204784

For Dad, who we loved and lost this year.

For greed all nature is too little.

Lucius Annaeus Senecca

Prologue

16° 51' 30.5" N, 88° 59' 15.6" W, Belizean Jungle, Central America

Eighteen months previously

Everything was wet. Colour Sergeant Bill Pagan's saturated fingertips were ribbed as if he'd spent too long in the bath. His jungle hat clung to his scalp like a swimming cap, its rim bowing downwards with the water that had soaked into the material. A small cascade of drips ran off the rear of the hat's wide rim and onto his combat shirt - which was damp with sweat and leaking rain that had found its way around and through the overhead camouflaged poncho. His olive-green roll mat was also sodden.

He and Mike had done their best when they'd set up the OP eight days ago. But the jungle floor was already soaking from the incessant afternoon rain. Rain which you could set your watch by. And whilst the warming sun had worked hard to dry out their position the following morning, it had started raining just as things had begun to get comfortable.

Rain.

At least it was warm rain.

The problem wasn't that the water got into everything. That their equipment, even though it was double-wrapped in decent sealed bags, still suffered from the 100 percent humidity. That the optics of their cameras and binoculars needed constant wiping - and their HF radio, a back up to the mil-spec Iridium satphone, was only working intermittently.

They and their kit were designed to cope.

It was seeing the target through a wall of water that was, when the rain was at its heaviest, next to hopeless. Mornings were good. Lunchtimes OK. Late afternoons, pretty poor.

The OP was set high on a rising, jungled hill above a curving dirt road looking over a junction that led away from their position to a heavily-guarded ranch complex. He and Mike had spent three hours choosing the right location before clearing the floor of rainforest debris and cutting a discreet observation window in the canopy. They'd been through the procedure countless times before - in training in Kenya and for real in nearly every country in Central America. The Special Reconnaissance Regiment's (SRR) ability to insert observation and recce teams into small, hard-to-get places made them as much sought after as their more brutish cousins, the SAS. The SRR had an invaluable talent. They could observe almost any location for any length of time. Bill had survived a week bent double in a slim hedgerow with a long-lensed camera in Sheffield. Another four and a half weeks on a bare-arsed, sun-drenched mountain top in Syria. And, more recently and most bizarrely, two weeks in a bathroom of an unfinished hotel on the Albanian coast.

They always operated as a team of four, with a larger extraction and support section set some distance from the OP - in this case 12 klicks back at a derelict Mayan temple. There was no hard and fast rule on how the OPs operated, although common sense dictated a 'two-on, two-off' regime. For this op he and Mike, with George and Darren, were working eight hours on, eight off. George and Darren were 25 metres behind them in a small jungle clearing. The choice of the OP's location was all about the views onto the target; the selection of admin and rest area was secondary. Hopefully George and Darren were sleeping. Dusk was an hour and a half away and the pair would start the fifth overnight stint at 7.30 pm. The next changeover wasn't until 3.30 am tomorrow. Everyone needed their sleep.

The routine was monotonous, but workable. According to the Regimental brief the target was graded A5: *utmost national importance; drugs*. They knew no more than that. For Bill a mission with an A5 designation was the easiest to remain focused for. His younger brother, a promising musician, had passed away at a festival 18 months ago. The culprit: ketamine. Sure, his brother needn't have taken the drugs. And there was some intelligence that pointed to a bad batch being distributed among the revellers. But ketamine had killed him. And every time an operation came along designated '5', he never had a problem staying the course. Anything he could do, any photo - any sliver of intelligence - that would help bring the sods to justice went some small way to honouring the memory of his little brother.

It was all worth it.

The saturated conditions.

The insects - a buzz in his left ear a constant reminder he was never too far from some biting fly laying its larvae under his skin.

A painful nip from a predatory spider.

Not washing, nor cleaning his teeth - one of the worst aspects of undercover operations - and peeing in a bottle and pooing in a bag. All necessary to prevent non-jungle smells alerting the enemy.

The tiredness. The discomfort. The sores from wet cloth rubbing against saturated skin.

And missing home.

And Christmas away.

It was all worth it.

Just a couple of decent photographs of Xavier Turner, aka Individual A, with some unknown actor. Or Individual A's workforce, recorded here at the ranch and then matched with equivalent images from Bravo Three-Two's OP at the plantation. Money on a table on the covered balcony. A long-barrelled weapon. A pistol. A rocket-propelled grenade. Anything.

Everything.

With their specially adapted Leica S DSLR camera and a long telephoto lens, so far the four of them had dispatched 723 photographs to the Special Force's secure cloud. They also had four and a half hours of HD video. In their pair Mike took the photos. He was better at it. Bill's job was to acquire the target. For this, in daylight, he had five grand's worth of Zeiss stabilised binos. At night he had a two-tube, mil-spec scope which operated as an image intensifier and a thermal imager. He also had a laser rangefinder, which they'd only used once to establish exact distances to eight points - from the track junction, up to the ranch and around the grounds. Lasers were fabulous at telling you how far away things were. They were also good at letting the enemy know you were lighting them up. If Bill were Individual A, he'd have spent £75 on Amazon and bought a suite of laser detectors. The OP would have been rumbled within an hour if the ranch could had been bothered.

Bill reached for a semi-dry microfibre cloth and wiped the lenses of his binos. He peered through. It was as good as it was going to get.

A drop of water had somehow found its way down the bridge of his nose and was now ready to launch itself from its tip. He pushed his bottom lip forward and blew hard. The drip spat into the air and was quickly enveloped in the curtain of rain beyond the front edge of the OP.

He looked.

And listened.

The problem with the rain was it obscured noise as well as vision. At the moment it wasn't quite like having Phil Collins and his drum kit besides them in the OP. But if the last week was anything to go by at some point in the next hour the rain would be so heavy any thought of hearing passing traffic before it reached the track junction would be lost.

But ...

... hang on.

'Mike.' A whisper.

'Yep. Got it. A car/small truck coming from the left.'

Bill tensed. He looked over the top of his binos, struggling to pick out much through the rain-pixelated image.

There it is.

A white Toyota Landcruiser. But not white. Mostly brown from the mud from the track; like a pint of frothy beer. It slowed at the turn. Uncertain. And then pulled off the main track into the one that ran up to the ranch. After 20 metres it was stopped by the large, red-brick arch housing a double metal gate.

Just forward of the gate was a video intercom. The driver's window lowered and an elbow appeared; it was immediately soaked. Bill then had a stabilised, times-sixty view of the rear of some of the driver's torso, his left arm and a partial view of the left side of his face.

White. Sunglasses. Panama. Beige cotton jacket, morphing to brown where it was damp.

How Grahame Greene.

But wetter.

The OP's Leica was in constant click mode. Bill didn't say anything to Mick. Mick liked silence when he was working.

The brim of the Panama was out of the window for no more than fifteen seconds. Then the automatic gates opened, the driver's window closed and the Landcruiser headed off towards the ranch.

Bill checked for a number plate on the rear door. It was a muddy smudge, but readable. He memorised it through the constant stream of rain - although he knew Mick would have an image.

They lost the Toyota here and there as it wound its way between a combination of palms and other non-indigenous trees. A minute later it was at the entrance to the ranch. Individual A and a couple of his henchmen were already waiting for the visitor under the protection of the ranch's canopy. The man in the Panama got out of the Landcruiser; Mick was now sure he was travelling alone. Carrying nothing but a brown suitcase he quickly, but casually, made his way around the bonnet of the vehicle. As he approached the canopy he extended a hand to Individual A, who met his offer with an outstretched arm.

The Leica clicked.

And clicked.

There was a short exchange. Pointing at the sky, Individual A appeared to make some quip about the rain, immediately after which there were smiles. And then the entourage went into the villa.

The clicking stopped.

And the heavens opened all of its doors.

When it rained this heavily Bill knew he could shout at Mick and someone a couple of metres away wouldn't hear him.

'Who the hell was that?' He half-shouted at Mick.

'No idea. But I should have some decent images. Give me a couple of minutes.'

Mick pushed back with his hands and, on his stomach, retreated deeper into the OP where he could check and transfer the latest images in a transparent dry-bag. Once on their ruggedised tablet, Mick would delete those which were either duplicates or out of focus, and then upload the pictures to the cloud via the Iridium. The whole process normally took less than ten minutes.

Bill was struggling to make out anything through the deluge; the ranch now a hazy smudge in the middle distance. The only difference in the past couple of minutes was some lights had come on in the buildings. If routine was followed, other than the odd patrolling guard, he didn't expect to see anyone outside the ranch until tomorrow morning.

But he remained vigilant anyway.

With a couple of grunts Mick was on his way back up to the platform.

Bill didn't take his eyes off the target area.

'Anything?'

'No. Not really. I have the vehicle details and one half-decent shot of the man's silhouette; the sunglasses did for any facial recognition. The team should be able to size and age him, but not much else.'

'Hopefully we'll get something decent tomorrow? Maybe they'll have champagne on the terrace?'

Mick scoffed. 'Maybe.' He was silent for a couple of seconds. 'There *was* something. Probably irrelevant.'

'What's that?' Bill replied.

'Our "Englishman abroad" was wearing a double-cuff shirt.'

'What do you mean. Like a city banker?'

'Yea. Which is odd, considering the weather. And the conditions.'

'Posh, then?'

'Yeah. Probably. And …' Mick paused for a second. '... he was wearing distinctive cufflinks.'

'Go on.' Bill encouraged.

'Small flowers. Like daisies. You know. White petals with a yellow centre. Among all of the images it was the only thing that might allow the int guys to nail him.'

'Daisy cufflinks? Hardly the stuff of international drug dealers?' Bill commented.

'Yeah, that's what I thought.'

Grief

Chapter 1

Present Day

Ping.

> *Ping.*
> *Ping.*
> No ping.

Sam absently re-swiped the white and clear plastic package across the barcode reader.

Nothing.

She looked up at the oversized woman whose shopping she was scanning. The woman had one hip lower than the other, her hand planted firmly on a fold of fat struggling to escape the confines of her pink t-shirt. Her free hand held a Tokyo Cat purse that was being slowly strangled by the woman's grip. Her demeanour was one of impatience. There was a lot of shopping. And there was only so much time.

Sam grimaced a smile whilst launching the package through the red laser zone for a third time. Still nothing. She shrugged her shoulders in the direction of the woman, looked at the package and found the barcode sticker. It had a ridge running down its centre, obscuring some of the thick and thin black parallel lines. Sam squashed the raised area with a finger and ran the package through again.

Nothing.

She let a gentle sigh escape through her nose and immediately tapped in the barcode number into the consul. She had seen the number once. She didn't need to be reminded of it.

PORK CHOPS: £3.54, the till's display announced.

Moving on.

As Sam re-engaged the woman's eyes – a sort of cash-till face-off - her left hand reached for six mini-Battenbergs. They were next in the jumble on the conveyor. As deftly as a poker player the Mr Kipling sugar fest shifted to her right hand and, as it did, it registered with the red laser. *Ping.* Next, a second pack of six Battenbergs. *Ping.* Then six more. *Ping*

I'm not saying anything, but someone has a marzipan fetish.

Then a six-pack of Felix cat food, all whilst holding the gaze of the large woman. Who couldn't cope. She fidgeted, muttered something under her breath along the lines of, 'You're friggin weird', and then looked in her purse for her credit card.

Sam continued the motion. Package – transfer – *ping.* Package – transfer – *ping.* It was a perfect example of mundane efficiency. She was good. *Very* good. If there were a supermarket till competition somewhere she would have a good chance of winning. A European record. World leader. An Olympic medal.

Being efficient - getting better and better at swiping the items - kept her mind occupied. She needed that.

In less busy moments she made up stories about the customers. One was a major drug dealer. Another a prima ballerina. A late middle-aged couple, the centre of the largest swinging club in western Leicester. Car keys on the ornate hardwood coffee table. Now take your pick.

Today she'd spotted a Russian. Probably a spy. He was different from all of the usual eastern European crowd: the men all upright and fit, with outdoor hands and chiselled faces; the women, angular and smart – in a 1980s fashion-sense sort of way. The Russian she'd spotted had that same distant look as the Poles and the Romanians. As though he hadn't quite got accustomed to living here. But the familiarity ended there. He was less manly; more scruffy thug. He wore a black collarless jacket with elasticated, woollen cuffs. Under that was a fading blue and red check cotton shirt, covering a Muscovite belly. His trousers were black polyester, the bottom of the legs not quite meeting his brown plastic shoes with fake stitching. His face wore a white, oily sheen that probably hadn't seen the sun for years. And he looked furtive.

Their eyes had met briefly, before he waddled off down the potatoes and veg aisle.

A spy.

For sure. She'd worked with a few.

But the imagineering wasn't always enough. It may distract her most of her time when she was at work, and she worked as many hours as 'Tony the Tills' would give her, but that still left the early mornings. The late nights. The 'awakes' at 3 am. The days off.

It had been a torrid time since Venezuela. She had pressed hard to mend her broken bits. Her calf with a hole in it. Her insides with a chunk removed by a surgeon's scalpel. Those were things she and time could fix. Things within her control. Plenty of hills. Trekking. And the running. It all helped. After eight months she was close to top form. Her five-kilometre run time was back down to just over 20 minutes. Not her best, but not far off. She had jogged to the top of Scafell without a break, carrying a pack loaded with all she needed for a night on the mountain. She'd picked up an Achilles niggle a couple of months ago, but that was on the mend. Physically she felt good.

But upstairs? Now, there was a problem.

She didn't want to think about it. She tried not to think about it. The succession of events over a number of years had continuously flung her down an abyss, followed by a short spike of elation that came from surviving a nasty fall. It was a rollercoaster. Up. And then down. Up again. And then crash: a brick wall. A ditch.

Each drop was deeper than before. Each up, only so high. It was a downward trend.

Camp Bastion. Kenema. Berlin. Rome. Miami and Caracas. The outcome of every one: lower than before.

She didn't want to think about it.

And she *really* didn't want to think about the 'triple-tap' in the jungle.

Bang, bang, bang.

You're dead.

Ralph Bell's mate - in the cell next to the satellite block in Venezuela. Bell was dead, killed by Austin Rogers using a rope and his bare hands. After that Rogers was out of it. Then Bell's pal. In through the door. Armed. Ready to kill. Sam, sat exhausted on the floor, had steadied her aim.

Bang, bang, bang.

The sound of death. At her hands.

He deserved to die. He did. He would have killed both of them. Her and Austin. But he couldn't then. Not when he was lying face down, his chest framed by a pool of blood. Not a chance.

She had killed him. Her first. Her only.

She didn't want to think about that.

Ping.

Ping.

The last item was a triple-pack of Asda's own frozen pepperoni pizza. £2.99. Isle 3. Bottom freezer. Next to the garlic bread. Barcode number: 908 526 1927.

Sam pressed the red summary button on the console. The total was £137.79. It lit up in LED-green on a stalk facing the large woman.

'Cash back?' Sam asked. Business-like. Neither kind, nor direct.

'Uh, no.' The large woman was already putting her payment card in the slot.

Tap in the PIN. Get the receipt. Then out of here. As far away as possible from the weird till woman with the intense stare.

The problem for Sam wasn't the death. It wasn't that she had pulled the trigger, three times. No, she could cope with that.

What dogged and dragged her down was she didn't feel anything. Nothing. She had taken another person's life and it hadn't registered. A void.

Bang, bang, bang.

Death.

Couldn't care less.

That pressed hard in the back of her skull. It gnawed at her. Made her feel worthless. It coloured everything a shade of grey. It left no vibrancy in her life. Just sludge. Noises were muted. Songs she may have once hummed along to were dirges now. Her taste buds failed to highlight flavour. It was all school food again: mince and potatoes. Semolina pudding. Corn-beef sandwiches.

Sam had been here before. And before. And before that. She'd had help. Lots of it. Some of it at the insistence of her first SIS boss, David. No help, no job. Doctor Latima was the worst. He knew which questions to ask. He knew how to dig. There were plenty of things Sam had been prepared to talk about. But, no. Latima wanted to talk about Afghanistan. And the mortar rounds. And Chris's death. Chris. Outside of her family the only person she'd ever loved. But Latima insisted. She declined where she could. Pushed back. Latima didn't get far.

And she'd got help after Berlin. Again it was a prerequisite before she took the SIS job in Moscow. Then the doc had been a woman. Kind and sincere.

And hopeless.

In tandem Sam had done her own research. Apparently the best thing was to be busy. To have a focus. Something tough. Something that occupies all of your mind. You can't feel sorry for yourself if a bunch of people depend on you for an answer that might save lives. Even less chance of being morose when you're running to save your own.

'A good war, that's what the young'uns of today need. That'll sort them out.' Her Dad's answer to the woes of just a few years ago. He'd been in the Falklands. A signals operator. Up at the front. There had been shells and shots. He'd lost his boss to an 'Argie sniper'. He understood war. Although she wasn't as sure he understood the youth of today.

For her it wasn't as simple as PTSD and depression – that's the label the quacks had stuck on it. Her upstairs was already different from everyone else's. She saw things others didn't. She had an eye for detail that hurt. It filled up her head, even today. A face here. A number plate there. The complete Chinese takeaway menu. All beautifully registered and available in an instance. The need for order manifested itself in day-to-day tasks. She worked best in straight lines. She couldn't leave a pair of scissors open. Her kitchen drawers were works of art.

But, then again, her mind was crazy enough to warp around problems. She didn't play chess, but if she did she reckoned she'd be good. She could see ahead – well ahead; around corners. And she learnt quickly, not necessarily by trial and error, although she did that as well, but she picked things up by watching others. As a skier she was parallel-turning at the end of day one. She just did what her instructor did – not as he said. She'd followed him down the slope and mimicked his movement.

She'd been able to strip the Army's SA80 rifle to its constituent pieces in under seven seconds - on her second day of training. She learnt that by watching her recruit instructor do it.

After one demonstration.

'Do that again, Green.' He was standing on the opposite side of a wooden trestle table. A brown Army blanket laid over the top. The parts of the rifle were set out side by side.

Sam noticed the main spring assembly wasn't perfectly in line. She nudged it so it was, and then returned to 'attention'.

'Put it back together first, Sarge. Please'

The sergeant looked at her nervously. And then, with his eyes closed and the whole platoon watching, he reassembled the weapon: two forward gas parts inserted; assemble the breach block and firing pin; slide into the body; cocking handle into the small recess in the rifle's casing; main spring – *press and clip*; push in the rear holding pin; pull the stock to the body and close; push in the front holding pin. *Cock and hold.* Feel inside the chamber with your little pinkie. 'Clear,' he whispered under his breath. He released the working parts forward and fired off the action.

Sam hadn't missed a thing. And she had counted. Nine seconds. Blind.

The sergeant, whose eyes were now open, thrust the rifle into her hands.

'Do it again, Green.'

Sam took a deep breath and then breathed out slowly through her nose.

She closed her eyes. And counted to herself.

One, one thousand; two, one thousand; three, one thousand; four, one thousand; five, one thousand; six, one thousand; seven, one thousand; eight, one thousand; nine, one thousand; ten, one thousand; eleven, one thousand; twelve, one thousand; thirteen, one thousand; fourteen, one thousand; fifteen, one thousand.

She handed the fully assembled weapon back to her instructor. Eight seconds earlier it had momentarily been in pieces on the table.

Disassembled and assembled in 15 seconds. In the dark.

The military classroom was silent. The sergeant's mouth was slightly ajar. Then he gave the weakest of smiles.

'You're going to be a problem, Green, aren't you?'

Sam braced up, turned smartly to her right and went and sat back down on her chair.

Her brain was wired differently. That had proved to be a useful tool. It had helped her through all manner of scrapes and had unpicked and glued together some crucial intelligence. It had helped save lives. But when it wasn't busy, bothered and tasked by other things, it was a plague.

It got so bad that three weeks ago she'd gone and seen her GP. Two nights before, she gathered together 48 paracetamol tablets and a bottle of cheap vodka. After a couple of glasses of the spirit, frothed up with some room-temperature coke, she'd fingered at one of the packets of 16 pills, still in their silver plastic wrapping. The underside was two rows of eight little white bumps, like a miniature Lego board. She pushed one of the tablets clear of its wrapping through the silver foil and held it between a thumb and an index finger. She rolled the tablet left and right, a bemused frown on her face. She put it down on the arm of her settee and pushed out seven more. She lined them up in a row, like good soldiers. She poured herself another drink, the coke's bubbles reaching the lip of the tumbler and then losing momentum. She drank it in two swigs. She took out the other eight tablets and followed the same procedure: row two. Before long she'd have a platoon's worth. Then a company.

Another glassful, and down it went. More vodka than coke.

Whoops. The room moved a bit.

Then the same procedure with another pack, although this time the tablets seemed less inclined to escape their wrapping. But she was persistent. Eight tablets. Row three. A shot and some coke. Down in one. The tablets again. She was a bit finger and thumby now, but she prised them free. Eight more. *One, two, three ... six, seven, wait, there you go: eight.* To her frustration she didn't quite get the row in line. And soon she'd run out of room on the arm. Then one of the tablets defiantly made a break for it, slipped and fell into the crack between the cushion and arm.

'Shit!'

What the ...? God, that's frustrating. How can that happen?

How could she have been so careless?

Man down!

That's not like me.

Hang on. Whoa. Hold still for a second. Stop moving it all about. Concentrate.

Breathe.

You can't have a tablet all on its own down there.

And this messing about. That's not like her - at all.

Mind you, she was in altogether new territory.

More drink.

No. Get the tablets sorted first. And careful. One man is AWOL and we don't want to lose a second.

Feeling slightly less agitated, even though order had not completely returned to her universe, she gingerly pushed all the pills out from the third board with her right thumb and let them fall into her left hand. She now had too many pills and not enough parade square. She looked around the room. *Where now?*

Ahh. The cushion next to her.

Yup, that'll do.

And then something happened that broke through the haze.

Her Mum was sitting beside her on the sofa. Just there. Sam could've reached out and touched her. Her smile. That warmth. The tenderness. The overwhelming love.

And she was gently shaking her head. She didn't seem disappointed. Just caring. Helping … and consoling.

Sam choked. She didn't know which way to look. Her tongue made an impromptu appearance. Her eyes brimmed with tears.

And then the floods.

Streaming down her cheeks, tracking over her chin and cascading onto her lap. She didn't move. And didn't shake, as some people do when they cry uncontrollably. She just sat there open mouthed, clutching a handful of tablets and within arm's reach of a half empty bottle of vodka. And a lapful of tears.

It was a mess. She was a mess.

Tablets. Vodka. Memories. Pain.

And nowhere to turn. Nowhere.

And then her Mum disappeared. Gone. Just like that.

Sam shook her head, tears sprayed sideward like badly positioned windscreen washers.

It was a sign. *Wasn't it?*

Her Mum had come to see her. To pass on a message: *I'm not ready for you just yet, pet.*

Roger out – to use the military vernacular.

That had been that.

She hadn't mentioned the pills to the doc.

The kindly Asian female doctor had asked her some straightforward questions.

'Do you have difficulty getting up for work?'

'No.'

'Do you feel lethargic. Overly tired?'

'No.'

'Do tears come easily?'

Sam paused for a moment.

'No.'

It was the doctor's turn to pause.

'Have you ever thought about, maybe, taking your own life?'

What sort of question is that?

'No.' She lied.

The doctor typed something on her keypad. Sam was too polite to look at the screen.

'Well, we don't have any previous records for you, Miss Green, I'm afraid. I'm not quite sure why that's the case …'

Sam knew. SIS were reluctant to release any.

'… and from what you have told me, I think I can rule out clinical depression. But, let me prescribe you some antidepressants. They're mild, but they may help lift your mood a little.'

End of consultation.

Three weeks later she still felt as flat as laminate flooring. But, give the doc some credit, she hadn't reached for the paracetamol.

'How are you getting on, Sam?'

It was 'Tony the Tills'. He was standing behind the DVD rack at the end of her aisle. He was wearing black trousers, a white shirt and an Asda green, logo'd fleece. He was smiling at her and had a thumb up.

Sam smiled back. Having seen off the large woman, she was currently serving a middle-aged fitness fanatic. Pasta, onions, garlic, lots of leaves, a bottle of top of the range olive oil and a carton of passata. He was obviously carbo-loading for a weekend marathon.

'I'm fine thanks, Tony.'

The final items *pinged* through the laser. Sam pressed the red button and the slim man with the shopping bag of goodness put his card in the reader.

'Do you need a break?' Tony hadn't moved.

Bless him.

She was pretty convinced Tony, who didn't appear to be married and probably lived with his mum, was keen to get in her jeans. Not in a pushy, insensitive way. Just in a, 'I've only ever kissed one girl before, and that was my cousin at my twelfth birthday party' manner. Sam reckoned he was early thirties, reasonably well educated and pretty much a gentleman. But he was a bit paunchy, had pallid skin and crooked teeth, and what was left of his hair was held firmly in place by plenty of masculine lacquer. And whilst he was a caring boss to all of the till staff, he lacked social confidence - particularly with the women, some of whom teased him mercilessly. Which was a shame, because Sam liked him despite his teeth and his stuck down hair.

Frankly, she could do with some kind, bodily warmth. Since the entanglement of limbs in Alpbach two years ago, she'd not been with anyone. The closest she'd got to a date was with a fellow walker whom she'd met up Helvellyn six months ago. They had trekked together for half an hour until they'd reached the summit. Then she had descended one way and her brief partner, another. And that was the end of that.

Tony was hardly her type – if indeed he were the right gender. But she was sure he would be gentle and giving. So, it was a thought. And it was definitely a better bet than an evening with Mr Vodka, Mrs Coke and their countless paracetamol children.

'No thanks, Tony. I'm fine. I'm off in half an hour. I'll keep my legs crossed until then.' Any innuendo was unintended, but she could see Tony struggling with the image.

'OK then, Sam. If I don't see you, have a safe trip home. Be careful in the dark. You know what the streets are like round here.'

I will Tony. I will.

Forty minutes later she had her walking jacket on over her Asda uniform and was ready for the 'off'.

Acknowledging the weather she wore her favourite black beanie – the one she had bought in a rush in Austria. Head down, she strode off into the dim light of afterhours Leicester. Council cuts had switched off the streetlights, and a dank drizzle made her hunch her shoulders and quicken her step. She had some leftover lasagne in the fridge, some bagged salad and a bottle of Asda's best Malbec which had been picked, pressed, fermented and bottled just for her. She knew the outcome of all of it would be bland, but one of these days she'd taste something.

After washing up, she'd watch half an hour of the latest *University Challenge* on BBC iPlayer. She enjoyed watching Jeremy Patronising mock overly intelligent twenty-year-olds. She would get close to 20 questions right. Probably two of the picture ones with some geography on them. And a couple of obscure science questions that she might recall from the back end of a textbook from school. And other irrelevant facts from a brain overfilled with the unnecessary. There were never any questions on military weaponry - or photo IDs of IS terrorists. Or barcode numbers of Asda goods. But she always did OK.

Her lack of education frustrated her. She'd been rubbish at school, and university was never an option for this working class girl. If she'd spent some time learning important facts, stuff worth knowing, she reckoned she'd be a polymath. And she'd put Jeremy in his place. *No, Jeremy, I think you'll find you've pronounced* 'Fick Dich' *wrong. The local dialect pronounces the* 'ch', 'ck'. She mouthed that thought out loud, as if she were really there.

Of course, she wouldn't. She wouldn't put Jeremy right. Not really. Not if she were actually on the show. She'd be too embarrassed to press the buzzer in the first place. She'd be the fringe student on the left end of the four, two down from the captain – the one who never answers a question. And if she did, she'd interrupt early, feeling very pleased with herself, she'd get the answer wrong and lose the team a valuable five points. Jeremy would glance up over his question card with a look of withering disdain.

'I'm afraid you lose five point for an incorrect interruption …'

That would be her. The misplaced geek who blows the team's chances.

A polymath? *Give me a break.*

Her head was full of useless rubbish. Numbers. Headshots. Car makes and models.

Useless.

Just useless.

After 20 minutes she turned off the main road that linked Asda to the centre of Leicester, into Shaftesbury Road. A few minutes later she turned right into Luther Street – her street. Thirty metres further down on the opposite side of the road was the hairdressers: *The Final Cut*. Nigel, the owner, had let her the first floor apartment. It was a one-bed and another room affair, with an adjunct of a bathroom. Small, clean and perfectly formed. You got to it through a brick arch between two identical terraced houses. A short, dark passage, followed by a flight of stone stairs with a metal handrail. Then, hey presto: her front door.

Her road was quiet. It was gone 10.00 pm and tomorrow was another working day. Mums would be doing their best not to scream at the kids to get them to bed. Dads would be watching the news and wondering what new catastrophe had befallen their world since they'd glanced at morning TV over a bacon sandwich and a cuppa. The recent upsurge of minor terrorist incidents across the world seemed out of place. She bet her old SIS boss, Jane, and her analyst pal, Frank, would be scratching their heads.

Not unusually, either side of the road was packed with cars, bumper to bumper. The houses on the street had small front gardens, none of them deep enough to concrete and turn into a space for a car. She remembered the details of all the vehicles; both sides - all the way up and all the way down.

In unnecessary deference to her past, she varied her route to work. From her front door there were two choices, left or right down her street. Then the options got broader, with multiple selections. She was now up to 15 different walking routes. She had no idea why she did it, and she cursed herself every time she added another five minutes to her journey. The only plus was she now knew this part of Leicester really well.

Actually, that was hardly a plus.

Sam could recall all the local cars' number plates in the area and describe any bumper and window stickers. The metallic blue, 2004 BMW 3-series across from her now had a small dent in its rear wing and a series of stone chips on its bonnet. Other than that it was in pristine condition – the pride and joy of Mr Bashkar. He owned a local carpet cleaning company. His wife was Parminder, and they had three kids: Ben, Sanjeev and Meera. Even though she'd never spoken to them, she knew how old they were and what schools they went to. She picked these things up, almost by osmosis. She'd seen an open notebook on the passenger seat of the Beemer; glanced in through the house's front window on a clear day. She'd overheard the kids playing in the street - and Parminder chatting to her neighbour. Parminder went to spin classes on a Thursday. And she fancied the hell out of the instructor.

Hang on.

There was the new Ford Transit van five cars down from her flat. It was … an Avis rent-a-car. *Tick.* She didn't like the new model Transit. The big, oval grille reminded her of a cartoon mouth – something out of *Wallace and Gromit*, when Wallace was heading for danger and all you could see was teeth and a couple of beady eyes.

Sam had not seen a rental vehicle in the street before. That was unusual, but hardly conspiratorial. Someone was moving stuff about. One house to another.

That was it.

She stopped in her tracks, stood on tip toes and craned her neck. She had the registration number.

Relaxing, she sighed to herself.

Pathetic. What is wrong with you?

A few seconds later she crossed the road. Then she was at the hairdressers front door. She turned, heading under the brick arch and into the darkness - before climbing the stairs. She was hungry. The tasteless lasagne was shouting at her.

But she didn't make the steps.

Instead, in darkness where recognition was futile, she was met by a wall of bodies and limbs. She had no time to think; less to fight. A number of strong arms held her tight and a chloroform rag was pressed to her face. She remembered her eyes popping out in surprise.

Then black.

Academy of Fine Arts, Naples University, Naples, Italy

Gareth dragged his mouse so the cursor on his screen danced to the bottom of his manuscript. He tapped the left hand button, waited for the thin I-shape to settle, and started typing. The university issue laptop was old and slow and, loaded with Bill Gates' latest incarnation of Windows 10, it struggled with even the simplest of tasks.

Never mind. It was free.

As was most of his stationery and, surprisingly, his lunch. *Pranzo* was either a pizza of some description, or pasta, in one of many versions. And it was all good. With it came an obligatory miniature bottle of white wine. The wine was a surprise addition to the main meal of his day and, whilst it tasted like it had soured a couple of years ago, it was 12.5% proof and didn't touch the sides. Just what Picasso would have ordered for a third-year Fine Arts student.

He typed earnestly, glancing often to his notebook. At the end of the current paragraph he purposefully placed a full stop, lifted his hands from the keyboard and pushed back in his chair. He looked to his left, out through the second floor window across the narrow *Via Broggia* to the building opposite. It was a four-storey, nineteenth-century block and plaster neoclassical monolith like all the buildings in the quarter. It looked impressive and appeared strong enough to withstand the next earthquake. But it was tatty with flaking paint and its ground floor was half-full of businesses hanging on by a paperclip: an out-of-date computer shop; a tattoo parlour; an internet café. The other half was unoccupied, their plywood-boarded fronts covered with adverts and graffiti.

It was scruffy.

Naples was scruffy.

But it *was* Italy.

When he'd learnt that Naples had accepted him on a third year secondment from the University of Wales, Trinity Saint David - or, as he liked to call it, Swansea Poly - he'd been on a bus heading into the city centre. The email from *Accademia di Bell Art di Napoli* had been forwarded by his tutor, Adam. Gareth had read it out loud, just to make sure. The final line of Adam's covering email was written in his inimitable style: *If you fell into*

31

the lav, love, you'd come up with a five pound note, you lucky s**t. Unlike Gareth, Adam didn't swear. But he always got as close to the line as he could.

'O.M.G! I'm going to bloody Naples!'

He'd looked across at the old woman who was sitting on the bench seat opposite him.

'I'm. Going. To. Bloody. Naples!' His right index finger tapped his chest in time to the words.

The woman gripped the chrome handle in front of her - staring directly ahead.

Gareth remembered he had a couple of fivers in his pocket, the winnings from a sweepstake in his digs as to who was next to be booted off *Love Island*. He immediately pressed the red 'stop' button, launched himself onto the pavement and found the nearest bar. What a night that had turned out to be. His hangover had been so legendary he'd missed one of Adam's tutorials. That had cost him a bottle of gin. But it had been worth it.

Naples was everything he'd hoped it to be. And so was the course. He was taking it seriously. That is, in a Gareth 'seriously' way. Academically it wasn't a problem. He was bright: two A*s and a B at A-Level, without much revision. His Dad had pushed him to take maths and the sciences when, what he had wanted to do was play around with a couple of art subjects and then bugger off to London and find an acting job; or enrol in an arts school somewhere.

But Dad knew best. He always did.

Or at least he thought he did.

It hadn't lasted. Gareth knew it wouldn't.

They'd fallen out the day he'd got his A-level results. He'd made the grades to meet the offer from Durham - reading some kind of engineering. But Gareth had turned them down. After a shouting match with Dad, and with Mum busying herself in the kitchen, Gareth had stormed out of the house. He walked down to the town centre, bought himself four cans of cider from Tesco Express and found a bench in the park. Then he'd called all the clearing organisations. An hour later, without an art qualification to his name, he had a place at Swansea. Fine Art. It wasn't acting and it wasn't London. But it was away from the Valleys - and his Dad - whilst still being close enough to Mum.

So, he was working hard – as hard as he needed to to keep out of trouble. It didn't help that the Academy's bureaucracy and administration was typically Italian - a cartoon character in a sharp suit and designer sunglasses. It seemed to go out of its way to dampen a lot of his endeavour. Lecture timings were vague and often amended at the last minute. Visiting artists turned up late, or not at all. Or early, only to be met by an empty studio.

But he could cope. All he had to do was stay sober for the four-and-a-half-day student week. And then Naples, God bless her, made up for any weekday frustrations.

For the lucky few at Swansea who were given the opportunity to apply for third year secondments, the choice of overseas unis covered much of Europe. Gareth instantaneously reduced the choice to two; Rome and Naples.

Italy. It had to be Italy.

The culture. The rolling Umbrian hills. The artists. The fashion and the style. The passion.

The men.

He'd applied for both. Rome had turned him down within a couple of weeks. So he and Adam had kept everything crossed for Naples.

'If you get the position, I'll be coming out in the Spring to check on your dissertation!' Adam had threatened.

'Come anytime you like, Adam. Just don't come empty-handed,' had been his response.

Depending who you asked, Spring was about four months away. And Gareth was 6,000 words into a 40,000 word dissertation. He was on track - just. He reckoned he'd have something ready before the beginning of March. He'd make sure of it.

He turned back and faced his desk. He let his hands float above the keyboard.

No. Can't.

He was at a loss.

He pressed the 'Page Up' key, holding it down so what he'd already written span downwards in front of him. A few seconds later the scrolling stopped. And there was the title. Sixteen point; Times New Roman.

In bold.

The Mafia's Influence on Italian Art.

The subject choice had been his. His Italian tutor was immediately uncertain and had told him to go away and think about it over the weekend and confirm his choice the following Monday. In the meantime, his tutor would think of some more appropriate titles for Gareth to consider.

Unfortunately, much of the weekend was spent in a sweaty embrace with Giorgio, his newest Italian best friend - and lover. They'd met at a seafront restaurant the previous week, just off *Via Nuova Marina*, down from the cruise liner terminal. Giorgio had been waiting on the outside tables and Gareth was eating – alone. They'd connected immediately. Gareth, whose Italian was getting better by the day, had left Giorgio a ten Euro tip and his phone number, followed by a single kiss. Giorgio had texted him the same evening. The rest was delightful, and ever so sultry, history.

On the hot Sunday afternoon when he should have been reconsidering the title of his dissertation, and after a couple of bottles of Giorgio-recommended *Aglianico*, he'd left Giorgio's lithe, Vesuvian body asleep on his bed, walked naked to his desk-cum-kitchen table, booted up his laptop and penned a note to his tutor:

Dear sir, The Mafia's Influence on Italian Art. Confirmed.

He'd pressed 'return' sporting a crooked smile.

An hour earlier in a moment of calm, he'd quizzed Giorgio about the title. His response had been. 'No. Not good. Warning!' Giorgio's gorgeous face, his dark floppy hair and even darker eyebrows, easily made up for his staccato English - which could at best be described as basic. But his tone and demeanour were clear.

Gareth had laughed at him, picked up a pillow and hit him with something more than boyish exuberance. That had led to a play-fight and more fabulous indulgence.

The thing was he'd plucked the title from nowhere; almost for fun. He was in Italy. On an arts course. And they had the Mafia. It was a simple connection.

But Giorgio's 'warning' had cemented something in Gareth. He'd always had a ruthless inquisitiveness, and whilst initially the title had no particular attraction, his tutor's reticence combined with Giorgio's wonderfully naïve, boyish response, had fired something in him. At that point whether the Mafia had any involvement in Italian art was a complete mystery to him. But he intended to find out.

So far, an eighth of the way in and still laying down the groundwork, he was pretty sure over the centuries no one in the Mafia could tell the difference between a paintbrush and a sculptor's chisel. And with the Mafia a secretive organisation, other than a few notable arrests over the centuries, nobody really knew who was who. That, surely, was the point. That's how they did their business.

That may work for them, but it was making piecing together a decent dissertation more difficult than Gareth had intended.

His largest footnote so far was the seizure of 125 paintings over a period of four years from, what was thought to be, a fine art collection belonging to Gioacchino Campolo. Campolo was a businessman with ties to the 'Ndràngheta Mafia, the largest, still-functioning Mafia organisation in Italy. The paintings, which included works by *Dali* and *Caravaggio*, were now on display in the Palace of Culture, in Reggio. (Gareth had not been to see the collection, but he intended to. He hoped Giorgio would be brave enough to come with him.) Campolo, on the other hand, had been sentenced to 16 years house arrest in 2011. The police were still unsure if they understood the breadth of his art collection or where it was all being held.

With respect to Mafia artists, men and women from Mafia families who had actually made any art, Gareth was struggling to uncover anything useful. It was painful. What was well documented was the amount of art, most of it twentieth-century and most US-based, which depicted the Mafia, or 'the Mob', as it is known in the US. He had made notes and references to this, but it hardly fitted.

Exasperated, he was almost at the point of revisiting the title and turning to something which had plenty of source material.

But, before he took that step he had one final opportunity. A friend of his Italian tutor had set up a meeting with a Neapolitan journalist for tomorrow. The woman, Chiara, worked for a local magazine called *Napoli Scoperto*. She'd agreed to meet him at a café in the *Via Lavinaio* at 10.00 am. Apparently she might have something of interest. His tutor hadn't been any more forthcoming, other than the journalist's name, the place and the time. He was probably still sulking over the fact Gareth had gone ahead with his original title.

A meeting with a mysterious journalist in a café in downtown Naples? It was all very *Pink Panther*.

Between now and then Gareth would look over a couple of Italian art books he'd found at a local second-hand bookshop, tap away at a few more keys … and dream of an upcoming evening with Giorgio, once the Adonis had got back from work.

Chapter 2

The Chief called the cabal to a close. Jane turned off her tablet, gathered her notebook and pen and, with her spare hand, took hold of her empty coffee mug. She smiled at the mug's decoration: *I'd rather be Knitting.* Her niece had given it to her for Christmas. She didn't normally get presents from nieces and nephews but last Christmas was different. Normally she'd have gone to Mum and Dad's. It was a family ritual for as long as she could remember. Apart from one forgettable occasion she always arrived boyfriend-less, so more often than not it was just the three of them. Mum bought the food and Jane provided the drink; an Ocado order rattling nicely as the delivery man struggled up the front path on Christmas Eve. On Boxing Day either the hoards arrived, or Jane would drive her parents to her brother's for cold meat and bubble-and-squeak.

Sadly she'd lost her Dad the previous summer. As a result Mum had been invited to her brother's for Christmas; the ritual well and truly broken. The idea of being alone in her flat on her first Christmas without her Dad horrified her. Thankfully her brother Kevin had extended the offer to her and, whilst work had held her attention to the very last moment, she'd caught a late train from Waterloo and made it to Godalming before Christmas Eve had morphed into Christmas Day.

It had been both a joyful and a sad time. Mum put on a very brave face and Kevin and Ros had made their place look especially Christmassy. It helped that they lived in a wonderful old cottage off a sunken lane, surrounded by fields. Fields that, last Christmas, had put on their own festive display, with sharp frosts and ice-blue skies framed with deep-green-and-red holly borders. Everyone missed Dad terribly, but they all tried very hard not to let it spoil the atmosphere for the children. Mum, all tweed, wool and flashing Santa earrings, sipped at her sherry, pausing every 20 minutes to ask if she could help. Ros, who was as efficient as a recently oiled multi-tool, wouldn't have any of it. So they had a really enjoyable time, whilst quietly missing Dad's calm and warming presence.

The mug had been her favourite gift. It certainly beat her Mum's effort, which was eight pairs of M&S big pants. Jane wasn't quite sure what message her Mum was sending. Jane thought she was still slim and, for an uber-busy 40-year-old, still squeezed in as much exercise as she could. OK, she wasn't getting to the gym as often as she used to, but she had remained a yoga fascist, hardly ever missing her 30 minutes a day. The pants were probably a result of her Mum's failing eyesight that had either misread the knickers' label or, maybe, Jane's hips.

Perhaps it was Jane who was kidding herself? After all, the big knickers hardly fell off her.

The mug, on the other hand, had hit exactly the right note. In what spare time she had Jane had taken up knitting. She wasn't very good, but had managed a red and white hooped cardigan with traditional leather buttons for Sophie's - Ros and Kevin's daughter - tenth birthday. According to Ros, Sophie loved it. And that seemed to be the case over Christmas. Apart from bedtime Sophie had worn it for the whole of the 36 hours Jane had been at her brother's.

She had intended to stay for a second night. Unfortunately an IED attack on the British Embassy in Cape Town had dragged her back into work. She was at her desk before the BBC had had chance to air the *Doctor Who* Christmas special.

And that had been the start of it. Eight months of sporadic, seemingly uncoordinated, worldwide terror activity. The attacks were mostly low key – and almost exclusively carried out by lone wolves. Significantly, out of 47 physical attacks so far, only two were suicide events: a waistcoat bomb at an army checkpoint in Cairo; and a failed rucksack attack on the Oslo T-bane metro. The latter was a disaster for the terrorist, Jakob Halvorsen, a Norwegian right-wing activist. The bomb's lack of sophistication meant the homemade explosive had to be primed at the last minute, otherwise it would have gone off in transit. Unfortunately for Halvorsen the detonator had exploded as he tried to prime the bomb. He'd lost an arm and was temporarily blinded by the blast. An old man who had been sitting next to him in the carriage, received minor injuries. There were no other casualties. The Norwegian police did note that if the bomb had gone off as many as 20 people could have been killed.

What was interesting was Halvorsen was an unknown. His internet profile was low-key, and whilst his

Facebook page made mention of Norway's defunct National Socialist Movement, Zorn 88, no one had been able to establish a motive. Least of all the Norwegian police as the man had committed suicide shortly after his arrest whilst recovering from his injuries in hospital.

The Christmas Cape Town Embassy attack was a simple pipe bomb: half a kilo of low-grade industrial explosive, shoved in a short, plastic tube, wrapped in duct tape, and primed with an industrial detonator attached to an unsophisticated burning fuse. Delivery had been a 'lob' at the front gate of the Embassy. No one had been hurt and little damage had been done. They still had no idea who the perpetrator was, or what his motives were – he was never caught, and no organisation had claimed responsibility. CCTV imagery showed a black local, with a bandana covering his nose and mouth; the rest of his face disguised by dreadlocks.

And that was the only thing connecting the attacks: there were no discernible motives. Out of the 47 attacks, from Quito in South America to Tokyo in the Far East, there was no unifying cause.

There certainly wasn't any Islamic underpinning. Jane's AO (*Area of Operation*) was the Middle East and Afghanistan. None of her 17 SIS stations had prior intel before any of the attacks. Significantly there wasn't a hint of intelligence before the seven carried out in her AO. But that made sense. The targets had been unlikely Islamic terrorist hits. Whilst IS continued to attack western and Shia hubs in Iraq, Syria and Yemen on a regular basis, the 'notable seven', as they had been coined in Babylon, were hardly IS's scene.

The latest, a handheld rocket attack against Dubai's tallest building, the Burj Khalifa, was carried out by a Bangladeshi worker. The rocket was an ex-British Army *Carl Gustaf* 84mm rocket-propelled anti-tank grenade. The low-powered rocket had an effective range of 700 metres and carried a small shaped charge which was designed to penetrate the side armour of older Russian tanks. The rocket had struck a second-floor window, travelled across a small and exclusive atrium, and blown up in a *Rolex* boutique - frightening the life out of a shop assistant and sending $7,000 watches in all directions. The firer, who had been disorientated by the blast at his end, was arrested at the scene. He'd stuck to a story that he was making a stand against capitalism for all poorly-paid immigrant workers in The Emirates. Under pressure, he claimed he worked for an organisation called the NDRA, but had no knowledge of what the acronym meant, nor where they were based - or who his operative might be. Not known outside of intelligence circles was the Dubai police had almost killed the man under interrogation. But he hadn't wavered from his story.

From Jane's sources, it seemed that ISIS, al-Qaeda and their offshoots were as much in the dark as the world's major intelligence agencies. In fact, the latest word was that ISIS were as frustrated by the maverick attacks as those trying to stop them. It hadn't taken the world's press long to coin the new wave of attacks as 'neo-terrorism', a term which begun to dominate the news cycles. Seasoned terrorist organisations needed media outlets to amplify their own brand of hurt. Now that they were having to share those platforms with a burgeoning list of unknown cells, they weren't happy.

And the attacks weren't all physical.

The hacking of governmental systems, financial institutions and big industry was also on the rise. It was difficult to differentiate attacks carried out by criminals for financial or industrial gain, from those by terrorists hell-bent on spreading havoc amongst the users and beneficiaries of the systems that were attacked. In the UK, The Service (*The Secret Service/MI5*) were now clear the website failure of a major UK bank earlier in the year, which had caused systems to crash resulting in accounts losing, and some gaining, cash, had been a deliberate act to undermine the financial system - rather than just an almighty cock-up by the bank involved. Whilst the connection had not been made the press, The Service was placing that meltdown under the banner of 'neo-terrorism'.

Political systems seemed no less susceptible to attack. Whilst the UK and US had its longer-term, self-generated divisions carved between Europhiles and Eurosceptics in the UK, and between the conservatives and the liberals in the US, other countries were also struggling with the rise of destabilising politics. If it hadn't been for the 'neo-terrorism' label, it would have been easy to suggest that this was just the way things were. A global push-back against decades of the elite few leading the less privileged masses for their own gains: the rich making themselves richer, whilst the poor spiral into debt, hit the floor and spill out onto the streets.

But by the Spring the governmental view was that it was more sinister than that. Election meddling was widespread - all for no apparent discernible gain, other than breaking the status quo. It certainly wasn't right versus left; or Christian versus Muslim. In the past six months two countries in South and Central America had voted in quasi-communist parties, and a third, a nationalist, right-wing organisation. There was no pattern.

In Botswana, a stalwart of African democracy, the recent election was so badly called – with final ballot sheets looking nothing like those called at the polling stations - the election had to be declared null and void. The rerun was planned for the week after next. In the meantime the country was on tenterhooks, so much so an unprecedented night-time curfew had been called in its capital Gaborone. GCHQ's review of the election e-processes discovered a small team of hackers working out of Algeria had interrupted, and then discarded, the poll results as they were transferred electronically to the Botswanan electoral commission. The hackers had then substituted the original results with new ones. Surprisingly, the forged result gave no one party a majority, so it wasn't as though the infiltrators were hoping to influence the decision – they were just disrupting it.

SIS had a small team working out of the British Embassy in Algiers. Within 24 hours, and with support from the CIA and direction from GCHQ, they'd raided the location of where the hack had originated. They found a three-by-three metre square room on the top floor of a crumbling apartment block. In it was a single desk and two chairs – nothing else. On the outside wall, by the only window, was a new metal bracket with nothing attached. SIS immediately shared photos of the bracket with GCHQ. After less than a minute's worth of consultation in the Doughnut (*the nickname for GCHQ*), they'd concluded the bracket was designed to hold a small microwave dish - probably no more than 30 centimetres in diameter. Such a dish would have a maximum range of 1000 metres – and connect, by line-of-sight, to a second dish. 'Could you guys find the target dish?', was their question.

With a pair of binos it took one of the SIS case officers less than five minutes to find the connecting dish. He was convinced that it was one of about 50 on a large communications tower toward the edge of the city. With the distances involved and the equipment they had available, they had little chance of finding the exact dish. Even if they could, GCHQ's view was it would be wired to an rx/tx mobile phone antenna, which was how they had found them in the first place. In short they'd be no further forward. As a result the team had little choice but to close the in-country operation. They had hit a dead end.

By the time the post-op report was written, the conclusion was no more than two people, working with reasonably sophisticated, but commercially available, equipment, had undermined the Botswanan election. They'd hacked the system from a distance, routing their disinformation via microwave, UHF radio and then satellite, around the world. They'd been swift and clean, possibly without motive – other than to undermine the election results. And they had bugged out within 12 hours, leaving little trace of their existence.

Jane had an intelligence officer still working the case, but so far they were no further forward.

It didn't end there. The list of potential 'neo-terrorist', non-physical attacks were endless. Fake news continued to test even the most open minded person, with spurious but highly plausible new events popping up on every media outlet. Twitter had increased its security identification requirements for its 'blue-tick' users, but even these had been 'botted'. Bots were regularly hacking blue-tick accounts, tweeting untrue and spurious comment until Twitter had closed them down.

Both the BBC and CNN's websites had been hacked. Fake news reports of seemingly incidental - but locally explosive - events were subtly included in news feeds. '*Army veteran murdered by deranged farmer*', was one BBC report that stuck in Jane's mind. The story was completely false, even though the particular web feed looked wholly realistic. The fictitious report was from Humberside. Almost immediately Facebook and Twitter were alive with ex-military and local farmers having a go at each other. In the evening, post the afternoon report, a small group of ex-soldiers marched on their local dairy farm. There was a stand-off and the police were called, but not before the farmer's barn had been set on fire killing 25 cows.

The intelligence services had found the originator of the breach. That is, they found his domain name: *NineTenReadyOrNot*; nationality unknown. By then the name was no longer in use. It only took five days for the BBC website to be hacked again, after which the site was closed for a week whilst further safeguards were installed.

The UK was far from alone. Fake News everywhere, on all social media platforms, continued to chip away and enrage sensitivities throughout the world

Mixing the physical attacks with the electronic painted an almost dystopian canvas. It was as if causing terror had become a new sport, like paddle-boarding - or a child's hobby, like Loom Bands. There was no central tenet. No defining mantra. People just did it, because they could. For the fun of it

Or that's what it seemed like.

But SIS profilers at Babylon didn't agree with that diagnosis. And their CIA counterparts concurred. Yes, there was an element of copycat about what was happening. But the whole thing was too unsystematic, not to be systematic. Bangladeshis do not buy second-hand Carl Gustaffs on the black market, train themselves using YouTube, and then take a pot-shot at the tallest building in the Middle East. Especially knowing they'd almost certainly get caught and end up hanging by the toes in a Dubai jail.

Something was behind the chaos.

And that meant, someone was gaining from it.

Unfortunately, so far nobody had any idea who or what that was. Which was uncomfortable for all of the security services - everywhere. Because, just now, the world felt like a very unsafe place indeed.

'Jane?'

She was still staring at her mug.

It was the Chief. He and she were the only two left in his office.

'Yes, Clive. Sorry. I was deep in thought.'

'That's OK. There's a lot to think about at the moment. Look, I reckon by tomorrow I'll be ready with a blueprint to extend your domain.'

This was news to Jane. She said nothing.

'I've decided to start to move away from geographical departmental boundaries. I think, for you, it makes sense to extend your remit to include all economic and refugee migrants headed for the UK. Not just those from the Middle East and Afghanistan. In particular ...'

'Sub-Saharan Africa.' Jane interrupted.

'Exactly. I think it's obvious that, however we cut this, we end up with a mix of nationalities in northern Europe. At Calais, Brest, Le Havre, Bremerhaven, etc. All along the coast.'

'And it would mean that for once, here, we'd have one point of contact with the Border Agency, CT police, the Joint Intelligence Maritime Unit and, of course, The Service?' Jane added.

'Yes, indeed. Good. You've got it. Have a chat to your oppos. 'Neo-terrorism' may be the current flavour, but preventing all would-be terrorists crossing our borders will be with us forever. Indeed, they may well be connected. And start to think who, within your team, might lead in this area. Give them a heads up. OK?'

Jane nodded.

That'll be Frank then.

Sidestrand, Cromer, Norfolk, United Kingdom

Sam listened to the *slap* of the waves and waited for the delayed *rush* as water backpedalled through pebbles back into the sea.

Slap ... rush. Slap ... rush.

It was melodic. Hypnotising.

It was also the only thing she could do – listen. She was in a wooden hut, still wearing what she'd been in when she'd left work. Her hands were tied behind her back. Her feet to the chair legs. Tied, but not so tight she was losing circulation. And she was gagged: a cotton material, not polyester; easier on the mouth when wet with spit. The material was folded on itself a number of times, and knotted behind her head. It was tight, but not so much she couldn't make a small amount of noise. It was a professional job. Very competent. She was sitting in an upright, cushioned chair which was bolted to the floor. She was tied to it with orange and green climbing rope, strapped around her waist. Again, tight but not so it dug in. She couldn't move, but she wasn't uncomfortable. And she hadn't been hurt.

Professional.

All of her bits were they should be. Her stomach, always the first to remind her she was not invincible, didn't ache.

She had been kidnapped – but not abused. Somebody wanted to talk to her. Somebody who wanted her intact; unbroken. That didn't mean that pain wouldn't come. Just none had been inflicted up until now.

Was she scared?

Not really. Hurt was an old friend of hers. It was quantifiable and most of the time she could see it coming.

Much worse were her demons. Ralph Bell was dead, but he was still with her. In her dreams. On the TV news, a face at the back of a crowd.

And … the unknown man from Croatia. The mastermind of the failed cruise missile attack on Mecca: *Freddie*. Known of – but never seen. No one had any idea what he looked like. But she had seen him. In the periphery of her vision. A fleeting movement; his eyes on her. A man without form.

The devil.

Am I scared?

What was left to be scared of?

She was worn out. Bored by it all.

On a slope heading downhill. Nothing mattered.

A shingle beach? She could be anywhere along the British coast. Large swathes of the coastline was shingle. She'd read an article, 'The best beaches in England', a couple of months ago whilst the UK had basked in an unusually hot summer. It seemed that pebbles were preferred over sand. Less bits of beach hiding in unnecessary places. Among the list were: Chesil Beach, the spit of pebbles that linked the Isle of Portland with the Dorset coast; Watergate Bay in Newquay;

Blackpool Sands, surprisingly not in Lancashire, but in South Devon; West Wittering in Sussex. Among others. She'd not been to any of them.

As a kid she remembered her Mum and Dad taking her to Sheringham, in Norfolk. That had a pebble beach. A short carriage-ride from The Queen's pad at Sandringham, Sheringham felt very posh. Their accommodation was more caravan than castle, but the whole place was a bit of a leg-up from Skeggie, where most of her friends holidayed.

She could be in Sheringham, or close by?

None of that was helpful.

She could be anywhere. She reckoned she'd been knocked out for about eight hours. She'd been taken in the dark – close to 10.30 pm. Looking at the poorly boarded up window – the only one in the single-skin, wooden hut she was in – it was dark again; probably about 8 pm, almost a day later. She'd come to about 12 hours earlier. At that point she was hungry and had a headache. And she needed a pee. But she was alone and there was no one to listen to her demands, let alone meet them.

Now, as the sea continued to slap the shore and then rattle back from where it came, she was still hungry but the headache was gone. And thirst was a new sensation.

And she still needed a pee.

During the day she'd tried to find the sun through the cracks in the boarded-up window. The only other opening was a tongue and groove, wooden door. It fitted its frame tightly: no cracks. But there was no sun. Nothing to help orientate herself to a particular coastline. Mind you, in the eight or so hours she'd been unconscious her kidnappers could have taken her to any coastline in Europe. If she were facing west she could be in Wales, the north coast of Devon, Sutherland in Scotland … or Denmark. Or Finland? The possibilities were endless.

God, I need a pee!

She really didn't want to wet herself. She bounced her right leg up and down to relieve the pressure on her bladder. She felt the skin reddening as her right ankle rubbed against the chair leg.

Apart from the rubbing, the only sound was …

… slap … rush. Slap … rush.

She closed her eyes and concentrated on sleep. She was surprisingly tired for someone who had been sitting on her backside all day. OK, she had tried to break her bonds and that had taken some effort. She'd moved her hands about, wringing them and pulling them in opposite directions. She'd wiggled in her chair, slipped off both shoes and tried to pull one foot then the other through the ankle tie. But she'd soon given up. Whoever had bound her had known what they were doing. She'd get free when they wanted her to.

One of the lighter moments of SIS case officer training had been a session on knots and trussing people up. This wasn't in preparation for their inevitable capture by some global master-criminal so they could free themselves, kung fu their way out of the building and then fly the pre-flight-checked, carelessly unguarded Apache helicopter into the sunset just before the nuclear laboratory was engulfed in flames.

It was much more practical than that.

As a case officer there was always a possibility an agent you were running 'just flipped'. Getting paid to rat on your own side was a high pressure job. For a few it became too much. SIS had countless examples of an agent breaking down in the presence of their case office. At that point the IA (*immediate action*) was to restrain them before they did themselves, and the operation, unnecessary harm. Often a hand on the shoulder and a strong cup of tea was enough. Sometimes it wasn't. At that point, knowing about ropes and knots was handy.

A different noise?

On top of the, *slap ... rush, slap ... rush.*

A car. In the near distance.

Sam strained her ears. It was tyres on gravel. From behind her. There had been little wind all day. She picked it up easily. A heavy engine. *Diesel.* Probably two-litre. *Maybe a small truck?*

Crunch. Silence.

The engine switched off. A number of doors opened, she couldn't tell how many. Then an additional noise. Light metallic clanking. Followed by a soft thud, like a mattress falling onto carpet.

Then she had it.

A wheelchair. Initially on gravel and then on a wooden boardwalk. It was rolling her way. There were two additional sets of footsteps. Three people. One of them unable to walk.

They'd reached the hut's door. A lock and two sets of bolts. It took fifteen seconds to open the Tardis. A *creak* – rusty metal hinge. It opened inward, towards her. The slatted, rectangular shape of the door came to a halt about the same time her mouth lost all of its moisture. Her heart rate picked up, but it was a soft beat. And her breathing shallowed. She could see very little so her body reduced internal friction.

She wanted to *hear* everything.

First round the door. A man.

What?

What?

It was a scene lifted straight from a *Len Deighton* book.

It was the Russian-looking man from Asda sometime yesterday, the one with the pallid face and Muscovite belly. Same grubby clothes. Same oily skin. He made room for the grand entrance.

Sam's initial shock was amplified ten-fold by the entrance of the man in the wheelchair.

He was in shadow. His silhouette was a fuzzy outline crafted by minimal light from a cloudy night that cheated its way into the hut through the open door.

But Sam immediately knew who it was.

'Hello Sam.' He spoke in English with a guttural, Russian accent.

'Privet Vlad.' A muffled, comic response. If she could have been heard through the gag, Vladislav

Mikhailov would have recognised Sam mimicking a mid-west Russian accent. It was one she could do easily. It would have matched the man in the wheelchair if his opening line had been given in his mother tongue.

A third man made movement behind Vlad, he found a switch by the door and there was light. Apart from three Russians - the one in the wheelchair a senior operator from the FSB and the other two, likely FSB support staff in whatever country they were in - nothing in the hut had changed. Four walls, a window, a door, an upright chair and her.

'*Zakroyte dver!*' Vlad shouted over his shoulder. The third man immediately pushed the wooden door too.

'*Razvyazhi zhenshchinu!*'

Asda-Russian leapt forward and attended to Sam's gag. He then started on the rest of the ties.

'I'm sorry, Sam.' Vlad spoke in Russian. 'I hope you are unhurt?'

Sam, who was now close to being free, took in Vladislav Mikhailov. A couple of years ago they'd been gathering intelligence in a much bigger wooden cabin when they'd both been shot. Vlad had been left in the cabin to die after Sokolov's men had set it ablaze. She'd been taken from the scene and dropped on the oligarch's yacht. She didn't want to think about what happened after that. Ever.

She'd not spoken to Vlad since the incident. From SIS sources she knew he'd lost the use of his legs. She had assumed he, his wife Alena and the kids, had retired to The Black Sea.

Obviously not.

'I need a pee.' Perfect Russian from Sam. Vlad's English was poor. Whatever he had brought her here for would have to be sorted out in Russian.

The three men went silent.

'Now. Otherwise the Russian government will owe me a new pair of slacks.'

'Go then.' Vlad flicked his head over his shoulder to the door.

Sam half-stood, and then hesitated.

'Aren't you worried I'll make a break for it. Find someone in authority and have you and your hoods arrested?' She was standing now, although she was a bit wobbly after the enforced rest. She placed a hand on back of the chair to steady herself. 'By the police, of whoever's country we're in?' She added.

Vlad closed his eyes and shook his head.

'We're in England. Do you think I have a submarine offshore, or a flight of jets on call to whisk you off to a country of my choice? I work for the FSB, not for the Bank of Russia.'

Sam, having now taken a couple of strides to the door, stopped by Vlad's side and looked down at him; he met her gaze. She put a hand on his shoulder He looked much older than she remembered. Closer to 50 now, rather than heading to 40 as she remembered him. The top half of his body had put on weight - his legs, clearly useless, were as thin as sticks.

'How's Alena', Sam asked.

He smiled and blew out through his nose.

'She's fine. Now go and pee.' He waved a hand. 'I'll make sure the boys don't look.'

She stepped through the gap that had opened up between the two men.

'And come back! I have a proposition for you ...'

Twenty minutes later Sam was clear why the FSB wanted to talk to her.

'But why didn't you catch me in the street. Text me? Why the heavy hand? This ordeal? The gag and the ropes?' Sam brought her fists together as if they were still tied.

'For a start, I knew you would only listen to me. And then, only face to face. This evening was the earliest I could get here. And, as I said, we only realised we had a problem two days ago. At that point we knew where you were and we didn't want to lose you. You know, up a mountain somewhere. Or trekking in the woods. We had to bring you in as soon as we could.'

Trekking? They'd been following her.

'You've been keeping a close eye then?' Sam didn't know whether to feel flattered.

Vlad answered the question with a shrug of his shoulders: *sort of.*

'But how did you get in the country? You're PNG. The system would have picked you up. Border Force would have been all over you like chickenpox.' She was sitting back on her chair with an empty bladder and feeling much more human.

'Correct.' Vlad replied. As if to release some tension in his upper body, he rolled the wheelchair forward a touch, and then back again. He continued with a half-smile. 'It depends which airfield you fly into.'

Sam nodded.

'So, you *do* have a flight of private jets on standby?' She teased him.

Vlad scoffed. 'If only. We have an old Gulfstream that all of the departments fight over. This week, I won.'

There was a pause. Sam was mulling over what Vlad had told her. He was waiting for an answer. She was still processing it all. She wasn't sure. At all.

'Show me a picture.' She asked.

'Of what?' Vlad replied.

'Of your field officer. The one I'm meant to be replacing.'

'Why?' Vlad was defensive.

'I'm not a good facsimile, am I? You want me to do the job because I'm expendable.'

That was the conclusion Sam had come to. It was the only one that made any sense. The Russian internal intelligence organisation, the FSB, feared an upsurge of Islamic-based violence on its southern border with Georgia. A new terror cell, naming itself Freedom for Oppressed, or FFO, had gained traction in South Ossetia, a small satellite state of Russia. Or, if you belonged to any Western government or most members of the United Nations, an integral part of the sovereign country of Georgia. The Russians feared Islamic fundamentalists as much as any nation and they were very keen on keeping the mainly Russian-speaking South Ossetia in tow. And with their own, large and disenfranchised Muslim population in southern Russia, the last thing they needed was a new banner under which that already subjugated grouping could muster.

Vlad had come to her because the Russian intelligence services had no idea where the leader of the FFO, Hasan Kutnetsov, was based. Their intelligence had the FFO as a small, tight grouping. Maybe ten to fifteen strong at its core. According to Vlad the FSB had a female operative on the cusp of meeting Kutnetsov. Her cover was as a Reuters journalist. The FFO and Kutnetsov, clearly seeking all the publicity they could get, had agreed to meet the journalist in three days' time. FSB had an RV just south of the Russian/Georgian border. The FFO had the details of the journalist. Everything was set.

Except it wasn't.

Unfortunately they no longer had a journalist. The FSB woman had been badly injured in a car crash last weekend.

Vlad had been clear with Sam. FSB couldn't afford to miss the chance to meet with Kutnetsov. They would get something from the meeting – something that would help them track down and destroy the grouping. And they had very few female field officers and certainly none capable of stepping in at short notice. So they had to find a replacement. Sam was it.

That was the nub of it. What Vlad hadn't mentioned was if she failed, FSB lost nothing.

I am expendable.

Vlad got out his smartphone and swiped and pressed. He then rolled his wheelchair forward and passed his phone to her.

Sam took it. It was a headshot of a middle-aged woman, possibly a passport photo.

It was the right gender. *Tick.* But the similarities ended there.

'Is this what the FFO have?' She asked.

Vlad nodded.

'How tall is she?'

Vlad scrunched up his face.

'I don't know. 165. Maybe 170.'

Her height. Sam looked again at the photo. She studied it for ten seconds, turning the phone ever-so-slightly left and right. She wasn't the girl in the photo.

'No. It's not me. And both you and I know there is no time for any cosmetics. And even if there were time, why would I work for Russia on this case - in a country where your imperialistic overtures are not coincident with those of the West? I would be considered a traitor. It's not happening. Sorry. It's not.'

Vlad took the phone, put it in his pocket and rolled his chair back.

'Speak to Jane Baker. Call her now. Your phone has her number on speed-dial. Tell her everything. It's in everyone's interest to quell the rising of any Islamic-extremist organisation in central Asia. The Taleban is confined to Afghanistan. Al-Qaeda is a spent force throughout the world. The West and Russia have restricted ISIS operations to small enclaves in Syria and Iraq – there is no Islamic Levant. We are all struggling with what the Western media have coined, 'neo-terrorism'. Let's nip this new grouping in the bud – before it grows a tail and whips us all with it.' He paused. 'Phone her. Phone her now.'

It hadn't crossed Sam's mind that she might still have her mobile on her. It was in her jacket pocket. She took it out and stared at it. The battery level read 45% and she had three-bars of 4G.

She looked up at Vlad.

'Where are we?' she asked.

Vlad didn't answer straight away.

Then … 'Sheringham. Just down from where your family had the caravan. I brought you home.'

What?

It was too much.

A multitude of thoughts flashed through Sam's mind. She welled up. Childhood images. The sea. Ice cream cones: vanilla with a chocolate flake. Dad. Mum, *for the second time in a month*? The static caravan: green and beige with a TV aerial pointing towards a tower in Cromer. Dad had checked. When was it? 1994? That's it. Her first taste of war – TV footage of the aftermath of the Serbian mortar attack on a market in Sarajevo. Three hundred innocent people dead. She'd wanted to be a soldier from that point onward. Anything to help prevent that sort of horror.

She sniffed, pulled the phone away from her face, closed her eyes and rested her chin on her chest.

Asda?

South Ossetia?

She sniffed again and wiped the smallest of tears from her eye with the hand carrying the phone.

Then she dropped both hands to her lap and lifted her head. Vlad was looking directly at her.

'If anyone can bring something useful from a meeting with Kutnetsov, it's you, Sam. You'll see something. How do you say? Something that should be there, that isn't. This is what you do, Sam. You are the expert.'

She sniffed again and pinched her nose with a finger and thumb, her eyes closing momentarily.

Then she unlocked her phone and pressed the blue phone icon.

Chapter 3

Café Napolita, Via Lavinaio, Naples, Italy

Gareth supped at his *double espresso*. Short, strong and black; he couldn't stop himself from bending innuendo around that description. The caffeine had already started to work its way through his system, chasing down the errant alcohol molecules and giving them a good talking to. Victory would be swift; soon he'd be feeling human. Another late evening with Giorgio, a bottle of amaretto, pasta, and clean, crisp sheets had left him tired and elated. They didn't talk a great deal. It wasn't just the language, although that was part of the problem. He was working hard on his Italian and between them they could order a take-away, ask about each other's day and make complimentary remarks as they removed each other's clothes. It was that Giorgio worked late and they had better things to occupy themselves with. Anyway, they had only known each other for three weeks. It was early days?

As he walked from his digs to the café the issue of the lack of meaningful conversation did cross his mind. On reflection he realised he didn't know a great deal about Giorgio. Gareth was 21, Giorgio was … well, he wasn't sure. Giorgio looked younger than him, but his actions and mannerisms were older. Gareth, who at 1.87 centimetres tall, had his Dad's build: the size and shape of a small-town, second-team flanker. Giorgio was more a 'winger'; slimmer and less bulky.

He had no idea where Giorgio came from. Currently he was renting, as he described it, *un appartamento della spazzatura* – a rubbish flat, in the north of the city. When Gareth had suggested they stay at his place, Giorgio, looking startled, had blurted out, *'No, no'*, his hands waving like two small windmills. Gareth hadn't suggested it again. In any case, he much preferred his place - it was close to the city centre and a short walk to the Academy. As to where Giorgio actually came from, all Gareth had was, 'down south', with Giorgio cheekily pointing to his own groin.

Gareth knew that Naples was considered 'south' to Italians. After Naples, other than the beautiful Amalfi Coast and the historic island of Sicily, southern Italy was an underpopulated spine of white mountains with some flat bits of earth laid down here and there to make up the toe and heel of the Italian boot. It was known to be church-mouse poor; and almost lawless. As part of his acclimatisation Gareth had read *Christ Stopped at Eboli*, a Carlo Levi memoir published in 1945. The book had many wonderful descriptions, but in short Levi portrayed anywhere south of Eboli, which was not that far further south than Naples, as somewhere by-passed by God, and even history itself.

So that was a vague description of where Giorgio came from: Godless and lawless.

Which made sense as it was *Mafioso* country. Which, by a stroke of luck, tuned in nicely with Gareth's dissertation.

But he still didn't know *exactly* where Giorgio came from.

Neither did he know if he had any siblings, where he went to school, what degree – or indeed any qualifications he might have … and what his favourite colour was. He might know every contour of his body but, thinking about it, not a great deal more.

Note to self – less sex, more talking.

Gareth stretched, forcing his arms down and pushing out his chest. He felt his shoulder blades touch.

He checked his watch. It was 10.05 am. Chiara was late.

How Italian.

He finished his coffee, caught the waitress's eye and was just about to order a second when a sunglasses-adorned Italian beauty stopped short of entering the café's patio area and took in the clientele.

Gareth sat still. Looking. Chiara was late. If the woman was her, she could find her own way to his table.

Then he remembered the waitress. She was standing impatiently beside him.

Sod it.

He raised his chin and called across to the woman who had just arrived.

'Chiara?' He nonchalantly lifted his hand off the table and waved his fingers.

The woman pulled her sunglasses off her nose and looked across at Gareth under her beautifully manicured, pencil-thin eyebrows. She smiled, and then looked for the easiest way to negotiate the chicane of tables and chairs between the pavement and Gareth.

'*Posso farti un caffè?*'

'*Si, si.*' She was gliding through the assault course, her feet hardly touching the ground.

'*Due caffè, per favore.*' He acknowledged the waitress,

As she moved away, Gareth stood and met Chiara. They feigned a double-cheek kiss and Gareth pulled out Chaira's chair, making room for her delicate legs which graced the floor with Ferragamo, banana-yellow flatties. She was wearing a black cotton, Emilio Pucci skirt and a half-silk, lime green open-necked blouse. Gareth couldn't recall the designer. Her handbag was a delicate Valentino Marilyn cross-body and she sported a Gucci watch.

The *pièce de resistance* was a string of larger than usual, beautifully-matched pearls, set off with accompanying earrings.

Gareth did a quick sum in his head. If he had five hours to spare and had been parachuted into Milan, he reckoned he'd need close to two grand to put together what Chiara was wearing. He was flattered.

She smiled at him, casually flashing her eyelids in a non-flirty way. She was lovely to the eye. Wealthy. And had that confidence that comes from being both.

'Do you speak English?' His opening line.

'Of course.' A slight grimace. He hadn't affronted her, but he had come close.

'*Il mio Italiano non è così buono.*'

She smiled again.

'That's not a bad start.' Her English was excellent; just a hint of that wonderful Italian lyricism. 'Your accent is awful, as though you swallowed a couple of toads. But it's always good to meet a foreigner, especially a young one, who is willing to try.' She was speaking quickly, like all Italians. So many words; not enough breath. 'But your accent … you have to imagine you are underneath Juliet's balcony. Love is coursing through your veins. The words, they come out quickly, like a …'

'Machine gun?' Gareth suggested. It just came to him.

Chiara hesitated. And frowned.

'That wasn't the metaphor I was searching for, but it works. Yes, a machine gun. No. Better. A tommy gun, like the American mafia.' She brought her hands together as if she were holding a machine gun and sprayed the nearby tables with bullets, accompanying the actions with a staccato sound as each bullet left the gun.

Gareth couldn't stop himself; he roared with laughter. Chiara joined him, dropping the weapon and raising her hand to her mouth to suppress further giggles.

'I'm sorry.' She apologised.

'Please, don't.' Gareth shook his head whilst showing a 'no more, thank you' flat palm to Chiara.

As they both regained their composure the waitress returned and placed their coffee in front of them. As the woman turned to leave, Chiara asked, 'You're gay?'

The waitress was unsure if the question was meant for her, but soon realised that it wasn't. She quickly left the two of them to their very direct conversation.

Gareth, now back in control, rested his chin in his hand and studied the reporter closely.

'Yes. How do you know?'

Another smile.

'We've been sitting at the same table for over two minutes and you haven't looked at my cleavage once.'

That was true.

'But you've studied what I am wearing, and are impressed?' She added.

Gareth had been watching Chiara's face intently. He dropped his eyes to her cleavage. It was *very* impressive.

'You have a fine cleavage. And you are impeccably dressed, although I can't make out where you bought your blouse.'

'Etro.' Chiara replied.

'*Ovviamente.*'

'No. More passion. Like a tommy gun. And more hands!'

As she gave Gareth a lesson Chiara wrung hers together.

'*Ovviamente. Ovviamente*!'

'Got it. Got it.' Gareth nodded. 'More passion.'

'Like a tommy gun.' Chiara added.

'Like a tommy gun.' Gareth repeated.

They both had a sip of their coffee.

'Can you help me with my dissertation?' Gareth asked.

'Maybe? That's why I'm here.'

'I need something, someone who has links to *gli Mafiosi*, but is also a recognised name in art. Could be historical. Might be present day.'

Chiara finished her coffee and dabbed her lips with a napkin. It left a red stain on the white cloth. She opened her handbag and took out a business card. Gareth made out her name, the newspaper's details and a telephone number before she put the card on the table, face down. She then pulled out a Montegrappa ballpoint pen and wrote a name in capitals. She turned the card through 180 degrees and slid it the short distance across the table to Gareth.

Gareth picked it up and held it a comfortable distance from his eyes.

He recognised the name immediately.

He shot a glance at Chiara. She had a single, delicate finger to her lips.

Matteo Monza.

Matteo Monza?

'Are you sure?' His response to the card was soft; quiet.

Chiara had lost her smile – and she had dropped her finger. She held his gaze.

'Isn't this newsworthy?' A whisper from Gareth, laced with incredulity.

She nodded, slowly.

'Then why aren't you investigating this. It's a huge story. National level – maybe international?'

Chiara took out her purse and placed a two Euro coin on the saucer of her cup. She then put her pen and purse back in her handbag, pushed her chair back and stood.

'You are an attractive man, Gareth. And I hear you are tenacious. But …', she leant across so that her lips were close to his left ear.

'*Stai attento, signore. Very* careful.'

She stood back to her full height.

'More passion.' She said.

'Like a tommy gun.' He added.

'*Si.*'

And then she left.

Headquarters SIS, Vauxhall, London

Frank rested his forehead on the palm of his left hand. He used his right to manipulate the 32-inch screen in front of him. In the top right corner was a hazy headshot and torso of a man. In the distance was the familiar London Tube logo. Running through the centre of it was the station's name: East Putney. That was south of the river and not far from where he was sitting. The DTG (*date/time/group*) on the security camera showed that the still had been lifted from the tape at 5.15 pm yesterday. Frank looked down to the bottom right of his screen. It was now 9.32 pm. The photo was over 24 hours old.

The image had been dropped in a 'to see' folder earlier today by The Metropolitan Police (*The Met)*. The 'to see' folder was part of a new, collectively-shared database he and a pal of his in The Service, and another in Counterterrorism Police, had been setting up over the previous months. Those with access to the database were: The Secret Service; Secret Intelligence Service; Counterterrorism Police; The Met; Border Agency; and Border Force. It was early days, but he and his two pals' 'Migration Terrorism Mapping Tool' (MTMT for short) was already proving very useful.

Frank hoped the database would earn its keep again today. The man he had on his screen was of particular interest to all of those with access to MTMT. He was sure of it.

Frank twisted his chair to his right and faced a second, smaller screen (there was a third to the left of the big, central monitor; *you can never have enough screens*). His hand swiped and dabbed and a map of Eritrea, north Africa, appeared. Frank thought the country looked like a stick of broccoli, titled to its left a bit. Its right side was all coastline; the Red Sea. The vegetable's 'canopy' bordered Sudan. Its left side joined Ethiopia. Its short base, a border with Djibouti. Despite its very strategic position, facing Saudi Arabia on the west side of the Red Sea, the country was dirt poor. Much of this was down to a 30-year fight for freedom by indigenous Eritreans against Ethiopian 'invaders', who'd annexed the country in the 1960s. Since Ethiopia had been ousted in the 1990s by the Eritrean Liberation Front, the country had been autocratically and poorly run. It had amongst the worst human rights records in the world, and press freedom was a joke. A very recent thaw between the country and her 'big-brother', Ethiopian neighbour had been the first positive sign for over 60 years that something was on the up.

But Frank had seen the latest intelligence assessment. Eritrea was still a basket case. And, importantly for the users of the MTMT, a breeding ground for exporting all manner of criminality.

He was pretty sure he had one such criminal on his central screen. No longer in Eritrea – now in East Putney.

He expanded the map of Eritrea so that the Red Sea port of Mersa Fatma, which was about halfway down Eritrea's 1,000 mile coastline, loomed large. A finger moved to the top right of the screen and found the terrain icon; it prodded and the latest satellite overlay appeared. The date on the overlay was just two days ago.

Mersa Fatma wasn't really a port. It was a place where some people lived between the hilly desert and the sea. The main coastal road dissected the village, which comprised a mosque, about 40 houses on the desert side of the main road and a further 20, including two large (*and new?*) warehouses, on the seaward side. A dirt track joined the coast road to the water's edge, at which point Frank thought he made out a slipway. To the left of the slipway was a long, thin pier, probably made out of wood and concrete. In the sea, bobbing around the pier were, Frank counted, 27 fishing boats.

And a large RIB.

Throughout Frank's manipulations of the Eritrean mapping there had been a constant: a small red, filled-in circle. It rested in the approximate centre of the village, hilly-desert side of the coastal road. He tapped it. A drop-down box appeared detailing a list of 47 names, all of which belonged to one of two 'nasabs', or family names: Khaldun and al-Rasheed. There were plenty of 'bin', sons of, and 'bints', daughters of, on the list. Six - all al-Rasheed and all male - were displayed in red font.

Frank touched on red-fonted, Abir al-Rasheed. A further box appeared. It contained a list of the man's family and character details, including height. Importantly there was also a photograph. It was a mugshot, probably from an Eritrean police file.

Frank put two fingers on the box and flicked it to his left. It shot across the screen, jumped the electronic boundary between right and central monitors and settled in the middle of the screen Frank had been studying earlier. He now had two photos, side by side. One from East Putney. The other from Mersa Fatma.

Frank hoped they were one of the same.

'Hi Frank, how's it going?' Jane's voice over his right shoulder. She broke his concentration.

He looked up at her. 'Fine, thanks, yeah, fine. You?'

Frank thought Jane looked tired, but wouldn't say so. Mind you, she always looked tired. Recently, with the upsurge of 'neo-terrorism', they both worked beyond an acceptable number of hours. He was strictly a Monday to Friday man – unless there was a lockdown - but they were long days. He knew she was in most weekends, and he never saw her leave the office before him. She was dedicated, very good at what she did and a brilliant boss.

Long may that continue.

'I'm fine, thanks, Frank. What have you got there?'

Bless her. She didn't need to ask him. He would brief her when he had something, but it was her way of engaging him: boss to not boss. It took time and energy from her, but gave something back to him. He admired her for it.

'Come with me,' he said.

He was on his feet, heading away from his desk to one of the corners of his piece of open-plan Babylon. He made the corner a few steps later, stopping in front of a massive, 80-inch LED. He assumed Jane was behind him.

He touched the screen and it energised. It displayed a map of Europe, North Africa and the Middle East, including Afghanistan. The map showed country boundaries, capital cities and around 100 small, red and green circles – much like the one he had manipulated at his desk. There was also a little less than 50 filled-in squares – all of them yellow. In the bottom right hand corner of the screen was a navigation box.

Frank pressed an icon in the box and the whole screen came alive with hundreds of ultra-thin blue lines.

They crisscrossed their way diagonally from the bottom and right of the map – North Africa and the Middle East – heading up and left, towards the UK. Nearly all of the blue lines passed through a red or green circle, or both. Many made it to one of 43 yellow squares. The squares were all on the north European coast.

Frank turned to face Jane. She was in deep thought.

'Can I sit down?' Jane asked whilst pointing at the very obvious chair in front of the screen.

'Sure. Sure.' Frank motioned with an open hand to the chair, and then moved to his left so that he wasn't in Jane's line-of-sight of the screen.

'How long has this contraption been here?' Jane pointed to the screen.

She hadn't noticed?

'About two weeks. I paid for it from the operating budget. It was cheap as chips.'

Actually it cost £2,300 but, as lead analyst, Frank controlled a budget 40 times that. And he was well within limits for this year.

'Oh. I'm just surprised I've not noticed it before.' Jane muttered.

I'm not; you're a busy bee.

Jane had been head-down on the neo-terrorism malarkey since Christmas. His area, migration and associated criminality, was tight as a drum, and getting tighter – and, so far, there didn't seem to be a great deal of overlap between criminal migration and the upsurge of unattributable, worldwide terror attacks that were keeping everyone else awake at night.

Frank was about to say something when Jane continued.

'This is a migration map.' A statement, not a question.

'Correct.' Frank answered.

'How long have you been working on this?'

He went for an oblique answer.

'You know you sent me on that conference to The Hague. Remember? A couple of months ago. You said I needed a break and this Europol thing came up. You glanced at the agenda, booked me on it and told me I was going?' Frank's words came out a bit too quickly.

Jane thought for a second.

'Yes. I think so. The one you had to buy a suit for?' If Jane were taking the mickey, it wasn't showing. Actually Frank hadn't bought a suit, although he'd told Jane that he had. However, when he arrived at the conference and discovered he was the only delegate wearing black jeans, a Genesis t-shirt topped with a blazer he had borrowed from his Dad, he did reflect that maybe he should have.

'Yeah. That's the one. Well, it was a migration conference. Economic and conflict migrants. Definitions, rationale, current position – the future. Sharing data. All that sort of stuff. And …'

'And, this was the outcome?' Jane interrupted.

'No. No. No. Not really.' He paused, gathering his thoughts. 'See, Europol have a brilliant database, tracking - where there is suitable information - migrants from Europe's eastern and southern borders, to final "resting" locations.'

'Resting?' Jane asked.

'Well, yeah. The French were keen not to designate where the migrants stop and sort of call their new home as "final". The Germans agreed, so we all said we'd call it "resting", on the assumption that is was temporary ...'

'But, politically you couldn't call it temporary either.' Jane interrupted again.

'Yeah. No, no. You're right. That could mean fewer funds for integration. And the migrants would lose benefits if they were "temporary".' Frank used both hands to demonstrate the quotation marks. 'So we all agreed on "resting".'

'And that's the UK's position?' Jane asked.

Frank thought he saw a grin emerging on Jane's face.

'Well, the Border Agency woman didn't make the conference for some reason, so I flew the flag, so to speak.'

Jane was nodding. And smiling.

'Go on, Frank.'

'Well, the database is brilliant. But, ehh, messy. And not very Anglocentric. It also didn't have everything we have, that is SIS, The Service, etc. That's because until I went on the course, the only agency with access to the info was Border. And they hadn't shared it.'

'So this,' Jane spread her arms, 'is the UK's souped-up version of Europol's database, *a la* Frank.'

Frank thought for a second.

'And Vernon. And Fi.' He added.

'Vernon and Fi?'

'Yeah, well, Vernon's a pal of mine from The Service, and Fi works at Counterterrorism. Fi's an expert with the front end ...', Frank tapped the top of the screen, '... and between Vernon and me, we did the modelling. Simples.'

Jane was nodding again. She looked pleased.

'Go on, then.'

'OK.' He took a deep breath. 'It's complicated. If you look closely you'll see that the red circles are terminals. That is, the blue transit lines stop, or, more accurately, start, at a red circle. They're "originating locations", where the migrants come from - originally.' He added unnecessarily. 'As you can see, they're spread everywhere in the east and the south. Most of the known documented migrants are from Afghanistan, Iraq and Syria. You know that. Using Europol data fused with our own, that's everything from all of our agencies and services, we have around 1,800 discrete "originating locations". Villages. Towns, Cities. Quite often down to house numbers, although whether the house is still standing, or a pile of rubble, we couldn't say.'

He picked the red circle that was centred on Mosul in Iraq and touched it. A new insert box appeared: an expanded view of Mosul, around 100 kilometres square. The one red circle had morphed into dozens and dozens.

'At city level, there are 73 separate locations in Mosul.' Frank paused to let Jane take it in. He touched one of the new red circles. A dialogue box appeared like the one on the right-hand screen back at his desk. Except this box had 127 names. Seven names were in red,

He stabbed at one of the non-red names. A further dialogue box appeared. Some subsidiary information dropped down, but there was no photograph. However, at the same time as the migrant's details were presented, one of the blue transit lines lit up brighter than the others. It left Mosul, travelled northwest through Baghdad, then due north to a green circle on the Iraqi/Turkish border. It stopped there.

'This guy ...', Frank leant forward to see the man's name, '... Mohamed Ibrahim, originates from Mosul and ...', he used a finger to trace the highlighted blue line to where it stopped, '... he's, as far as the intelligence tells us, currently in the Andac refugee camp.'

Jane had leant forward so she could get a better picture.

'Turkish side?' She asked.

'Correct.' Frank said.

'Where did this int come from?' Jane looked confused. 'Unless he's been picked up by our people in Iraq, we'd have no record of Ibrahim. We don't have access to the refugees in the camps. And I can't imagine that Europol do either? Unless he was a previously known criminal.'

Frank let out a long breath. He had a lot to do and it was starting to get late. He needed to eat something. And he never went to bed without watching at least two episodes of *The Big Bang Theory*. He wouldn't be in bed before midnight.

'DfID (*Department for International Development*). They have access to most of the camp's registers. For no other reason than their own bookkeeping. They only have boots on the ground in six or seven; Jordan mostly. But they have contacts with The Red Cross, The Red Crescent, Save the Children, etc.'

Jane was sat back in her chair now.

'I'm surprised they would want to share that. A leak of their information attributed to us would drive a wedge between them and the aid agencies?' Jane asked.

'Actually, not so much. We played the "national security" card. And, when they need to, they have access to this database. The know we're keeping it close to our chests. Currently everyone's fine with it.'

Jane nodded. But Frank thought she wasn't completely comfortable with them abusing their DfID contacts. He was sure she would check with her oppo at the Department sometime soon.

'Why are some of the names in red?' Jane asked.

Frank didn't reply. Instead he touched one of the red names. A new dialogue box appeared; this one had a photo. And a second blue transit line lit up. It led all the way from Mosul, through Turkey, across the corner of

The Black Sea, north to Bulgaria, then Serbia, Austria, Germany, stopping at a yellow square in northern Germany.

'That man, or woman, has made it all the way to the German coast – Bremerhaven, I guess?' Jane asked.

'Yeah. That's right. If they make it to a yellow square, we're assuming they're looking to cross to England. And if I pick another ...'

Frank touched another red name. This time the illuminated blue line transited through Jordan, across the Med to Greece, then Italy, France, up to the French coast, crossing the channel and ended in London. The yellow box, the point of departure from France, was down a touch from Calais.

'That man ... woman, crossed south of Calais. Boulogne?' Jane asked.

'There, or there abouts. The original dialogue box here ...', Frank pointed back to Mosul, '... will detail the transit itinerary.' He looked. 'No, we think the crossing was by a chartered yacht from Wissant, between Calais and Boulogne. Where we can, we have attributed a degree of accuracy to the detail. We have 65% on Wissant. And, wait ...', he looked again at the screen, '... 80% on him landing just down from Brighton.'

There was silence for a few seconds. Jane stood and walked to the window just down from where the screen was. The views from this side of the building were unremarkable. Frank knew that if she craned her head she might be able make out one of the four towers of

Battersea Power Station. Although, probably not tonight as rain was draining diagonally across the window.

'By the way,' Frank continued, 'We know much of this because Border Force closed down the particular yacht charter. The guy's in court next week. They did a good job.'

If Jane heard him, she didn't respond. She just kept staring out of the window.

He waited.

She turned back to him. She looked stony-faced and then, as if he'd caught her looking glum, she smiled.

'This is a huge piece of work, Frank. Well done you lot. How many migrants?'

He paused to get the numbers straight in his head.

'There are 845,000 on the database. Most of whom we have just cut and pasted in, letting Cynthia (*SIS's AI mainframe*) piece together much of the detail. The three of us have carried out a one percent gross error check over the last three weeks, that's 8,500 names. We've only found a handful of anomalies. It's pretty watertight.'

'And how many have made the UK – illegally?' She asked.

'If you believe the database, and The Met and Border are still inputting their own known names, since 2014 we reckon 4,300. That doesn't include the 15,000 or so legal migrants the government has allowed into the country from Afghanistan, Iraq and Syria since the start of the crisis.'

'4,300 illegals! That's a huge number. Do the politicians know?' Frank thought Jane deserved to sound shocked.

'I haven't told them.' He couldn't think of a better response.

There was a further silence.

'How many of these are thought to be involved in criminality, or indeed terrorism?'

That's a good question. It was difficult to answer. Counterterrorism Police and The Service, The Met and the other police forces, would only know of those they'd arrested. Or had tagged.

'We've taken the view that all of the 4,300 are economic migrants. Whilst that doesn't tell us a great deal, it does mean once they're here they are likely to do anything for money. And, nearly all of them are poor, so susceptible to radicalisation. Of course, when they're here they're The Service's bailiwick - the migrants are on their turf. So you'd get a better overview from speaking to a pal over there. But, my mate Vernon reckons 75% of economic migrants are either immediately or, pretty soon after they arrive, on the wrong end of modern-day slavery. The men in illegal, poorly paid chain gangs, or as servants; the women as sex workers.'

Frank didn't like to think about it. He could cope with these sorts of things happening overseas – in his work domain. But not in his own backyard.

'And is the movement slowing?' The obvious supplementary from Jane.

'Yes, and, well, maybe not.' He pressed a button on the top of the screen and it went blank. 'Come with me, please.'

Frank led Jane back to his desk.

'Do you mind?' He was pointing to his chair.

'No, of course not, Frank. Sit.'

He sat and touched his middle screen, which had switched to power saving mode. It lit up again showing the same two photos.

'We reckon illegal migration is down to no more than 50 a month, maybe less. Border Force, and indeed all of the overseas border and coastal services, from Portugal through to Denmark, are getting much better and preventing people getting on boats. However …'

He pointed at the two photos of the man on the screen.

'A good number of economic migrants are part of a chain. Somebody - or a group of people, normally a village - raise enough cash for a singleton to make the perilous journey from Afghanistan, Iraq, whatever, across Europe and into the UK. Once here, their job is to raise money. When they have a wodge they transfer it by, say, Western Union, back to their village. The village elders save that money until they have enough for the next one to make the same journey. And so on.' He paused for breath. 'The Met busted an operation the other week where there were eight members from the same village in Afghanistan – five men and three women - living in a one-up, one-down in Brixton. The house was a shoebox. The eight were living with 12 other migrants. Twenty altogether. On interrogation, other than the first, all of them had travelled on the back of money raised by those here in the UK.'

'Eight? From the same village, one after the other?' It wasn't really a question from Jane.

'Eight.'

'And they were all in modern-day slavery or involved in some form of criminality?'

'Both. The Met were busting a drugs ring. The six men were low-level carriers. The two women, sex slaves for the badly organised cartel. Apparently the conditions they found them in were squalid.'

'That's…' Jane didn't finish her sentence. 'But we think we're getting better at stopping this?'

'Yes. Except.' Frank looked back at his screen. 'Look at this guy.'

Jane bent over and read the name from the mugshot Frank had taken from his right hand screen earlier.

'Abir al-Rasheed.' She glanced across at Frank's screen which still showed a blow-up of a small portion of Eritrea. 'He's from … Somalia?'

'Eritrea.' Frank corrected Jane. 'But a good guess. I haven't corroborated the two photos yet. But if they are the same man then he's a migrant from the village of Mersa Fatma.'

'What's so special about him, Frank.'

'Our people in Asmara, the Eritrean capital, have Abir al-Rasheed fishing, just off the coast from Mersa Fatma, about two weeks ago.'

'Two weeks? But the journey normally takes months?' Jane sounded incredulous.

Frank didn't say anything for a second. Instead he focused on his screen, placing his index fingers on the two men. He moved the images so that they were touching. *Are they the same man? Could be.* He had three others like al-Rasheed, and they all needed corroborating. He wasn't quite ready for Jane … yet.

What the hell.

'If I can get Cynthia's facial recognition programme to make a match, then I think we have a new type of immigrant. Let's call them "fast-tracked".'

Jane didn't say anything for a second.

She stood upright and stretched her back, and let out a little yawn.

'Sorry,' she added. Then she asked, 'Why?'

He turned to face her again.

'Because the cost of moving them here quickly must be worth their value, plus some. They must have a special skill, or skills.' His expression lost its intensity. 'Although, the view from our people in Asmara is Rasheed is just a plain old fisherman.' Frank answered.

Jane blinked. And then shook her head.

'It doesn't make sense. If there's plenty of money available, why not just pay for decent forged documentation, get al-Rasheed the bus to Cairo and fly him here?'

Frank mused for a second.

'Because then we have him, or at least a facsimile of him but with a different name. On our records. He'll be tagged coming through customs. He'll not be completely invisible. If he comes overland and by boat, we don't know he's here.'

'Good point, Frank. Good point. That makes sense.'

Jane looked at her watch. Frank knew it was close to nine-forty-five.

'Look, I've still got lots of stuff to do. And I haven't asked you what I originally came over here for.'

'What was that?' Frank asked.

'Have you ever heard of the FFO, a South Ossetia Islamic terror group?'

No.

'No, sorry. Should I?'

'No. Not really. Never mind.' Jane put a hand up. 'And I need to talk to you about this whole migrant thing and you coordinating migration work with the sub-Saharan desk. But that can wait.'

Frank glanced over his left shoulder to the 80-incher in the corner. What Jane had failed to pick up were the blue transit lines that fell off the screen due south, as if into an abyss. Those lines had terminals in sub-Saharan countries such as Guinea, Sierra Leone and Ghana. Whatever she was going to ask of him, he was pretty sure he was already onto it.

Appartamento VI, Via Mortelle, Naples

Gareth unlocked the front door to his flat with his spare hand and used his bum to push it open. His free hand was carrying the shopping he'd picked up from the local *Conad* supermarket. His bag of goodies, which included fresh clams, would knock up a superb *spaghetti alle vongole*. It would be hot on the table in about three hours when Giorgio got in from work. And, over the meal, rather than fantasise about him wearing the sauce, they'd have a long and in-depth conversation about each other. They would.

After this yesterday's meeting with Chiara, it had been a frantic and reasonably interesting afternoon – so much so he'd worked until 7 pm. At which point the caretaker had thrown him out.

Matteo Monza.

The name on the back of Chiara's business card. The Mafia's influence on Italian art.

Couldn't be.

He was huge. A young Italian protean artist – no medium was beyond him.

Originally Monza studied at the Florence Academy of Fine Arts. His brilliance was quickly recognised and after two years he was offered a place at the Rhode Island School of Design, a top-ranking art school in Boston, US – known for its more modern and maverick approach to art and design. If you were into art, Monza's work was already legendary - even at the tender age of 28. His most recent work, which Gareth thought was easily his best, was an immersion piece put together in Amsterdam. Monza had taken over the whole top floor of a disused warehouse, creating enclosed narrow corridors and much larger 'domey' rooms from polystyrene. Entitled *Death in Paradise*, it was all blue/black - as if you'd been dropped into the ocean. Whilst the corridors and the display rooms were exhibits in themselves, the art they held had a dystopian-aquatic theme. There was one room filled with thousands of fish – all blue, set off against a black background. When you looked closer, small white plastic balls floated around the fish, delicately balancing on almost invisible wires. Then you noticed half of the fish were portrayed as being dead; floating upside down. Dead fish and plastic. It was shocking.

Moving through an all-blue corridor you were met by the huge mouth of a whale, its small teeth made of discarded plastic bottles, its tongue from dark blue plastic bags. As if you were Jonah, the passage through the exhibit led you down into the whale's throat. You popped out the other side into a new room with even more startling work displaying the effect of plastics and debris on our oceans and rivers.

It was the most remarkable thing Gareth had ever seen, amplified by the fact only one person could enter the exhibit at any one time – you were let in, on your own, at intervals. To enhance the effect, the rooms were cold and the accompanying soundtrack had been recorded in the depths of the Atlantic Ocean. He had travelled to Amsterdam during his Spring break to see the exhibition; it was brilliant.

Monza was currently working on a new exhibit in Chicago. Its theme was a secret, but everyone expected it to be some form of anti-popularist, anti-climate change – maybe even anti-religion? – piece, to highlight the US's current slide away from centrist politics towards isolationism. It was due to open for the Christmas break. Gareth was doing all he could to find the airfare and get a ticket.

But Monza having some Mafia involvement? If it were true, as Gareth had commented to Chiara this morning, it would be a huge revelation. And it would surely destroy his reputation.

Gareth had spent the afternoon on Google. He'd pieced together Monza's childhood and career. He was born in Turin – hardly Mafia country – to professional parents. His father was an engineer; also from the north. He'd met his mother, a Swiss national and a half-decent artist, whilst he was skiing in Cortina; seemingly no Mafia influence there. From what he could gather Monza's schooling had been unremarkable, but he had shown a real ability for art, winning a couple of local competitions. Pushed by his mother he'd earned a place at Florence's Academy of Fine Arts where he had thrived.

But it was at Rhode Island where his true talent unfurled. His ability as a traditional artist now mixed with an almost explosive creative pallet. Strange, thought-provoking and, for some, heart-stopping exhibits followed. Since he'd left Rhode Island he'd had major exhibitions in Berlin and Beijing. Amsterdam followed.

But none of it pointed toward a Mafia connection. As far as Gareth could tell he'd never travelled further south than Florence. And Boston was hardly the centre of 'the Mob'. It didn't make much sense.

Running out of ideas he had managed to unearth a list of sponsors for the Amsterdam set. He recognised one of the businesses and a couple of the names, but the list was a couple of pages long. By the time he started Googling each one the caretaker had stuck his head round the door and asked him to leave.

He'd pick up on that piece of work tomorrow.

In four strides Gareth was in the centre of the flat, a quarter turn right and he was at his kitchen table. It was three rooms. A kitchen/sitting room, a decent sized bedroom and a bathroom. Best for him, though, was the obligatory narrow double doors leading out onto a concrete Juliet balcony where he could just fit two folding, metal chairs. From there, if he strained his neck, he could see Vesuvius in the distance. Perfect.

He put the bag of groceries on the table … and noticed something.

In the middle of the table, next to a small vase with a single, plastic red rose, was a small brown parcel, no bigger than something his monthly contact lenses were delivered in. He picked it up and studied it. It was neatly wrapped and marked with his name in capitals, scribed in black felt tip. There was no stamp – no postage details at all. But, of course, there wouldn't have been. Along with all the other flats his post was delivered to a small mailbox in the tatty lobby of the apartment block. He checked it regularly by putting his fingers into the hole where the mail would be dropped. He'd looked on the way in; there was nothing there.

And no one had a key to his flat, apart from him and his landlord. He'd made a note to get one cut for Giorgio, but hadn't got round to it.

Oh well. It was clearly something from his altogether vacant landlord. He'd never met the man. On arrival he'd been let in by a neighbour. And he paid his rent via the Academy. If he thought about it, he wasn't sure who his landlord was.

A cup of tea first?

He was about to put the package back on the table when inquisitiveness overcame him. He lifted the box to his ear and shook it. There was a sloshing sound.

Mmm. Good. An alcoholic, belated, 'welcome to Naples' from his landlord.

He nodded and smiled to himself.

With box in hand he walked across the room and opened the balcony double doors, which pulled toward him. He was met by the noise and smells of the city. Fish and unburnt fuel. Air conditioning. Cars, mopeds and the constant chatter of Italian talkmanship. A woman opposite was hanging out her washing on a metal airer that hung from the railings of her own balcony. She was shouting at high speed to someone behind her, failing to overcome the noise of the TV inside the room.

His tiny brick and tarmac garden had its own particular atmosphere. It was fantastic.

He stepped onto the balcony and sat on one of the chairs. The sun, now low in the sky, was a distant memory to the street below. But the bricks retained their heat. It must have been 28 degrees in his particular piece of shade.

Gareth looked at the package for the final time and then unwrapped it.

Inside was a white box. It was second-hand and had Italian markings. It looked like the packaging from a clothing shop; possibly a box for some socks, or similar?

He turned the box on its end and opened the lid. He peered inside. There was a see-through plastic bag; maybe one inside another. The bags were what was holding the fluid.

This is very odd.

Squeezed between the bag and the side of the box was a piece paper. He didn't know what to go for first.

So he pulled out the plastic bag.

And almost dropped it.

It was disgusting. His stomach gave a lurch, but he steadied himself. Between a finger and a thumb he held the specimen at arm's length, pulling his shoulders away from the bag so that it was as far away from him as possible without dropping it onto the pavement below. He turned his face to one side and grimaced.

Inside the bags, suspended in clear liquid, was an eye. A whole eye. Like someone had ripped it from … well, what? A human? *Someone's eye?* Surely not? It must belong to an animal. *Or it's fake?*

He had no idea how big his own eyeball was, but he could guess. About the same size as the one in the bag …

A human eye? What kind of sick joke was this?

His brain went into spasm. All manner of scenarios filled the gap between his ears.

What? Well ... no, surely not?

The note!

That might help.

Still holding the bag at arm's length and with the box now between his knees, he took out the note. It was written using the same felt tip that had scribed his name on the outside of the brown packaging.

It read:

LEAVE HIM ALONE!

What the ...?

Gareth felt his stomach weaken.

Him? Who?

Monza?

How did they know? Who were 'they'? How did they get onto him so quickly? He'd only met with Chiara this morning. Were they listening at their table? Did they know Chiara was going to talk to him about Monza? Were they monitoring his computer?

Really?

And they'd got into my apartment!

My apartment!

And ... for God's sake.

Who were they?

He didn't have time to consider that question any further. His stomach had a clearer and more present danger. He had to make it to the bathroom.

Chapter 4

Bolotnikovskaya Ulitsa, Moscow, Russia

Sam picked up a bowl from the plastic rack on the draining board. She wiped it dry with a gingham tea-towel, half turned and placed it on the wooden table behind her, next to the other items she had just finished drying. The kitchen was clean and simple. But there was no dishwasher.

'It's a lovely apartment, Alena.' Sam said in perfect Russian. 'How long have you, Vlad and the children been here?'

Alena was washing a big pan which an hour earlier held the largest pork and dumpling stew Sam had ever seen. Sam had ladled onto her plate as much as her stomach could cope with – Russians don't do small portions and she was very keen not to appear rude. Vlad, just as she remembered from having shared a restaurant table with him before, ate more than enough for three men. The two kids, a lad and a lass, followed their Dad. Alena, who untypically for a middle-aged Russian woman had the body of someone 20 years younger, ate less than she did. Which was good news. Sam didn't feel so bad about turning down seconds.

Alena stopped mid-scrub. She stared absently out of the ground floor window. It was getting dark. Sam had caught the end of the news as she'd arrived at their apartment. Rain was expected in Moscow any time soon.

Maybe snow overnight. It would be turning colder and staying that way for, well, possibly until next April. The weatherman hadn't said the last bit, but having spent a winter in Moscow Sam knew what to expect.

'About eighteen months, maybe. After Vlad came out of hospital.' Alena looked over her shoulder, through the kitchen door and into the small sitting room. Sam followed her eyeline. Vlad was on the settee. The daughter, whom Sam reckoned was around 12, was sitting on his lap. The son beside him. They were watching one of those madly-painful Japanese athletic shows, where men attempt almost impossible assault courses before falling in the drink. All three of them were shouting at the screen.

Alena continued. 'He couldn't make the stairs up to the old flat, so we had to find this place real quick. It's nice enough. And the local schools are good.' She was scrubbing the pan again now. Sam, efficient as ever, was waiting for her.

'It's good to see him again.' Sam meant it. A couple of years ago she and Vlad had worked together for six months on various SIS/FSB collaborations. That was before they'd both got involved in the Sokolov affair. He was the only member of the FSB team who showed her, a woman, any respect. Until the cabin fire separated them, they had been a good team.

Alena stopped washing and turned to face Sam.

'Will you promise me something?' Alena's face had anxiety sketched all over it.

Sam knew what was coming, but didn't pre-empt what Alena would say next.

'Of course, Alena. If I can.'

'Please keep Vlad safe. I know what happened before wasn't your fault, but we can't afford to lose any more of him.'

There were tears in her eyes now.

Immediately Sam felt out of place. This wasn't her thing – displaying empathy, even though somewhere deep inside she felt something stir. She had absolutely no idea what to say - or do - so she answered the question as honestly as she could.

'Vlad and I are not, strictly speaking, working together. You know, side by side. Not this time.'

She tried to sound natural – caring. But she knew she was talking to Vlad's wife as if she were briefing a senior officer. Any normal person would have given the woman a hug. Or held her arm gently whilst they chatted. She'd seen them do that on TV.

But no, not me. Not Sam, bloody-hopeless, Green.

'We are travelling south tomorrow. Together. But Vlad is staying in Russia. I'm going "overseas", as it were. He'll be quite safe … I'm sure.' She added the last bit as an afterthought, realising as she spoke she had no way of guaranteeing Vlad's safety.

Still uncomfortable, Sam smiled, leant forward and touched Alena's arm. A pat, that was all.

Like how an allergy-ridden idiot would treat a moulting dog.

Alena smiled back and nodded, dabbing her eyes with the dishcloth. She didn't seem convinced.

'Thank you. Thank you. Vlad tells me very little.'

There was a lot Sam could have told Alena. She'd had the full FSB briefing on the FFO this morning. It had answered a number of growing concerns that Sam had about her part in Vlad's plan.

And she wasn't the only one who was dubious. As Vlad had suggested, she'd called Jane from the hut on the beach. Jane, who was surprised to hear from her (they hadn't chatted for over six months) was even more surprised when Sam had put the, 'would it be treasonous if ...' question to her. Their conversation hadn't been a long one. Sam wasn't one for small talk, and stuck in a wooden hut on a shingle beach in Norfolk with the FSB for company, it probably wasn't an appropriate time. What had caught Sam off guard was Jane - and therefore, she guessed, the whole of SIS - had not heard of the Freedom For Oppressed. After a couple of supplementaries Jane asked to be given some time to consider the question.

Putting a hand to the phone's mouthpiece, Sam had asked Vlad, 'How long do we have?'.

He'd looked at his watch and replied that the Gulfstream's flight plan to Moscow would be void in 85 minutes, and the airfield was 30 minutes away.

That would be none, then.

In the end Jane had told Sam to fly to Moscow. She would brief the staff in the Embassy to expect her in country. And finally she and Jane had agreed to talk again this morning.

Jane had phoned mid-morning after Sam had had the FSB brief. As Sam knew they were going to be discussing classified information, she'd phoned her back on one of the SIS/FSB secure links.

Once live, Sam'd asked, 'You remember the Moscow suicide-bus bomb in February?'

Jane came straight back. 'Yes. Filevsky Park. Twenty-five dead. FSB attributed the attack to Chechen rebels. They arrested five of the group after a highspeed chase on the E30 motorway to Smolensk. The court case in currently ongoing. It will be a whitewash.'

'Exactly.' Sam replied. 'That's *exactly* what happened. Before the attack FSB had their eyes on a new Chechen grouping. The bomb goes off and, as if by magic, five of the new Chechen team go down. Classic FSB reaction: incident – then round up anyone you want, as soon as you can. Everyone's happy.'

'That's their MO, Sam. But, as you know, they also undertake a thorough investigation and, in their own time, find the real culprits.'

'Yes. And they've done that. This time it's the FFO - a new, tightknit terror cell. They're South Ossetian Muslims, but with Georgian blood. They hate the Russians, who have their *Kirka* Army boots trampling all over their homeland – and they hate the mostly secular Georgian government, who still think they run their country. And, according to the FSB, they have lots of

Muslim fans on the Russian side of the border. It's a tinder keg down there.' Her briefing was sharp.

Sam waited for an answer. One came a few seconds later.

'But it's not our fight, Sam. If the Russians want to take apart a terror cell across the border in South Ossetia, there may be some murmurs in the UN from, say Iran, but against the backdrop of the latest terror cycle it'll be lost in the noise. *However*, an ex-SIS case officer getting caught in the process … well, that would leave us with some very uncomfortable questions. At the highest level.'

Jane was right. So far.

But she didn't have all the intelligence.

This morning, once the general briefing had been completed, Vlad had led her into another room which was full of filing cabinets and a standalone safe. He'd taken a thin file out of the safe and passed it to Sam – it was tagged at the highest level of FSB security clearance. Sam had read the three pages in less than a minute: two folios of words, three photos and a map.

The first photo showed a Russian military convoy. It had been ambushed. There were dead soldiers lying around three *Kamaz* trucks. A caption said the convoy was a detachment from 21st Guards Motor Rifle Brigade on its way to a live-fire exercise in Elista.

A second photo was of the inside of a military warehouse. Pride of place were five 82 millimetre *Podnos* mortars. An insert to the photo showed 12 pallets of high explosive rounds. A caption explained that this stash was a replica of the weapons and munitions that had been taken by the raid on the convoy. There was a paragraph in the blurb which highlighted the lethality of the mortars. Sam didn't need to read it. She knew the detail. The *Podnos* was a copy of the British Army 81 millimetre mortar. It broke down into three parts: the baseplate; the tube; and the tripod. It was man-packable - if you'd spent all your time in the gym and didn't want to lug it too far. Both mortars had a maximum range of around six kilometres. But, as you reduce the C-charges – the propellant that's shaped like a broken ring-doughnut; they slip on a rod at the bottom of the mortar round – and point the tube skyward, you can hit a target which is very close. Mortarmen don't like it when you ask them to do that, though. A small miscalculation and they get back what they've sent up.

And that's the thing about mortars. They're 'area' weapons. You can't take out a small target, like a tank, with a mortar – unless you're really lucky. But, if you want to level a sizeable building, cheaply and effectively, then pop along to Mortars-R-Us. And take a big shopping trolley with you.

The final photo was of the *Novovoronezh* nuclear powerplant in Voronezh, Oblast, about 500 miles north of the Russian/Georgian border. Again, Sam recognised it immediately. SIS Moscow were constantly concerned about the theft of nuclear fuel and waste. The whole team was alive to that possibility. When she was there they ran four agents in *Rosatom*, the Russian agency that oversaw the plants. Sam's view was four was nowhere near enough.

The map was a 50 by 50 kilometre overhead of the same power station. Whoever had produced it had drawn on two concentric rings, with the powerplant at the centre. The inner had a radius of 500 metres - the second at six kilometres; between them was the effective operating space of an 82 millimetre mortar if the centre was the target. Apart from the nuclear facility and the odd hamlet, inside the outer ring was nothing but fields, forest and hills. Sam had done a quick calculation. She reckoned the space between the two rings was 110 square kilometres. That was a mighty amount of real estate in which to hide five mortars each of which was not much bigger than a wheelie bin.

The written part of the briefing put together a very plausible case that the FFO were responsible for the attack on the convoy and they now had in their possession five *Podnos* mortars and enough ammunition to blow up a small town. In addition, FSB had intelligence that suggested a recent grenade strike on an Army checkpoint in South Ossetia had actually been a mortar attack. A sort of 'practice run', to familiarise themselves with the equipment - and get their eye in.

Frighteningly, and the key to the dossier, was that there was additional intelligence, picked up by mobile-phone intercept, that showed the FFO were primed to attack the power station at any time. The latest prognosis was an attack within three weeks.

Sam couldn't verify the intelligence – she just had the folder. But it all looked sound. She had to trust it.

Vlad had added the reason Hasan Kutnetsov wanted to talk to a reputable journalist was so the moment the FFO hit the site there would be someone out there who knew who they were, and believed they were capable of such an attack.

Sam had briefed all of this to Jane.

Who said nothing.

'Are you there, Jane?' Sam couldn't hide her impatience.

'Yes. Look. If the FFO wants to make the headlines, then why not come out and claim responsibility for the Moscow bombing?'

It was a good question. She'd posed the same one to Vlad.

'It's a question of credibility. You can only boast when you already have a reputation. They wanted the FSB to track them down *first*. They laid a trial from the Moscow bombing to them. FSB made that connection themselves. Now they think they can be taken seriously. And a chat to a *bone fide* journalist will seal the deal. It make sense if you look at it that way.' It certainly made sense to Sam.

There was more silence.

'Look, Sam ...'

Sam didn't like the way this might be going. She wanted to meet with Kutnetsov - with the full support of SIS.

'... look. I had a chat to the boss this morning. He was, like me, dead against this. But, maybe with the nuclear thing, and with the FSB seemingly being open with us about this, I think we might be playing a whole new sport.'

That was better; but Jane paused further.

Sam waited.

She could hear the cogs turning.

'Go ahead, but keep in touch. I want this on paper before you leave Moscow, mind. And I want the Director of the FSB to phone C. Clear? I'll brief him now, and if you don't hear from me, then you can assume it's all green.'

Brilliant.

That's what she could have told Alena. That and the fact she knew more about Reuters and how their freelance journalists work than she'd done 12 hours earlier. And that she was due to be met at 4.00 pm tomorrow by a member of the FFO, at a specific point in South Ossetia close to the Russian border - where a dirt track meets a paved road.

Alone.

But Sam didn't tell her any of that.

Instead she dried the pan, which was the last of the washing up, and put the cloth on the radiator by the door.

'If you go into the lounge, Sam, I'll make us all some coffee.' The wetness in Alena's eyes had gone. But her smile was forced. Alena probably liked her, but Sam thought she didn't trust her; that Sam favoured mission success over her husband's remaining limbs.

If she'd asked Sam that question, her husband's safety versus mission success, she wasn't sure she could have answered. She didn't think she knew the answer. She didn't have that sort of capacity. Not for deep thinking. She just did what was right when the time came along. She never wanted anyone to get hurt, but she couldn't say she had any well thought-through principles. No particular mantra. Things happened and she reacted. As best she could.

And with all the other things going on in her head, dwelling on something was the last thing she was capable of right now.

Anyhow, thinking about stuff like that made the end of her fingers tingle, and she wasn't sure that was a good feeling.

And coffee sounded like a decent idea. And she was pretty sure Alena had turfed out her daughter so Sam could use her room. She'd argue strongly for sleeping on the couch once they got to that point.

Headquarters SIS, Vauxhall, London

It was late again. *Late, late, late.* Jane was shattered. Last night, after she'd finished with Frank and his 80-inch screen with the blue spider's web, she'd spent another hour sifting through papers she hadn't had chance to look at during the day. And then today. Another day playing master juggler. Her phone call with Sam. The revelation that the FFO looked like a joined-up Islamic terror group after all, with an eye on a big prize. Then clearing Sam's support to the FSB with the Chief, something no one in the building could recall ever happening before. There was plenty of recent history of FSB and SIS joint operations, but nothing where the UK's support was being provided by a 'mercenary', ex-SIS case officer. Neither she nor the chief had come to a conclusion as to whether or not Sam was actually working on behalf of the SIS - 'in from the cold', or she was working on her own with their tacit approval. They'd checked with the lawyers who, in the first instance, couldn't agree on a preferred line. Apparently they were going to come back tomorrow with a quorum.

And then the latest terror attack - 10.22 am local in Singapore. The attacks were getting more and more bizarre; more and more difficult to fathom.

That reminded her. She needed to update the map.

Jane stood and moved away from her chair. She had a quick glance in the long mirror on the wall opposite her chair.

Jane Baker. Head of SIS Operations: North Africa and Mid-East.

One level below the chief and the deputy. For someone with her experience, the plum job in Babylon.

In my opinion.

Some might argue to be head of station in Beijing or Moscow were better posts; manipulating British government foreign policy with the 'big two'. Using of the minute intelligence extracted from local agents to second guess what China or Russia would do next. Does Russia have ambitions in the Baltic States? Are the

Chinese manipulating their currency so their goods were cheaper abroad? SIS recruited agents from every strata of society – every level of government. Those agents risked everything for money, or for fear of being exposed by the very hands of the case officers who were running them.

Wheels within wheels.

Moscow and Beijing: semi-independent stations wielding massive influence.

The best job?

No.

My job is better.

She oversaw multiple smaller stations, some with as few as two case officers, with no admin staff – blistered onto Embassies where the Ambassador was often embarrassed to have them work out of the same building. Nobody likes having spies in their midst.

She coordinated intelligence from across a fractured and war-torn region. She briefed the senior echelons of British government, the remaining intelligence agencies, the police, Special Forces and the rest of the military, on the fusion of the intelligence that came from her people. People who were in danger *every day*. They risked their lives meeting agents at RVs in dangerous and sordid locations. They took photographs, listened to phone calls, made voice-recordings, sifted through realms of data and, hardest of all, groomed new contacts. She knew how hard that was; a painstaking job lifting up plenty of rocks. Exposing other human beings' mistakes and frailties. And then exploiting them.

There was some glamour. Undercover as an Embassy-badged employee, case officers sometimes wined and dined with the higher echelons of society, hoping to finger that government worker, or industry bigwig, who was ripe for turning; an indiscretion here – a bounced cheque there. It was rarely about ideology; it was nearly always about money.

But most of their agents were low level contacts. Easily bought; often unreliable. And from those agents came more information than her staff could manage. Information was raw data - like tons of gravel in a riverbed. Most of the time it was dull, repetitive and unrewarding work. What they needed was useable intelligence, an often irregular occurrence - the nugget of gold gleaned from a sift of the pebbles.

Unlike Russia and China where diplomatic immunity gave SIS staff some comfort, nearly all her staff worked in broken countries, or where governments turned a blind eye to the rule of law. Every time her staff ventured outside of the Embassies to which they were attached, their lives were in danger.

Every time.

No wonder, as she looked at the mirror, she saw a different Jane to the one she remembered. Older. More haggard.

Her Mum was right. She had started to migrate south.

She was a wearer of big pants.

Ho hum.

Jane dismissed the mirror and walked around the small conference table that took up the centre of the room. She stopped in front of a traditional paper map of the world. It was big, probably three metres by one, and it was sitting just off the vertical on a wooden easel. Jane thought someone had probably had to pop out to a local art shop to buy the easel, and possibly to IKEA to get the map big enough to cover a small wall. On the lip of the easel were a couple of folios of sticky stars in two colours: blue and red.

Blue was for physical attacks; red for cyber. On the map were 47 blue stickers and 38 red. And they were distributed reasonably evenly across the map - on all five continents, save Antarctica. There was no key, or any explanatory remarks. It was just a map of what SIS had classified as neo-terrorist incidents.

Still only seven stars fell within her AO. Technically they were the ones she should be interested in. And she was. She had a new, cross-agency team trying to establish if there were any connection between the seven. Was there a theme? Could one organisation be behind the attacks? Or were they just random acts of violence and destruction, spawned from a new world order? An order where those wanting to make statements got off their soap boxes, stopped Tweeting and gathering hordes for riots and demonstrations via Facebook, and resorted to terror?

Yes, she had four of her best on the case. And so far there was no news.

But she needed to see the bigger picture. See all the dots. Get the global view. Even if her technology was from the '70s.

She peeled off a blue sticker and placed it on Singapore.

About eight hours ago in the MacRitchie Reservoir Park in Singapore, two men blew up one of the stanchions holding up a hiking attraction: The Tree Top Walk. The attraction did what it said: it allowed visitors to walk among the canopy. The highlight of the walk was a suspension bridge between the tops of the trees. Before the blast hikers experienced the world from 25 metres above the ground. After the blast, the bridge collapsed. Two people were dead, falling with the metal and wood as it plummeted to the ground. The perpetrators escaped into the park; they were still at large. One eyewitness had seen the men. She'd told the authorities that they looked like Singaporeans.

Jane stood back and rested her chin in her hand.

It doesn't make sense.

What was their point? Why The Tree Top Walk? Sure, it's going to make the news. You can't bring chewing gum into city, so blowing up a minor attraction and murdering a few tourists was going to be a huge headline. Clearly you don't mind killing people. And, by the look of things, you're not so keen on getting killed or apprehended yourself. *But they could've killed more.* Singapore was a centre for technology. If you can put together an IED capable of bringing down a pedestrian bridge, why not remotely detonate it by mobile signal?

Place a backpack in the centre of the VivoCity Mall, walk away about 50 metres and press 'Send'. One hundred dead – maybe more?

Two dead and a broken bridge that went nowhere. It seemed pretty pointless; futile, almost.

Jane stepped back a pace and took in the whole map. She reminded herself of the attacks so far, starting in the northwest moving south and east. She pointed at each dot as she did.

'Anchorage bar bomb, Alaska; quarry grade explosives; three dead; no one has claimed responsibility; no arrests. Cyber attack on the Vancouver City Bank; no casualties; fall out unknown or well protected by the bank; SIS assessment is one billion Canadian dollars lost in the ether; no arrests. Cancun beach shooting, Mexico; twenty-five dead; two perps shot dead at the scene - one was a local, the second from Miami – native US, Mexican grandparents; no allegiance or affiliation known; only usable int was that both men had significant debt. The Machu Picchu bombing; a large amount of homemade explosives with considerable damage to the outer wall of the temple (how they managed to get the bomb there in the first place was a mystery); bomb was remotely detonated at sunset when there was a large group of tourists in situ; thankfully the tour was in a different part of the attraction to the bomb; no fatalities, only minor injuries; no one had claimed responsibility; apart from rebuilding, the major outcome was the closing down of the temple; a number of local tour companies had gone bust.'

It took Jane ten minutes to recall everything she knew. The last in the bunch was another bar bomb, this time in Suva, Fiji. It was a small device, no bigger than a hand grenade. But it was sophisticated and had a tamper-proof digital timer. Unfortunately for those in the crowded bar, the explosives were tightly packed with ball bearings. Only two people died from the blast, but there were countless injuries as the ball bearings indiscriminately took out eyes, tore muscle and lodge themselves in fleshy tissue. Again, no one had been arrested, and no one had claimed responsibility. Fiji's tourism, however, had taken a hit.

Jane closed her eyes.

A pattern?

No. Not that she could think of. Not in type or manner of attack. No one was admitting to orchestrating the attacks; three separate perpetrators arrested at the scenes of their attacks had claimed affiliations to seemingly fictitious terror organisations, but none of them could be matched to any known grouping. As such, there was no obvious driver. And there didn't seem to be a religious connection.

Nor did the attacks look state sponsored. It could be Russia; they were certainly capable of laying down this sort of terror in these places. But what would they gain?

That, of course, was the question.

If this were systematic, who wins?

She didn't know. She didn't.

And then she remembered something Sam had taught her – something that was rooted in military intelligence. *Don't look for things that shouldn't be there, but are. Look for things that should be there, that aren't.*

Something twigged.

She opened her eyes.

And stared at the map.

There were dots everywhere.

Everywhere?

Try Europe.

Every country in Europe has suffered an attack except ...

Jane moved closer to the map, her head centimetres from a two-dimensional, paper Europe.

What should be there, that isn't?

She ignored the micro states: San Marino; Andorra; Monaco; Liechtenstein; Vatican City; Malta.

Should I? Yes, it made sense.

Every country in Europe had suffered a neo-terrorist attack.

Except ...

She read them out loud. Slowly. Carefully.

'Latvia. Sweden. Hungary. Switzerland. Italy.'

Did that tell her anything?

No. Not at the moment.

She was about to move onto Africa when there was a tap at her glass door. It was Frank. He waved at her. She motioned for him to come in. He did as she beckoned.

Frank was dressed like … Frank. Same black jeans, but a different t-shirt which hung over the top of his jeans. It was one she'd not seen before. It was as black as his jeans and had 'Ask Me About My Beard' stencilled in white on its front.

Go on then …

'How's your beard?' Jane asked.

'I haven't got one.' He looked confused.

Jane got it. She thought.

'Can I help?' She asked.

'Eh, no, not really. It's just we haven't spoken since last night and you asked about the FFO? I have something on that now.'

'Islamic terror cell based in South Ossetia?'

'Oh. OK. You know, then.' Frank's tone was whimsical.

'Yes. I do. And it's a bit ahead of us now. The thing is I spoke with Sam the day before yesterday …'

'What? Well I never. How is she?' Frank's face lit up.

Jane knew Frank had the hots for Sam. It wasn't a surprise. If you knew Sam, you couldn't help yourself. She was easily the most annoyingly endearing person she'd ever known. She was like a pet dog who could do so many tricks it would win *Britain's Got Talent*. When it wasn't surprising you with its latest performance, it looked at you all floppy-eared and brown-eyed, with its head on one side: a look that demanded you give it something to do – or take it for a walk.

Endearing. Loveable.

Brilliant.

Maverick.

What Frank probably knew was that Jane had a softer spot for Sam than he did.

'Other than the fact she's been kidnapped by the FSB and then coerced into working for them in central Russia, she's fine.'

Frank was bobbing excitedly.

'What, you mean she's playing with us again?'

'Well. No ... no, actually, not no. Maybe. We won't know until the lawyers get back to us tomorrow. It's complicated.'

'That's great. And that's why the South Ossetia/FFO question?'

'Correct. She's going to meet with the leader of the group – hopefully tomorrow. As a Reuters journalist. The FSB hope she'll be able to uncover something about their intent; maybe their location.'

Jane wasn't going to give Frank the whole story – even in Babylon, 'need-to-know' held good.

'Oh. Well. Good. If you need someone here to ride shotgun – I've done it before, as you know. I'd be delighted.'

Frank was still excited. And he was right. He'd worked as Sam's anchor a couple of times before, one of which almost got him killed. He was certainly up for the job ... if it were needed.

'Thanks, Frank. I'll bear that in mind. Anything else?'

'Eh, no. No. That's it. Thanks. I'll have something, a proper briefing, on the fast-track migration issue in the next couple of days, maybe sooner.' He was making his way to the door.

'Thanks, Frank. Let me know.' Jane put a thumb up. It was time for Frank to leave, because she needed to make a few notes from the map – once she'd listed all the countries who had yet to suffer at the hands of the neo-terrorists.

Whoever the blooming hell they are.

Appartamento VI, Via Mortelle, Naples

The light was doing the tango on his ceiling. Gareth's blinds in his bedroom didn't close properly, so the Naples night was an accompaniment to his waking hours. There were shadows and colours, and colours and shadows. Even on the fourth floor the light from a passing car's headlights somehow managed to force their way in through the cracks. And the constantly changing, green neon sign of the *apothekry* from across the road posted a kaleidoscope of lime on his ceiling. And the noise. It was movie script stuff. If he could concentrate long enough to separate words from cars, from scooters, from cats, from industrial sounds, like the hum of air conditioning, he could write the opening of a decent *film noir*.

But whatever his imagination could script, it wouldn't get anywhere close to what he'd been through over the past four hours.

The brown paper; the box; the note.

And the eye.

Just horrific.

And then Giorgio.

Oh, Giorgio. Wherefore art thou ...

Shakespeare wasn't his thing. *Wherefore art thou*, along with, *Alas poor Yorick I knew him well*, and, *Once more unto the breach dear friends, and we'll fill this gap with our English dead* - or something along those lines - were the extent of his Bardisms. But he knew Shakespeare wrote tragedy. And the old man would have had to have his imagination in overdrive to quill the past four hours.

You couldn't have written it.

Gareth hadn't known what to do with, nor what to do about, the eye - in the fluid, in a bag within a bag, out of a box, wrapped in brown paper. Once he'd sorted himself out he'd gone straight to the bin in the kitchen and put his foot on the lever to open the lid. The double-plastic bag monstrosity hung from his finger and thumb grip, ready to join last night's supper.

Then he thought better of it.

He went back to the toilet, where he'd just spent an uncomfortable five minutes. The seat was up. He started to untie the granny knot that held the bags closed. Then he stopped. He didn't want to open the bag. He didn't know why, except it would release the thing into the atmosphere. Maybe only for as long as it took to tumble into the pan, but it would have escaped - momentarily. And what would happen if it didn't flush?

And kept bobbing around, looking at him? He have to pick it out. And …

His stomach had turned again at that point. Thankfully relief was close at hand.

In the end he put the bag and the note back in the box of socks and loosely wrapped it in its original brown paper. He found a rubber band to secure the wrapping and put the thing behind the sofa. He wanted it somewhere close, so it wasn't hidden in the depths where it could multiply and create havoc. *Or, worse still, disappear …* and then pop up again on his kitchen table. But he also didn't want it on display, staring at him.

And he hadn't wanted Giorgio to find it. He didn't want his rashness, to pursue Matteo Monza against all advice, to upset their relationship. Not tonight. Not after *spaghetti alle vongole* and his plan to talk, and to listen. To replace physical intimacy with closeness borne from understanding. To learn more than just the location of his g-spots.

He'd tell Giorgio about the package later. Tomorrow. That was the plan.

But it was now tomorrow and none of that had happened. Having put the package behind the sofa he had helped himself to a bottle of *Peroni* and had the longest hot shower in history. Cleansed, but not completely free from distracting images, he'd opened a bottle of *Nero d'Avola* and started cooking.

Nearly all pasta dishes take no more than 20 minutes to make. Knock up a sauce, this one with fresh clams and cream, cook the spaghetti *el dente*, throw the sauce in with the spaghetti, toss and serve. In his case, out of the pan. He'd planned to leave cooking the spaghetti until Giorgio had crossed the threshold, so it wasn't overdone. In the interim he'd spent the time mixing a dressing, chopping and dicing the salad, as well as making the table look nice.

The problem was ... Giorgio didn't arrive.

10.30 pm. 11.00 pm.

He'd SMS'd him at eleven; the restaurant might have asked him to stay behind to help with some chores. There was no reply.

He waited.

At midnight he'd phoned Giorgio's number. There was no response.

He now felt panicky. Since their first night together, he and Giorgio had texted each other three or four times a day. Not hearing from him since lunchtime was unheard of.

He prepared another SMS:

Where are you? Really worried. If I don't get a reply within 5 mins I'm walking to the restaurant. Hope u r not in a ditch. Luv. G xxx

He pressed 'Send'. The word 'now' appeared next to his text. It had been sent and received.

He sat at the kitchen/dining table like a distraught housewife waiting for their husband to return from a long day at the office. He had his phone in his right hand. He stared at it.

It vibrated. *SMS from Giorgio.* Relief flooded through him. He opened it.

Am not coming. I will not see you again. Do not phone or message. Giorgio xxx

Gareth had stared at the phone - for five minutes.

He'd then prepared three different texts in reply to Giorgio's. And sent none of them. He'd walked round and round the room. He finished the bottle of *Nero d'Avola.* Made himself a coffee. Then another.

And every time he looked at Giorgio's message, it read the same.

Which didn't make any sense. Last night they'd had a wonderful evening together. Giorgio had left for work this morning after coffee and 'you know what' for breakfast. Before he left he'd kissed Gareth with a bruising intensity, holding his mouth on his for an eternity. He left as a lover. Gareth had no doubt about that.

And the text. He'd signed it '*Giorgio xxx*'.

Why the kisses?

And why today, of all days? The day he gets a package from The Mafia ordering him to stop working on Matteo Monza. Was this a coincidence? Were they – *who the fucking hell are they?* – using Giorgio to get to him?

Is Giorgio in danger?

Was this all his fault?

He was sober and sensible enough to know that he'd achieve nothing until he'd slept; until he had a clear head with which to be objective.

Sleep.

But he couldn't sleep. Not now. Not with the lights playing chase on his ceiling. Not with his emotions in the washing machine. Fear. Passion. Anger. Frustration. Pity. They all spun about in the tumble.

He needed to sleep. He had to sleep. Wake up with a clear head. Be sensible. Objective.

And, about then, sleep came.

Chapter 5

Sam raised a hand to the departing red Lada Vesta. It was, considering the history of the marque, a surprisingly good ride. And what a ride. They'd left Vladikavkaz airport, a municipal hub hoping for international recognition, four hours ago. Until they'd hit the main Caucasus mountains, the vista had been interminable Russian steppe. Dull, flat plains of forests, corn and root crop, broken up by decaying towns and belching industry. This part of Russia, like much of the Siberian west, hadn't seen investment since the fall of communism. If you lived in a town, it was very likely that you were housed in a state-owned, concrete and 'peeling paint' apartment. And you probably worked in a 1950s-style industry making industrial-sized equipment for the factory in the next town. Which, in turn, was making industrial-sized equipment for the next city. Or you were digging and drilling – for anything the land would give you: oil, natural gas, bauxite, iron … gold. It was men's work, undertaken in all weathers and every season. Hard and physical. That didn't mean the women weren't hard and physical – nor did it mean the women didn't work on the industrial complexes; they did. They administered and book-kept; cooked and cleaned. And they took on some of the less physically demanding grunt work. It was work Sam knew would add years to her, if she were to last a year.

Timber was huge. Millions of square kilometres of forest carpeted the steppe. And the Russians were now adept at scything it down. Huge machines felled, cut and shredded trees in minutes that must have taken decades to grow. Sam had read somewhere that the worldwide trend for laminate flooring had stepped up the decimation of hardwood forests. Whilst the Russian climate hardly encouraged replacing felled trees with an oil-rich plant, such as palms, their choice of softwood to fill the gaps still took years to grow.

Old forests being usurped by new ones.

As the scenery flashed past her all Sam saw was green and brown wallpaper, with the odd break for yellow and green crops.

Until they reached the Caucasus.

She'd experienced the steppes before. But the Caucasus Mountains were definitely new territory for Sam.

These were tall mountains, rising to over five and a half thousand metres, spreading themselves between the Black Sea in the west to the Caspian Sea in the east. A natural barrier between Russia and the Middle East, the range has always protected both sides from each other. After the second world war Russia increased its influence and added a further layer of protection to its soft underbelly by bringing its southern Caucus neighbours, Georgia, Azerbaijan and Armenia, into the Soviet system.

Since the fall of communism, the three states had reclaimed independence. Now, after a series of local, but bloody wars, an uneasy truce was in place.

Over the past century the mountains hadn't flinched. They'd seen fighting with tank and artillery, they'd protected non-combatants as they escaped from the wars. And they'd allowed terrorists and freedom fighters to exploit their ravines to ambush their enemies.

And Sam loved them.

Once they'd left the small village of Nar, where the road split, they headed further into the mountains. The Roki Tunnel and the Russian/Georgian border was their next destination, and their progress slowed as the gradients increased and road disintegrated. But that didn't mean it wasn't used; Sam reckoned she saw a couple of dozen logging trucks climbing and descending the mountains. Every time they squeezed past a big truck on a road now suitable for a single vehicle, Sam felt herself breathing in involuntarily. It was as though the Russians hadn't bothered to keep one of the few main routes to Georgia in good order. Or maybe they couldn't afford it.

As they climbed Sam soon spotted snow on the side of the road and, in the near distance, it covered all of the peaks. Even in early autumn it was winter here. And there was no way they kept the road open in the winter.

The tunnel itself, which Vlad had told Sam was at a height of 2,000 metres, was in good order – and it took them only a few minutes to navigate the unlit three kilometres before they emerged, south facing, into sunlight.

Wow.

The view was outrageous. Ahead of them the mountains on either side dropped away precipitously. Rocks and scree littered the vista, trees only making an appearance when it was safe to do so. The valley fell dramatically in front of them, before bearing right in the distance at the edge of Sam's ability to focus. And the road was straight out of *Top Gear*. Hairpin bend after hairpin bend like a grey snake on a brown and beige carpet. It was all spellbinding.

And she had a chance to study the view in some detail.

As soon as they got out of the tunnel they were met by a concrete block chicane; poorly painted in red and white stripes. Off to one side was a small military encampment which appeared to provide the guards for the border crossing point. There were men in untidy, olive-drab uniform everywhere.

The car came to a halt by a sandbagged, machine gun post. Poking through a horizontal slit between the bags was the foresight and barrel of a weapon. Sam recognised it immediately. It was a *Kalashnikov PKM*; 7.62 millimetre short, belt fed. Not a bad weapon if it were properly maintained. Which, looking at the state of the man who was operating it, she thought unlikely.

One round and then a stoppage.

The belt would seize.

Soldiers forgot that belt-fed machine guns were the sum of two parts. The weapon, which they knew to keep as clean as a newborn baby. And the belt of rounds -

brass casings and mix-metal slug bullets held together by black steel clips - that feeds the gun. Which they don't.

After each shot the steel clips and the empty case split up and are discarded – and this happens at great speed. For any machine gun manufacturer this is a complex piece of engineering. The complete belt feeds in one side, the bullet leaves the barrel and the spent case and clip eject separately, on the opposite side of the feed. It is the engineering equivalent of applying lipstick whilst doing your hair. There'd be red everywhere.

If you don't keep the belt clean – and oiled, if the weather is cold and damp – then it won't feed and the gun will only fire the first round. And then stop.

But soldiers, especially poorly trained ones, don't get that.

Vlad wound down the window. A bearded and badly dressed soldier, who wouldn't have passed muster in any first world army, barked an order in Ossetian, a dialect of Iranian.

'Get out!'

Sam's Iranian was not great, but she had a handle on a number of key phrases. She understood that one, especially as it was accompanied by spittle and the sharp wave of the barrel of an AK47.

En route Vlad had explained that, at the border, they'd be met by the South Ossetian army, such as it was. They'd be asked to pay for the privilege of passing through their checkpoint. Having a small army and then fleecing trade through the Roki Tunnel was one of the few independences Georgia allowed her errant region to enjoy.

Vlad pointed to his legs. And then over his shoulder to the wheelchair that was in the back. The guard was confused. He looked from Vlad to the wheelchair and back again.

'Papers!'

Vlad calmly reached inside his jacket and took out some papers. He passed them through the window to the guard who studied them carefully. In an instant his demeanour changed from 'man with a gun' to 'man under the cosh'. There was a further soft-toned conversation, and Sam thought she spotted a bow.

Vlad took the papers back and put them in his jacket.

'What's so special about your papers?', Sam asked.

Vlad turned to Sam.

'I'm a good friend of the Chief of the Staff of the Ossetian Army.'

'That's impressive. Are you a Godparent to one of his children?' Sam was playing with him.

Vlad snorted and turned the Lada over.

'I haven't got the necessary paperwork for that …'

With that they headed off down the most dramatic road she'd ever driven on, at the bottom of which the Vesta's brakes were smelling like they were about to set the tyres on fire.

And that was about an hour ago.

Now, here she was.

Alone.

Thick cotton trousers, t-shirt, blue Buffalo top, hiking jacket, decent boots, ski gloves, a cheap Casio watch and her favourite beanie. In deference to the fact she was a journalist, she was also carrying a notebook, two pens and a Dictaphone. She had an FSB-issued mobile, which Vlad told her could be tracked even when it was switched off.

'But what if they take it apart and find some of your clever jiggery-pokery in the workings? They'll know I'm no ordinary journo.'

He'd assured her someone in the FFO would have to have a PhD in micro-electronics to spot the difference between her new phone and a shop-bought one. She wasn't convinced. In any case, she wasn't sure Georgia Telecom would be providing a signal where she might be going.

And she was carrying a passport. It was Russian and had her new name on it: Varvara Koslov. It was good as an original. As were the 30,000 roubles she had in her pocket.

Other than that she was all alone on the side of a road, in the increasingly cold Caucasus Mountains - waiting for a ride. She checked the time: 4.20 pm. She was 40 minutes early. With the sun now behind thick cloud and the temperature dropping a degree every 15 minutes, it was going to be a long wait.

She stamped her feet and wrapped her arms tightly around her chest.

She rehearsed the questions she was going to ask Hasan Kutnetsov.

She stamped her feet some more.

She thought of Vlad. Sam had told Alena Vlad wasn't travelling with her outside of Russia. Because that is what Vlad had told her. When they'd got to Moscow Vnukovo airport this morning – just the two of them – she'd asked, 'Are we meeting someone when we get to Vladikavkaz?'

'No, It's just us.' He'd replied.

'But I thought you weren't travelling into South Ossetia with me?'

'Did I say that? Sorry.'

And that had been that. She'd inadvertently lied to Alena, and Vlad was now heading off to South Ossetia's capital, Tskhinvali, where he would wait for her call. He reckoned if at the end of the meeting the FFO dropped her where she was now, he could be with her in under two hours. She hoped that that wouldn't be in the middle of the night. Not unless someone had lent her another jacket. Or a bottle of Vodka.

She danced up and down a bit more. Her toes had stopped speaking to her.

A car? From her left; the south - down the mountain.

She checked her watch. It was 4.56 pm. Could they be this efficient?

It was getting dark, but Sam recognised the small 4x4 immediately. It was an old Lada Riva. Cream. Petrol – two-door. She reckoned mid '90s. Not heavy, it was a really decent off-roader, although bits did have the tendency to fall off when the driver least expected. In the half-light Sam made note of the registration. *Tick*.

The Riva drove past her on a wide track, turned and then stopped with a gravel skid next to her. Left-hand drive, the driver was half a metre from her. The face belonged to a thin, old man. His skin was wrinkled and weather beaten, with a scruffily-clipped white beard and plenty of nose hair. He was wearing oily blue coveralls and an un-logo'd, red baseball cap. He looked miserable, as though he'd rather be at home watching TV.

He wound down the window.

'Varvara Koslov?' Russian. Sam wasn't surprised. Under communist rule, by edict all Soviet states spoke Russian. The man would have grown up with Stalin's long arm reaching every corner of the USSR.

'*Da.*'

He didn't reply. Instead he flicked his head in the direction of the passenger seat. Sam walked around the back of the Riva, checking for any signs that might give away ownership. There were none, but at least the rear number plate was the same as the one on the front.

It took them 20 minutes to make their way further down the mountain before the man, who hadn't said a word – nor replied to any of Sam's questions - pulled off left and drove the Riva another couple of klicks up a gravel track until they stopped outside what appeared to be a single-storey house. It was black-dark now, so Sam could make out very little. But it looked like the house was on its own, surrounded by trees.

'*Podpisyvaytes na menya.*' A bark.

Sam got out of the 4x4 and was about to take in more of her surroundings when the man grabbed her arm and pulled her to the door and then inside the house.

She took it all in. Dim light and smoke. A mid-sized room. Peeling paint. A wood table, Formica top. Four chairs. A simple kitchen. Some pots and pans; a copper kettle. A fireplace with the remnants of a fire, but with plenty of wood to make more. A black and white TV which was switched on, but with no sound. The picture was fuzzy. It might have been showing the news. Two windows, heavily curtained. And a further door, heading into – it was anyone's guess.

The other door opened. It was a woman. She was a bit younger than the man, but with the way weather aged people round here, Sam couldn't be sure. The woman had more flesh on her than the man and she was wearing denim dungarees and a greying flowery blouse. Her hair, which was mostly hidden under a chequered scarf, was tied back with a piece of garden twine.

Initially she looked as miserable as the old man, but as she approached Sam her expression softened.

'Take everything out of your pockets.' Russian. The woman pointed to the table.

Sam didn't move.

'Am I going to meet with Hasan Kutnetsov here?' Perfect Russian.

The woman's face turned sourer.

'No. Someone will come and collect you. Soon. First you must be searched.'

Sam spotted the woman's face change again. Some of the sourness had gone. There was a glint in her eyes which Sam couldn't place.

She emptied her jacket pockets: notebook and pens; mobile; cash; every last thing. She placed them on the table. She straightened the pens up so they were in line with the edge of the small book and perpendicular to the side of the table.

'Jacket.'

Sam did as she was told. She hung it on the back of one of the chairs.

'Top.' The woman pulled at the strap of her own dungarees.

Sam stared at the woman. Just for a second. And then she slipped her Buffalo over her head and put it neatly on the back on a second chair. Other than when her face was covered by the Buffalo, she hadn't taken her eyes of the woman.

The woman took a couple of steps forward. They were now standing less than half a metre apart. Sam stayed focused on the woman's eyes ….

… which looked Sam up and own. It was quick. Like a farmer assessing a lamb for the abattoir. Sam thought the woman momentarily dwelt on her crotch. Looking back at Sam she licked her lips, but quickly put her tongue away. Sam thought she recognised anticipation.

'T-shirt.'

No. That's not going to happen.

'No.' Sam replied.

The woman's eyes – small and piercing – darted round the room. Then back on Sam.

'If you want to meet Kutnetsov, then I must search you. No search – no meeting … now, t-shirt.'

This is not good.

'Please.' A statement, not a question from Sam. She wanted a delay. She thought she knew what was coming and she didn't know how she would cope. She needed time to prepare herself.

The woman stiffened, her brain in a spin. Then she smiled. She got the game.

'Please.'

Sam slipped off her t-shirt revealing a workmanlike bra. Thankfully some of the heat from the dwindling fire had been retained by the room.

The woman's pupils grew perceptibly larger.

'Drop your trousers.'

In all of this Sam had forgotten about the man. She glanced towards him. He was standing to one side with his hands in his pockets. If he was fiddling, he stopped as Sam shot the glance. But he was definitely an accomplice. They were in this together.

'The man leaves the room. Otherwise I tell Kutnetsov he's employing a filthy pair of perverts. And that this is no way to treat a Russian journalist.' Sam nodded toward the door.

The woman thought for a second and then, without taking her eyes off the prize, she nodded to the door. The man sighed petulantly, but did as he was told.

'Now drop your trousers.'

Sam undid her belt, the top button and the zip. She pushed her trousers down to her ankles as benignly as she could. She stood up again.

The woman moved forward, neatly stepping around Sam and stopping so that she was directly behind her. She was a couple of inches shorter than Sam, and Sam knew that in a cat-fight she'd probably come out the winner. But with her trousers around her ankles, she'd be at an immediate disadvantage.

But it was an option.

Shit! The woman's hand were cold. They were on her breasts, but not under her bra. A couple of seconds, no more. Sam had flinched, but not moved.

A pause.

Then the woman's hands were between her legs. Inside her pants.

She's not wearing any sodding gloves!

Sam had to make a microsecond choice. Let the woman finish her fetish, or stop her in her tracks.

…

She held still. It was over in four or five seconds. The woman's fingers pushed into her vagina. Cold, clammy fingers against unlubricated, internal skin. It was horrendous. Painful. An assault. She gasped, and involuntarily locked her knees together.

And then her backside. The same fingers? She clasped her buttocks together. She couldn't stop herself.

And. That. Fucking. Hurt!

Sam clenched her fists. Her teeth locked and she fought every instinct to turn and beat the living crap out of the old woman.

But then it was over.

Finished.

The woman was back in front of her. She wore the face of victory. Her head tilted to one side. A shallow smile, with wet lips. I've done what I wanted. I'm in charge. You do as I say.

'Get dressed. And leave the phone, your passport and the money here. You can have it back when Hasan Kutnetsov has finished with you.'

Sam didn't move.

The woman stared.

Sam's brain was whirring. Trying to reconcile her horrific ordeal - and that she hadn't tried to escape, or prevent it.

She didn't get that. It didn't compute. Right and wrong. Fight and flight.

Do nothing.

Acceptance.

I don't get it. But …

In some strange way she was proud of herself – allowing herself to be abused … for the mission. In another, she hated herself. Despised her own weakness. Enabled a filthy violation.

Some small part of her had been shattered. Snapped by the hands of a wretched woman.

Fingers all over her. In her ...

The woman broke the impasse.

'The driver will be here in five minutes. Get dressed.'

…

Sam closed her eyes for a couple of seconds. And then opened them quickly. Everything was as she had left it. Room. Table with her stuff on it.

Abuser.

She shook her head.

And got dressed.

Academy of Fine Arts, Naples University, Naples, Italy

Gareth pressed his hand against the windowpane. He spread his fingers out in a wide span. He stared at his knuckles for a few seconds. Then he dropped his hand to his side. His focus altered, his eyes taking in the building opposite. Dirty windows seen through dirty windows. A browny-grey tinge. Opposite looked like an apartment. There were decorative curtains hanging down, not quite reaching the bottom of the glass. Probably a rental. The landlord unwilling to put in new drapes that fitted the frame. He couldn't make out their colour. Striped of some form. Could be blue or green, and white. But through two pairs of dirty windows the outcome was brown and grey.

Grey and brown.

Dirt.

Curtains that don't reach.

This was Naples. It was Italy. Dull colours - and things that don't fit.

How could his mood about this place have changed so dramatically - so quickly? Twenty-four hours ago he couldn't have been any happier. Giorgio. His year at *Accademia di Bell Art di Napoli*. The strange and colourful meeting with Chiara. *Like a tommy gun.* His apartment with the comfortable double bed and …

… Giorgio … oh, Giorgio.

Everything came back to Giorgio.

Now he hated the place. He seethed. All of that taken away from him in a period of six hours. The box. The bags. The watery eye.

And then no Giorgio.

What was he to do?

He'd got up at six. He'd had a quick coffee, put on his trainers and walked – south, towards the harbour. Giorgio's route from the restaurant. By the time he'd got to the waterfront the sun was a ball of fire rising just off Vesuvius's left shoulder. The shadows of the yacht masts in the marina clambered over their neighbours and then lost themselves in the depth of the dark blue water

On any other day it would have been the perfect morning walk.

But not today.

It was already warming up; a tingle of sweat spread under his arms.

As he approached Giorgio's restaurant he took off his linen jacket and slung it over his shoulder. He caught a glimpse of himself in a full-length shop window. Even in mourning he looked the part: white, Jameson Carter straight jeans; dark grey, K-Swiss men's trainers; a black Mensch t-shirt (with a chest logo in rainbow colours); and gold-rimmed, Samjune Aviator sunglasses. His jacket was linen - and lime green; no label. He'd picked it up from a charity shop in Newport. A wonderfully chanced find.

Not bad.

Even if he said so himself.

He had no idea what he'd do when he got to the restaurant. It would be closed and there'd be no one to talk to.

Talk.

Is that what he wanted to do? Talk?

And did he really want to find Giorgio? Did Giorgio want to be found? His lover had been clear last night: no phone; no text. Giorgio had split up from him. In the coldest way possible.

People get jilted.

Shit happens.

Did that still make any sense, though?

Did it?

It sure as hell didn't make any sense last night … and whichever way he cut it, it still didn't make any sense this morning. It just didn't.

He stopped outside of the restaurant, put a hand on the window and peered in.

Nothing. Why would there be? It was just gone seven.

He paced up and down for a few minutes in deep thought. Does it make sense? Lovers. That long, goodbye kiss … and then nothing? Was he such a poor judge of character?

Lost for what to do next, he dodged traffic across the busy road and ended up right on the waterfront. He found a bench and sat, facing the sea.

And thought about not much.

And listened.

It took a while, but then the yachts and boats started to sing to him. He wasn't a sailor and knew little about the water - as a family they hadn't spent much time by the sea, even though it was only a 40 minute trip down the valley. But he recognised the song from somewhere. A gentle wind dancing through the taught wires of the masts – one pitch here; a different pitch there – discord and harmony together as one. The slosh of water against hull. Other clicks and cracks as the wind turned small turbines and fluttered ensigns. The music wasn't as loud as the traffic behind him, but he tuned out what he could and listened to the track from the boats

…

Giorgio.

What?

He was sure he heard his name.

He strained to listen.

…

Click, whine and crack; song and hymn.

…

Giorgiooo.

He shook himself. Was it a sign? Was he making things up?

This is nonsense.

It was nonsense. It was the red wine talking. He was a fool. A stupid sodding fool.

He stood, shook his head as if to clear the noisy bloody boats, turned and crossed the road; avoiding cars again, but this time one or two of them got too close and he got a toot for good measure.

He'd made it to the university much earlier than usual and had spent a frantic last couple of hours searching the net for any reference of Giorgio. Gareth didn't have a Facebook page, so it hadn't crossed his mind that Giorgio might. He typed in Giorgio's full name, Giorgio Pacenti, and found four Facebook links - none of whom was his Giorgio. He checked on Twitter, Instagram and tried every other avenue he could think of, but to no avail. Either Giorgio wasn't Giorgio Pacenti, or he led a very quiet life indeed.

It was all very frustrating.

He then thought hard about typing in Mateo Monza, which he'd done countless times yesterday. Just for the hell of it. That would teach the bastards; show them who's boss. Maybe he'd get a pillow full of horse's head next?

But he paused.

Am I scared?

Was he scared? Did he really think that they'd come after him - and do him in?

And does that bother me?

Of course it bothered him. He dwelt on that for a minute.

Scared? His right knee shook up and down. He told it to stop, which it did. He looked above the laptop's screen, staring at some old BluTac on the wall. His knee started to rock again as his mind moved on.

Decision.

He opened his top drawer and started to empty it.

Into what?

Onto his tidy desk? He had nothing to put stuff in. Was he leaving?

Now?

What would he tell his Italian tutor? Should he tell his Italian tutor?

Should I phone Adam? Would Adam know what to do?

Possibly.

Probably not.

His Dad?

No. Not a good idea.

He stopped emptying his drawer, leaving it open. He stood and walked to the window - and stared at the grey and brown curtains across from him.

Anger grew again.

And frustration.

And hatred.

He felt like an animal in a cage. Freedom, whatever that was, was on the other side of the glass. Freedom he could touch but couldn't reach.

His mind raced.

It seemed to him he had three choices. Abandon everything. Get on and complete his dissertation, knowing that he'd never be sure what piece of what animal's anatomy might be left on his kitchen table next. Or pursue Giorgio. Go back to the restaurant tonight and find him. If he's not there, then maybe someone will know where he lives.

But …

… Giorgio didn't want to be found. Not by him. He'd made that clear.

That doesn't make sodding sense!

Giorgio had left him yesterday morning …

He didn't complete the sentence in his head. He knew how it finished.

And the song. This morning by the waterfront.

Don't be a Welsh prick. The boats weren't talking to you.

He pulled away from the window and looked back at his desk, with its open drawer and the contents strewn about, messing up his normally tidy desktop.

Run away. Dissertation. Giorgio.

A choice of three.

Or phone Chiara?

Option four. He had her number. On the business card. Where was it? There. By his wallet.

Gareth picked it up, turned it over and found the number. He took out his mobile from his jeans pocket and dialled.

It rang … three long tones. Then she picked up.

A splurge of Italian. He got her name, but nothing else.

'It's me, Chiara. Gareth. We met yesterday for coffee. You gave me a name …?' he spoke in English.

'Ah, tommy-gun man. Yes, of course. Gareth. Yes, Gareth the gay. Good looking, but unattainable. How can I help you, Gareth the gay?' She was playing again. Did she always play?

'This going to sound really strange. But …', he hadn't thought through what he was going to say. He was unsure if he wanted to tell the whole story … what the hell. '… I got home late yesterday afternoon and someone had left a package on my kitchen table. Someone who had a key to my apartment.' He paused.

'Yes, go on.'

'Inside the package was an eye. A whole eye. Like it could have been mine. Or yours. Suspended in water. And there was a note. It said, "leave him alone". An eye and a note. Isn't that absurd?'

There was quiet for a few seconds. Gareth heard Chiara's shallow breathing. She was unusually quiet.

'Well?' His patience broke.

'I don't know. How would I know? What have you done?' Three sentences as one. No punctuation. English as Italian. Her tone was accusatory. Blaming him.

Gareth returned at speed. 'I didn't do anything! I just, well, did some internet research. That's all. Using the name you gave me.' He didn't want to mention Mateo Monza's name – he didn't know why.

Did he sound pathetic? Like a child who had broken his Mum's best vase?

But, she sounded worried – as though he'd crossed a line – and it was all his fault.

What had she expected him to do?

Her anxiousness had added to his. What had he started?

There was more quiet from the other end of the phone. He didn't like it when she was quiet. She was a woman of words. Lots of them. Quiet meant thinking – concern.

Then, 'This sounds so unreal. It just can't be? These people have friends, who have friends. And those friends have friends. They are good at what they do. They extort – and they launder. They bully and they befriend. Nothing is for nothing with them. Everything has a price. They're brutal, but, they're not efficient. *Non sono la CIA.*' The Italian pronounced with passion. And she continued. 'They don't reach every corner of my country. This is ... the speed of this. The eye. It doesn't make sense.'

Gareth was breathless listening to her.

'What do I do? What would you do?'

'I don't think you have a choice.' She paused. 'If I were you, I'd go back to my own country and forget about Naples. If you don't do that, forget about Mateo Monza. Forever.'

Gareth closed his eyes and lent his head right back. His mouth naturally fell open. He let out a sigh as he thought. There was a finality to Chiara's words which betrayed her occupation. She was a journalist. This may be the biggest story of her lifetime. It would certainly blow the art world apart. And yet ... and yet she was telling him to run away.

Run away. Away from Naples. Away from his hitherto fabulous life.

Away from Giorgio.

Away from Giorgio?

No.

No, he wouldn't do that. He wouldn't run away.

He straightened his neck and opened his eyes.

'Thanks, Chiara.'

'Well, what are you going to do?' There was still immediacy in her voice.

'I don't know.' He did. 'I'm probably going to sleep on it. But thanks for your help and advice.'

A further pause.

'OK, Gareth the gay ...', she was calm again now, '... but be careful, mister.'

The phone went dead. He looked at it for a second and then placed it on the table. He sat at his desk, swiped the finger pad of his laptop to wake it from its slumber and checked the time. It was 1.45 pm. He'd work for a couple of hours and then walk down to the restaurant and take an early tea. Some seafood. And a couple of bottles of Peroni. If Giorgio were there, he'd have it out with him. If he wasn't, he'd ask around. Somebody would know something. He would find Giorgio. He would find him and they would talk.

In the meantime ...

... he typed in the Google search box:

'Mateo Monza – current works, galleries and exhibitions in Italy'

Tomorrow was the weekend. He needed to get a bellyful of his nemesis's art work as soon as he could. He was sure some of his work would be on display somewhere within a train ride of Naples. He just needed to find it.

Headquarters SIS, Vauxhall, London

Cynthia had come back with a positive response on the two images. They were the same man. Abir al-Rasheed. The man by the tube station two days ago. And the man from Mersa Fatma in Eritrea, the fishing village with 27 boats and the large RIB. He'd been spotted by SIS staff two weeks ago getting off his fishing boat; very much at home. A casual pick up – 'tourist-snaps' taken whilst the SIS team were asking around. Apparently their cover had been as ex-pats looking for someone to take them to sea for the day so they could fish for grouper and snapper. Casual. Frank could imagine it – all bonhomie and slaps on the back. Snaps of a fishing port, and selfies with men with boats to take them out.

In a village on the Red Sea - which had two new warehouses and 27 boats.

And a big RIB.

Frank knew that's what SIS case officers did. They, and the local analysts, pore over satellite imagery. They spot something unusual. And then go and investigate.

The images showed that the warehouses were metal, well put together and unmarked. This had caused the SIS team concern; as a result they would need further investigation. When they'd asked around they'd been told the village had paid for them. It was about expanding the fishing business. There was more money in fish than emaciated cattle. And they were saving for a new pier. One which would take bigger boats. And a refrigeration unit for one of the warehouses. To keep the fish cool until a bigger boat comes along and takes the fish away.

The village was on the up.

Unlike most villages in Eritrea.

Among about a hundred photos of boats and warehouses taken by the SIS team, Frank had fourteen - mostly men - out of 47 documented village members.

One of the photos was definitely Abir al-Rasheed; one of the SIS team had asked him his name as he waded out of the sea, the details recorded on a hidden voice recorder.

And Frank had found Abir al-Rasheed in East Putney, just two weeks later. Frank knew that now. Cynthia had attributed 87% to the match. That was as good as it gets.

Abir al-Rasheed. A man who had moved through the migration system quicker than a Jack Russell down a burrow. Currently the only 'fast-track' Frank could pinpoint. But he was after more.

It was a result. And knitted into a developing, wider picture.

The Met were certain they had one of the other five al-Rasheeds from Mersa Fatma in the UK; but no photos. They'd picked up his name through a SO (Special Operations) contact, but they had no idea where he was – or what he was doing. The Service had notes on two others – again, picked up from cascons and a single phone tap. But still no photos. It seemed that four al-Rasheeds were in the UK. Only one of whom they could positively identify: Abir.

And Frank, whose job was to match cross-continent migration with those turning up in the UK, had him down as 'fast-track'. Currently the only migrant in the past 12 months who had made it from east to west in under a month.

He thought that made Abir special.

The MTMT was open on Frank's right screen. It showed four of the six al-Rasheeds highlighted in red. They had the one – dead cert. What route did he take? When did the other three leave Mersa Fatma? How did they get here? Were they 'fast-track' as well?

And could Frank match any of the photos taken by the SIS team with the three relatives who were now doing God knows what in the UK?

He got to work.

His first job was to investigate every database that might help piece together how Abir al-Rasheed got from Eritrea to the UK; uncover his route. Establish a pattern the others may have followed: a refugee camp here; a point of entry there.

He opened the SIS mapping software on his central screen. It was Google Maps based, but included a number of layers that Cynthia could launch. She could show things like crime statistics, terror cell analysis, data-access points to allow for interrogation of other countries intelligence networks, and other links to commercial detail such as hire-car data and airline manifests. Plus many others.

He looked to the MTMT on his right hand screen. He separated and dragged until Eritrea was at the bottom right corner of the screen and the UK, top left. The blue transit lines told their story – showed the available routes. Frank counted … and then stopped counting at 15 east/west transits. There were far too many permutations to consider.

He pushed back on his chair.

What now?

He took a more pragmatic approach. He reduced his options to three: longest time at sea; least time at sea; shortest route.

The first took Abir al-Rasheed from Eritrea by boat up the Red Sea, through the Suez Canal, across the Med to southern France. And then by vehicle north, cross-country through France to The Channel. Frank tried to imagine the journey. What would it be like? How many times would you want to swap vessels? Wouldn't that length of boat journey take longer than two weeks?

He did a fag-packet calculation: 4,500 kilometres at 15 knots. Almost 300 hours, and that was without getting off and getting onto a new boat. It was too long.

He dismissed it for now.

The next was overland – Sudan, Egypt, Israel, Syria, Turkey, Bulgaria ... he stopped there. Already there were too many borders to cross. Too many people to bribe. Too many chances to get caught. Too long.

Finally, and by now he was thinking he was wasting his time, he looked at the shortest route, assuming a vehicle was quicker than a boat. He used his finger as a trace and called out under his breath,

'Overland. Sudan – Libya – Tunisia. Sea journey across the Med. Where to? Italy, yes, that makes sense. Then into France – and ... the UK.'

He reckoned that getting from Eritrea to Tunisia overland was easy provided you had some firepower and were prepared to bully your way through. It was all pretty lawless: Sudan, Egypt, Libya, Tunisia; although you could miss out Egypt if you drove through the Sahara. With money, a couple of trucks, some uniform and guns, it wouldn't be unworkable. And it would be quick? He Googled it: 5,200 kilometres to Tunis if you used decent roads. At 40 kilometres per hour, that would take about a week's driving.

Now the sea route.

The MTMT showed that refugees often travel northeast from Tunisia and hit the Sicilian coast even though they weren't as welcome on the island as they were on the Italian mainland. But it was a shorter journey at sea. However, since the new anti-migration government were in power, landing anywhere if you are remotely refugee-like was close to impossible. So you'd have to travel more incognito. Say, a fishing boat as crew.

Or on a container ship?

Frank wasn't quite sure why that thought hit him. But …

… container ships were big. Easy to hide on. Most have multinational crew. Probably easy to bribe. And container ships berth at bespoke docks. That were well controlled. With fences and guards. But less random. Easy to bribe the dock staff?

Try it.

He asked Cynthia for the latest list of container vessels to sail from Tunis to Italy.

It took her less than 30 seconds.

In the last two weeks 52 container ships of all of shapes and sizes had left Tunis and berthed in Italy.

Make some decisions.

He discounted those that had sailed from Tunis in the past five days; anyone travelling would need that long to make it across Europe having landed in Italy. The list was shortened to 34.

Frank then crossed off those that had travelled via Valetta, in Malta. If he were planning this, he'd want to make a direct route and not have to berth at an intermediary. He was now down to 29.

Italian mainland, west coast only. A shorter route. He ignored Bari, Ancona. Ravenna and Venice, which were Adriatic ports. They were east coast.

Now there were only 17.

He spent the next 45 minutes looking at port logs which Cynthia provided for him. It was a long shot – actually the fact he'd restricted the list to just container ports when you could land any small craft along Italy's massive coastline and disgorge a couple of passengers, was a long shot. But he had to start somewhere.

And that's what he did for a living. He started somewhere.

He stopped at ship 14. He needed a pee; and a hot drink.

Five minutes later he was back with his Goofy logo'd mug and a steaming cup of Red Bush and soya. He started again.

Boat 15.

A small 13,000 tonnes container ship - the Marks Cross, flying the Guatemalan flag. It was carrying all sorts of products, mostly fruit, from West Africa. It had sailed from Tunis 12 days ago and had berthed at Gioia Tauro, a relatively new port on Italy's shoelaces, two days later. Frank checked the map. It was the shortest time at sea, if you ignored Sicily, from Tunis to the mainland. *Check.*

The Marks Cross inventory was uninteresting. The list was predominantly bananas, coffee, pineapple and mango. But there were eight passengers who boarded at Tunis and alighted at the port. Their names were a mixture of nationalities, and none of them came anywhere close to Abir al-Rasheed. He wasn't surprised. Unfortunately there were no photographs. He'd have to email the Embassy in Rome and get one of the SIS analysts to do some digging. He could wait.

He then tapped an overlay tag on the monitor. The AISE's (*Agenzia Informazioni e Sicurezza Esterna* – MI5's Italian cousins) terror and criminal incident list for the whole of the Calabria washed over the screen.

Bugger.

He wasn't expecting that.

Chapter 6

Vlad placed the cardboard cup on the table in front of Sam. It was mid-sized. The type Starbucks serve their 'small' Americanos in. But this wasn't Starbucks. This was the Russian equivalent. Micro-coffees were the norm. Thick, treacle-like liquid that tasted like nothing you could describe. Sam had had the same in Afghanistan, and, as she thought about it, Turkey. You might as well inject caffeine into your veins and smear your teeth with creosote.

But it was just what she needed right now. Caffeine. And warm liquid. Even if it were just a thimbleful.

'How did you sleep?' Vlad had sat opposite her. Either side of the table. As if he were going to interrogate her.

Which he is.

She looked around the room Vlad had acquired on arrival at the airport. He'd flashed his FSB card and barked. Minions of minions had rushed about as if the Queen had dropped in. Five minutes later they were in a small back room with polyprop chairs running down two sides and, in the centre, a table with a red and white chequered vinyl top with two further chairs. Two doors -

in and out. No windows - just a two-way mirror. And two shitty cups of coffee.

Their return flight to Moscow was in an hour and a half's time.

Plenty of time for a debrief.

'Did you put sugar in this?' She replied. She was too exhausted for pleasantries.

'Yes. Three as you asked.'

Good.

'Thanks.'

'Did you sleep well?' Vlad's tone was soft; genuine.

Sam had slept continuously since she'd got in the Vesta three hours ago. The choice wasn't hers. It had been a very long and stressful night and her brain had shut down as soon as she felt the warmth of the car's heating.

'Yes, thanks. Sorry. I couldn't keep awake.' Sam finished her coffee. She put the cup down, and then moved it so it sat perfectly in the centre of one of the chequered squares. She didn't get it right first time, so she adjusted it - until it was right. She looked at Vlad's cup. It was misaligned. She fidgeted in her chair, and then stared at the mirror.

'Is someone watching?' She asked casually.

'What? You mean, "who watches the watchers?".' I bloody hope not, or someone will be out of a job.'

'Juvenal.' She was staring at his cup again.

'What?' He replied.

'I read it somewhere. It's actually, "Who watches the watchmen". But it's a good point. He was a Roman poet.' Why was she mumbling on about nothing? Vlad had a job to do. She knew that.

Tiredness?

Apathy?

Lows after a high? That happened to her a lot.

Come on.

'You've got a recorder?' She asked

'Sure.' He reached into his pocket and took out a Dictaphone. He turned it on.

Sam put her elbows on the table and rested her chin in her hands. And then she let it all come back to her. Moment by moment. Word for word.

'After you dropped me off, I was taken to a house which I know I can find again, although you've probably got it from the mobile's location. An old man. I can describe him. No blindfold. I have the car details.' She gave the make and registration number. 'I was searched … by an old woman,' she stuttered; closed her eyes and held back tears. Would they have been tears of anguish? Or tears of frustration. Never mind. *Push on through.* 'Same again. I can describe her. I had to leave everything behind accept my notebook and pen.'

'It's a good job you've got a retentive memory.'

She opened her eyes.

'Yes.' She nodded. 'About 30 minutes later I was picked up by a third man. Who I can also describe. Younger. More brutish. The car was a Mark II Ford Focus. Dark in colour. I couldn't get the registration number.' She didn't add she was still in shock having been assaulted by the woman. The act had temporarily done something to her brain. 'I was hooded. We drove for 32 minutes, give or take. I have no idea where to. I tried to remember the route, but he was clever. We could well have ended up back at the same place. Or close to. It was up and down, round and round. I didn't see the outside of the building - he kept me hooded until I got inside. In fact I only saw two rooms inside the building. Not much, I'm afraid.'

Sam stopped. Everything was compartmentalised. She'd done track one. She now needed to do track two.

Vlad was sitting perfectly still.

'Any chance, with decent imagery, you'd be able to follow the route? Find the place?'

'Wait. Don't put me off. Let me finish everything and then you can ask questions.'

She started again.

'The main room was the size of a small hall. There was a simple but fulsome spread of food laid on for me on a table at one end, against the wall. Chicken legs. Cut ham. Soda bread. There were some casual chairs and a second, dining, table. A kitchen in one corner.' Sam pointed around the room they were in, as if in comparison. 'The other half of the room was set out a bit like a throne room. There was a large ornate chair, painted poorly in gold and red, against the far wall, a coffee table with fruit, and two standard wooden chairs facing the "throne". That's where the interview was going to happen. The room had three doors - again I can sketch it for you - and two heavily blacked out windows. One of the doors led outside. It was half-paved; no blind. A second was the one I came in through. And the third, by the feast, led to, let's call it, "the mortar room".'

'So they've got the mortars?' Vlad interrupted.

Sam sighed and gave him a withering look.

'Sorry.' He added.

'I'd asked countless questions of the first old man and then the second driver on both the journeys, but they didn't talk - other than issue orders. Once in the room I had my hood removed and was told to eat by the second man. I asked him when I was going to meet Kutnetsov. He said I'd meet him once I'd eaten.'

Sam stopped again. This time it was to reach across the table and move Vlad's cup so it was in harmony with the table top. It was doing her head in.

She thought as she spoke. She could do that. She could recount something whilst thinking about something else - the next sentence, or another thing she might need to sort in her brain.

The whole thing had been a bizarre experience. All, she reckoned, three hours of it.

First was Kutnetsov. He certainly wasn't your regular Islamic terrorist.

She'd eaten - on her own - at the dining table. It seemed polite and, following the Army's maxim of 'eat when you can', it also seemed sensible. Whilst she scoffed, and made a mental note of every inch of the room, the driver had paced impatiently around the hall.

After half-an-hour Kutnetsov had made a grand entrance. He was all big gestures glitzed with smart jeans, Nike sneakers, an open-necked shirt, off-white bomber jacket, gold necklace and sunglasses. Sam reckoned he was late-thirties, slim but strong, crew-cut dark hair and a minimal beard.

And he came in alone. No entourage, less her driver who stayed with them.

'You must be Varvara Koslov?' Good Russian with an accent she thought was southern Ossetian. He thrust out a hand, showing off two heavy gold rings. 'So good to meet you.' He continued. Sam shook his hand. 'Please, please, sit.' A sweeping arm movement pointing to one of the chairs by the 'throne'.

He let her get ahead. She sat - but he stood by his chair. And then, with a grandeur that almost made Sam laugh, he sat. Then it came to her. It was if Sacha Baron Cohen was playing the leader of a terror cell. Reuters journalist meets fake freedom fighter; but she had seen through his disguise.

Don't worry, it'll be my secret.

They spoke for over an hour. Sam didn't recall every word for Vlad. Just the salient points. They'd spent most of the time talking about him. His childhood. His schooling. His country. His parents and his brothers. He even told her that he liked The Beatles. 'You know. Love, love me, do.' Sam had nodded. *If only you knew*. It was like being on a chat show - she was James Corden. And he was, well, some celebrity there to promote his new TV series.

And then, with a glance over Sam's shoulder to her driver, and as if he remembered he was responsible for killing 25 people with a bus bomb in Moscow, he changed tack. The benign banality ceased. Now he was all bravado and menace. Although in an Ali G fashion.

It started ideologically. For Vlad, Sam recounted what she considered was the odd key phrase. Word for word.

'The world has forgotten us. We will not be forgotten. We are a nation not defined by the imposition of other people's boundaries. We are a brotherhood. Ossetian Muslims live here. And there. Everywhere.' His unbounded geography accompanied by plenty of hand gestures. He paused in thought, as if remembering something important. 'We are a people. We will not be confined by the vagaries of others. We will do as we wish. We will do what is right. We will march. And we will fight.'

Up until this point Sam had only asked the odd question to keep him talking. She'd made notes as Kutnetsov had talked, although, unless someone sucked her brain out with a straw, she didn't need notes. But it seemed the right thing to do.

'And you were responsible for the Moscow Bombing?' She interjected.

His eyes lit up in recognition.

'Yes. And there will be others. We have weapons and expertise. We have guns and killers.'

They continued for another half an hour. Sam interrogated him on the size of the FFO, which Kutnetsov seemed to make up as he went along. And then change. She moved onto weaponry, likely MOs, timings - targets.

'You think I'm stupid?'

Well ...

'We have targets. But I will not share this with a journalist.' And then a light came on upstairs. 'We have one big target ...' He stood as his hands demonstrated a large explosion. '... yes, we have a big target.' And then, abruptly, he sat. It was like watching a kindergarten nativity play.

Another glance behind her. 'It could be anywhere. Anywhere!', as though he'd just shared state secrets. This time Sam glanced over her shoulder and found her driver. He had a face of granite and looked much more like a man who would pull the trigger than Kutnetsov.

She looked to her front. Kutnetsov seemed to understand what was going through Sam's mind.

'Come, let me show you.' Action was required.

The next 20 minutes was an armoury display. Sure enough the FFO had five 120 millimetre *Podnos* mortars and 453 high explosive rounds. She'd counted. In the corner of the 'mortar room' were 12 pallets, each of which carried 40 rounds. There were 27 empty spaces – probably rounds fired at the Russian Army checkpoint, and maybe a couple for practice in the local forests. In addition there was a wooden rack holding 14 AK47s, 15 cases of Russian Army 7.62 millimetre shorts - each of which carried 600 rounds, and three pistols of varying makes. The AKs looked in good nick, as did the mortars.

The pistols, not so much. But that wasn't an issue. Pistols with a top-loading magazine rarely seize unless the spring in the magazine had gone soft.

Sam made appropriate noises and asked some journalist-type questions.

'Aren't those green tubes, mortars? How do they work exactly?'

What was amusing was Kutnetsov made up most of his responses. He overplayed the mortars' range - by double, as he did the explosive effect of a single high explosive round on a well-built structure. Mind you, 453 rounds landing within 100 metres of each other would do a good job of bringing down a nuclear power station. As he spoke Sam again felt the presence of her driver, over her shoulder. He was clearly the power behind the throne.

Why had they chosen Sacha Baron Cohen as their front man?

After the weaponry display, and now at God knows what hour of the morning - Sam had left her watch with the woman and there was no clock in either room - they had 'tea'. Her driver did the honours; there was a sink and a workbench by the outside door. She and Kutnetsov retook their positions: throne and questioning seat. The tea was served in small china cups; no milk, but already heavily sugared. Sam was running out of puff, so she was glad of the sugar infusion.

'Where do you think the FFO will be in a year's time?' There was no refill of tea. The meeting was drawing to a natural conclusion.

The question caught Kutnetsov off guard. It was as though he'd not thought it through. As though there was no campaign. It was violence for violence sake.

'An Islamic Ossetia - with an expanded border to the north, beyond The Caucasus Mountains.' The words came from behind her - from her driver. Raspy and steel-edge.

The power behind the throne.

'Yes, exactly.' Kutnetsov added quickly. 'An independent Islamic country. Bringing together all of the brothers.'

'And you will be their spiritual leader?' Sam was pushing it now. She knew Kutnetsov was uncomfortable with the balance of power in the room.

'Of course! Why not?' He was indignant. Like a child reminding everyone who owned the only bicycle. 'It's time for you to go now. I think that's enough. I'm tired.' He stood quickly. Sam let him stand. *Unbalance him further*. Then she did the same.

She was bored of his bravado - and his access to five 120 millimetre mortars and more rounds than were necessary.

'You will report this? All of it?' He snapped at her.

Sam was heading for the door where her driver was standing, holding the hood. She needed to get out of there before she said something that forced him and her driver to interrogate her. Inquisitor becomes inquisitee. She stopped by the door, turned and offered her hand.

'Of course. My editor will make my report available on the international feed within 24 hours. And then we'll see which news agencies pick it up. I'm sure there'll be a lot of interest from Russia and Central Asia.'

He smiled tentatively. And shook her hand … then she was hooded.

'You can ask questions now.' Sam checked her watch. She and Vlad had been in the room with the mirror for 40 minutes. It was definitely time for another coffee.

'The whole thing sounded really strange, as though he wasn't an ideological terrorist at all?' Vlad asked.

'I think that's right. He's a front. And what's pissing me off is I can't make out why. And, if you discount the old man and woman, I only saw two of them. Kutnetsov and the driver. And there was another thing …', Sam paused.

'What was that?'

'The iconography was all wrong. I've studied terrorist locations before. And they're much more basic. Stark. Bleached. There might be the odd picture of Mecca hanging on the wall. Maybe a likeness of Mohammad, although hard-liners don't like to second-guess what their prophet might have looked like. But not much else. Last night there was a poster of a mountain range. There was a painting of a local scene with a farmer and an ox. Above the sink was a calendar. It was unmarked, but at its top was the logo for a garage - like you and I might have in our kitchen. And the food was too grand, and there was too much of it. It all very … well, Western. It wasn't right. As though they'd hired the village hall and been told not to mess with it.'

Vlad didn't say anything for a second.

'So, if they're not Islamic terrorists, then what's their point? Why plan to bomb a nuclear power plant in Russia?' He asked the obvious question.

'I don't know. Unless …' Sam paused.

'Unless what?'

'Unless they're not terrorists as we remember them? Maybe they're part of this whole neo-terror shenanigan. You know. Terror for the sake of it?' It didn't make much sense to Sam, but it was an option.

'Well whatever they are, we need to track them down before they create the worst nuclear disaster since Chernobyl.' Vlad had stood. He'd taken Sam's cup and now picked up his own. 'Can you find it? The village hall?'

Sam looked at Vlad and smiled to herself. She really liked him. She trusted him; she always had. She was glad she had taken the assignment. And having had a couple of hours sleep and with another coffee, she'd be ready to help him further.

'Maybe. I've got some markers. One or two details which might help. What I need is the best satellite imagery you have of the area. Maybe 120 square kilometres of where you picked me up? Can you get that?'

'Sure.' He paused as he opened the door. 'Can you get onto your people? You and I both know the CIA have much better definition photographs. And they'd probably be more up to date. Whatever, I'll get on to my team. We'll have any imagery that's available in the system on my desk before we touch down in Moscow. OK?'

Sam didn't say anything. She just nodded. She'd get in touch with Frank now. She was sure SIS would get her the images.

As the door closed she put her head back in her hands and closed her eyes.

She hadn't told Vlad about the abuse.

What would be the point?

And she hadn't told him what had happened when she'd been dropped back at the first house.

Still hooded, her driver had taken her to the front door where, now with dawn struggling against the gradient of the mountains, she'd been met by the old man. He'd shown her in and pointed to her stuff which was still lying on the table. It was all there - except she was 10,000 roubles short.

'Where's the rest of my money?' It was tired question. She knew where it was. And she knew she wasn't getting any of it back.

'Expenses.' The man smiled a toothless smile.

Sam raised her eyebrows, collected her stuff and put it in various pockets. She picked up her phone last and texted Vlad.

Come and get me. Please. S.

'You'll take me back to where you picked me up?' She asked the old man.

'*Da.*' He looked ready to go.

Sam thought for a second.

'Where's the old woman?'

'Sleeping.' He pointed through the second door.

'I need to use the toilet.' Sam asked.

The old man pointed to the same door.

'Be quiet. She doesn't like to be wakened. And be quick. We need to go.'

I bet she doesn't.

Sam tentatively opened the door. It led into a single room that was partitioned with a curtain. She was sure the drapes rippled with the old woman's snores.

The loo was a further door ahead. She could just make it out in the half light. As she opened it she spotted two orange and rust gas cylinders to her left, half hidden by some old wood and newspaper. One had a hose leading back the way she had come. *Probably to the cooker.*

She opened the loo door and pulled it to - leaving just enough of a gap for some light. She dropped her trousers and peed.

Finished, she sorted herself out and didn't flush.

Back in the partitioned room and with a real desire not to wake her abuser, she stopped by the gas cylinders. At first she didn't know why. And then the devil whispered in her ear.

Sam gripped the tap of the cylinder that didn't have a hose attached. She twisted it a half-turn. The smell of LPG was instant - as was the high pressure whine of escaping gas. Quickly she twisted the tap so it almost closed. The whine slowed to a hiss, but didn't stop

Then she was through the door to the main room, shutting it swiftly behind her.

'Let's go.' She said.

Joint Intelligence Committee (JIC), Whitehall, London

'Well, Tristram, what have we got?' The chair of the JIC, Grahame Mills, shot the question across the table to Tristram Michael, the Director General Capability of The Security Service - better known as MI5. Within the rarefied atmosphere of the UK's intelligence services the title was abbreviated to 'The Service'. Between them and SIS the more colloquial terms 'Box' or 'Thames' were often used. Jane preferred 'The Service', and it had stuck with her. Whilst most of her colleagues referred to SIS, or MI6, as 'SIS', she was very fond of using SIS's Vauxhall address 'Babylon' to describe where she worked. There was still plenty of discussion as to how that term had come into use. SIS's headquarters was a modern, pink-block pyramidal structure right on the Thames. It was built in a 1930s modernist style on the site of the old Vauxhall Pleasure Gardens. And whilst there was little foliage hanging from the stepped structure, it didn't take much imagination to transport yourself back over millennia to Mesopotamia - and spot the connection.

Babylon worked for her, so she forgave anyone for using any term they wished for SIS or MI5.

Tristram Michael - *no decorations*, which Jane thought probably hurt as he'd been in The Service since Oxford - had an open tablet in front of him. He tapped at it and the briefing screen at the end of the teak oval table burst into life. The opening slide was The Service's logo, a blue crown and portcullis perched on a lion, surrounded by a circle of hieroglyphics that Jane had never attempted to decipher. Tristram swiped at the screen and the first slide appeared. It was an empty map of the UK.

'This is what we have.' He nodded to the screen - and paused. 'Before you ask for my resignation, let me explain. We have a verified threat, that is three separate unconnected sources, of a planned Level 4 or 5 attack on the UK's infrastructure. Within the next 48 hours. The three sources are all "gold" and their handlers are working them into a frenzy to try and establish exactly what "UK's infrastructure" means. There is no attributable organisation, no links via the Prevent programme and nothing from our city centre open-connections, mosques and similar. It's all blank. It's as though whatever is being planned is being enacted by a new grouping, maybe one of the neo-terrorist cells - spawned out of thin air.'

'When did you get corroboration?' Grahame Mills again. He was both a *Companion of The Most Distinguished Order of St Michael and St George*, CMG, and had been awarded an OBE earlier in his career. Impressive, though hardly a chestful.

Stop it - that's two more than I have.

Jane was distracted. It was a heady meeting of 'greats and goods'. No matter how many times she crossed the river to attend the JIC she was always on edge. Apart from being the youngest in the room, she was also the only woman - other than the scribe, who sat off the table. Her name was Susan. When the weight of what they were discussing made her shoulders ache, Jane sometimes wondered what it must be like to have less responsibility - such as Susan. But that thought never lasted long.

She attended the JIC on behalf of C. She was the senior operational director in Babylon and, whilst C did attend on occasions, The Service and SIS both sent second-tier officers. It wasn't a case of belittling the committee, it was more that Jane had a better handle on the detail of operations, certainly in her AO, than C. It made sense for her to attend.

'Last night. Hence this emergency meeting.' Tristram continued. 'I know all of our teams have been talking, but the PM wants a brief before lunch. We need to get out heads together and come up with something.' Tristram opened his hands to the room. 'Before I go on, has anyone got anything?'

First up was Mike Bevill, Head of UK Communications at GCHQ (*no post nominals - yet*). He raised his hand.

'Just to clear our deck. We have nothing. Sorry. The thing is, we've been awash with chatter since Christmas. Non-specific, highly threatening and in the

UK, apart from the Rochdale bomb and the Glasgow supermarket shooting, none of it materialised. Hoaxes - wishful thinkers. That sort of thing. With all the noise we could well have a feed that might be linked to the threat, but there's just too much going on. It's a case of wheat and chaff, I'm afraid. And our services abroad are not much better. Sorry. Again'

'What about Counterterrorism. Bradley?' The question from Grahame was to Bradley Smyth: Head of Counterterrorism Police. An OBE and the *Queen's Police Medal* - for gallantry.

That's impressive.

Bradley Smyth was a touch older than Jane, but still younger than everyone else in the room by about a decade. He always looked permanently tired and ready to bite anyone's head off. His reputation, on the other hand, was different: considered and calm.

'We gave Box the first of the three leads. We've been working together on this. It's a girl, out of Dagenham. She's on the job, but is high class enough to mix it with some money. She has clients in the City, as well as some extremely well paid low-life. The talk is of something new; something different. The place is abuzz with speculation. Even the hoods want to know what's coming. It's unprecedented. Like some sort of reality TV show. And it's only come to a head very recently.'

Jane would be asked next, and then Brigadier Johnny Walters CBE DSO MC and bar - Director Special Forces. The CBE was for hard work at a senior level. The DSO - *Distinguished Service Order* - for leading a large number of Special Forces soldiers on dangerous operations. And the MC - and bar. Two Military Crosses; one level down from the Victoria Cross. That's bravery under fire. *Twice*. And the Brits don't give out gallantry medals without very good reason. Jane had seen Johnny in his dress uniform. As well as the three major decorations he had two rows of medals from every conceivable conflict the UK had been involved in in recent years. She'd heard he was the Army's most decorated soldier. That *was* impressive.

'Jane?' Grahame asked.

'Nothing from overseas. We have a number of foci: next week's Botswanan election for example. The view is that the original attack was a one-off, part of the NT's (neo-terrorism's) network of spreading random terror around the globe. Also, in conjunction with the intelligence services of India and Argentina, we're still mopping up yesterday's attacks on the hydroelectric plant north of Patna, India, and the extraordinary arson of a major ranch in Reo Negro province, Argentina. That attack, which killed 850 cattle, has, we think, an NT marker: expect the unexpected. So, sorry, we have nothing to add to the detail. Other than, whatever we are looking for, think outside the box.'

Grahame nodded. He looked across from Jane.

'And Johnny? Anything from Special Forces?'

'No.'

Not even a shake of his head.

Jane knew that was coming. Not that Johnny had nothing to add, it was just if he didn't he wouldn't elaborate unnecessarily. Why use ten words when one will do.

'So …', Grahame summarised, '… what am I going to tell the PM?'

Tristram raised a finger.

'I hadn't quite finished.' He swiped on his tablet. The map of the UK was now alive with colour; lines and dots all over the map. 'It's difficult to get in the mind of these particular terrorists as we have no idea who they are, or what MO they might use. Stepping back from the here and now we at The Service have come to the same conclusion as SIS. 'Neo-terrorism' is a coordinated phenomenon. Pulled together by some extraordinary global power. Could be the Russians, although unlikely. Could be a cartel of some form …'.

'With the aim of?', Grahame interrupted. 'There must be an ambition to all of this?'

There was a pause. Jane filled it.

'Not sure. But our profilers have developed a sophisticated mind map which leads to one of two possible conclusions: revenge or money. They've dismissed ideological.'

That drew silence from the team.

'Revenge?' Johnny eventually asked.

'Someone, some party, with money and resources …' Jane continued, '… is going out of their way to punish the world for having being blighted in the past.'

Jane looked directly at Johnny.

He scoffed. 'That's fantastical. Something from a Bond movie. Has anyone given Daniel Craig a call?'

A thin smile then broke on Johnny's face. If his comment was meant to be cutting, Jane didn't let it sink too deep.

She continued. 'We're currently looking at the world's 100 richest individuals. Take Reyansh Ahuja, the Indian billionaire, for example. He's in the top five. He recently lost badly in the Indian elections, his wife died last year of cancer and he has no children. He has made countless bitter comments in the Indian broadsheets about the state of his country. He's a possibility.'

Jane smiled for the Director of Special Forces, and added, 'And C's got an interview with Daniel this afternoon. Pierce and Roger have slots for tomorrow morning.'

There was a chuckle from around the room.

'OK, everyone. Let's park that for a second.' Grahame pointed at Tristram. 'Finish what you started.'

'We have, as Jane suggested, thought outside the box. The schematic shows what *we* would attack if we wanted to create the greatest havoc, for the least effort. Something extraordinary. Headline catching. Pulled off by a team of two, maybe three, no more. But with plenty of access to cash.' Tristram swiped again and much of the colour disappeared. What was left was an overlay showing the regional airports.

'Air travel. If you ignore the London based internationals, we have 38 regionals that fly internationally, that is those where you can travel overseas on a passenger plane with capacity of over 100 - say a 737. To make an attack, all you need is fifteen grand. With that you can buy yourself a gen-two heat-seeking missile from the black market. Another twenty will get you a handheld simulator. So you can practice before firing the real thing ...'

'You mean, like a US Stinger or Russian SA-14. Both fire-and-forget, heat-seeking missiles, launched from the shoulder?' Johnny asked dryly.

'Yes, or the UK's defunct Blowpipe.' Tristram added.

'Indeed.' Johnny again. 'You have to understand they are notoriously difficult to use. It seems simple enough: acquire the target in the optics, place the crosshairs on the fuselage and fire.' Johnny made the noise of a missile leaving the tube. 'The missile heads off to the target and if it's lucky it recognises what it's heading for is hotter than the surrounding sky and tracks using infrared. But nine out of ten missiles go rogue, unless they are in the hands of a practiced operator. It's about the launch. You should try keeping a fast moving jet in the crosshairs. It's a real skill, although I grant you that 737s are pretty sedentary.' He paused, as if thinking. Then, 'And at 25,000 feet the target is too high and too far away for both the shooter and the weapon - so you're looking at placing the operator close to the airport. Maybe within a couple of klicks.'

'We think so. Say within a 2-mile radius. Not too close. Not too far.' Tristram added.

'And, in terms of terror, we're talking reliving nine-eleven.'

Tristram nodded, waited for the gravity of Johnny's comment to sink in and then swiped at his tablet.

A different set of dots appeared. Jane recognised them immediately. They were the UK major power stations.

Tristram continued. 'Moving on. This is a schematic of all of the UK power stations over 1,000 megawatts. Same sort of detail in terms of attack, although you would need to spend less money. Possibly a handheld anti-tank rocket fired at a nuclear power plant. Maybe a couple. Finding the radioactive core is not too difficult. Google would give you that if you looked hard enough. However, the shooters would have to be very lucky to affect a nuclear catastrophe. The core is very well protected. But ... if they had an insider with detailed knowledge of the site they could target the waste area. If they were lucky they might be able to disperse some contaminated material.'

Jane raised her hand.

'Yes, Jane?' It was Grahame.

'If we're short of resources, which depending on the number of slides Tristram's got, I guess we will be, I'd discount an attack on a nuclear power plant.'

'Why?' Tristram asked.

'Because what we've learnt so far is if you ignore small time bombings, shootings and vehicle attacks, NT never strikes twice. Their major targets are all different and left field.' She paused for a second. 'We're currently in liaison with the Russian FSB about a possible attack on the *Novo Voronezhskaya Aes* nuclear plant, north of the Caucasus Mountains in southern Russia. The MO is very likely to be mortars. On that basis I'd discount an attack on a UK nuclear facility for copycat reasons. However, I wouldn't dismiss mortars as a weapon of choice. They're easy and cheap to procure - and can put down a lot of firepower, really quickly. As we know the IRA used to make them in their garden sheds and weld them to the back of a flatbed truck. Ignore a nuclear plant. Don't ignore mortars as an attack method.'

Jane had spoken with Sam on the way over. She was just about to get on the plane and fly to Moscow. It seemed her trip to South Ossetia had been a success ... in that she had got in and out again without injury. Sam's line was that the FFO were a pack of cards, short-term funded and resourced by whoever the NT kingpin was. She was unconvinced of any ideological rigour behind their existence. It would be just another terror attack. And a significant one too. Sam had added that she was unsure if the FSB agreed with her. But Jane and Sam concurred that the FSB needed the FFO to be a functioning Islamic terror group because it added grist to any heavy-handed action they took in the region.

The room agreed with Jane's prognosis, and nuclear power plants were removed as potential targets.

Over the next ten minutes Tristram threw up slides of motorway services, major malls, train lines and sidings, all local government hubs, and major ports. All in all there were 237 potential targets. They then discussed recommending closing down some of the targets for 48 hours until the threat window closed. Choices included regional airports and some major train routes. But they quickly discounted any such action.

'And what about the current threat level?' Bradley asked the group. 'As at now it's at SUBSTANTIAL. Do we raise it to SEVERE, or even CRITICAL?'

The committee knew the decision would be the Prime Minister's, but they had to offer a recommendation.

'I'm going to recommend SEVERE when I meet the PM in about an hour.' Grahame concluded. 'But, I'm also going to ask you, Bradley, to call a press briefing. Give the public as much as you need. Sixty million eyes on the case will help a lot.' He paused for a second, then added, 'Do we have any choice?'

Grahame let the question hang for a couple of seconds. But there were no dissenters. An alert public were easily the best intelligence service.

'Before I close the meeting, has anyone got anything else?'

Jane was tempted to talk through her work from the printed map in her office. She now had a list of the countries which had yet to be subject to an NT attack. There were 42 across the world. Twenty-four hours ago there were 43 but, after yesterday's Argentinian ranch attack, that had been reduced by one.

At her own meeting this morning one of her team had pointed out that one effect of the last six months had been a gradual reduction in the value of the world's stock markets. The Dow Jones had dropped by 22% since May, and that was against very strong economic data. Markets liked certainty; they hated turbulence. She thought this was important.

'It might be worth keeping an eye on the markets.' Jane said. 'The Dow is currently just over 21,000, that's down 15% this year. And the FTSE is well below 7,000 for the first time since January. If, say, the NT motive was financial, it might be worth the Treasury or GCHQ looking at who's buying as the market drops, as opposed to who's selling. If you drive the price down with global terror, and then buy at the bottom, you could make 25% overnight?' Jane didn't think it was a stupid idea.

'But is 25% enough? How much has it cost the NT mastermind so far? He, or they, need to recoup his cash - and some?' Tristram interjected.

'It's a good point, Jane.' Grahame raised his hand to stop the discussion. 'Let me finish with a tasker. Rough order stuff. Jane, I want SIS to cost the terror attacks so far. Assuming the NT network can hire the staff, shooters and bombers - how much money would you need to buy terror at this level of intensity. And, maybe if you match that with one of your disaffected billionaires, you might get lucky? Happy, Jane?'

That made complete sense to her.

We're on it.

MAXXI Museo nazionale delle arti del XXI secolo, Rome, Italy

Gareth checked his watch. It was 2.30 pm. He needed to finish up. If he were lucky he could get back to his apartment before it was late. First, though, he wanted to spend a final five minutes with *Extinction*, one of Mateo Monza's very best works.

He was sitting on a concrete bench, surrounded by white concrete walls lit beautifully by natural light from the glass ceiling. It was the perfect gallery. For the perfect picture.

For the uninitiated, *Extinction* was just splodges of primary colours on a huge canvas. Swirls and straight lines. Big blocks of red, and swathes of royal blue. But there were also blacks and whites. Yellows and greens. It was a cacophony of colour.

Squint your eyes and you could pick out a coastline. Maybe a field and some farm animals. A mountain here. A valley there. Or, it was all of humanity - all colours and creeds - mixed together? The global village on one canvas.

If that were the finished article then it was a very well executed picture. A map of everything. On a grand scale.

But that wasn't all. Mateo had added something else. *More accurately taken something away*.

The canvas had been slashed - in six places. Like it had been vandalised, but the museum had decided to leave it hanging where it had been attacked. A desecrated masterpiece.

But the knife had been wielded by Monza. To make a significant point.

It showed the world - but at the same time portraying its demise.

Death of the humanity.

Extinction.

It was genius. And Gareth let it sink in for a few seconds more.

…

I must go.

He stood, picked up his well-weathered satchel which he threw over his shoulder, and headed for the exit. As he passed works by Enrico Del Debbio and Vittorio De Fao, he revisited last night's trip to Giorgio's restaurant.

It had been completely fruitless.

Nothing. Not a dickie-bird.

It was as though Giorgio had never worked there. He'd pestered every member of staff he could find, but they'd closed ranks.

'No, scusa.'

Sorry.

Nothing.

It didn't make any sense. None at all.

After 20 minutes the manager had asked him to leave, and ushered him out of the restaurant. He was being a nuisance. Asking too many questions.

On the street he turned to take one last look at the restaurant. The manager, who on first meeting seemed like a really nice man, had stood in the doorway with his arms crossed. Sweat was dripping from his brow. He was agitated. Upset.

Then he mouthed, *dimenticalo*.

It had taken Gareth a few seconds to translate.

Forget him.

Forget him?

Gareth couldn't forget him. He couldn't forget his passion - his love. And he couldn't forget the mysteriousness of everything that surrounded the last twenty-four hours.

He couldn't.

But he could be distracted. For a short while.

He'd found a suitable gallery. One within a train's ride of Naples that allowed him to get near to Mateo Monza. To soak up some of the atmosphere. To be energised by his work. To enable him to overcome any fear he had. And to allow him to start to unpick the question he'd set himself for his dissertation: *The Mafia's involvement in Italian art*.

He was being irresponsible. He knew that. He should leave well alone. He knew that too. That's what they'd told him to do. Them; whoever the hell *they* were.

The manager and the staff of the restaurant. They'd joined the list of 'them'.

But, do you know what? Fuck them.

Fuck them.

He wouldn't be terrorised by a bunch of Mafia lunatics. He had lost his love. Gone.

But he had found *Extinction*.

He now had something to fill some of the void.

So, fuck them. All of them.

With added energy he passed through the museum's entrance hall and skipped down the steps into the harsh light of Rome's mid-afternoon sun.

Which way?

Left. About 100 yards to the nearest *metropolitana*, and then connect to Rome's *Termini* station, and a train home.

He felt strong. Alive. Invigorated.

But he didn't make 100 yards.

He hardly made 20.

As soon as he left the museum, a Vespa carrying a pillion pulled up behind him. The passenger, with a rucksack, got off. As he did he pulled out a short baseball bat from this sack.

Gareth sensed something wasn't right; something peripheral. But it was Rome. It was busy. Cars. People. Scooters. There was noise and movement. Sounds and colours.

What was that?

A scream from across the street?

And then an overwhelming sense of pain.

Fuc…! His mind didn't complete the expletive.

The bat smacked the back of his head as such a rate it cracked his skull and sent his brain into vibration; soft tissue against hard bone. Capillaries broke and blood seeped into spaces it wasn't meant to go.

An image. Colours. Primary. Everything. The whole world.

Slashed.

Someone with a bat that seemed to glisten in the sun.

Then the colours were gone. All was dark.

The man with the bat was unrecognisable. Mid-sized and unremarkably dressed. He wore a full-faced helmet with a tinted visor. His approach was casual. Arrogant. He had time on his hands.

So much so that before he jumped back on the scooter he placed a small rectangular card in Gareth's satchel.

It read: *Lascialo solo*.

Leave him alone.

Chapter 7

Sam stretched her back and closed her eyes. *What a day.* She'd been sitting on her backside for over eight hours. Vlad's interrogation. The three-hour flight. An hour in Moscow traffic. And now two and a half hours into - she didn't know how long - a mad dash trying to find the 'village hall'.

Vlad had been as good as his word. On arrival at FSB Headquarters she'd immediately had access to some decent satellite overheads of the area around last night's drop-off point. The images were ten days old, but the resolution was good enough for what she needed. As a precaution she'd phoned Jane before she'd boarded the flight to Moscow. She'd updated her on her meeting with Ali G and asked if she could put a bid in for some SIS imagery. Jane had quizzed her in some detail about her 'interview' - and Sam had gleaned a few things in return. Jane couldn't elaborate too much as the line was insecure, but apparently things were coming to a bit of a head in the UK and what Sam had given her might well be useful for an emerging threat in the UK. The upshot was that Sam should liaise with Frank and ask for what imagery she wanted … within reason. Each 100 square kilometre overhead came via Langley and cost SIS $1500. Jane wasn't prepared to give Sam a blank cheque.

Her chat with Frank had been a frenetic combination of, 'God, it's good to speak to you, Sam. How are you?', and, 'Look, Frank. I've got a plane to catch. If I give you some lat and longs, could you get me the best imagery you can of a 1600 kilometre square box? I need normal and IR.'

Frank was a sweetheart and a superb analyst. He was also uber-reliable and worked outside any boundaries he'd been set. He'd been electronically at Sam's side through some of her most difficult moments with SIS. And had never let her down.

Frank told her the overheads would be with her by midnight tonight - Zulu. That would make it 3 am tomorrow, Moscow time. Sam was pretty convinced she'd still be awake, or at least attempting to stay awake, at that point. Unless she was lucky and the Russian images gave her what she wanted.

She focused back on the screen. Unfortunately the FSB hadn't yet been issued with high-definition monitors. But, as she'd begun her analyst's life looking at printed black and white photographs using a handheld magnifying glass, being able to zoom in with a mouse and having half-decent image correction software to sharpen any pixilation, was definitely a bonus.

Sam had decided to search a forty-by-forty kilometre box, centred on where Vlad had dropped her off. She reckoned, as the crow flies, the farthest distance to the old man and woman's house was five klicks. Then, if you drove at twenty klicks an hour - the speed her second driver would have managed on the local roads - it gave a maximum arc of an additional 15 klicks. That had formed a clear image in her head: forty-by-forty it was.

She'd used an e-gridding tool to break the available mapping into kilometre squares; 1600 blocks in all. She'd discounted anything north of the Russian border - that had removed 273 blocks. Using the FSB's terrain overlay she was able to strikethrough a further 1125 blocks where the gradient was too steep for habitation.

That left 202 blocks, each one kilometre square.

She'd got that far within 30 minutes of acquainting herself with her new office - a pokey room with a single door and a window that wouldn't open. The view was of the Lubyanka's quad. It was hardly inspiring stuff.

Vlad had booted up the computer and assigned her necessary access. Then he wheeled himself out and returned with a thermos of coffee and some rubbish Russian biscuits, made of sand and lard. But it was sustenance for now.

'Have you found where you were first taken to? The house with the old man and woman?' He'd asked whilst peering over her shoulder as best he could with his limited movement.

Wait.

She was concentrating - and raised a hand to shut him up. And, *come on*, she'd only been on the system for fifteen minutes …

… but she was close.

'There.' She pointed at the screen. 'This is the route we took.' Whilst keeping a finger on her right hand marking the location, Sam used a finger on her left hand to plot out the drive.

'If you hover the mouse pointer on it and right-click, you'll get coordinates. And we can then check those with what we got from your phone.'

I know.

Sam moved the mouse, clicked and read out the lat and long of the house.

The one with the gas cooker and the leaky bottle.

Her brain instantaneously went to mush. She felt her pelvic floor slacken and she was petrified that she was going to wet herself. It was all too much. She needed proper sleep in a proper bed. She needed normality. A life away from abuse, violence, guns and terror; where she didn't feel the need to try and kill another human being with liquid petroleum gas.

Get a grip. The woman's not worth it.

Vlad seem to notice Sam's short descent into the abyss. He scribbled down the coordinates on a scrap of paper he had in his hand. When he'd finished he rested a hand on her forearm.

Focus resumed. Just.

'Are you going to do something with that now?' She didn't look away from the screen.

'Yeah. Sure. I've got a team on standby. If your two old people are there, then they can be interrogated … and, how do you Brits say? "Bob's your uncle?"'

She caught his smile from the corner of her eye.

Sam stopped looking at the screen and turned her head to face Vlad. He was washed out; as on edge as she was.

She hesitated.

'I'm not sure that's the best thing to do. You'll spook them. There'll be some form of immediate contact procedure. Hit the house and the mortars will be on the back of a *Kamaz* before you have time start pulling their fingernails out …'

'We don't …!' Vlad protested; Sam interjected.

'Whatever. Give me five hours. Have your team on standby for a dawn raid. Either I'll have the coordinates of the village hall by then, or your people can take out the old folks' home.'

Vlad thought for a second. He clearly wasn't convinced. He had a target. He had the men. It made complete sense to him. A large magnet was pulling the two together. And subtlety wasn't FSB's strongpoint. Bigger the problem, bigger the hammer.

'OK. OK.' He looked across at a non-existent clock on the wall. 'We'll have them ready to move at 3 am.'

'Four.' Sam replied.

'What? Why?'

'I should have more up to date imagery coming in from London at three. That'll give me an hour on the new stuff. Please.'

Vlad scrunched his face up.

'OK. Four. But you'll let me know if you get anything in the meantime?'

'Sure. Where will you be between now and then?' She asked.

'I'm popping home for half an hour, and then I'll be in my office supplying you with coffee.'

Sam was back on task now. Pleasantries were over. Her mind blocked out the rusty gas canisters and her eyes filled with the pixels on the screen.

'Good. And keep those lovely biscuits coming.'

Sam glanced at the digital clock on the bottom right of the screen. It read 1.30 am. It would be another 90 minutes before the Langley overheads arrived. She really needed them. She'd completed a strip review (starting top left corner and then 'reading' the images like a page, ten metre line by ten metre line) of all of the 202 blocks. Twice. She'd been able to discount 75 percent of the terrain where it was clear there was no habitation. Five blocks of the remaining 25 percent clearly contained buildings. *Tick*. The remaining blocks had so much tree cover it was difficult to tell if there were buildings under the canopy. That's why she needed the infrared imagery from Frank. It would look under the leaves and show stuff that was currently obscured.

But that may not be enough. Even with the buildings she could see, she hadn't been able to discount 16 of them as potential targets. She was looking for a house/building of at least 25 metres by 15. Something village hall size. She had 16 potentials. And who knew how many additional ones under the canopy?

Shit.

She stood and stretched. She walked to the window and looked out at the gloom.

Come on.

She thought. Stared at the dirty glass; condensation eating at the putty of the single-glazed windows. Eight pains. Two-above-two, twice.

Window. Panes of glass. Two-above-two.

Hang on.

There was something peripheral. Something oblique. It was nagging her. Something she par-saw. A glimpse. Something that would unlock this puzzle.

She sat down and moved the keyboard away from her to create some space. Then she reached for a notepad and a biro.

And started to draw.

The image came from nowhere. Accessed from the most bizarre of corners of her mind.

She scribbled frantically, like a fax machine on three-phase power.

It was all blue. The colour of the pen. A rectangle. No, not quite all blue. Blue squares.

Like?

She wasn't sure, but it was free-flowing now. The drawing child-like but accurate. It took her a couple of minutes to complete the picture.

She put the pen down and stared. In front of her were six blue squares. Portrait. Two on top of two, on top of two. But there was a slash across the middle and bottom squares. A diagonal. Forty-five degrees - ish. Top right to bottom left.

She stood again. And walked back to the window. It was raining now, so heavily she couldn't make out the other side of the quad.

Think.

What was the picture?

Think.

...

Got it!

Yes ... that's it.

I know what I'm looking for.

Sam rushed back to the seat, sat, pulled the mouse and keyboard back towards her and started again.

Sixteen buildings.

Sixteen potential targets.

Sixteen. Just maybe one of them might have a child's swing or climbing frame in the back garden. Lit up by a fleeting outside security light, probably activated by an animal. A snapshot through the back door of the village hall. She'd seen it, or something like it.

But it hadn't registered at the time.

Ten minutes later and 16 buildings down she was no wiser ... and much more frustrated.

She looked at the clock. It was 2.14 am.

She half stood. And sat down again.

Relax. Wait for the Langley images.

Watch the news.

She clicked on the Google icon, typed in 'BBC news' which threw up a live feed. The red ticker tape said the talking head was Bradley Smyth: Head of Counterterrorism Police. He was finishing off.

'Please, therefore, could every member of the public be particularly vigilant in these difficult times. Thank you.'

That must have been in response to what Jane had told her this morning.

Following that the BBC switched to a reporter in Hungary. The headline was 'Hungary to follow the UK out of the European Union'. The presenter described Hungary's continuous anti-EU leaning fuelled by the refugee crisis and the rise of nationalism supported by popularist politicians. Sam could have written the report herself. There was nothing new about Hungary's growing disdain for the EU, but as far as she was concerned it was bravado - playing to the home crowd. Hungary received far too many benefits from the EU for any sensible politician to follow through and leave the pact.

The screen switched to a clip of the Prime Minister, Viktor Molnár. He was a member of the right-wing, Fidesz party. Sam thought he was a more moderating influence in that party, and rarely offered anything more than jingoistic commentary for his base.

She thought she knew what was coming and almost closed the video box.

Then Viktor Molnár said something that surprised the hell out of her. She didn't catch all of it, and she could have been mistaken. But she was pretty sure …

The clip closed. The news switched to a minor terror attack in Namibia. A knife attack in a popular coastal town. Three dead …

But she wasn't interested in that. She needed to hear the Viktor Molnár clip again. To be sure.

She typed into Google: *Viktor Molnár - leaving EU* - and today's date.

There it was, at the top of the listing. She opened the link and pressed play. In among the anti-EU diatribe, Sam heard what she thought she had heard a few moments before.

'… We are a people. We will not be confined by the vagaries of others. We will do as we wish. We will do what is right.'

What?

That was nonsensical.

Ping!

Sam's spinning mind was stopped abruptly by an alert from her machine.

A dialogue box had popped up in the middle of the screen. She had new mail - from Frank. It had a link.

Let's get on with this.

She opened her mail and clicked on the link. A door in the firewall between SIS and FSB opened, and there they were. Daylight and IR. Seventy-two files.

It took her ten minutes to sort through the imagery, and a further five to pick out the areas where she needed the IR to look below the canopy.

Twelve minutes later she had it. A solitary building, accessible by road. Room for five cars. A single pitched roof.

And a swing and a slide in the back garden.

To be sure she measured the building and compared it against what she remembered. There was easily enough room for the hall and the armoury. Plus some other, smaller rooms. The measurements fitted.

She checked the route her driver might have taken. There were two possibilities. One was 12.3 klicks; the second, arriving from the opposite direction, 21.6 klicks. Both worked, depending on how fast you drove. The building was the right distance from the rusty gas bottle.

That was it. She had the village hall.

'Vlad!'

Port of Dover, Dover, UK

'Toffer' Hawley gazed out of the side window of his Volvo. There was a slightly battered white van in the lane next to him. Ahead of the van was a motorhome of some description, then a coach full of kids. In front of them was a man with a high-viz vest and a walkie-talkie. Holding them in place.

He looked to his front - his lane. Six cars. In the middle distance a recently arriving ferry.

The cars were various makes and colours. He wasn't a car buff, so he couldn't tell what they were. He guessed, like him, they were packed full of kids, suitcases, grips and the odd cool box. It was the first day of the autumn half-term. Exodus-day for those lucky enough to have the wherewithal to head onto the continent to find some sun before the reds and browns of autumn became the greys and blacks of winter.

Radio 4's *News at One* programme was reminding him of the state of the world. There had been three more unattributable terror attacks in far-off corners of the globe; places like Montevideo, where the city's metro had been hacked causing a train to run into the back of another. Result - 12 dead. He guessed that even Radio 4's discerning listeners would struggle to find the capital of Uruguay on the map. After the world update, the programme's lead had been the replaying of a senior policeman's call for vigilance among all the public. A terror attack was imminent in the UK. Everyone needed to report anything they thought was suspicious. As soon as they could.

He was so glad he was taking his kids to France for a week. Away from the madness.

He checked in his rear-view mirror.

Two kids. Two *beautiful* kids. Amy and Sophie. Twelve and nine. The only thing in his life that mattered. They were going to have a great time. A French farmhouse *gîte*, a pool, fizzy drinks and croissants ... and a couple of bottles of decent white wine. Perfect. The two girls were both ensconced in something on their tablets. Earphones in. Them and their machines. Everything else was peripheral. A tunnel of focus - eyes to screen. The whole world was on the back foot to hell and they didn't care. He wasn't sure they noticed.

He smiled to himself. They were in the best place.

It would be different in France: the pool, barbeques, smoothies in coffee shops, Moorish castles with imaginary princesses, a trip to the sea. The first act: ending with iPads exiting to muted applause. Second act: Dad would enter stage-left to rapturous cheering. It would be a short second act. Just a week. But it would steal the show.

Toffer looked left, through the passenger window and slightly behind: a newish 4x4. A Range Rover? He commended himself for recognising the marque. The tailgate was open. An older couple were standing at the back. The man, dressed as if he were about to get on a yacht, had a glass of fizz in his hand. Toffer strained his neck to see better. The woman had a glass too. She was passing the man a sandwich. Brown bread and something. The man was smiling. He leant forward and gave the woman a peck on the cheek. She smiled back. They were in love.

A lump grew in Toffer's throat. He swallowed and snapped his head back to the front. He closed his eyes; breathed out. He realised he was gripping the steering wheel tightly. Tears were not far away. He relaxed his grip.

He could *feel* the emptiness of the passenger seat. It was tangible, as though, with Chloe not sitting beside him, there was a vacuum into which he was being pulled. The void hurt. It hurt so much.

This time last year it was different. The four of them. The team. Off to the *gîte*. It wasn't their two week summer break, flying somewhere exotic. Or to Florida to immerse themselves in a world of cartoon characters and rollercoasters - the kids' favourite. But this week in France had become a family ritual. It had always been special. And it was *his* favourite.

Even more so just now, with Chloe no longer part of his life. Initially at her Mum's, and then into a flat. The kids too. She couldn't live with him anymore. Not after what he had done.

He got that. What he'd done had been stupid and reckless. Heartless. It was more than a one night stand. But it had never been a substitute for what he and Chloe had had. Never. It was the act of a fool. A selfish and self-centred idiot. Driven by an uncontrollable lust. Downwards and away. Away from the family - from the loves of his life.

He'd got what he'd deserved. And, having received a letter from Chloe's solicitor a couple of days ago, he was going to pay for it.

Bloody fool.

This was probably the last time he could afford to take the kids away to France.

So he was going to enjoy it.

They all were.

Noise. Something mildly incomprehensible over a tannoy. Their boat had docked. They would be boarding in 20 minutes. Could all passengers return to their cars.

News at One had moved on. It was an editorial of sorts. Some reporter he didn't recognise was talking about a series of rallies planned for Sunday. There was one in London. Sister ones were planned in many cities across the world: New York; Toronto; Tokyo. There was even one planned for Beijing. The reporter said there didn't appear to be any central organisation making these things happen. It seemed to be a benign uprising against the wave of terror that had gripped the world. One of the unifying hashtags was *#enoughisenough*. A second was *#orderfromchaos*. They expected hundreds of thousands in London, even though the police were strongly advising this was the wrong time for a major public gathering when the threat of a major terrorist event was so high.

Apparently, whilst they could expect the rally in London to attract the usual fringe groups, the reporter had just interviewed a 'millennial'. The young woman had said that their generation had had enough. They were disenfranchised and being led by an age group who didn't understand - or care. And now she and her friends couldn't even guarantee to live their lives free from terror because the so-called leaders of the world were incapable of providing even the most basic of necessities.

'Do you think they are responsible for the terror attacks?' The reporter had asked.

'Well, they're not pulling the trigger, so to speak. But, yes. And d'you know what? It wouldn't surprise me if they weren't secretly encouraging the terrorists. To keep us in our place.'

That didn't make sense to Toffer, but he could understand how they had all got to where they were.

And, as for the madness, these people didn't know the half of it.

He was a banker. In the thick of the markets. And it was a system on the edge.

The FTSE was down another 70 points this morning and the fall would continue until trading stopped at 4.30pm. Unless things improved his firm reckoned on another 300 point loss next week. Maybe a further 200 the week after. And then, unless the economic factors changed, they would hit the bottom. That's what they were telling people, anyway.

But he had insider knowledge. He sat on the bank's emergency futures committee. And their analysis painted a much more dystopian landscape.

From its height in the New Year, the system had liquidity enough to stand a shock of losing 20% of the value of all stocks. Maybe 25%. They were already at 20%. And 25% was where they predicted the bottom. But the housing market in most western countries was overvalued and household debt across first world economies was unnaturally high. GDP had flatlined and was set to fall as consumer confidence look likely to plummet. And whilst unemployment was low, around ten percent of those employed worked in the gig economy - their positions were not safe.

And government borrowing, especially in the US, was a huge burden on the system.

It was a tinder keg waiting for a spark.

The committee's view was all they needed was one spectacular terror event and the 2008 crash would appear a minor tremor in comparison.

Their bank wouldn't be able to stand the jolt. It would follow maybe ten others in the city not strong enough to cope. There would be chaos. Trillions of pounds would be lost. And the rally at the weekend would be a shadow in comparison to the uprising that would follow.

Chaos.

Maybe the beginning of the end. Whatever that meant.

Just before he'd left to pick up the kids this morning, he'd had a chat to a long-term client of his. Obviously he wasn't able to share the committee's most gloomy predictions. But he was able to tell him what he was doing with the money he'd taken from his own share portfolio.

Buy gold.

The price of gold had shot through the roof after the banking crisis ten years ago. For three decades it had fluctuated between five and ten pounds sterling a gram. The collapse of the Lehman Brothers had put a rocket under the price; it reached a peak of just below £35 a gram in 2012, dropping briefly below £25, before rising again above £30 a gram last year. This morning it was at £39.53; a 420 percent rise in just over ten years. In the same time the stock market had risen just 37 percent. Even the most speculative of stocks would struggle to match a 400 percent rise in ten years.

Any sensible investor would have thought the price of gold had maxed. In 2008, with gold hovering at £15 a gram, they all talked about the £20-a-gram ceiling, as if there were no way their generation would ever see gold at those heady heights. Now the talk was of £50. A new ceiling. Unreachable. Unbreakable.

Unthinkable.

But Toffer didn't think so.

You just had to look at the stats. If market forces could affect a 400 percent rise in ten years, then anything was possible. You just needed one almighty shock on top of the current political situation and gold would go nuclear, whilst stock markets melted.

This morning he'd told his client to put all his cash in gold. All of it.

His daze was broken by movement to his right. It was four men and a woman walking down between the row of cars, vans and buses. They were headed for the battered white van. As they got close he couldn't not stare at them.

The five were black. In an earlier life he and Chloe had been on safari to Kenya. To him most Kenyan's looked 'normal', like the black men and women who worked in his bank. Like Kyle, a good friend of his.

But in Kenya's hinterland, where they travelled for the safari, the indigenous tribes were different. They were taller - less bulky. More like long distance runners.

The four who were now getting into the van looked like the rural Kenyans on the safari - except they were taller still. The woman, who was strikingly beautiful, was a young Grace Jones. Tall, angular. Distinctive. The men were similar. And a little bit scary.

The woman and a man got into the back of the van via a sliding door. The driver was already behind the wheel.

The man in the passenger seat had the door opened, but hadn't got in. He was looking directly at Toffer, his head to one side. No sign of emotion.

And then he did something that made Toffer shiver involuntarily. He made a pistol out of his right hand and fired an imaginary shot in the direction of the car.

Bang.

He then raised the imaginary barrel to his mouth and blew away imaginary smoke. And smiled a non-imaginary smile.

Toffer couldn't stop himself. His head whipped around to check on the kids …

… who were happily immersed in whatever it was their tablets were engaging them in.

He brought his head back to the front.

The man was gone. And the van door was closed.

Headquarters SIS, Vauxhall, London

Frank was sitting on a soft brown, faux-leather armchair that he would struggle to fit through the front door of his house. He was in, what the team called, 'the mood room' - a Googlesque meeting and relaxing space designed to declutter the mind and allow for 'big thoughts'. There was one on each floor of Babylon and he was one of only a few people who used it for what it was designed for: thinking. Others escaped into it when the pressure seeping out of their phones and keyboards was overwhelming, or for somewhere quiet to eat their lunch. And he'd known three or four folk use it as a bedspace when they'd worked so late it was almost time to come back in again.

All of those uses seemed fair to him. But he popped in when he needed to declutter and focus. And he needed to do that now because ... *it had been quite a day.*

Last night's examination of the potential routes Abir al-Rasheed might have taken to get from Mersa Fatma to East Compton, established that ten days ago eight people (according to the manifest, six men and two women) had disembarked a small container ship, Marks Cross, at Gioia Tauro. First thing this morning he had pinged a request to an old SIS pal of his, Justin, who worked out of the British Embassy in Rome. He'd given Justin a date and time and asked him to pull whatever favours he could to get any info they had from the container port of Gioia Tauro. He was looking for eight passengers. Ten days ago. Marks Cross. Any images, or any details they could get.

And then it all got a bit strange.

Justin had called him back two hours later. Having received Frank's email he'd spoken to one of his contacts in the *Arma dei Carabinieri* (Italian armed police). Details were passed and promises were made.

The same policeman had just come back to him. There was confusion all round.

'Are you sure about the date, Frank?'

'What? Yeah. Let me check the email I sent you.'

It took Frank 15 seconds to throw up the missive he'd dispatched to Justin. He then crossed-checked it with his notes he'd taken last night on the freighter's movements.

'Hi, Justin. Yeah. That's correct. Why, is there a problem?'

'Well, maybe. It's just my contact in the *Arma dei Carabinieri* has been in touch with the security operations at the port and they have no record of a Marks Cross docking within the last two weeks. According to them your ship doesn't exist - not on the southwest coast of Italy.'

What the ...?

'Hang on, Justin. Let me check.'

Last night Cynthia had found Marks Cross for him. He was pretty sure she used *marinetraffic.com*, an online, minute-by-minute worldwide ship tracking programme to scope the problem. He could have used the website himself, but Cynthia had built-in AI and was a million times quicker than he was.

Maybe she was wrong?

This time, instead of using Cynthia, he opened up *marinetraffic.com* and searched for Marks Cross - sailing under a Guatemalan flag.

What?

There it was.

In the mid-Atlantic.

How strange.

He glanced at his notebook and then back at the screen.

And then the terrorist notes on the Gioia Tauro area that had been overlaid by AISE came back to him.

I wonder ...

'Justin, can you do me another favour? Could you see if you could get any CCTV footage from or close to the port, at the date I've given you - that was when Marks Cross was meant to have berthed in Gioia Tauro - let's make the window 24-hours. I'm looking for either eight passengers ambling about, or anything that could transport eight people. Probably not hidden. In plain sight. Maybe a minibus.'

Frank closed his eyes. *Think.* 'And, if possible, don't use your *Arma dei Carabinieri* contact. Can you go straight to the *Carabinieri*?'

There was a pause on the end of the line.

'Hang on, Frank. Do you think someone's messing with this?'

Definitely.

'Possibly. Last night Cynthia did a trawl for me looking at sailings between Tunis and Gioia Tauro. Among others she came up with Marks Cross. I wrote the name down in capitals on my notepad, ... ', he had the pad in his hand, '... and then double-underlined it. Before I left the office I e-copied the details from Cynthia and dropped them into a draft report, a copy of which I have open on my screen.' Frank glanced at the central monitor. 'And that's the same document I cut and pasted into the email to you a couple of hours ago. There's no error between the three. In short, last night Cynthia had heard of Marks Cross and had plotted its route between Tunis and Gioia Tauro - 10 days ago. This morning, according to *marinetraffic.com*, the ship is in the mid-Atlantic. I would say that's suspicious. Wouldn't you?'

'Unless you've made a mistake. Maybe?'

I don't make mistakes.

'I think that's unlikely, but it is a possibility. The thing is, there's a time constraint on this. So whilst I check again, could you put your best man on it ... please?'

'OK. Sure thing. I'll get on with that. And I don't need to contact the *Carabinieri*. The Embassy's embedded Italian police LO has access to all of the government-owned CCTV. I'll go upstairs now and see what he's got. I'm on it.'

After that Frank had called the Southampton-based, Maritime and Coastguard Agency. Within a minute the officer he spoke to had found Marks Cross. It was as Cynthia had described last night - a 13,000 tonne container ship. But that's the only thing the officer and Cynthia agreed on. As for location he was with *marinetraffic.com*. The ship wasn't in the Med. It was sailing from the Panama Canal to Conakry, the capital of Guinea, West Africa.

'Are you sure?' Frank had asked.

'Yes, of course.' The officer sounded a bit put out.

'Is there anyway …' Frank didn't have time to complete the sentence.

'Hang on.'

Frank waited. Either the officer was busy checking something, or he had been distracted. Frank didn't need distractions at the moment.

'That's not right. No. Something's not right here. There's an anomaly. The ship was on the cross-Atlantic route two weeks ago headed for Guinea. Cargo … cheap goods from China, as far as I can make out. Picking up fruit. Its itinerary was the Med: Tunis, Italy and then back again. It left …'

It sounded to Frank as the man was poring over a spreadsheet of infinite detail. He knew what that felt like.

'..., uh, Conakry for Freetown, Sierra Leone. And then, hang on, and this is where it gets weird, as if by magic it's back halfway across the Pacific - steaming east for Panama. It time-jumped, backwards, like a Tardis. Is this why you spooks are interested in it?'

'Possibly. Thanks.' Frank was leaning back in his chair, chewing his pen. 'Does this thing happen often? You know, ships being somewhere, but then not.'

'I've never come across it before. No. Ships' VHF and satellite tracking systems are bomb-proof. But, I guess, systems break.'

The officer didn't sound convinced.

'Can you find out where Marks Cross actually is?' Frank asked.

'Not immediately, no. But I can trawl the databases we have access to and check where it last *really* berthed, and what its actual route was. Can you give me an hour?'

'Sure. Sure. You have my number?'

'Yes, I do. I'll come back to you as soon as I have something.'

In the end Frank didn't need corroboration that someone had interfered with Marks Cross's positional data. Because they'd found Abir al-Rasheed.

Justin had called him back at lunchtime. There was a CCTV camera at the traffic lights of the container port slip road heading onto the north-south, E45 motorway. Justin had sent through 27 clips of 'vehicles large enough to carry at least 8 people'. It was a combination of people carriers, minibuses and coaches.

Immediately after the phone call Frank got to work. He started with minibuses joining the motorway, heading north.

His logic was that Abir al-Rasheed was precious cargo - with, maybe, seven others. He wasn't paying for his own trip and wouldn't be taking chances inside a packing case in the back of an articulated lorry. Or in a sealed, metalled grain container. Or any of the other horrible methods refugees used to illegally cross Europe. Abir al-Rasheed had taken two weeks to make a three month journey. Somebody wanted him in the UK quickly.

In one piece. If he were on Marks Cross, his agent would have paid a lot of money to get him off the boat and out of the port, almost certainly with decent, albeit forged, papers. Outside of the port's perimeter the chance of getting stopped by the police until he reached the northern European coast was minimal. So Frank would definitely be making sure his cargo travelled in some sort of luxury.

In a 24-hour period nine minibuses had left Gioia Tauro, heading north. Five were empty; four had passengers. The CCTV imagery wasn't good enough to make out who the passengers were, but he had the vehicles' registration details. Significantly, only one of the four with passengers had left the port at night.

He'd got straight back on the phone to Justin.

'It's great work Justin. Can you do something else?'

'Yes, of course.'

'I need to track a single minibus, …', he read out the number plate of the van that had left in darkness. 'It went through your CCTV at 1.13 am. It's heading north. I would guess eventually crossing into France at Nice. But I can't be sure. It's probably making best legal speed, but will need to stop at a couple of service stations. Let's assume a range of between three and five hundred kilometres. Can you get CCTV imagery of any fuel stop on the east coast motorway? I need a mugshot of the passengers. They will need to get out and pee.'

'I'm on it, Frank.'

Most of the time being an analyst is days and days on painstaking effort with no reward. Every so often a hunch pays off. A lead comes good. Today was such a day.

Justin had called back three quarters of an hour later. Frank was brushing custard cream crumbs from his jeans. He almost dropped the phone.

'Bingo, Frank, bingo. I've just sent through some stills.'

Frank stopped brushing, found his mouse and opened the mail.

There he was.

Abir al-Rasheed.

At a service station just north of Salerno. And Justin had three full-face and four glancing shots of the other passengers. They were all northeast African. Tall, slim with very dark faces.

From the same village?

Frank just about found the time to thank his pal. He was too busy opening up the images taken by his SIS colleagues from Asmara.

Fifteen minutes later he had two certains and one likely.

It was clear. Abir al-Rasheed, a fast track immigrant from a sleepy fishing village in Eritrea, and very likely at least three others, had made the same speedy journey at the same time to London.

What now?

Frank needed thinking time. So he'd made himself another cuppa and retreated to the 'mood room'.

Unfortunately his thinking time was interrupted by Claire, Jane's PA. He was relaxing in a chair big enough for three of him when she tapped on the glass wall.

Frank glanced across at Claire, then round the room. He was on his own.

She mouthed, 'Jane. Now.'

Frank mouthed back, 'Me?'

Claire raised her eyebrows and tutted silently.

'Yes, you.'

Greed

Chapter 8

They had a system. He and Sophie carried all the gear - a picnic, pillows and a couple of rugs - and Amy ran ahead to the family bar at the pointy end of the boat and bagged a table, two chairs and bench. It worked every time, even when there was a ferry-load of coaches. And it had worked this time. Right in the middle of the boat, looking out on a beautiful autumn day. Light blue sky, darker closer to the heavens, with a pale half-moon leading the way. It would be a better view if the ferry company knew how to clean their windows, but it was still pretty spectacular.

The kids were in their own version of heaven: sausage rolls, Doritos, dips, breadsticks, cucumber cut in chunks and small bread rolls, buttered with salmon paste. Coke Zero, of course, and dark chocolate digestive biscuits. The picnic had developed over the years and this was the agreed outcome. Toffer had gone out of his way to make it so again this year. Of course it wouldn't be complete without being plugged into your tablet - playing on your favourite game. Sophie was tucked up on one of the chairs, with her legs under her bum. Amy was laid flat out on the bench, her head resting on a pillow. And he was on the second chair, a bar-bought coffee in his hand

and his eyes fixed on the horizon - which didn't budge. The sea conditions were perfect.

But he couldn't get *that* image out of his mind. The tall, dark … African? With a hand doubling as a pistol. That veiled threat. The fleeting sense of imminent horror.

Was he aiming at him? Or his children? For some reason that made him look around.

Wait …

Shit!

There he was. Walking through the bar. Casually, but with purpose. Grey joggers, a black hoodie with a white rope cord. And a backpack.

He's coming this way. Towards the centre of the bar: a large circle of arc-like benches, facing inwards. The area was full of chairs and small round tables, much like the ones he and the girls were sitting on. In the middle there was a small round space that wasn't filled with furniture. If they moved a few tables and chairs it could have been a dance floor.

The man stopped there. He took off his backpack.

And then …

… what … shit!

Toffer instinctively lunged towards Sophie and pulled her to the floor.

She screamed … which cut through the noise in the bar.

He didn't care. Only one thing mattered.

Sophie was on the ground; he was on all fours. Amy's head was level with his. She was staring at him, her face wrenched away from the screen, reacting to her sister's scream. He grabbed her by the arm and pulled at her; his strength overcame the minimal friction between his daughter's clothes and the plastic of the seats. She slipped off the bench and fell in a heap joining them on the floor.

'Dad! What are you doing?!' It was a shout. Louder than the surrounding background noise.

He had to get them to be quiet. He had to get them safe.

He pulled Amy towards him, she instinctively moved closer.

They were now one bundle under the table. Toffer had thrown his body over the girls. The small circular table gave some protection. His back was facing the bar.

Between them and the man.

The man who had taken an imaginary shot at him and his family. And had blown away the imaginary smoke.

The man who, seconds earlier, had pulled a gun from his backpack.

A gun.

A proper gun.

From his backpack.

There was nothing imaginary about this now.

Toffer clung on. The girls asking, probing … protesting.

And the noise level grew.

Screams. Shouts …

… and then …

Bang! Bang! Bang!

The loudest noise Toffer had ever heard.

It was three shots. One after the other. Toffer expected to be hit. To feel pain. The tall black man had singled his family out for punishment before they had got on the ferry. He was now seeing that through. With a real gun. And real bullets.

They were going to die.

Please, no.

'Are you OK? Sophie? Amy?' He screamed the question, his face muzzled against one of the backs.

'Yes, Daddy. Yes.' A stereo response. 'What's happening Daddy? I'm scared!' He couldn't make out which girl was saying what. He was so glad they were talking - still with him. Unhurt.

Bang! Bang! Bang!

Toffer flinched. He held the girls tighter. Tried to make his shoulders wider.

No pain. Not that he could tell.

Screams. Shouts. Movement. They were in the scene of a disaster movie.

Then ...

'SHUT UP! AND DON'T MOVE.' A huge voice, above the screaming. Loud and clear. Dark and thick with an African accent.

Bang! Bang!

'SHUT UP! You …', Toffer imagined some pointing, '... shut up! DON'T MOVE.'

A piercing scream … the sound of panicked movement ...

… and then ...

Bang!

No scream.

'Oh God!' A plea. Above the background noise which had been reduced to a murmur.

'Oh my God! She's been hit.' A pause. 'You've killed her!'

Bang!

A gurgling noise. Then nothing. Quiet. Heavy breathing.

A whimper.

Noisy tears.

The silence of fear.

Toffer held the girls tighter still. Really tight.

He whispers.

'Don't talk. Don't scream. Please. Shhh.'

Toffer listened.

Muffled crying. A sob.

'You're next.' African. Thick, but clear.

Toffer was working with only what he could hear. He had been expecting to die. But he was alive. Still. He could feel Amy and Sophie breathing under him. They were alive.

Now, cowering beneath the table, he didn't know what was happening. He couldn't see. He needed to see.

He carefully lifted his head and turned it so he could make out the centre of the bar.

The man was there. Tall. In the middle. He was circling on the spot, his big metallic gun pointing at the crowd.

Toffer could see the smoke this time. It hung above head height. Real smoke. And he could smell the smell. He'd never experienced gun smoke before, but if he got out of this alive it would be a sensation he would never forget.

'Daddy?'

That broke his concentration. It was Amy, He quickly moved his hand and found her mouth. He pressed lightly, leaving room for her to breath.

'Shhh, darling. Shhh. Everything's going to be OK. Be still. Please' A whisper. The tall man couldn't have heard.

Everything's going to be OK.

He was reassuring himself. He had to feel that way.

For his girls.

Ferenc Liszt International Airport, Budapest, Hungary

Sam stood patiently in the customs queue. She was in the line marked 'EU Arrivals'. There were eight people ahead of her. She had no bags to collect. She'd brought nothing with her from the UK and picked up nothing from Moscow. She needed a change of clothes, for sure. Once through customs she'd find a taxi and head off to a guest house she'd picked from the internet. She reckoned she'd be there in time for some evening grub. Then she'd get her head down. She'd work out what to do next tomorrow.

After she'd bought herself some clothes. And some deodorant.

It had been a bit of a whirl.

Vlad had accepted her logic on the location of the FFO's hideout. Twenty minutes later a *Spetsnaz* team were *en route*. Vlad had said they would take out the 'village hall' first, sending just a team of two to provide overwatch on the old man and woman's house. Once the first target had been stabilised, the other pair would assault the first house Sam had been taken to. He reckoned it would all be over in a couple of hours.

They'd got the report back just as Sam was halfway through a small plate of pig meat and toast - the only thing on offer at 7.00 am in the FSB canteen. That, and coffee you could seal a fence with. Vlad was with her. His phone had rung. Throughout he was mainly on receive, but it was clearly good news. He finished the call and carried on eating.

'Well?' Sam was frustrated.

He took another mouthful. And a swig of his coffee.

She smacked him on the hand.

'Oi!' He feigned hurt. And then he smiled.

'You did good work, Sam Green. We got Kutnetsov - we think, the mortars, the mortar ammunition and a number of other weapons. He's in custody, claiming he knows nothing. They're sending through a photo of him. Could you ID it?' Vlad forked some more meat.

'Sure. What about the other man? My driver. Or was it just Kutnetsov?'

Vlad finished chewing.

'He was on his own. No one else. The team reckon, having been given your very clear description of the armoury, they're a couple of AKs short. But it's still a really good haul.' He picked up his coffee and finished it. He placed the mug on the table and sat completely still. Staring at her. Not an unpleasant stare. Just a stare.

And then the smallest of nods.

'You're something else, you know?' He said. 'To go in like that. With all the inherent dangers. They could have done anything to you. We may never have seen you again. But, you made it. And you made a connection none of my team would have made. The swing in the garden. Amazing. And you found it. Amongst all that detail on those pictures. It's impressive. Fabulous.'

Sam didn't know what to say. Or do.

It was nothing. Not really.

She just did what she did. She didn't think about it. In any case, what else was she to do? It was either South Ossetia - or Asda. Simple as that.

Except ...

... what Vlad didn't know was what she'd gone through whilst she was in the old woman's hands. The ignominy. The abuse. The pain.

The memory made her stomach lurch

'What about the old folk's home? Did they manage to get the man and the woman?'

Someone who Vlad recognised had just come into the canteen. He raised his hand to the man, who nodded back.

'Yeah, that's strange. The two-man team went in. There was nothing there. The place had been razed. By fire. It was still smouldering. Too hot to enter, apparently. They thought maybe there was a body towards the back of the shell - on a bed? But they couldn't be sure.

Sam's stomach lurched again - pork and coffee. It wasn't a great combination.

'Are you all right?' Vlad asked.

She swallowed and held her hand to her mouth.

'Loo? I need …' She pointed at her mouth with her free hand.

Vlad was ahead of her. He indicated over his shoulder.

'Out left, then first left. Can't miss it. Are you OK …?' The last sentence trailed off as Sam dashed out.

She made it to the first pan in the first cubicle. And threw up. And again. She took some deep breaths. And threw up once more. Just bile. And one piece of pork. Brown, disgusting. The smell was rancid. Her stomach wretched again, but there was nothing left.

Exhausted, she stood, wavering uneasily. She steadied herself with her hand on the wall. She pulled the lever, the contents of her stomach flushed away. She turned, moved out of the cubicle and faced the basins. Six, side by side. Mirrors above. She looked at herself.

Ashen. Off-red curls that needed a gardener. Dark, functional clothes and a face the colour of an unwashed pillowcase.

She was trembling.

What have I become?

What had she done?

She had killed again. Probably. Certainly. The woman who had abused her. And her husband?

She doesn't like to be woken. The man's words.

The woman wasn't awake now. For sure.

There was a knock on the door.

'Sam? Sam! Are you OK?'

She turned on the tap, bent down and took a gulp of water. She rinsed her mouth and spat it out. Brown fluid. Water and coffee tinged with flakes of pork.

She did the same again. The result looked more like water this time.

The door flung open. It was Vlad.

'Are you OK, Sam?'

She didn't answer him. Instead she stared at the mirror.

She saw a woman. Mid-height, slim build. Unremarkably dressed. A woman she didn't recognise.

'Sam!'

The tap was still running. She formed her hands into a bowl, caught some water and splashed her face; the face of the woman in the mirror.

'Sam!!' Vlad was beside her now. He placed one hand on her arm. That broke the spell.

She turned to him. The woman in the mirror did the same.

A grimace of a smile. It was all she had.

'I'm fine Vlad, now, thanks. I need some coffee. And I need to work out what to do next. I think I have somewhere to go today.'

'Where? Where's that?' He sounded confused. Flustered.

'Hungary. But first I need access to your files, please.'

'You haven't slept. You must get some sleep.'

'I can sleep on the plane. I'll book it now. And then if you could get me access to your files on the Hungarian prime minister, that would be great.'

He chewed over her request.

'Sure, OK. This is all a bit strange ...'

Sam ushered his wheelchair towards the main toilet door.

Just before she followed him, she had one last look in the mirror.

There was that woman again. The one she didn't recognise.

The woman spoke to her.

Busy. Keep busy.

The first flight to Budapest was in four hours. That was probably enough time to do the work she needed. Vlad had quizzed her as to what she wanted, and then, as he had a number of other things to do - like write a report on the previous evening's events - he handed her over to one of his team. Vlad's man had set up the necessary permissions, asked some overly detailed questions, which didn't surprise her - he was a spy, after all - and then left her to it.

The FSB had a big file on Viktor Molnár, Hungary's prime minister. It was clear to Sam she was only seeing so much detail. She tried to follow a reference in the file, but came up with '*неразрешенный*': unauthorised. This happened a number of times.

What was clear was Viktor Molnár had been, as she thought, a moderating influence in the Fidesz party. Until very recently. Hungary's erosion of the influence of their judiciary, and the closing down of a lot of the left-wing press, had been ongoing for a couple of years. Recently, additional powers had been afforded to the prime minister, with new pro-Fidesz judges passing the necessary legislation. The EU had become so incensed with Hungary's anti-democratic actions they had formally sanctioned Budapest via the European Court of Justice - something which had never been done before. Over the summer an uneasy truce remained. Throughout Molnár had said one thing to his own base, and something different when he was in Brussels. Hungary needed EU financial support - only a fool would upend that.

But that's exactly what Molnár had done. His tone had changed about three weeks ago - the files Sam were reading pointed to a single day in September. On that day, and for no discernible reason, Molnár had changed his tune. His anti-EU rhetoric stepped up a couple of gears and this appeared to culminate in last night's announcement: Hungary was pressing ahead with their own legislation to leave the EU. And it was Molnár who was leading the charge.

It didn't make a great deal of sense. Nothing in the files made it clear. There was no revelation. Molnár had crossed the Rubicon and nobody knew why.

The files gave her access to his background, travel, bank accounts and his property. He was moderately well off - a single bank account with the Hungarian OTP Bank. It was constantly in credit, with his main income being his official salary. His travel was particularly unremarkable. He spent most of his time in Budapest. In the past year he had visited Brussels four times, and Slovakia, Finland and Poland once. He owned a small estate just outside Budapest and took an annual family holiday to Calabria, Italy, with his first and only wife and two sons. He was originally a lawyer, his father a soldier and his mother a doctor. It was all very normal.

And yet ...

... *and yet.*

Sam didn't know. It was *too* normal. There were files she couldn't access - but they didn't appear to be recent. She'd check with Vlad, but sensed what she wasn't seeing said more about FSB's surveillance activity than it did about something nefarious Molnár was involved in.

And yet ...

Last night on TV. In Molnár's speech. He had said, 'We are a people. We will not be defined by the vagaries of others.'

What did that mean? It was out of context and meant nothing.

But much more mysteriously, why did he utter exactly the same words, in the same order, as Kutnetsov had twelve hours earlier?

Exactly the same words.

Two men. One leading a country on the brink of political and financial suicide. And the other, the leader of a four-man cake and arse terror cell, that was now defunct.

Exactly the same words.

'We are a people. We will not be defined by the vagaries of others …'

Was it coincidence?

Could be?

But Sam didn't like coincidences.

Not when it came to 14 words in two languages. Out of two mouths, separated by 2,000 miles and just 12 hours.

There was only one other explanation.

Someone was telling them what to say. Someone was making them do things they weren't comfortable with. Molnár wasn't a hard-liner. Kutnetsov was no more Islamic extremist than she was lion tamer. This was part of something. Something bigger than both of them. The new terror, maybe? Break up the EU. Blow up a nuclear power station. Set the world ablaze. And watch it burn?

But then she thought she was mad. She was distracted. Dislocated from reality. She'd seen too much of her own horror. Experienced the very worst of the very worst people. Been tangled up in conspiracies so bizarre and unbelievable, that now she thought anything was possible. Planes brought down, killing hundreds, just to hide the murder of a single person. A biological bomb set off in a British underground station - laid by Muslim hands, but orchestrated by the Christian far-right.

She saw terror everywhere. Religion against religion. Man versus man. Her own mind against itself. Hatred. Disgust. Fear.

Sam felt all of those; she saw it writ large in the face of the woman in the mirror.

Coincidence?

There was only one way to find out.

So here she was.

In Hungary. At the centre of the dismantling of the European Union. In a country caught up in nationalistic fervour. Driven by anti-migrant fear. And led by a man who, until recently, had kept a very tight lid on it all.

Vlad had added little to the sum of all knowledge. What was hidden, he reassured her, were FSB protocols. There was nothing she needed to know. Of course Russia was courting Molnár, encouraging him. Whilst Vlad didn't necessarily agree, his country would be happy to see the breakup of the EU. If it went further, they would be equally delighted if NATO followed suit. And if Hungary left the EU, then that might well precipitate a collapse in both organisations. Moscow would be the winners. Their old satellite states would be easy pickings.

The Soviet Bloc might well resurge. Certainly that's what his premier wanted.

The thought almost paralysed her.

She had to do something.

As of yet, Sam had no idea what that something was. What was she was going to do in Budapest?

Her MO had always been the same. Be there. Where the action was. Make some noise. Watch the ripples. She'd have a much better chance of working things out if she were in the thick of it. And she had finished her job with the FSB. The FFO was no longer a threat. And the woman was gone. It was over. And they had paid her well - not that that was the point. She had some free time. Budapest was a lovely city - she'd visited before, a long time ago. And why not have another poke around? Lift up some slabs. Scratch at the sand. See what comes up.

She had no idea what that meant, but it had never stopped her before.

So that's what she'd do.

And now it was her turn at the front of the queue.

She handed over her passport. The man in the kiosk looked her up and down. And then stared at the document.

A light went on behind his eyes.

What?

He looked at her again, and then fidgeted. Sam thought he reached for something under the table. She couldn't see.

He smiled. If it had been more forced it would have popped off his lips and stuck to the glass that was separating them.

It was Sam's turn to fidget now. She looked left and right. Then back at the man with the unnatural smile. He was sitting bolt still. Not moving. As if breathing would unhinge the natural order of things.

And then she spotted them. To her right. Two men in cheap suits heading her way. Out of an unmarked door behind the kiosk. They were big. If they were military they would have been paratroopers. And they were quick. She had nowhere to go, but even if she had they would have been on her before she had chance to move.

One grabbed her arm. The other had taken out a black card case. He let one side of it hang, It was film-script stuff. There was an unrecognisable badge and Sam thought she saw the initials, TEK.'

The Hungarian counter-terrorist police.

Brilliant. Just brilliant.

'*Terrorelhárítási Központ.*' The man barked.

She was right: the TEK.

'What? What do you want?' Sam. In Russian.

'Come with us Miss Green. We have some questions.'

Sam didn't have a chance to argue. The paratrooper in the shitty suit who was holding her arm lifted and pulled her so her feet were almost off the ground. Thankfully he hadn't chosen the arm that popped out of its socket if you looked at it in a strange way. That would have hurt.

He dragged her to the door.

The unmarked one.

She glanced behind at the man in the kiosk. His mouth was ajar and his head was following her frogmarch to the door.

She waved at him with her free hand.

At least I've made it through customs.

Joint Operations Room, Dover, UK

'Situation, enemy.' The Special Boat Service (SBS) major had a laser pointer. He sprayed the red light about on the screen, highlighting each section of the briefing. 'Current int has three men, one woman.' The screen changed; a new slide. A white van, no side windows. 'Driver and passenger. Black. Coming through customs.' The major pointed the red laser at the two men in the cab. Then another slide. Two men and a woman standing in a queue. 'Another shot of the driver.' The pointer was on the man's half-exposed face. It moved and danced a circle around the other two. 'A black woman and another black man. In the queue at Burger King, in the ferry terminal.' A further slide. Blurry CCTV footage of four people entering the ferry terminal ... the video tripped ... and the same four leaving the building.

A new slide. Four headshots.

'These are the passport photos provided by Border Force.' The major waited. Another slide. 'And here are photofits of the four dressed as they were in their van. Note the height scale. The three men are taller than 185 centimetres. The woman, more like 170. They're slim. We guessing East African.'

The slide changed. Two words: ENEMY INTENT.

'Intent. Absolutely no idea.' The major looked to the back of the packed room. 'Spooks? Met? Border? CT? Anything yet on what these bastards want?'

Frank wasn't expecting to be asked a question. He was sitting in the back of a room the size of half a tennis court. It was dominated by a dissected model of The Pride of Eastbourne, a P&O cross-channel ferry that was currently carrying 823 passengers, 370 vehicles and 119 crew to Calais. Except it was no longer heading to Calais. It had turned left and was steaming out into the North Sea.

He reckoned there were 100 or so soldiers - *sorry, highly-trained Marines* (he'd been put right earlier; they were dressed like soldiers and what did he know?) - seated around the model: all of SBS's M Squadron. They were the maritime counter-terrorist grouping. It was their job to handle things like this.

Sitting at the back with him were a mixture of non-soldiers - *sorry, non-Marines*. They all wore badges bearing their names and their organisations. It had been such a rush to get into the briefing room he hadn't had chance to work out who they all were. Listening to the major's question there were obviously reps from CT, the Met and Border. There were at least twenty 'suits', so the list in his head wasn't comprehensive.

A number of them said, 'No.'.

Frank thought he had something to add - but couldn't be sure. And, as SIS's LO (liaison officer) in Dover, after a short hesitation he gave as confident a reply as he could muster.

'Nothing from SIS.'

There is something?

After Jane had dispatched him to Dover he'd had no more than five minutes to update the MTMT with the photos from the service station of the three men from Mersa Fatma. He'd grabbed his denim jacket off the back of his chair just as he pressed 'send' on an email he scrambled together to his pals in The Service and CT, Vernon and Fi. The last line read: *We need to find these. They're looking for trouble.*

Frank wasn't 100% certain, but he thought it likely he'd just found three of the men. And trouble was an understatement.

So 'nothing' was not an accurate answer from Frank. But it would do for now. He knew where they came from and how they'd got to the UK. He didn't think that was necessarily helpful. What the major needed to know was what were their weaknesses? What did they want? What was their MO? Stuff that would help his squadron rescue a huge ship full of scared people, at least two of whom were dead, without causing further casualties. In that respect 'nothing' was a perfectly adequate answer. He'd speak to someone in uniform once the briefing was finished.

The major had moved on.

'Mission. Neutralise the terrorists in order for the ferry to be returned to port. Mission. Neutralise the terrorists in order for the ferry to be returned to port. Execution.' A new slide. 'Five phases …'

The major's briefing style was clipped. Exaggerated. And incredibly clear. He exuded confidence. There was no arrogance and the whole process lacked the American bravado he'd seen in so many films. Here there were enough words at the right tempo. And given in a tone that ensured success. Frank was ready to get his kit on.

The major moved to the model. He pointed when he needed to.

'Phase one. Prelims. Over the horizon. One-two-alpha. In the air with dogs. Circling at 22-kay. South of target.' Frank noticed the major looking at six men sitting middle-left. They weren't dressed as soldiers. They were wearing olive-drab coveralls. Flying suits? 'Can you get in the air by then John?'

One of the pilots replied, 'Sure. The Herc's at 30 minutes.'

The major nodded.

'One-two-bravo: in the SDV on HMS Ambush. You know the score. Deep and close. The ferry people tell me their sonar's good for five klicks and 1000 metres depth.' A pause for effect. 'The rest of One Troop and all of Two Troop, 17 klicks out in the RIBs.' The major exchanged a nod with a Marine in the front row.

'Three troop. Airborne in two Chinooks. Seventeen klicks. But cut that if the weather allows.' More nodding.

'Phase two. Foothold and gather. One-two-alpha. Drop on the top deck. Dispatch the dogs. One-two-bravo. From the rear, scaling both sides. Powerplant is your baby.' He was pointing at the model as he spoke. 'The rest of you, move to within five klicks. One Troop: you are our eyes and ears. We've got an AWACs in the air from 8.00 pm this evening, and will get whatever SAR readout we can. But my bet is you're it.' The major was now talking to the whole room. Everyone was silent. Many were taking notes.

'Phase three. Assault. Simultaneity is key. One Troop - you're inside by now. You call "power down". I want Two and Three Troop alongside and on deck exactly at that moment. We know the drill from there.'

The major paused. The room was waiting.

'Phase four. Consolidate. Again, usual drills. All passengers and crew, including the captain, in two locations. Deck seven, family lounge. Deck eight, food court.' More pointing. 'If any of the terrorists are standing, they're on deck here. Mike-three-four ...', he was looking to one of the other men in a flying suit, '... we'll call you in when we're ready.' The man in the flying suit nodded.

'Phase five. Reorg. Once we're secure, we'll get the stand-by crew out by Chinook and they'll drive us in. Any questions so far?'

There was a gentle murmur around the room. But no questions.

It took the major another ten minutes to reach the end of his briefing. Frank knew what was happening - in principle - but he guessed the overwhelming confidence of those in the room grew from rehearsing scenarios like this a hundred times.

'Finally. A reminder. Key to this is surprise. London has a small negotiating team trying to establish comms with the terrorists. That team are not aware of our timings. They will not know that we assault this evening. The terrorist will not be expecting us. They will have not slept for 36 hours. They will be fidgety. They have killed at least two pax and, now out of phone coverage, we have no idea if they've killed more.'

The major walked around the model. Frank thought he managed to look every one of his team in the eye as he did.

'Let's bring this to an end ... by strength and guile.'

'By strength and guile!', was the chorused response.

Frank caught up with the major five minutes after the briefing. The major had a thermos in one hand, and a small mug of coffee in the other. Frank was second in line. The major was currently talking to one of the pilots. He spotted Frank, and glanced at him, raising his mug.

'Wait one.' The major said.

Frank nodded. It took ten seconds for the pilot to finish and he moved away.

The major extended his hand.

'Colin Hall. How can I help ...', he looked at Frank's badge, '... Frank?'

Frank shook the major's hand.

'Thanks. I'm not sure this is going to help. Could you put the mugshots back up?' Frank motioned to the screen which currently displayed SBS's logo.

The major turned and faced the screen. He played with his pointer. The slides flashed back until they stopped at the mugshots of the four men.

Frank looked. He said nothing.

The major glanced at the screen, and then back at Frank.

'Do you know these people?'

Frank was SIS. He followed leads that led to certainty. Or not. Outside of the building he only worked in certainty. The three men's faces were not exactly facsimiles of his men from Eritrea. But that wasn't a surprise. They could be using original passports of a decent lookalike. Originals were always easier to use than a fake. And when you wanted to hijack a ferry, you really didn't want to get picked up because your passport didn't pass muster.

And, as we all know, every passport photo makes you look like a convict.

Frank answered the major's question with a question.

'Do you have the names of these four.'

'Sure.' The major walked to the front of the briefing room and accessed a keyboard. Within a second the slide had reduced in size and under it was a set of briefing notes. In the notes were four names. Frank took out his notebook and wrote them down. He didn't recognise any of them.

'Can you share the slide pack with me?'

'I don't see why not. Speak to my IO. He'll be in the Ops Room. And, are you going to tell me whether or not you know these hoods?'

Frank was still looking at the screen.

'I need our facial recognition programme in Vauxhall to look over all of the images to attribute a level of certainty …' Frank started.

'Cut the crap, Frank. I've got things to do.' The major's interjection showed neither signs of impatience nor anger. It was business like.

Frank wasn't offended.

'The three men come from a coastal village in Eritrea. I know the name of one of them, the driver. He's Abir al-Rasheed. I think I know the names of two more. I don't recognise the woman. They travelled to the UK within the last two weeks, clearly with the intent of hijacking this ferry. It's highly unusual … no, that's not right. I am SIS's lead immigrant analyst in the UK.' He clarified. 'We have *never* seen immigrants move this quickly from domicile to the UK. This is hyper-organised. A one-off.'

'So what?' The major asked. 'Sorry. That's a military term. It's not meant to sound derogatory. So what? What do I need to know from that information? How can it help me with my mission?'

'I have absolutely no idea at all. Sorry. But I'll get onto that now - once I have the slides.'

Frank was about to leave - he'd taken up too much of the major's time. But something from the briefing poked at him.

'Dogs? You mentioned a team … and dogs.'

The major was gathering some things.

'Yes. They drop in with the freefall team. Strapped to their chests. We've been using them for almost a decade.'

'Are they attack dogs?' Frank was amazed.

The major laughed.

'They're spaniels, Frank. They would piss on you before they bit you. No, they carry a pack of sensors. Visual, IR, comms. They're trained to get inside the boat and trot about. The squadron gets immediate feedback. If the power's off, the dogs will have given us a really good set of infrared images of the passenger decks within five minutes of landing. They're special.'

I bet they are.

52°31'56.8"N 3°12'48.3"E, North Sea

Toffer was struggling to keep the girls quiet. There was a woman with a gun in the centre of the bar now. She wasn't demanding silence like the original man. So far she hadn't fired her weapon. And thankfully no one else was dead.

Both girls were sniffing. He held them in the crooks of his arms. Tight, but not suffocating. Over the past five hours he'd tried to make sense of it all to them. Not that it made any sense to him.

'These people probably have a grievance. They want or need something in their own country which they can't get.' He whispered. 'And sometimes, they think the only way to get what they want is to hurt people. Random people. By getting the world to notice.'

'But why ...' *sniff*, '... us. Daddy?' Amy had whispered back. She was still crying. He was surprised she had any tears left.

'I don't know, darling, I really don't'

They'd spent the first half an hour being reorganised by the man with the gun. Toffer reckoned there were about 100 of them in the bar room to begin with. By the time the man with the gun had finished there were more like 500. They were tightly packed around the edge of the large three-quarter windowed room, with the central area and the bar frontage empty. He and the girls were squashed tightly between a couple of lorry driver types and an extended Eastern European family. Sat on the floor in front of them were a bunch of kids and, he guessed, some teachers. There were arms and legs everywhere. And there was a dreadful smell of sweat - and urine.

The two bodies, both women, had been dragged to the foot of the bar by passengers, under orders of the man with the gun. They had been abandoned unceremoniously in the middle, one of their faces looking towards the crowd. The other corpse had its back to them. Initially the partner of one hadn't been able to let go of the body. It had been pathetic to watch. The two male passengers who were lifting and carrying, gently pleaded with the man who was being asked to let go of the woman he loved. Everyone else turned away. There was more sobbing. But the man couldn't let go. A few seconds later he had no choice. The man with a gun put a foot on his shoulder and jabbed the weapon's barrel into his face. He let go of the corpse at that point.

Early on an elderly woman to his left had stuck up her hand and asked 'to go to the lavatory, please'. The man with the gun didn't understand - the word lavatory was probably new to him. 'Toilet. Please.' The woman had added.

'No. Nobody moves.'

There had been an immediate outbreak of discontent.

The man with the gun's response had been to fire in the air. The huge noise, even louder than Toffer had remembered from the first dreadful bursts, caused everyone to cower. Amy and Sophie, who at that point had their arms around his chest, squeezed him so tightly he struggled to catch his breath.

'Daddy ...', a whisper from Sophie.

'Shhh, darling, shhh.' She had lifted her head. He looked at her. She pointed downwards. There was a wet patch on the floor.

Grief almost overtook him. He lifted his chin and stared ahead, holding both girls with as big a hug as he could. And then a tear made itself known from the corner of his left eye. Just one. He could feel it. It dribbled down his cheek, hung on his chin, and then dropped to his jeans.

'Shhh, darling. Please.'

Since then four hours had passed. And those who couldn't hold on, hadn't.

Whilst the woman terrorist had ignored the room as it filled with whispered conversations, she hadn't allowed anyone to move.

A loud snore broke through the quiet melee. Nervous laughter followed. Then near silence.

The original man with a gun returned. Toffer felt the room wince. He was accompanied by an elderly man in a ship's uniform. Blue trousers, white shirt and a tie. The new man was carrying a large bundle of keys. He looked petrified.

'We are going to lock the doors. On both sides.' The man with the gun used his head to indicate both sides of the bar where double doors lead to corridors running down the side of the ship. 'The door in the bar will be locked as well.' The uniformed man was nervously nodding his head. 'You will stay here. You will not try to escape. We will be on the other side of the door. We will shoot.'

The man with the gun stared at them all.

They got the message.

'Do it.' He said to the uniformed man.

The elderly man jogged off to the right of the bar and locked the double doors. The woman followed him and checked his work by shaking them. He did the same to the door behind the bar. The woman checked again.

The three of them then left the room, closing … and locking the double doors behind them which shook, making a rattling noise. The woman was probably checking again.

Silence.

And then …

… *bang!*

…

Thud.

The noise was slightly quieter than the gunshots in the room, but no less horrific.

Toffer could only imagine one explanation. An elderly, uniformed man lying in a pool of blood. A bundle of keys still in his hand.

The room broke out into uproar.

Toffer sat still - dumbfounded. As hysteria caught on all around him, he pulled his girls to him, tighter still.

Chapter 9

'What the bloody hell do you think you're playing at?' The man from the British Embassy was pacing around the small cell - shouting at Sam as if she were an errant child. 'And how in the name of God did you get that black eye?'

Any more questions?

Sam didn't want to answer the shouty-embassy man. She just wanted to get the hell out of the tiny room in which she was incarcerated: her, a bed, a metal sink, a pot, four walls and the shouty man from the Embassy. She didn't do small spaces. Not since Berlin. Not since she and Wolfgang had spent 48 hours in a freezing cold shipping container on the edge of death.

Her current cell was different, in that there was a barred window which she could reach with her hand if she outstretched her arm. The walls weren't closing in. She could imagine life outside. But it was still four walls and not enough room to swing a cat. And a shouty man from the Embassy.

He was wearing a city suit and decent shoes. But his shirt needed an iron and his tie didn't quite reach his top button. And there was an odour. The sweat of frustration. A long day in the office and then an unwelcome trip to the cells.

'The Ambassador has made some calls. And I'm expecting you to be released at any moment. But mark my word, you're on the first plane home, that's for sure.'

Sam was staring at the floor. Her feet were tapping and she was picking away at the wick of her thumb. The man's noise was just that. It washed over her; didn't penetrate. Like an annoying fly you couldn't swat. Her containment didn't help. Everything was amplified. Annoyances became grievances. A loud voice became a shout. Her Mum wouldn't be proud.

Whatever - she'd deal with it all once she'd got out of the cell - and had some paracetamol. Her head was throbbing as if her eye had been plucked from its socket, twisted around its optical nerve, and stuck back in again.

The TEK were a blunt instrument. They wanted to know why an ex-British spy had come to their country to undermine their prime minister. *How did they know?* Her latest FSB helper must have got on the phone. That's gratitude for you. You can't trust anyone. Sam had applied SIS interrogation training and said nothing - then something … just enough to keep them from pulling out her fingernails. But that hadn't stopped them from smacking her about a bit. It was nothing fatal, but it hurt like hell.

'I just … I just can't believe we're having to bail out an ex-spy.' Shouty-embassy man was venting again. 'You're PNG, you know that. Your record makes that clear. "Services no longer required". If I had my way I'd leave you in here to rot.'

Persona non grata? Really?

After all she'd done for SIS.

Typical.

Shouty-embassy man was a senior diplomat of some description. He was her way out of here. Unfortunately, he was also beginning to wear her down. She didn't want the red mist to descend. She couldn't afford to thump the man responsible for securing her freedom.

Clunk. Clunk.

Saved by the bell.

The door opened. A man Sam didn't recognise came in. He was casually dressed: jeans and a sweat top. He was carrying Sam's rucksack.

He and the shouty man had a conversation. Sam didn't speak Hungarian but picked up the odd word. She was to be released now. That's all that mattered.

Shouty-embassy man turned to her.

'Come on, Miss Green. We have to get you out of the country. Now.'

He was through the door first - *chivalry obviously lost on today's diplomatic corps?* Sam followed on, collecting her bag from the man in the jeans and the sweat top. She didn't pause to say thanks. She needed to find space. To breathe fresh air.

'There's a plane to London at 8.15 pm - that's in two hours' time. We've just got time to make it to the airport. Come on ...'

Shouty-embassy man was five steps ahead and his pace was quickening. He communicated with a casual glance over his shoulder. Sam was in tow. She was moving quickly - a light at the end of the tunnel now in view. But she didn't overly rush. She didn't want him to think he was in charge.

Three corridors and two metal doors later and they were on the street in downtown Budapest. Sam had no idea exactly where - she'd not rehearsed the map - but it was no further than an hour from the airport.

She stopped at the bottom of a small flight of steps. Shouty-embassy man was ten yards ahead. He pinged his key fob at a Discovery three cars down. Its lights flashed.

'Come on Green. You've got a flight to catch. Come on!' The passenger door was already open on the Disco. He was pointing at it insides.

Sam ignored him. She took a couple of deep breaths. And closed her eyes for a second. Then she reached into the side pocket of her rucksack and picked out her phone. Thankfully it still had some battery left. She found Jane's number on speed dial and stabbed at it. It rang twice; Jane picked it up.

'Sam! Good to hear from you. How did South Ossetia go? I've had a read-out from Moscow. But no detail.' Very Jane. Straight in.

Sam didn't have chance to reply. Shouty-embassy man was at her shoulder.

'Green, I told you to get in the car!'

'One second, Jane.'

Sam dropped the phone to her side and looked at the man. He was red in the face, turning to blotchy. He had a touch of spittle on the end of his bottom lip. He was about to say something else when Sam raised a finger and pushed it to his lips.

'Shhh,' she said quietly. 'I'm on the phone.'

The man pulled his head back.

'What the …?' More spittle.

Sam turned away so her back was between shouty-embassy man and her phone call.

'Hi, Jane. Sorry. I have an irritating guy from our Hungarian Embassy here.' She shot a quick glance up and down the road. 'I'm going to put you on speaker for his benefit.'

There was a pause. Jane's cogs were dealing with Sam being in a new country.

'Sure, Sam.' Loud and clear.

'Who's that on the phone?' Shouty-embassy man had come round the front of Sam. He was even more red and more blotchy. She was convinced his tie had dropped a further couple of centimetres.

'South Ossetia was fine. I'll call you with the details when we're at the Embassy …'

'We're not going to the Embassy, Green, we're going to the airport!'

Sam had had enough.

'One second, Jane.' She sighed a nasal sigh. 'Look. Me and my ex-boss from Vauxhall are having a conversation about matters of national importance. In a second you can drive me to the Embassy and I will get out of your hair.' *Not that there's much of it.* 'In the meantime, be a good chap and give us time to talk.'

That was too much for shouty-embassy man.

'I don't know who you think you are, but I'm the Third Secretary. And I couldn't give a damn who you are talking to. You're in my country and I'm taking you to the airport.'

He put his hand on Sam's elbow. Sam inwardly flinched. The last person to get within her personal space hadn't survived the fire.

Calm.

Jane chirped up.

'Hi. Who am I speaking to?'

Shouty-embassy man was at a loss. Who should he speak to?

'Uh. It's Ralph Lansom. Third Secretary. And who is this?'

'I can't give you my position over an insecure line, Mr London.' *Did Jane get his name wrong on purpose?* 'But rest assured I out rank you and your Ambassador. And, you may not have heard but we have an ongoing situation in the North Sea which requires my best attentions. Now, be a sport and let me and my operative finish our conversation in private. Then take her back to the Embassy. I will have spoken to the Ambassador by the time you get there, and he will sort all this out. Happy?'

Sam pulled her arm away from shouty-embassy man. He shook his head, bewildered.

'Yes, yes of course. Mind you I will be speaking to the Ambassador about this. Whoever you are.'

'Not before I do, Mr London. Rest assured. Sam? Take us off speaker please.'

Sam did as she was asked.

'Where were we, Sam?'

'Ossetia was fine. I'm in Hungary. I was picked up by the TEK at customs. I think there must have been a leak between my Moscow contact and Budapest. I was set up. I was looking into the activities and background of Viktor Molnár. Again, I need to talk to you on a secure line, but I'm pretty sure there's a link between his recent behaviour and the 'neo-terrorism' threat. It's obscure, almost unbelievable, but somehow I think there's a clear connection. If I'm right it might help you identify a common cause, unless you have one already?'

There was a pause on the line.

'That's interesting, Sam. Do you think the FFO might be part of the NT scene?' Jane asked.

'Yes, obscurely. It's to do with Viktor Molnár's "leaving the EU" speech the other night. At one point he used exactly the same language as the man in South Ossetia did when he was describing their future. *Exactly* the same words. There's no way it could have been a coincidence. And I think my prelim investigations in Moscow set in train a series of events which led to me being arrested.'

'OK, Sam. Get to the Embassy. I'll speak to the Ambassador and clear your stay. And I'll get in touch with "B" and ask her team to give you whatever assistance you need. It's late here now and I have a bag of things to do. Unless there's something key, phone me tomorrow?'

'Sure, Jane, sure. And, Jane?'

'What, Sam?'

'Thanks.'

'No probs. Just stay safe - and help us. We need some oblique thinkers. Currently we're running into a minefield with no identifiable safe route. And the mines are getting bigger and more deadly.'

'Will do, Jane.'

Sam hung up.

She looked over her shoulder. Shouty-embassy man was sat in the driver's seat of the Disco. He was on his mobile.

She sighed. She was only just beginning to feel human again. And she desperately needed something for her headache, some coffee and access to Budapest's SIS files on Viktor Molnár. She really hoped she wasn't to get any more shit from the blotchy man with the tie at half-mast.

53°51'59.4" N; 3°12'41.3" E, North Sea

The lounge area had quietened. After the initial uprising once the external doors had been locked, two men and a woman had taken control and the untuned orchestra of screams and shouts and cries had died down. Toffer thought the three were probably off-duty British military who had realised someone needed to get a grip of the braying crowd before it descended into *Animal Farm*. The three of them had quickly brought order to a group of hugely distraught people who needed someone to grip the chaos.

'Will you quieten down!' One of the men, who had stood on a chair, had raised his voice.

The cacophony continued.

'SHUT UP!' It was the military woman. Her female scream piercing through the noise like a javelin. She was shorter than the man, so had made it onto one of the small round tables in the centre of the room. Toffer thought she had looked incredibly natural … born to lead.

Her scream had dampened the noise.

The woman had control.

She continued.

'Help - will - be - on - its - way. Soon.' She spoke slowly, seemingly aware of the multilingual audience. 'We - need - to - remain - calm. We don't want to attract unnecessary attention to ourselves.' She pointed to the two bodies by the bar. 'We have seen what these people are capable of.' She paused.

God, she's good. Even Sophie and Amy had lifted their heads from his chest.

'Has - anyone - got - a - blanket? A rug? To cover the bodies?' She looked around the room. There was a murmur from Toffer's right. A man had a picnic rug. He was making his way through the crowd.

'Good. Thanks.' She let the man get on with putting together the makeshift morgue. 'Next - we - need

- to - establish, sorry, *find* - an - area - to - use - as - a - toilet. *Toilette.*' People had remained calm. They waited to see what would happen next.

One of the military men had moved to a corner of the lounge area. He picked up a couple of movable chairs and formed a small enclosed area next to the bulkhead. He stood on a chair and pointed at his creation.

'Toilet. *Toilette. Baño.*'

Toffer thought three languages was impressive.

The crowd naturally looked back at the woman. She was alone now. The second man had moved behind the bar.

'We will run the bar. Please - only - one - person - *une - personne* - from - any - family - at - one - time. We may be here a while, so we must make the food and drink last.'

Toffer looked at the man guarding the bar. He had a crew cut and his blue polo shirt only just held his large frame in place. Nobody was going to argue with him.

The woman then continued with some encouraging words. They would all be OK. Provided everyone remained calm. We were in this together.

That was six hours ago. Nothing else of note had happened. The two terrorists had not returned. Nobody had been shot. People had found their own spaces and a bizarre routine had set in. People used the toilet area - which stank to high heaven, even from this distance - and a steady stream of mostly men had formed an orderly queue at the bar and taken away food and drink for themselves and, where they had them, their families. There had been no harsh words. A refugee camp came to mind.

Amy and Sophie were back in their respective chairs and Toffer had found a space between them on the floor, giving up his chair for a pregnant woman; her partner initially sitting on the chair's arm, before making himself comfortable on the floor. People were keeping themselves to themselves, but there was a growing sense of camaraderie.

The ship was pitching a bit and Toffer thought if they were under steam, they weren't travelling very quickly. Ten minutes ago he'd been for a stretch around the lounge, which was two-thirds windows, one-quarter bar and the two locked exits. All he could see outside was black. There was no horizon and no lights. That was no surprise as the sun had disappeared a couple of hours ago. But he expected to see something, surely? A ship? A lighthouse?

But there was nothing. It felt oddly surreal, almost unbalancing. It was as if the ship had been transported into space. He suspected cloud cover blocked out the stars, so there was no help there. There was nothing tangible to hold on to. Gravity was the only certainty.

He'd just sat down and had started to try to get some sleep when he heard a noise that sent his brain into spasm.

It was a quiet noise. Distant.

But deadly?

Beep. Beep. Beep ...

It was remorseless.

He could be wrong. It could be anything. There must be tens of different warning noises on a boat this big.

Beep. Beep. Beep ...

He could be wrong.

I must be wrong. Please may I be wrong?

Beep. Beep. Beep ...

He couldn't disassociate the sound from the picture in his head. A huge slab of orange and white metal - on its side in the water.

He was old enough to remember *The Herald of Free Enterprise*. The 6th of March 1987. Just outside Zeebrugge. A car ferry with hundreds of passengers had sailed out of the Belgian port ... with the car deck doors open. Water had breached the entrance - an open chasm. The ship's crew had tried to close the doors, but it had been too late. The boat tilted. The cars, coaches and lorries had followed that lead. The boat was on its side in minutes.

He couldn't remember the death toll. But he did remember the boat had not sunk completely because it had rolled onto a sandbank. It was almost submerged; but not fully. Lots of people had died.

During the day. Right by the coast. On a sandbank.

They were out of sight of land. Who knew where?

Beep. Beep. Beep ...

He could be wrong.

He remembered much of the detail because a friend of his had been on the boat.

And, just once, he'd told Toffer the story.

And once had been enough. For both of them.

His friend had been separated from his wife - she had been sitting at a table (*probably in the bar area, like where I am now?*) - and he had gone to the duty free. He'd told Toffer once the boat had tipped and he'd got his bearings, he'd battled his way to the bar.

Which was under water.

His friend remembered where his wife had been sitting. He'd half-walked, half-swum in that direction - he recalled that the water had been perishing. And filthy. Brown freezing liquid, plastic plates and cups.

An upturned body.

His wife's table was under him then; beneath the water - which was rising.

He'd dived down. Three times. He'd found his wife. She was caught by the table which had moved and pinned her to a bench. Her eyes had been open.

She'd blinked.

His friend had found strength he didn't know he had. He'd pulled and pushed - his lungs bursting. Something moved, but not enough.

His wife had shaken her head. *Go! Go!*

She had closed her eyes.

And opened her mouth.

Toffer had read somewhere that drowning is the nicest way to die. Just breathe normally and let your lungs fill with water. You pass out before you feel any pain.

Breathe normally?

His friend had found one last monumental effort.

His wife was free.

They made it to the surface - he had taken multiple short breaths, his wife lifeless in his arms.

He was a strong swimmer. He pulled and dug and swam and, eventually, walked. And dragged.

They were now above the level of the water; at an angle, standing on the wall which was sloping precipitously, the windows, which were letting in light, now an oblique ceiling.

His friend knew CPR. But first he had to get rid of the water? He should have known what to do. Why didn't he know what to do?

Then a Frenchman slid to his side. He took control. The man rolled his wife over, put his fingers in her mouth and slapped her back. Water dribbled from her lips.

The boat tipped! It was almost completely on its side. Water rushed about. Their world turning upside down.

All three of them slipped back into the water, His wife headfirst.

His friend's description of the next ten minutes had been frantic - a story told in panic. He and the Frenchman had pulled his wife from the water again and rested her on her back next to a diagram of the innards of the boat. They worked as a team. His friend had held her body steady whilst the man tried to breathe life into her.

It lasted a minute - maybe two?

And then magic. A cough and a splutter. Sick - all over the Frenchman. More coughing.

Tears from his friend, both then and as he retold the story.

And hugs … briefly ...

… and the final escape, climbing up and over the furniture that was screwed down. He'd implored the Frenchman to move on. *Vite! Vite!* The Frenchman had acknowledged his shout, and he'd quickly got ahead.

His friend had dragged his wife, and she had helped where she could.

Eventually they'd made it to an opening - a window above them smashed, shards of glass framing freedom.

And there was the Frenchman. He had his jacket off which he used as a makeshift barrier between the broken glass and the escapees. He held his hand down. *Voici! Allons-y!*

His wife made it first, after two attempts. His friend second, glass ripping at his side.

They were free. Out on the side of the boat. It was almost horizontal, lying flat in the water. His friend had turned around slowly. He described the indescribable. There were fifty or sixty people on the side of the boat, huddled together in small groups, sitting amongst portholes, rivets and orange paint. In front of him was the horizon. Behind him were … cliffs. So close you could almost touch them. His friend recalled people on the top of the cliffs looking back at him. He couldn't make out their faces, but he imagined their horror.

Terror and death - because they hadn't closed the bloody doors.

Beep. Beep. Beep ...

Toffer looked around. Someone who was sleeping on the floor had woken. Their eyes met. They looked confused; trying to establish the source of the noise.

Creak. The boat shifted unnaturally.

Toffer suppressed panic.

Creak.

His leg was wet.

What?

Cold tea was dripping off the table from an upturned plastic cup.

Drip, drip, drip.

Beep. Beep. Beep ...

The warning noise seemed louder.

And the angle of the boat was definitely not right now. He couldn't get the image of coaches straining on their tyres a few decks below out of his mind.

Creak!

The ship moved. It really moved.

And the screaming started.

Operations Room, Port of Dover, UK

Frank fought fatigue. It wasn't late, just after 10.30 pm, but it had been a long week and sitting waiting in a warm room for something to happen was sapping.

He'd got nothing back from the MTMT team. Everyone was searching for the three men and the woman; more accurately for where the group might have been working out of and, ultimately, who they might have been working for. The SIS team in Eritrea had been given the heads up on Abir al-Rasheed and any entourage. Frank thought the obvious approach was to get in a 4x4 and scoot on down to the village. And then keep asking questions until you got the right answers. However, as Jane had pointed out on the phone earlier, that may well uncover some of the background, but it would blow any semblance of cover SIS might have in that region of Eritrea. 'Quick and dirty' would've been understandable if they were rushing to prevent a terror attack. But they weren't; it was already in train. What they needed was a longer-term strategy. One that guaranteed they would find out who had sought out that particular village and those particular men ... and why. According to Jane that required patience. And procedure. Apparently SIS ran an agent high up in the Eritrean police force. He would be contacted ... and questions would be asked.

All of that meant Frank had nothing to add to the operation. The major had pressed him an hour ago, just before he'd left the building - all togged-up, black-faced and looking very menacing. Frank couldn't hide his disappointment that he'd got nothing new.

And now they waited.

H-hour was 11.30 pm. That was in 85 minutes' time. He wasn't sure he could keep his eyes open for that long. The ops room, square and about half the size of the briefing room, was busy with screens and operators. Front-middle was the model of the ship, which a couple of hefty Marines had effortlessly moved from the briefing room to centre-stage as soon as the major had finished his orders. Frank had no idea what each of the operators' responsibilities were, but he counted 15. Twelve of them were wearing uniform of some colour; the remaining three were in smart civvies.

The 'agencies', of which SIS was one, had seats along the back of the room. Power was provided for laptops etc, and each polyprop chair had one of those really annoying tables that fold up and then drop sideward, out of your way. Frank had never sat in one where the table had been perfectly horizontal.

He'd said 'hello' to most of his colleagues in the cheap seats and briefed them on what he knew of the three male terrorists. Frank was an introvert and never comfortable with making introductions. Even though he worked for SIS and knew what he did was important and valuable, that never seemed enough to give him the confidence to unabashedly stick his hand out and say, 'Hi, I'm Frank.' As a result all introductions were uncomfortable and awkward, but he always did what he had to do whilst his stomach churned. And he thanked his job for that.

He looked up and down the line of seats with wonky tables: five men and two women. Some were tapping away on laptops. Others were chatting. One, the Border Agency rep, was flat out; head back, mouth open. Calm before the storm.

That made Frank suppress a yawn. It was no good. He had to do something.

Coffee.

It would be his fourth cup in as many hours. Thankfully there was a toilet just down the corridor.

He stood and squeezed between the legs of his colleagues and the bank of operators. He got halfway to the door when somebody changed the plan.

'Hello Zero, this is Romeo Six. We're getting something on the SAR readout. Can you see it? Over.' The voice came from a speaker forward-left, on the desk of a woman who was wearing light blue - RAF.

SAR? Frank previous thoughts were interrupted immediately: Synthetic Aperture Radar; not Search and Rescue. Pictures taken in sequence from an aircraft at long distance - looking sideward - using tiny radio waves that bounced back and gave a very detailed image in something close to 3D. He wasn't sure, but he thought the RAF had a couple of small commercial jets fitted with those very capable radars.

'Sergeant Hollison, stick it on the main screen.' A snap order from the operations officer.

As Frank understood it the major, the squadron commander, led the troops on the ground. His second-in-command, a captain - the ops officer - controlled the operation from afar. There were a couple of senior hoods, one was a Brigadier, kicking around the room. But the success of the operation was down to a major and a captain.

The main screen, beyond the model of the boat, burst into life.

'Lower the lights!', the captain barked.

And there it was: the Pride of Eastbourne. A light grey image floating on a sea of black. The image was sharp, but inverted, like a negative from an old wet film camera. The boat was side-on. Looking just like the model in front of the screen.

Except ... what's that?

'Someone tell me what's happening?' The captain's voice was laced with impatience. 'What's that at the front of the boat?'

'The carport bow doors are opening.' The reply came from a woman in P&O livery who was sitting front right. Frank noticed her epaulettes showed three gold bars. She was obviously someone who knew a lot about the P&O fleet.

'What?' Only the captain said the word out loud. Everyone else must have been thinking the same, *surely*?

The P&O woman was on her feet. She was at the screen. Pointing.

'Here ...'. She stuck her finger at the bow of the boat. Sure enough, a large slab of something was sticking out of the front.

'They'll sink it, surely?' The captain had moved to the P&O woman's side.

'I'm sorry, captain, but that's exactly what will happen. Unless ...'

'Unless what?' More impatience.

'Unless, someone gets on the boat, or someone on the boat, lowers the doors.'

'How long?'

The woman stepped back and studied the whole image. It flickered. Frank reckoned it was being updated every 20 seconds or so.

'It looks like a force three or four out there at the moment. The water will have already breached. Ten minutes, maybe fifteen and then the vehicles will start to move ... maybe less.'

The P&O woman didn't have time to finish her sentence. The ops officer picked up a handset from the nearest desk.

'Hello, all stations this is Zero, Zero-Alpha acknowledge. Over.'

The squawky reply was immediate.

'Zero-Alpha, send, over.' Frank could hear the *clump-clump-clump* of the helicopter's rotor blades in the background of the major's reply.

'Situation change. The target's bow doors have been opened. We have confirmation of this from Romeo Six. And we have confirmed it here from the SAR images. Roger so far, Zero-Alpha, over.'

'Roger, send.'

'My view is this has now changed from an assault to a rescue. Repeat, now a rescue operation. Implement Plan Golf, over?'

The only other noise in the ops room was the RAF operator talking in hushed tones to Romeo Six. That exchange was so quiet Frank couldn't make it out. Everyone else was fixed on the horror unfolding on the screen.

Nothing came back from the squadron commander. The latest update on the screen showed the slab of metal sticking out of its front was now parallel to the water.

'Zero-Alpha?' The captain reminded his boss that he needed an answer.

'Wait … *clump, clump* …'

'Hello, all stations this is Zero-Alpha. Reference operation, cancel. Sierra Seven, acknowledge, over.'

'Sierra Seven, roger, over.'

Frank couldn't be sure but he thought that might be the Vanguard submarine.

'Enact Plan Golf. Sierra Seven, how long before you can get a team aboard, over.'

'Wait …', Frank imagined a guy with a periscope having a frantic conversation with men in dry suits.

'Six minutes. Do you want me to launch them now?'

'Yes. Now. All stations, move now. Move now. Make best speed. Do not, I repeat, do not worry about taking terrorists alive. Key now is rescue. Let me know when we have boots on board, roger so far, Zero.'

'Zero, roger.' The captain replied.

'Zero-Alpha, get every helicopter from Odiham in the air. And anything else. Make sure they've fitted with appropriate winches. Hold them at ten clicks. Once we have "boat clear", fly them in. Over.'

'Roger. Out.' The captain turned and spoke at the same time. 'RAFLO. Get Odiham on the line, now. Get every Chinook in the air.' He turned again. This time he stuck two hands out. One was pointing at an Army major. The second, at a civilian who was on the back row of the monitors.

'Kev.' The Army major nodded. 'Get hold of PJHQ. Any winch capable Army Air Corps birds - get them in the air.' He was now looking at the civilian. 'Steven. Lift the exclusion zone. Any civvy ships within 20 nautical miles - get them to steam to the ferry. Tell them the UK government will pay the bill.' He then put himself dead centre. 'Any questions, anyone?'

Frank had one.

What was that small black object heading away from the bow of the ferry?

A Marine officer in the front row beat him to it.

'Captain …'

Chapter 10

That's interesting. What's that noise?

Gareth's mind was well ahead of most of the rest of his body. It was like his brain was an independent spirit, floating around, unattached. And it was struggling to make the leap of faith required to connect to his torso and limbs. Even the casing of his skull, which had an extra hole in it drilled by surgeons to release the pressure from the bleed, was leaving him well alone. His brain was clever. It knew if it made that connection, then a whole load of hurt would join his consciousness. And it could do without that for a while longer, thank you very much.

'His eyes are moving. Can you see? Under his eyelids. There's something there.'

A female voice. It was one that Gareth thought he recognised.

'Oh my God! You're right. Gareth! Can you hear me? Gareth?'

A male voice. A Welsh twang. Soft, but instantly recognisable.

And then a touch on his arm.

An arm? I have one of those?

It came flooding back - most of it. In torrents. Wave after wave. Who he was. Where he was … *Italy?* And … *shit!, that hurts!*

He still hadn't opened his eyes. He wasn't ready; not for that new dimension. But it didn't stop them from weeping. Tears and tears. It was mostly about the pain. Which was like the worst toothache you could ever imagine, all over one side of his head. But something told him that maybe there were more reasons to fear consciousness.

'He's crying! Gareth, love. It's mum. Are you OK?'

Mum ... of course.

'Nurse! Nurse!'

The pain was overwhelming.

Please make it stop. Please.

His mind took that as a direct order.

And shut down.

Basement, British Embassy, Budapest, Hungary

Sam was sitting on a comfy chair in a small staff room just down from the open-plan office from where the 15-person, SIS Hungarian station was based. She'd just woken up. The inside of her mouth felt as if she'd just eaten a sand and Marmite sandwich. And her black eye was demanding a paracetamol reboot.

Give me five minutes.

She straightened her back, blinking - trying to moisten her eyes. She looked through the half-height window into the main office. Unsurprisingly, at this hour, it was empty - save in one corner. A man. She could only see the top of his head sticking out from behind a computer screen.

Probably the duty officer.

The staff room was small, but it had a coffee machine, six lounging chairs, a table with some magazines on it and a wall-mounted TV.

She reached across for the remote and pressed the red button.

Flicker. And ... *what the blazes?*

It was the BBC news channel. The picture was black with strobes of beams of light, like super-powered torches. If it hadn't been for the red ticker-tape headlines, Sam wasn't sure she'd have been able to work out what was happening.

Hijacked ferry close to sinking in the North Sea. Hundreds of lives in peril ...

It was a Lilliputian scene; like looking at a whale floundering on its side, lying in a black ocean. Above the waterline were scores of little people, huddled together - no, *clinging* together. And then the ropes, not tying the giant down, but dangling onto the body of the whale. It was difficult to tell as the spotlights kept moving, but Sam reckoned there were five helicopters working the side of the ship, hoisting people to safety.

The BBC camera then zoomed into one particular group. They got really close. It was a man and two girls. The man was passing the two girls to the rescuer who was hanging at the end of the rope. You couldn't make out facial expressions, the picture quality and the light made that impossible. But Sam sensed the man's relief as the winch did its job and the two girls started their elevation to freedom.

Shit, no!

The boat moved - toppled. Five degrees maybe. The BBC were still focused on the man and his departing girls. He fell. Dropped to his knees. And slid. The camera tried to follow him, but he moved too quickly, heading for the edge. It was a lowlight blur. Someone at the BBC pressed a button and a new camera angle appeared. It was the whole ship. It looked different. More of it was under water. And the people on the top had all been shaken around, like ants fleeing a nest that had been soaked with boiling water. It was distressing. Horrible.

Someone at the BBC agreed. The picture changed again. Now they were looking at a talking head. He was on dry land, outside a building. It was a reporter at Dover. He was asked a question by the woman in the studio. And he gave an answer which Sam knew he could only have made up.

But it filled time.

And took them away from the horror of the whale in the water.

And the ants. Scurrying and clinging. And falling. The man, having saved his daughters, now gone.

Sam pressed the red button. The screen went blank.

She felt her cheeks. They were wet. And the tears kept coming. She found a hanky in her pocket and wiped her eyes.

Shit! Idiot.

Her left eye was sore as hell.

What a night. What a week.

She was going to finish with, *what a year*, but gave up.

She was frustrated. And tired. And unbelievably sad.

What the hell was going on? What was it with a foiled attack on a nuclear power station in Russia? And, how many did Jane say yesterday? Eighty-nine unrelated terror attacks since Christmas, hitting almost every corner of the globe. And now this. Someone hijacks a ferry, drives it into the middle of the North Sea and then sinks it? Sam had no idea whether the terrorists had got away. Or if they'd 'gone down with their ship'. But, and she knew she'd be right, there would be no easy explanation. There'd be no ISIS video on Al Jazeera claiming responsibility. No clear link to a new terror cell demanding freedom for its people. Or the release of political prisoners. The only guaranteed outcome would be a world aghast that, yet again, a random act of terror had befallen them. Where would the terrorist strike next? Would it be their country? Our town? Would me, or my family be victims? No wonder the streets of the world's capitals were quickly filling with frightened residents demanding their country's government make their lives safer.

It was crazy. Inexplicable.

But …

… there is a link. Somebody, or something, is behind this.

Yes, they were clever. Uber-organised and incredibly secret. The internet and the dark web provided indecipherable portals and conduits for agents of terror to do their business. If you wanted to hire someone to do something unspeakable, or buy any weapon of choice, the dark web provided the people and the guns - and the secrecy. Sam reckoned a cell of maybe five or six people could work the dark web and find individuals and small groups who were willing to enact terror on this scale. It would take planning - lots of it. And each link would have to be utterly discreet and completely obscure.

And there'd need to be a lot of money. A huge amount.

Because that's what this was about. If there was no ideology, nobody on a soap box in a desert or a town square demanding their version of religion or their incomplete statehood be listened to, then this was about money.

Jane had mentioned 'revenge'. Someone wanting the world to fall apart. Longing for it to happen. Sitting behind a desk somewhere, stroking a fluffy white cat. Disinterested in the death. But relishing the mayhem. Watching with glee as governments and their security services chase non-existent leads. Getting off on the chaos because sometime previously they had been smited. Maybe they'd lost an election. Or had been sacked from the board of a huge global company. Or, just maybe, they'd lost someone. Death at the hands of a police force somewhere. And now, because they had money, the rest of us would pay.

Sam didn't buy that.

It would take a hugely unhinged person to want this level of terror and destruction *just* to get back at the world. And whilst those people may exist, their states of mind didn't match the micro-surgery needed to keep the lid on an operation of this magnitude. They'd be too fidgety. Too … mad. They'd take risks. Cut corners. And that would have exposed them by now.

No, she didn't get the revenge theory.

This was about money. Huge amounts of it.

And that's what frustrated her most; why the tears fell as they did. Mix unspeakable horror with tiredness and she'd shed a tear. Add in the frustration of not being able to see where this had come from, or where it was going, and she'd give you floods. She hated it. She hated not being able to see the journey - where she'd been, and where she was going. She couldn't cope with the unknown being so obscure - so opaque. She *always* knew what to do next, even if the direction were the wrong one. She always knew something about her antagonist. She always had a feel for her next decision.

I always have something.

But she didn't now.

Between arriving at the Embassy and falling asleep in the chair in the staff room two hours ago, she'd read every piece of evidence, every document both the Embassy and the SIS team had on Viktor Molnár. It didn't surprise her that they knew little more than she'd gleaned in Moscow. The Hungarian prime minister was, at heart, a moderate. Until two months ago he'd held the

275

country firm. He'd made conciliatory noises to the right wing of his party, whilst avoiding the calamity of taking the country out of Europe.

But something happened. In August. His mood changed. He became more belligerent. He curbed the press, shutting down left wing newspapers and websites. Both *Twitter* and *Instagram* had been turned off, although if you were clever enough you could bypass the government blocks. His language had changed. His anti-EU rhetoric escalated. And then, the night before last, he let the world know that Hungary was leaving the Union.

We are a people. We will not be defined by the vagaries of others.

The words rung in Sam's ears.

It was no coincidence.

Someone had got to Viktor Molnár, in the same way they had played Kutnetsov. It was part of a script; words on a page. It wasn't ideological. It wasn't that the Hungarians and the Ossetians were following the same creed. They weren't inspired by a common purpose.

It was a script. Shared by someone to two different people. Two people who were being asked to say things they didn't necessarily believe. They had to be told. And, whoever had briefed them had got lazy. They'd not checked the wording of the two handouts, probably sent at different times.

Two leaders. Separated by thousands of miles. One script.

It was a mistake. The person in the centre of this had messed up. Possibly for the first time.

And that was key.

She had to find the link.

Come on.

Sam stood. She held herself steady as her legs woke from their own independent slumber. And then she made her way out of the staff room and found the desk she'd been allocated the night before.

Ten seconds later her monitor was alive and she was all focus. She had a bullet point list in front of her. She scanned it. It was a reminder as to what she'd distilled so far: the perceived date of when Viktor Molnár had changed demeanour; a bank account with multiple statements; tax returns; a list of the prime minister's appointments over the past three months; his family details - a wife and two grown up children; his house - a satellite overhead; and a few key sentences lifted from his last ten speeches.

It was nothing.

Nothing.

Sam clicked on her SIS temporary email account. Her inbox dropped down. Earlier she'd pinged one of the local case officers who was running a cabinet minister in the Hungarian government. She'd asked if he had any idea why the prime minister had had such a dramatic change of heart. The case officer had been out of the building, but had responded within the hour. He was as bewildered as everyone else. She sent him a reply, asking if there were any signs Viktor Molnár was being bribed, or had been bought.

She'd had nothing back. Yet.

Money. *It's about money.*

Sam had 84 monthly bank statements and three annual tax returns. She'd been through them once already

It's about money.

She opened all of them again and worked chronologically; a line at a time.

It took her 15 minutes.

Nothing.

Wait.

She started again, taking more notes.

Twenty minutes later she had something. It was small; probably nothing. But worth further interrogation.

First, coffee.

The resultant mug from the staff room was out of one of those pseudo-espresso machines. The ones that force water through a metal-cased sachet. The result wasn't bad, but the unrecyclable by-product of metal and plastic had always soured the taste for Sam.

Whatever.

She had work to do and caffeine to consume.

She narrowed down her investigations to the three tax returns and three months of each year: March, April and May. The numbers were telling a story. They were.

Possibly.

She finished her coffee. And then started again.

Probably.

Ten minutes later she closed the spreadsheets and statements. And opened a new tab. In it she typed: *Villa Feradina.*

There it was. Four entries down.

She clicked on the link.

A pink-painted, medium-sized archetypal Italian villa stared at her. It was nothing overly grand - certainly not your *Gladiators* Tuscan villa, perched on a beautiful hill, surrounded by rustling fields and approached by a cypress tree avenue. But it was substantial - and neat.

And it was where Viktor Molnár and his family had spent two weeks every summer for the last seven years - maybe longer, if she'd had the records to check. The prime minister's bank statements showed a payment of around £2000 in Hungarian Forints to an Italian villa company on the same day every year from 2011 until 2017: the 31st of March. There was a small inflationary increase each year. Viktor Molnár had used it as a tax ruse. It allowed the family to pay for the villa in the previous year. The expense was reported in the following tax return as 'an occupational retreat' and was set against income. Sam wasn't an accountant, but she thought that may have been pushing the boundaries of fiscal honesty. But, it was hardly something he could be blackmailed for.

However, this year was different.

There was no 31st March payment. In fact there was no obvious payment at all. Not even multiple transfers that might add up to somewhere close to £2000.

And yet, this year, the family had holidayed in the same villa for the same two weeks last August. As they always did. She knew that because earlier she'd scoured both the Hungarian and Italian media. She'd found a video clip of Viktor Molnár outside the main gates of the villa. He'd been talking to an Italian news reporter about something uncontentious. It was the same villa as Sam had on the screen in front of her. Sam was sure of it.

No payment.

No £2000.

A free holiday?

Maybe.

Maybe not. Maybe it was something much bigger. The language the reporter had used painted a picture of its own. Sam had asked the local SIS mainframe to translate. The translation hadn't been perfect, but the reporter had finished his exchange with, 'Well, President Molnár, how do you like your new holiday home?'. To which Viktor Molnár had replied, 'We love it here.'

Your new *holiday home.*

And that wasn't all.

There was nothing in any of the bank statements that indicated the family may have spent, Sam reckoned, in the order of 300,000 Euros on an overseas property. However, there was a single line in his latest tax return which didn't make sense. It read: *Overseas property transfer. 36,000 Forints.* Sam did a quick exchange in her head: Hungarian Forint to British Sterling. That was about £100. For an overseas property transfer? Hardly the right amount to buy a large pink villa in southern Italy.

She pushed back in her chair. Tiredness again was the overriding sensation.

The last hour begged so many questions. Among others ... did Viktor Molnár now own a pink villa in southern Italy? If so, how could he afford it? Sam wasn't sure she was going to find suitable answers in a basement in Budapest. And with a PNG tag, she was hardly welcome to wander the streets.

So, what now?

She'd leave some questions with the team here - maybe speak to Frank.

In the meantime ...

... next stop, Calabria.

Fatebenefratelli Hospital, Rome, Italy

Gareth came to differently from last time. There didn't seem to be any detachment. His mind and body were as one. He didn't open his eyes immediately, but spent a few seconds registering he was who he thought he was. He remembered bits of his last foray into consciousness; mostly the pain. But that had subsided. Now it was a 'thud' at the back of his head, rather than a piercing scream which he hadn't been able to cope with.

'Gareth?' It was his mother's voice. 'Gareth? Are you awake?'

He didn't open his eyes. Instead he smiled.

That broke his mother. Sobs and cries amongst, 'We thought we'd lost you! Say something. Please.'

Gareth opened his eyes. And closed them. And then opened them again.

It took a couple of seconds for his new world to come into focus: hospital; machines that go 'ping'; drips; a window.

His mother.

'Hi, mum.'

'Oh … Gareth.' She half stood and leant forward to give him a hug. In her excitement she got caught up in the drips.

'Sorry. Oh, Gareth. How are you feeling, love?' She'd managed to disentangle herself from the tubes and was now in full embrace mode.

'Fine, mum. Just fine. Thanks. Bit of a headache. What happened?'

His mum sat back down, keeping hold of his hand. Her smiling face then lost its shine.

'You were attacked. In Rome. Someone hit you. Hard. On the back of your head. They broke your skull. The doctors …' She faltered.

Gareth was computing all of this. He remembered the museum. And then ... nothing.

He moved his free hand and reached for her forearm. He smiled his biggest smile.

'Don't worry, mum. I'm fine. Everything's going to be fine. Really.'

Will it?

'Was I robbed?'

'No, love. It's very strange. In fact the person who hit you, left you with something.' Her face was still one of consternation.

His dad came into the room. Gareth saw relief spreading across his face. And his mother's too - as though she'd been rescued by the cavalry.

'Hello, son. How are you doing?'

Gareth smiled again. Those were the kindest words his father had said to him for as long as he could remember.

'Fine, dad. I'm just fine. Look, mum was saying I wasn't robbed. That the person who hit me left me something. What was it?' His face switched between his mother and his father. She looked up at her husband. He back at her. The exchange was fretful.

His father took a breath.

'It's probably a gay thing, son. Something or someone you might have upset.'

Gay thing? What the ...?

'I've no idea what you're talking about, dad. What do you mean a "gay thing"?' A soft question hiding his frustration.

His father turned and picked up a card that was on a side table. He handed it to Gareth.

Who looked at it. And then flipped it over. And looked at it again. It was a familiar message.

Leave him alone.

Same message, different outcome. They had followed him to Rome. They had attacked him. They were very serious. More serious than a horse's head on his pillow. They had come close to killing him. They had cracked his skull. His mum and dad had come over to Italy to be at his bedside.

'What day is it?' He asked.

'Tuesday.' His dad replied.

He'd been out for ....?

Gareth closed his eyes and breathed out.

It was over. He'd get out of hospital and go home. Back to Swansea. Back to his humdrum life. That's what he'd do. He'd give up on Naples. On Mateo Monza and the Mafia. It had been fun ...

Buzz.

A phone. Receiving a message.

Is it mine?

His mother and father's mobiles didn't get messages as far as he remembered. Even if they did, their phones were ancient. They wouldn't give a buzz alert.

Who's trying to get in touch?

'Mum. Where's my phone?'

His mother stood and looked around. His dad had beaten her to it. He gave her the phone, and she handed it to Gareth.

It was his mobile which had buzzed - a tiny green LED flashed. He unlocked it with a swipe and was greeted by two things. First, it had almost ran out of battery. Second, he had 15 missed calls and 13 unread messages.

He swiped and dabbed, ignoring his parents; his mother looking earnestly on.

Shit!

The calls and messages were all from Giorgio.

He opened the latest message.

It read: *Plze, G. We need 2 talk. I'm in trouble.*

Xxx

Headquarters SIS, Vauxhall, London

Jane was cold. She'd forgotten to turn on the heating in the office and as the temperature dropped outside, her very small part of the building had followed suit. She was standing by the gizmo which controlled the air conditioning. It read 18 degrees. She knew that wasn't cold … it was just that she'd fallen asleep on one of her soft chairs and her body's heat had tried its best to warm the room to a more respectable 21 degrees. As a result, she felt like a hot water bottle in the morning: cold and clammy.

She pressed the 'up' arrow. A small number in the corner of the light-green and black display rose northward. It got as far as 30 and refused to budge any higher.

That should do the trick.

She reached for her coat which was hanging on a traditional wooden stand in the corner of her room. As she did she caught the muted television picture; she'd left the set on whilst she'd slept. It was closer to dawn in the North Sea than here in central London, but the cloud base there was low and heavy. The picture was of greys and blacks. There was no ferry. Just a foreign tanker, a couple of circling helicopters and some debris. Earlier, before she had fallen asleep, one TV expert predicted a normal human being, whatever that was, wouldn't survive more than nine and a half minutes in the water before succumbing to hypothermia.

Those caught inside the ferry as it went down would have drowned well before then.

The SBS had got on the ship before it had capsized. Two Marines had made it to the bow door override controls on the bottom car deck and had managed to partially close the door, which slowed the water ingress. Unfortunately one of them had been hit by a sliding truck. And the second had died trying to save his colleague's life.

It had taken the ferry 40 minutes to sink. In that time the SBS had found and released the two main groups of passengers who had been locked in the family bar and the restaurant. Early live SBS headcam footage, which Babylon had had access to, painted an eerie picture of empty corridors. That was until the Marines had released the passengers. Then all hell had broken loose.

P&O had 942 passengers and crew registered on the ferry. Reports currently showed that six passengers and four crew, including the captain, had been shot by the terrorists when they initially hijacked the ferry. Five hundred and seventy three people had made it out onto the side of the ship and had been airlifted to safety - which, considering the conditions and the number of available winch capable helicopters, was an extraordinary figure. The RAF LO in Dover said that the final Chinook load carried 114 civilians - in an airframe designed for 55. The pilot had described the journey home as 'harrowing'. The SBS had picked up 43 out of the freezing water in their five RIBs, which itself was a hugely difficult operation. Every inch taken by a civilian was one less for a returning Marine.

The remaining passengers and crew had gone down with the ship. The images were not shown on TV, but Jane had watched the ferry make its final turn, upend itself and then slip beneath the surface. As it did she was reminded of 9/11. The terrible shots of people throwing themselves off the Twin Towers, rather than suffer the pain of burning to death. The ship's motion catapulted some; others slipped; some hung on for dear life. The numbers were nowhere close to being reconciled, but so far the reports detailed that 87 bodies had been collected from the water. Everyone else was still lost.

Still standing motionless by the coat stand with her jacket in her hand, she found herself bowing her head. She wasn't a hugely religious person - but just then she did mouth a quick prayer.

…

On, on.

Jane threw her coat over her shoulders and moved to her desk. Before she sat, she caught sight of herself in her trusty mirror - the one that never lied. She looked rubbish; bedraggled. She needed a shower and her teeth were crying out for some minty freshness. Her own needs would have to wait. She had a long list of things to do.

First was to check her emails.

She'd had 27 in the two hours she'd been away from her desk. All of them were important. She opened the one from Frank.

Hi.

Things not good here. SBS down 17 Marines, including the squ comd. They're saying it's the worst casualty rate of any SBS operation, ever. They've lost fewer in Iraq and Afghanistan combined. Horrible.

There is little else I can do here. I need to talk to you about the Mersa Fatma three. Something's been bothering me that might help. Best to talk face to face. I'm on the 8.15 out of Dover unless you tell me otherwise.

F xx

Jane didn't know what to do, or say. She reckoned that 17 Marines was about one-in-ten of the squadron. That was a huge hit rate. She tried to imagine how she might cope if it had been her team. They'd struggle to fill the gaps and operate effectively; she hardly had enough people to do the jobs that needed to be done when they were at full strength. And that would be without the emotional impact that would reverberate around the desks if they lost so many.

What a horrible thought.

What a horrible day.

Next she opened up an email from her team in Asmara, Eritrea. They'd arranged to meet with their senior police agent at 10.00 am local. If nothing came from that meeting then they'd hot foot it down the coast and see what they could find with cascons (*casual conversations*) in and around the village.

Seven emails down was a briefing from Carla, the analyst she'd asked to look over the UK Treasury's version of the Forbes rich list - to see if there was anyone on that list who might be keen to set in train a nine month reign of terror. She scanned the four page brief.

Jane recognised seven out of the top 20 names: internet company founders, businessmen and a media mogul. The rest were, to her, faceless. Unknowns. Carla had annotated those on the list matching the Forbes equivalent. What Forbes couldn't show were the multi-billionaires who employed people to keep their wealth hidden. Carla had highlighted these, the non-Forbes names, in red. There were 17 among the top 100 who you wouldn't find without insider knowledge. Four of them were in the top 10.

Three out of those four had names. People who, if you Googled them, would register somewhere. According to Carla they were a Swiss banker, an Indian industrialist and an American in the pharmaceutical business. The fourth had a current worth estimated to be £73 billion.

That particular slab of money had no name, although the Treasury suspected the culprit to be British. Carla had included a link to a Service file. Jane clicked on it.

The MI5 report was half a page long. And was scant on almost every detail. The Service knew about the size of the wealth because the details had been leaked via the Panama Papers. They suspected 'the name' to be male, for him to be living abroad and, because there was no link to major business or industry funding, for the money to have been accrued nefariously. The last update to the file was over a year ago.

Might 'the name' be the one conducting the NT orchestra?

She closed the file and pressed 'reply' to Carla's email.

> *Thanks for this Carla. Get onto Service. We need something more than this. Let's assume the unknown Brit billionaire is behind NT ... providing the money. Lift every stone. Put a name to the file, and then find out where he lives. I'd like an update before COP tonight. Jane.*

Jane thought she was chasing her tail. That this mystery billionaire was unlikely to have any connection with the terror attacks. But it made her feel better that at least she was looking somewhere.

Ping.

A new mail. From Counter Terrorism's lead Inspector. It had been sent to all of the intelligence services. She opened it.

Dear Team,

Pride of Eastbourne Terrorists - Provisional Brief.

Thanks to SF we have 3 x male and 1 x female terrorists in custody. They are uncommunicative. We believe they took an uninflated RIB on board in the back of their van (stolen plates - still chasing).

Thanks to SIS we have the name of one of the men: Abir al-Rasheed. They assume the other two men originate from the same village in Eritrea and have provisional names. Action SIS. Any further details you have, post to all addressees please.

We need every assistance to confirm/find the names of the other terrorists, where they worked out of in the UK, and who they may have been working for/with.

We will be holding a meeting at NaCTSO at midday today. All addressees to send a rep please.

And that was that. The sum of a high speed RIB and helicopter chase. Four mute terrorists. Surely they knew they had little or no chance of escaping from the ferry? That they would end up in a cell facing multiple counts of murder?

What did they, or the people they work for, hope to gain?

She didn't know. And it was bloody frustrating.

Frank would go to the meeting. She closed the email down and opened the one she'd read earlier from Frank. She was just about to start typing when Claire came in carrying a coffee. It was only 6.50 am.

What was she doing in the office this early?

'Hi, Jane. Cold?' Claire was at her desk in a couple of strides. 'Really sorry about last night.' She put a motherly hand on Jane's shoulder.

That helped. Claire had been Jane's PA since she'd taken over the job from David Jennings who had retired a couple of years ago. Claire had been David's PA for a decade. She knew more about the inner workings of Babylon than anyone in the building. And, as an older woman, she was a perfectly gentle matriarch. She was always in at the point of crisis, she was always right on top of her game … and she was always kind to everyone. And they all needed that just now.

'Yes, thanks. There are no words …'

Jane had half-glanced at the TV and stopped herself. It was muted but the ticker tape told a story that made her feel very queasy, very quickly. She reached for the remote and turned up the volume.

'This will not be great news for the intelligence services. We have it on good authority MI6 knew the name of at least one of the terrorists who scuttled the Pride of Eastbourne well before the attack. Of course, the question that comes from that is, if they knew about the terrorist why didn't they stop them from committing this heinous act? I think everyone in the country will want to know the answer to that question …'

Jane tuned out. She looked to Claire, who stared back.

'Bugger.' Claire said.

'That's one way of putting it.' Jane paused for a second. Frank knew the name. He'd made the connection from looking at the footage of the terrorists just before they boarded. He had briefed Jane last night. She knew he wouldn't have leaked the details. But, clearly, someone close to the operation had.

'Is the Chief in?'

'Yes. I've just been chatting with Susan. She reckons, like you, he hadn't got home last night. Do you want to see if he's free?'

Yes, please …' Jane's thought process was interrupted for a second time. It was her mobile; the ringtone was *Moonlight Serenade*. She picked it up off her desk, at same time signalling to Claire with a forced smile and a nod that they had finished.

It was Sam.

Did she have time for this now?

I must email Frank.

She swiped the green phone icon.

'Hi, Sam. Got a lot on here. Can I help?'

There was momentary pause. Jane knew Sam didn't like to be ignored - especially as she only ever phoned when she had something.

'Sorry, Sam. The poop has hit the fan here. Someone has leaked that we knew the name of one of the terrorists on the ferry. This is going to take some mopping up.'

'Did you?' Sam, as always, used as fewer words as possible.

'Yes, but only at the last minute, and only because Frank had been a star and found the guy whilst chasing a completely different line of enquiry.'

'That's your defence. No more. The truth. You can't be bothered with judgement by the press. You have more important things to do.'

Makes sense.

'How can I help, Sam?'

'I'm in Italy, heading south. The Hungarian PM changed his tune about staying in the EU a few days after he got back from holiday. He had been staying in a villa which, I believe, he'd just "inherited". It's dodgy and I think there's an NT connection. I need Frank to provide me with backup.'

Jane had put the phone on speaker and was rehanging her jacket. She reached for her coffee.

'OK. Anything else? I need to get some stuff done before I head over to see the Chief.'

'Yes. Why Britain?'

'What?' That didn't make any sense.

'Why have NT carried out their worst attack - by far - on a British ferry? Why us? I'm up to date on the three earlier minor attacks from yesterday morning: Frankfurt; Melbourne and Cancun. But why pick us? This ferry. Why not one out of Bari heading for Igoumenitsa, Italy to Greece? There are countless others.'

Jane was sat back at her desk. She had pressed 'reply' to Frank's email and had started to type … but then stopped.

It was a good question.

'I don't know. But …', she was randomly joining the dots, '... we have a suspected British billionaire, no name, in fact no details at all, who has the financial wherewithal to make these sort of things happen. I have someone on that case.'

'OK. I'll leave you to it. There is a pattern here, Jane. We're just not seeing it. So, let me leave you with the perennial question: "who gains the most in a breakdown in trust and order across the world?" That's what's happening here. That's got to be the major line of enquiry.'

And with that she was gone. The phone hummed. Sam hadn't even given Jane the chance to say, 'Be careful.'

She'd call her back later. In the meantime she liked Sam's response to the leak. Admit it and move on. Fighting a press-fuelled rear guard action was going to help no one.

Chapter 11

Autogrill Po Ovest, Northern Italy

Sam woke with a start.

What?

Then clarity.

Motorway service station. Very Italian. Compact, clean in places, plastic table tops, unusual bright yellow decor, but decent coffee. *Tick.*

She had left Budapest at 9.10 am. The station had lent her a car on the proviso she dropped it at another Embassy somewhere in Europe once she had finished with it. She was heading for Calabria - the toe of Italy. It was a hunch. No more than that. She knew that's where Viktor Molnár spent his holidays. And, until this year, he'd rented a villa there. Now all the indications were he owned the house his family normally rented. And there was nothing 'official' in his tax returns or his only bank account to show he had purchased an overseas property.

It was during the last summer holiday that something had moved his political ambitions; had altered his mind on which direction Hungary was heading. His change of heart would likely have huge ramifications for the rest of Europe. *Losing one country from the EU was a misfortune; losing a second might be considered careless.* Leaving aside a badly plagiarised Oscar Wilde quote, Sam could only see one path from here. And that was the dismantling of the European bloc, a political pact that had kept Western Europe free from major conflict for seven decades.

What had happened in Villa Feradina? Who had got to Viktor Molnár?

How?

And why?

'Why' was the recurring question to which there appeared to be no sensible answer. To everything. Anywhere.

Sitting in the pokey cellar in the Embassy in Budapest, Sam could only think of one way to find out. And that was to see the place for herself. Touch it. Smell it. When the images on a computer monitor and associated data didn't paint the whole picture, it was her fallback MO. Blunder about for a bit on site and see who she upset. Shout, and wait for the echo.

That's what she was going to do.

She'd got as far as Ferrara, in the east of the River Po plain. According to Google Maps she was 743 kilometres from the villa. If she drove through the night she'd be there in the early hours. Which would be perfect.

Provided she stayed awake.

She'd had a couple of close shaves driving when completely shattered. A passenger had stopped her leaving an autobahn at a non-existent exit when she had been serving in the Army. And, heading south to a small village in the foothills of the Urals a couple of years ago, her Nissan Navara had driven into a ditch for far longer than was necessary before she'd woken and, somehow or other, made it back onto the gravel track.

When, a couple of hours ago, she recognised the ominous signs of overwhelming fatigue, she knew it was time to pull over before her brain switched to sleep mode. Like a computer, there were warnings but the final decision was instantaneous and taken without consultation. So she'd stopped at the next motorway service station, staggered to the loo, bought a double espresso, found a spare table in a corner of the Autogrill - out of the way, took a swig of her coffee and promptly fell asleep. Thankfully her head had pivoted backwards and hadn't dropped onto the table. One black eye was enough.

Sam scrunched her shoulders together and pushed the back of her head against the nape of her neck. She held that position for a few seconds before relaxing and reaching for the remainder of her coffee. It was, unsurprisingly, cold. But it was caffeine.

Her journey from Budapest hadn't been incident free. From the city centre she'd been followed by a dark blue, old-style Audi 80 all the way to the border with Slovenia. In it were two men, almost certainly TEK, seeing her off the premises. She would have done the same. Early morning Slovenia was lovely - as Slovenia was. She always thought any country that had the word 'love' within its spelling could only be fabulous. She'd visited once before and, leaving aside the fact it was pricey, she felt it easily met and surpassed its hidden logo.

She'd been in Italy for two and a half hours. From a driving perspective that was already two and a half hours too long. For all their supercar marques and racing heritage, the Italians all drove older, dented cars. So far she'd seen one supercar: a bright yellow Ferrari 458 and that had German plates. The Italians may love their cars, and their designers were among the very best in the business, but the Italian public drove battered cars, badly.

Why use two lanes when you can imagine a third?

That was another reason why driving when tired was currently not a great idea.

Come on then. Action.

She took her phone out of her pocket. The news.

She opened the CNN app.

First up was the latest on the ferry hijacking: 292 confirmed dead. She scanned the rest. There was nothing there she and Jane hadn't already discussed on the phone. And there was no government response to the press questions concerning SIS having prior knowledge of one of the terrorists. Whilst that report may remain front page news for a day or so, she thought the overriding sense the security services were well behind the curve on the whole 'neo-terrorism' story would stay dead centre until one of the agencies had a major success.

Next was a report titled: '#enoughisenough - a global call to arms'. It seemed there was now a coordinated effort across the world to demonstrate to all politicians that people had had enough of the terror.

Strikes were being planned and larger marches organised. Sam was initially cynical. She thought maybe fringe movements were exploiting the climate of fear to undermine governments - to forward their own agendas. But the headline acts leading the charge were not politicians or known activists. Businessmen, actors, musicians and even senior civil servants were all on social media demanding change.

In the US, for the first time in recent memory, there was a clear coming together of Republican and Democrat voters. Sam had tried to keep up to date with all of the terror attacks, and she reckoned the US had suffered six so far - the worst of which was a recent nail bomb lobbed into a restaurant in Kansas City. Outcome? Ten fatalities. It was hardly a Twin Tower moment, but the mood was the same. People were scared: black, white and brown - any race; and both red and blue - all political persuasions. The indiscriminate and random nature of the attacks was wholly unsettling. And, and this was being played out in the more developed countries, the economic impact was taking its toll. If you moved away from the headlines, such as the Dow Jones hovering just above 20,000 points - a 23% fall since Christmas, there were more fundamental numbers that were beginning to impact upon every household. The price of oil had jumped. Business and consumer confidence had dropped 15 points. People were hoarding staples, whilst ignoring big ticket items such as a new TV. Unemployment, which had been slowly dropping in most Western countries over the last couple of years, had started to rise as firms shed jobs, rather than create them.

And the outlook looked bleak.

The CNN report finished with a harrowing statistic. Since January the number of male suicides in the G7 countries had jumped by 17%.

Italy was a G7 country. The suicide statistic made Sam scan the motorway restaurant. She did a quick headcount. There were 58 men in the room. She remembered stats somewhere that showed the European male suicide rate was 11 per 100,000; higher still in the Baltic states. A 17% increase would take that figure to 13 per 100,000. She looked around the room again, this time briefly dwelling on a face and a frame.

Mid-50s. Haggard. Overweight. Wearing a suit, but not smart.

Could he be one of the two additional Europeans?

She checked herself. It was only four weeks ago that she had been staring across the room to oblivion: white soldiers lined up on the sofa. And way too much vodka and coke.

Her face flushed. She was embarrassed, even though there was no one with whom to share her discomfort.

I bloody hate this.

Tiredness enveloped her again. A touch of despair. Pointlessness. A lone, sad figure tilting at windmills. Knowing what's best, whilst knowing nothing at all.

She closed her eyes. But sleep wouldn't come. Not after an extended cat nap.

She should go. She stood. And then sat again, her phone ringing in her hand.

It's Frank.

She connected.

'Hi, Frank. How's it going?' She should try to sound more upbeat.

'Hi, Sam.' *God, he sounds tireder than me.* 'I'm fine. It's been, how would you say, "a shit time". But I'm getting through it.'

'Is it the four on the ferry?' They were on an open line. Sam didn't want to compromise herself, but still needed to communicate.

'Yes. I wasn't quick enough. I had the info on one of them a day earlier, but I needed corroboration. That took a little longer. By which time I was too late.' He paused. 'It really hurts.'

Sam knew how he felt. She'd help foil some attacks. And she'd messed up. She reckoned there'd be at least six people still roaming this earth if she'd been a sharper operator.

'I don't think you can count yourself responsible in any way. In any case, it's how you react now that matters, Frank.'

'What do you mean?' He sounded lower and tireder.

'Get to work, Frank. Do what you do. If you provide the vital piece of intelligence that brings this chaos to a close, then that's what you will be remembered for. So, come on, let's get to it.' It was a half-arsed attempt to help him out of a hole, delivered without true conviction. But Sam thought it worth a shot.

Silence.

'OK … thanks. I've just come back from an all-stations meeting at NaCTSO. There is currently little new news. The Service suggested they take responsibility for the ferry four and, if necessary, send them abroad. You know, a different country, different techniques. Desperate times and all that.'

Sam understood why some people would see some sense in that. But torture was not the way the British intelligence services did their business. Not now. It had, on occasion, proved its worth but there were countless more examples of how the process had backfired. One case study during her training was in the first Iraq war. A captured Iraqi intelligence officer had been 'put under pressure', from which two locations for chemical weapons had been exposed. Special Forces teams had been dispatched. One team found nothing, wasting time and resources. The second fell into a trap, with Republican Guards ambushing the patrol, killing one and injuring a second. They had been lucky to escape without complete catastrophe.

The bottom line was: torture didn't pay. And grown up countries didn't use it.

'I'm guessing there was a senior civil servant at the meeting and they put a stop to that?'

'Yes. In no uncertain terms. Although, the level of desperation in the room was palpable. I wouldn't have been surprised if the quorum had agreed to it. Anyhow,

Sam, Jane asked me to give you a ring. Help out. You're on the loose again?'

Sam gave Frank thirty seconds on where she was - and why.

'And, so, I'm heading down to Calabria. I'm not sure what I'm going to do when I get there, but I'll think of something.'

'Calabria?' There was surprise in his voice. *Recognition?*

'Yeah. You know, the toe of Italy. The bit kicking Sicily into touch.'

There was a silence from Frank.

'Frank?'

'Sorry. I don't know. Look, Have you heard of Gioia Touro?'

'Sure. It's a container port. Newish. Southwest Italy. In … Calabria. Hang on …' A penny found a slot. 'Where's this going, Frank?'

'It's the port where the three men landed. They came in from Tunis on a container ship. It took them just two weeks to get to the UK from Eritrea. That's a world record. I can send you a secure link. It's a short brief I prepared for Jane.'

Sam's mind was turning quickly. Villa in Calabria. Port of arrival … in Calabria.

Is there a connection?

She was about to question Frank some more when she spotted something that made her feel she had spent far too long at this service station.

A man and a woman had come in through the main doors. They were casually, but smartly dressed. Trousers and jackets. Not holiday makers. Nor tourists. Not in business - well, not in an ordinary line of business.

The man looked towards the shopping area. As his head turned Sam noticed a slight bulge under his jacket. The woman looked over the restaurant. They were neither buying nor eating.

They are looking for someone.

Me?

What?

Why?

'Frank. I've got to go.' She was whispering unnecessarily. The two were out of earshot and still an escapable distance from her. If she moved now.

'Wait. There's something you should now about the container port.'

Sam was on her feet, heading right, away from the two new potential thorns in her side ... between tables, glancing backwards.

'Oops, *scusa.'* She clipped an elbow of a beautifully manicured feminine hand that was, a moment previously, holding a full cup of coffee.

She didn't wait for a response. The woman had started to stand, her head bowed looking to the dark stain on her cream slacks.

'Tell me!' Sam still had her phone to her ear. There was a choice of two doors ahead. *One with a circular window led to the kitchen?* The other - she had no idea.

'Gioia Touro is run by the 'Ndràngheta Mafia. And it's not a well-kept secret.'

Sam had to make a choice.

Kitchen. There'll be a route out the back.

As she opened the door, she glanced behind. She met the non-business woman's eyes.

Was there a spark of recognition?

'Thanks, Frank. That may be useful. Got to go.'

She pushed her phone into her jeans pocket and legged it through the kitchen amid mild protests from a man in whites.

'*Scusa!*'

There was a door at the end of the kitchen. She pushed it.

Why am I being hounded in sodding Italy, of all places?

She was outside. She had no idea if the woman had followed her.

Sam's car was behind her, on the other side of the building. Potentially one of her two pursuers could have exited the way they had come in and be at her driver's door well before she could.

Make unexpected choices. Surprise yourself.

She jogged away from the direction of her car, every so often glancing behind. Coming up there were three concrete picnic tables on the grass to one side of a line of cars. They were all full. In the mid-distance was a truck park, packed with articulated lorries.

Three tables. Three families.

Tourists?

Third table. Blonde father. Three blonde kids - assorted school age. Attractive mother: 40s, brown dark hair. Could be Anna-Frid Lyngstad.

Knowing me, knowing you, ah-ha!

Sam found a small space at the end of one of the benches. Next to a young, blonde teenage boy. Facing away from the threat.

She sat down. The boy straightened his back and stared at her.

'Sorry. Thanks. I need a rest.' Sam tried Latvian. It was close to Russian, but crucially from a Latvian viewpoint, not Russian.

The boy looked confused.

That didn't work.

But the blonde father, who was two down on the opposite side of the table, spoke instead.

'Hello?' Balto-Slavic, probably with a Norwegian twang.

'Are you Norwegian?' Sam still spoke Latvian as she looked over her shoulder. The non-business woman was standing by the door from which Sam had exited. She was looking left and right. The man with the bulge appeared from the front of the building. She had seen their faces. She could match them in a line-up. Every time.

'Yes. But I have worked in the Baltic States. Welcome to our lunch?'

Sam faced the front and smiled at the man's sarcasm. Typically Scandinavian.

'Thank you. Look ...' She glanced over her shoulder again. The two non-business people were talking now. The man was giving the woman instructions. At any moment she would head this way.

'... sorry. I'm in a bit of trouble.' Everyone in the family had stopped eating their picnic. The boy she had squeezed next to had his mouth open; his pupils were slightly dilated. Sam could see a piece of unfinished smoked fish on his tongue.

She continued. 'Don't look, but there's a man and a woman by the side of the building ...' Sam nodded in the direction of the restaurant.

Her new boyfriend, having closed his mouth, had followed her nod. Sam felt herself ducking.

'Marcus!' The father barked at the boy, who sprung his head back.

'Are you a criminal?', the father continued.

'No. Of course not ... I'm a ... scientist.' *In for a penny.* 'I work for Nokia. On their latest mobile phone. And these people are industrial spies. They have been chasing me over northern Italy. I stopped for a rest. And then they caught up with me. Are they heading this way?'

The father looked over his wife's head.

'The man has gone. The woman is still looking. She hasn't seen you. Hang on ... she's on the phone, and now walking to her right. She's following the man ... away from us.'

Sam didn't wait for any further explanation.

'Thanks.'

And then she was off.

It took her twenty seconds to get to the lorry park. Just before she jogged round the front of the first cab, she looked over her shoulder. There was no sign of either the man with the bulge or the non-business woman, but she caught the eye of the Norwegian man's wife. Sam gave her a short wave. The wife smiled and gave a similar wave back.

Sam walked down the row of trucks. Three cabs down was a bright red Volvo Globetrotter - with Romanian plates. The engine was running. Sam walked round to its right hand side, mounted the two steps to the passenger door and peered in.

The driver was concentrating on the instrument panel. He was alone in the cab.

Holding a grab handle and leaning back, Sam pulled the door open. She slipped around its edge and got in the cab. She pulled the door too with a finality that made her intentions clear. The immediate smell of cigarette smoke was almost overpowering.

The driver, late-30s, mid-build, mid-height and a crew cut, obviously thought all of his Christmases had come at once.

'Where are you going to?' She took a chance: Russian.

'Bari.' Russian with an inexplicable accent.

Sam did her geography. Bari was a port on the Italian southeast coast. Close to its heel. It was a set of shoelaces from her final destination.

'I'll pay you. Two hundred Euros. Nothing else.'
Just in case you're working in a different form of currency.

The Romanian didn't add anything. He just smiled and nodded. Then he took out a packet of Carpați Green cigarettes from his shirt pocket and offered one to Sam.

'No, thank you.'

The driver shrugged, took one out and lit it. He found second gear, looked left and right, and pulled the bright red truck out of its parking place.

Next stop Bari.

If I don't succumb to lung cancer before I get there.

Appartamento VI, Via Mortelle, Naples

Gareth's mother stopped abruptly just as she got out of the old, metal-cased lift on Gareth's floor. As a result he bumped into her.

'What's up, mum?' He asked.

Gareth didn't need to wait for an answer. The entrance to his flat was a few feet forward left of the lift's exit. And it had a message on it, badly daubed in red paint:

leave him alone

He sighed, closing his eyes as he did. Up until now he'd managed to spin his parents a half-lie about the message on the card left in his backpack.

'Dad's right, Mum. It's a lover's tiff thing. Nothing more.'

'So much so the jilted party smacks you on the back of the head with a baseball bat and almost kills you?' His dad had asked. His reddening face an image of incredulity.

'Well, they're pretty passionate these Italians. You know how it is?'

His dad clearly didn't.

When Gareth had woken from the 48-hour coma he was definitely heading home. Enough was enough. There was nothing left to stay for. His life was worth more than a bit of sunshine and the odd romp with an Italian beauty.

Five minutes later he had changed his mind. That is, *Giorgio* had changed his mind. The series of left messages on his phone. His love was in trouble. He was crying out for Gareth to get in touch.

And he had. The first thing he'd done having read the messages was to reply to Giorgio's latest text:

sorry, been in hospital with no access to my phone. am getting better. will not let you down and will phone tonight. G xxx.

He had initially added, *luv u*, but deleted it. That may come in time.

His dad had been in a rush to get back to Wales and now he knew Gareth was on the mend he'd had a final cup of tea and left to catch a plane home. As he reached the door of the ward he'd turned, smiled and said, 'See you in less than a week, son. I'm so glad you going to be OK.'

Gareth had smiled back and waved.

But he wouldn't see his dad in a week. He wasn't coming home. Giorgio was in trouble. He needed Gareth. And Gareth wouldn't let him down.

And that had been Gareth's first lie. He'd told his dad he was coming home, once he and his mum had cleared his flat. The universities would understand and they'd sort something out.

That lie hung between him and his mum as the doctor cleared his release. He'd never lied to her before and he would have to tell her sooner or later. It was just a question of timing.

That discussion had been brought forward as soon as they pushed open his daubed front door.

The place was a mess. It had been vandalised to the point nothing in the flat, neither his stuff nor the landlord's furniture, was intact. Everything was broken, ripped or smashed. It was disgusting.

His mother stood in the middle of the main room surrounded by the broken table, bits of crockery and Gareth's favourite picture, a Picassoesque face by Nathaniel Mary Quinn which he'd bought a couple of summers ago having worked in a bar in Barry. The picture, not much bigger than a sheet of A4, was out of its frame and torn in half.

'What the hell is happening?' He couldn't stop himself. He spun around, oblivious to his mother, registering the contents of his short life laying about the floor in tatters.

His mother reached for his arm and grabbed it tightly. It stopped him, dead.

'Don't swear, dear. This is horrible, I can see that. We must phone the police.'

'No.' Gareth spat-out his response without thinking. He softened his tone. 'No, mum. No. Look ...' His mind was racing.

What do I do now? Is she right about the police?

But all of his thoughts coalesced into two words: *help Giorgio.*

His mother had both of his arms now. They were facing each other. Tears were welling up in her eyes. He couldn't stop himself. A lump rose in his throat and the corners of his eyes became damp.

'Mum. This is complicated.' He stupidly looked for somewhere to sit. So he could tell her of his plans in some degree of comfort. But there was nothing safe to sit on.

Was there anything left of his here?

No. Nothing. He already knew that everything was gone.

Fuck it.

A tear rolled down his cheek. His mother reached up and dabbed it with the sleeve of her blouse. He smiled.

'Mum. I'm in love. With an Italian man. He desperately needs my help. Whilst I was asleep I had 15 missed calls and 13 text messages from him. His name is Giorgio. He says he's in trouble. And I believe …'

His mother raised her hand and put a finger to his mouth. It stopped him mid-sentence.

'Shhh, Gareth. This is the boy they're telling you to leave alone?'

What? No! It's not like that …

He reached up and gently moved her hand away.

'No, mum, that's not it.'

He sighed and, standing less than a foot apart, he told her the whole story. This time there was no finger asking him to stop.

'And that's why I'm not coming home, mum. Not yet. I'll leave the Mafia well alone, I promise. But now I have to go and help Giorgio. He needs me. I don't know why, but he does. He's given me an address in southern Italy and asked me to meet him there as soon as I can. That's what I'm going to do.' He had another glance around the room. 'Look, as there's literally nothing left for me here, we should maybe go and get a cup of coffee somewhere. I'll then book you into a local hotel and make sure you're OK. And then I'll head off. I promise to keep in touch. And, once Giorgio's OK, I'll come home. Promise.'

His mother looked down at her feet.

'Are you sure this …', she pointed at the mess, '… isn't anything to do with him?'

'Sure, mum. Sure. I told you. Everyone said I was foolish to look at the Mafia art thing. And they were right. I made a mistake. And this is the cost.'

'Do you love him?'

Gareth didn't answer, because he didn't know how. He couldn't love Giorgio. They hadn't known each other long enough. But there was something organic, almost primeval, between them. Something unspoken. He felt it. And he was convinced Giorgio did too.

'No, mum. I don't know him that well. But, do you know what?'

She smiled a confused smile.

'Tell me.'

'He's gorgeous, mum. Think of an 18 year old Bruno Tonioli - your favourite. You wouldn't be able to keep your hands off him!'

His mother blushed, smacked him on the arm and smiled all at the same time.

'You fool. I wouldn't … nothing, nobody would come between me and your dad.'

Gareth smiled back. This time he held her hands.

'Let's go and get you booked into a hotel. And then I'll get on my white charger and gallop off into the sunset to rescue my prince.'

There was silence for a second. For the first time since they'd come into the flat Gareth heard the sound of Naples murmuring in the background.

'Don't fall off, Gareth. There's only one of you and it would break my heart if you got hurt more than you have been.'

Jane had two documents to look over. The first was a half-page report from Carla, the one she'd asked for this morning. The title was: *The unknown billionaire.* Unfortunately there was nothing of substance in the report. The Service had agreed to relaunch an investigation into the missing details; Carla would let Jane know if that avenue came up with anything. She'd also spoken to colleagues in the CIA to check if their list of the top-100 was anything like the one from The Treasury. Once she had the list, she'd make a comparison and come back to Jane. She reckoned she'd have something by the morning.

The second document was a response from a junior analyst of hers, Nadia. She had made a slow start in the building and Jane hadn't yet gained enough confidence in her abilities to let her loose on any major independent work. However, what Nadia had produced was excellent; just what Jane wanted. Jane scribbled a note on a separate pad: *give Nadia an independent task.*

Nadia had produced two animations. Both began with an ordinary 2-D map of the world, with the land in white and all the water in blue. The borders of all 195 countries were marked with thin black lines.

The first animation was time-lapsed. It ran for 266 days, starting with the Embassy attack in South Africa. Every attack was marked with a star which was colour-coded: blue for bombs; green for guns; etc. And each star was a certain size, depending upon the *most likely* number of casualties - not the actual number. Nadia was looking from the enemy's perspective. What was the expected result? A simple pipe bomb came up as a small blue star, with an expectation of no more than five deaths. A gun attack on a beach, a bigger green star: less than 20 deaths. And so it went on. The final star, which was given its own colour - purple, was the ferry hijacking. Centred on the North Sea, in comparison with the other stars, its size would have covered the whole map of the world, and some. But Nadia's scale was 'semi-logarithmic' and 300 deaths only produced a star as wide as the gap between Scotland and Norway.

Whatever, the effect was grotesque. The purple star eclipsed everything else.

Jane ran the animation twice. And then she read Nadia's comments and conclusion:

> *Comment. There's a crescendo. The size and speed of the stars increases over time. The ferry attack is a spectacular finale, particularly as there have been no new incidents for the past 24 hours.*
>
> *Conclusion. It would seem that, unless there are a spate of new attacks, the NT cycle might be broken for now.*

Jane ran the first animation two more times. It was like watching a fireworks display. *Bang, bang* ...

bang, ..., bang, bang, ..., bang, bang, bang, BANG! It was almost *too* perfect a sequence. You could have written a piece of music to the rhythm.

She watched the second animation. As soon as it started to roll she knew this was the original piece of work she'd asked for. And it was a much better and a much more informative than her paper map on the board in her office.

Well done, Nadia.

It followed the same logic and process as the first animation. Except this time there were no stars; just a red spot on the exact location of where the attack had taken place. And, once there'd been an attack on a country, that whole country colour changed from white to a mild pink. And once there'd been a second attack, the pink darkened to a rose colour. Then a light red. Then mid-red. Then blood red.

The final image was significant. Nearly every country in the world was at least mild pink. Most were rose pink. Many were darker still ....

... hang on.

She'd spotted a pattern at the end of the animation. Well, almost a pattern. She used her finger to trace over the completed map.

The blood red countries were ... she mouthed them as her finger traced over them from west to east, 'Canada, US, UK, France, Germany, Russia, and Japan.'

That's the original G8 countries, less Italy, which was starkly uncoloured.

She had something.

She checked Nadia's notes. Did she agree with her?

Yes. And she'd asked the same question: *why no Italy?*

It was an imperfect pattern.

Jane moved on.

What about mid-red countries?

Nadia had done the work for her. Her notes read: *as above plus - Argentina, Australia, Brazil, China, India, Indonesia, Mexico, Saudi Arabia, South Africa, South Korea and Turkey. And if you like, less Italy, the European Union.*

That was the G20 countries?

Jane read Nadia's conclusion:

Conclusion. The targets appear to be in first-world, wealthy nations. In order of GDP. The only anomaly is that Italy has suffered no attacks at all. This does break the premise.

Maybe, maybe not.

Where did that leave them?

For a start Italy wasn't the only country left uncoloured by a red tinge. Leaving aside the smaller principalities, there were now only two other countries in Europe that had remained white: Switzerland and Sweden. If this were about targeting rich countries for the greatest impact, Jane would have planted a bomb or two in those. North America was covered, as was most of central America and all of South America. Mainland Asia was covered, accept for Mongolia. Africa was more notable. Eritrea, Somalia and Libya had all remained white.

Eritrea? That was where Frank's terrorist, Abir al-Rasheed, originated from. *Is that a coincidence?*

Australia and New Zealand had both been attacked a number of times, as had many of the Polynesian islands. The Southeast Asian island nations had a smattering of different shades of red. All in all, apart from six notable exceptions, the world was pretty much red of one shade or another.

Whilst she was convinced the final slide demonstrated the attacks were co-ordinated and aimed at creating as much chaos in the richer nations as possible, she couldn't understand the anomalies. Unless it was just the way it was? Maybe the people planning this couldn't get the right contacts in the 'white' countries? Perhaps it was as simple as that.

And then there's the timing.

Could it all be over? The ferry attack had been the sum of all fears?

Jane was just about to rerun the first animation when she decided to turn up the TV. Currently BBC news was still focusing on the ferry attack. She switched to CNN. They were also dissecting the North Sea attack. There didn't appear to be any new news.

She picked up her phone and pressed '#7'. It was Frank's number.

He answered straight away.

'Hi, Jane.'

'Hi, Frank. Thanks for your note on the NaCTSO meeting. That's clear. Look, have I missed something, or have there been no additional NT attacks since the Pride of Eastbourne?'

There was a pause. Frank must have been looking at something.

'No, quiet as a mouse. Sorry, do you think they're spent? Or, that they're having an operational pause, as the military would call it?'

She didn't know. She really hoped so.

But ... there was part of her that wanted the attacks to continue. More attacks meant more intelligence. And more chances of the perpetrators making a mistake. If things stayed as they were they may never work out who was behind the terror.

'Possibly. I'm not sure. Anyhow, thanks, Frank.'

Jane put the phone down.

Could this really be it?

Or was there going to be one final catastrophe?

Chapter 12

Dockside, Bari, Italy

Sam woke. *Fish?* No, the sea. Then cigarettes. She looked across to her driver and new best friend, Marius. He was framed by his window and the artificial glare of the port lights that was turning night into day outside the cab. They'd talked for no more than twenty minutes over the last, Sam checked the clock on the dash, six hours. For the remainder of the time she'd slept in the red Globetrotter's very comfortable passenger seat.

Marius stuck up a thumb.

'I was going to wake you on the outskirts of the city, but you were dead to the world.'

Sam smiled.

'Thanks.' She glanced out of the window. The main seafront, which was dominated by a very tall and very thin shaft of ageing white lighthouse, looked to be no more than a kilometre away. 'That may have been better, but I can walk to the centre from here.'

Sam also needed to find a convenience store. She'd left her bag in the Station's car at the Autogrill. Whilst she always carried her essentials on her - rule one on her SIS case officer training course at Portsmouth - she was now short of a change of clothes, and a toothbrush. Her hair would have to remain unkempt, a state it wouldn't be surprised by.

'Did you sleep well?'

That was an interesting question to which Sam answered 'Yes, thank you.', when the truth was definitely a 'No. And don't ask me to explain why.'.

Until about a year ago her nights had always been a mixture of cold sweats, irregular heartbeats and unpleasant imagery. She never dreamt of nice things; green fields, blue skies and loved ones. Hers were always violent and haphazard. She'd be falling, or running and not getting anywhere. Or she'd be facing a firing squad, the makeup of which was grotesque monsters with big guns that would blow your head through the backstop wall. Worse still, they'd find her old wounds and exploit them. Her patched-up stomach. Her dislocated shoulder. The hole in her calf.

And then there was Ralph Bell. Her nemesis. The man who, until Venezuela, had stalked both the still of her night and the corners of her day.

He'd died in the whitewashed cell in Puerto Ayacucho. She'd checked. There, on the spot. With two fingers on his carotid artery, pressing so hard she thought if Austin's strangling hadn't killed him she'd have cut off the blood supply to his head. She'd checked again. In the hangar at the end of the Caracas airstrip. He'd been in a green body bag. Cold and clammy. And still dead.

Bell, more recently, had started to slip from her dreams.

But he'd been replaced. By another man. The one that got away in Croatia.

Freddie.

Sam shivered, even though the cab was warm as a winter duvet.

She had no idea what he looked like, so her warped, slumbering imagination made one up. He was white. In his forties. Slim - sometimes athletic. He was always well dressed and, whilst she could never make out his face, she thought he was attractive. He was in the shadows. Just off centre. Peripheral.

But he was there.

And he never attacked her - directly. That was someone else's prerogative. But it was his fault. He was the conductor; the puppeteer.

He was mostly the one currently spoiling her nights. Making monsters, and then setting them loose. It was he who made her fear sleep; who always joined her. He was her constant companion.

And she hated him.

So, no, she hadn't slept well.

Sam reached under her fleece for her tummy-bag. She pulled out 200 Euros and offered it to Marius.

'No, thanks. You keep it.' He put up a polite hand to reinforce his refusal.

'No, I insist. Please.' Sam tried to be kindly indignant. In a bastardisation of her second language she didn't know if she'd pulled it off.

Marius shook his head.

'You muttered in your sleep. Half-British, half-Russian. I picked up a few words. It seems to me you're in a lot of pain. It was upsetting to listen to - and I am sorry. If I have helped in any way, maybe brought you closer to ending your suffering, then it has been my pleasure.' He smiled a half-embarrassed smile.

Sam didn't know what to say. For as long as she could remember there had been a paucity of kindness in her life. So much dark … and so little light. As a result her driver's empathy took a knife to the grey blanket of torment that covered her and ripped out a huge hole. His accompanying smile filled the tobacco-scented cab. She wanted to hug him. To hold him close and soak up his warmth.

Instead she coughed - hiding her sense of confusion. Before she'd slipped into her nightmare-ridden sleep, he'd mentioned he was sailing to Greece to drop off and pick up some goods in the outskirts of Athens. And then he was heading home; Bucharest - overland. Now she was that close to asking him if she could join him. Surely it was going to be better than bungling around southern Italy in the vain hope she might help save the world?

As if?

Come on, who are you kidding?

It hit her then. That sense she'd felt before. The realisation that she wasn't anyway near as effective as she thought she might be. That she was a tiny pawn on a chessboard the size of a football pitch. Intelligence agencies across the world were dealing with everything. They were coordinated … she was a taskforce of one. They were automated … she was manual. They were thousands … she was a singleton; an unwired and emotionally crushed individual.

What the hell am I doing?

The cab was warm. And safe. She was hidden. And not alone.

'Can I ...' She stopped herself.

That compassionate smile again, from the angel in the Globetrotter.

'No.' He had read her thoughts. 'You cannot run away from whatever it is that is haunting you. You must confront this. You have to exorcise it. I am a good Catholic with a mother who knows best. This is what she taught me. Face your demons. Fight them. It is the only way. And God will judge you kindly on that. Now go, Sam Green. And take your money. You may well need it.' He put out a flat hand, pointing to her door.

Sam dithered and then she reached across and gave him the hug he so richly deserved. She held it for a few seconds.

'Thank you. Thank you.' She whispered.

She turned quickly so he couldn't spot the wetness in her eyes. And then she opened the door, climbed down the steps of the cab, focused on the lighthouse in the distance and strode off into her future.

Headquarters SIS, Vauxhall, London

Frank was back in the 'mood room'. This time he wasn't after thinking space; he needed some time to stop his head spinning. He'd just left the meeting Jane had called for her staff and a wider group of the SIS team. The aim was to redirect their efforts after the ferry attack.

Clearly it was considered important as the Chief had made the opening remarks.

'You are the brightest and the best. But you were selected to work here because you're more than that. You are oblique thinkers. Fertile minds that can outsmart any opponent. Wherever you were before you came into the room, ignore that place. Do away with any preconceptions. Avoid any precedent. Let's look at NT from every angle. *Any* angle. You choose. Unless and until we get new directional intelligence, I don't care where you search, what you look at, or to whom you speak. We have - as at now - to start to piece this together as quickly as possible from as many directions as we can. Jane … over to you.'

The Chief had left at that point and Jane had taken over.

She'd shown them two animations. One was of the escalation of attacks around the world, culminating in the ferry disaster. And the second showed that this was indeed, save a couple of countries, a worldwide phenomenon. Finally she'd asked the question, 'Why was a *British* ferry attacked at the end of this frenetic build-up of activity? And why have there been no new incidents in the past 36 hours?'

She then threw up a simple chart with side-by-side double bars covering the last 243 days. Each day had a blue and a red bar. Blue denoted an attack; red the number of casualties. In this case Jane had gone for actual casualties, rather than expected casualties which her animations had used. It surprised no one that the number of attacks and the corresponding number of casualties grew exponentially, the right hand side of the graph as busy as hell. But that wasn't her point.

Her point was the tiny but significant white gap at the end of the chart. It was only 36 hours, but it was an empty 36 hours. It was as if the ferry attack was it. The end. At which point the stats had fallen off a cliff.

Jane had used a laser pointer to highlight the gap.

'Every second that passes, this area becomes more and more crucial to the investigation. Why has it stopped? What's next, if anything? And what's the point?'

There had been murmuring around the room, but everyone realised that Jane's questions were rhetorical.

She then asked people for an update.

Carla had given them five minutes on the unnamed Brit billionaire. New news was GCHQ had established his wealth was distributed among 296 separate overseas accounts, the largest of which was a bank in Switzerland, AfH International, based just outside Lausanne. Getting more information was proving to be difficult, but GCHQ was on the case.

Frank had been asked to talk through where they were on the men from Eritrea. He didn't have much. SIS's in-country agent had been pushed hard. The senior policeman had come back with a provisional response: Abir al-Rasheed's details were not on the police database, so there was no record of any infringements. The policeman had taken away the mugshots provided by Frank of the two other men and the women on the ferry. He'd promised to look over police records and see if he could establish their details.

However, there was one significant new piece of intelligence. It had been uncovered by an SIS analyst in Asmara whose job it was to constantly scan Eritrean news. Mersa Fatma had recently come into some investment, which was unusual. The new-build warehouses on the waterfront had made page seven of *Alhaditha*, the Eritrean Ministry of Information's major newspaper. Details were scant, but what the analyst had found was that international investment had paid for the development of a small fishing factory. It had been hailed as 'good news' by the government, but there was nothing about who had fronted the cash to make it happen. Frank had asked the Asmara team to establish the link.

Finally he'd taken the opportunity to describe the route taken by Abir al-Rasheed and the two other men from Mersa Fatma to the UK. He'd mentioned the Mafia links to their Italian port of entry, Gioia Touro, but there had been no supplementaries from anyone at the meeting. He'd finished noting the Met had yet to find where the four terrorists had based themselves, although there was a lead they'd rented somewhere in Lewisham. As Lewisham had a population of over a quarter of a million people, that was hardly helpful. But it was a start. The 'Ferry Four', as they'd now been coined by the press, were still remaining shtum.

The Met LO at the meeting had not added much to Frank's summary. He'd gone on to briefly outline the

#enoughisenough protests arranged for the weekend. London expected close to one million on the streets - and police forces from around the country were being bussed in to help. Similar, smaller events were planned for Belfast, Edinburgh and Cardiff. Jane had added that these protests were being mirrored across the world.

With no more updates, Jane had called the meeting to a close.

'OK, everyone. You heard the Chief. There is no box to think outside of. We'll reconvene same time tomorrow. I know it's a Sunday, but that's the way it is.'

Frank had gone from the meeting straight to the mood room. He'd made himself a camomile tea, plumped himself in his favourite soft chair and opened up Twitter.

He flicked through a mixture of rock and news hashtags. The memes were the same as they'd been for the last 24 hours. He followed most of *Rolling Stones'* trends and 'artists to watch'. He did his best to keep up where music was going. The latest was Justin Timberlake was back in vogue. He didn't think that was a bad thing.

The news was a mixture of the ferry attack, the mobilisation of the world's population against NT and the state of the global economy. There was one report about a conspiracy theory that the attacks were all orchestrated by a single government. The title was '10 nations that could be behind the attacks'. Frank opened the link. And quickly closed it when the UK was third on the list.

What a load of rubbish.

He reached for his mug which was on the coffee table, whilst still scrolling with his free hand. And then he stopped. He scrolled back.

Two Twitter winners in the current terror climate.

He didn't need to click on the link, because the tweet told him all he needed to know. It read:

> @Pontifex *and* @DalaiLama's *twitter accounts have received a huge boost (63.3M and 92.5M). People are turning away from politicians (@realDonaldTrump - 55M) and looking for answers elsewhere.*

Frank took a sip of his tea. And then scrolled on.

What is the world coming to?

Pentone Village, Calabria, Italy

It was cold. Sam reckoned about five degrees. She hadn't managed to find anywhere to replace the stuff in her bag, which didn't surprise her. This was southern Italy, not the outskirts of Leicester with its Tesco and Asda open 24/7. As a result she was wearing the clothes she'd had on when she'd left the Hungarian Embassy: tatty jeans, grey t-shirt, a blue lightweight softie and her well-worn Doc Martins. Jeans were rubbish in the cold. And she could have done with her favourite beanie, but that was still on the back seat of the car.

And her teeth … her tongue told her they were as furry as velvet. And she hated that.

The journey to Pentone had been a mixture of overnight train, a short bus ride and Shanks's pony. The bus had dropped her off on the main road about a klick short of the village - uphill. That had warmed her up. But now, as she stalked the perimeter of the villa, her sweat cooled and her body temperature dropped. And she shivered. The sun was making itself known over the hills to the east, but it would be a couple of hours before she was comfortable.

Her ability to recce a target was borne from her time in the military as much as skills she'd picked up during her SIS training. Start from a distance and circle your way in, stopping regularly and making mental notes. She was looking for strengths and weaknesses. Putting herself in the place of the defender. Where would she put the security devices? Where were the blind spots? What's the enemy's best direction of approach? And if you recognise that, that's where you, the defender, cleared the foliage. Or placed an alarm.

The villa was on the edge of the village, set back from a very minor road. The track to the villa from the road was pebbly and bordered by short bushes. The main house and a fairly large garden was bounded by a combination of trees and shrubs, but hidden amongst the greenery was a six-foot metal fence, topped with razor wire. *Tick.* The fence was new and sturdy - not a surprise as it was the holiday residence of a European prime minister.

She looked for alarms as she approached. The fence was clear; there were no movement sensors on the wire or at the posts. *Tick.* Nor were there any tripwires in the foliage. *Tick.* It was difficult to be certain, but Sam couldn't spot any security cameras in the grounds or attached to the building. So far, so good.

Just the fence, then?

She thought the villa would be alarmed but, unless it was occupied and unless there was a live-in guard, she had 20 minutes inside the building before any alarm might bring assistance. Make that half an hour; it was still before dawn.

Half an hour for what?

She had no idea. She really didn't. Look around. Pick things up. Put them down. Look at photos. Rummage through drawers. Find something. Something that linked Viktor Molnár with a change of heart. A connection.

From where she was, the building was dark and looked unoccupied. But she couldn't be sure until she was close in.

Which was the next job.

The track from the road met the perimeter at a new, sturdy metal gate - the sort that slides sideward under its own power. The gate was six feet high and had spikes on the top. The gateposts were taller still and were decorated with unlit lights and more razor wire.

Choices?

There were two. Vault the gate and play truth or dare with the very pointy spikes. Or, go round the back, climb one of the trees close to the fence, shimmy along a branch and make a leap over the razor wire. Both looked likely to cause harm, either from impaling or from a ten foot fall.

She'd try the 'tree climb, launch and drop' approach. It had the advantage of not being in the full view of the villa should there be a camera ... or a guard. And she'd spotted the most likely tree. It was round the back of the house. It was tall and had a couple of decent overhanging branches.

Climb when ready.

It took her a couple of minutes to make it up the trunk to a suitable branch and, legs either side, shuffle along (tongue sticking out from the side of her mouth) until the branch was beginning to groan under her weight. And she was still a couple of feet from the fence.

Mmm.

Sam reached above her for a higher branch and pulled herself up so she was standing, albeit uneasily.

Creak.

Her branch didn't like that.

The razor wire was below and slightly in front of her.

Two footed jump. Like at school. See who has the best springiness.

She momentarily closed her eyes ... and then ...

Jump!

She hit the ground on the other side of the fence. Hands first.

Her chin followed on and took a chunk of turf, a heavy bump, but thankfully no real damage head-wise.

The problem was her right leg. Her foot had caught the top of the razor wire and slowed, just as the rest of her was gaining momentum. The wire gave, but only after it had ripped her jeans and sliced through her calf.

Shit!

That hurts.

She lay still, her hand reaching down to the wound. It was wet. She moved her toes. They responded. She bent her leg. It did as it was asked.

All good.

A flesh wound?

It was difficult to tell in the dark.

She ignored it, for now.

She looked up and across. The house was quiet. It still looked unoccupied.

On your feet.

Ouch.

She'd need to get that leg sorted.

The villa was surrounded by a wooden veranda, its white paint looking grey in the dark of the dawn. On the bottom floor, under the short tiled roof, the back of the house had three windows and one set of double doors. She dragged her leg across the grass as quickly as she could. Once on the veranda she had a search for any cameras - or any small LEDs that might betray a lens in the dark of a recess. *None.* She peered in the front left window. A kitchen? It was too dark to tell. It looked unoccupied. There were no lights, not even an LED clock or a machine on standby. Empty.

The next window was a dining room? Quiet and still. Next were the double doors - 12 small panes of glass, six next to six, in each door - and a normal lock and handle. She crouched and peered sideways through the glass. She couldn't be sure, but she thought the keys might be in the lock on the inside.

Before she stood she reached for the cut in her leg.

Ow! That was sore. And wet. More blood.

Next she tried the final window.

A study?

Sam pressed her face closer to the glass. There was a desk and a computer in the corner. A red glow on the floor to the side of the desk. *An extension lead?* There were a couple of bookcases and an old wooden bureau; a small sofa and a coffee table.

Wait.

A mug on the coffee table.

That wasn't so good.

Who locks up a house and leaves an unwashed mug on a coffee table?

No one.

The villa was occupied, or had recently been occupied. That made everything slightly more complicated.

Sam scouted the rest of the building and came to the same conclusion. Downstairs was tidy and packed away.

Except for the mug.

Whatever. She hadn't come this far ...

Round the back of the house she slipped off her fleece and created a barrier between her elbow and the glass closest to the lock. And then '*smack*' she hit the pane with her elbow ... which refused to break.

She tried again. Harder.

Smack. And then *tinkle*.

Sam stood still. And waited.

...

Nothing. No alarm. No feet on floorboards.

She crouched and carefully removed the remaining shards of glass that had made up the pane. She then reached in, found the keys and unlocked the door.

She stood, waited a few seconds and opened it.

No alarm. No footsteps.

But the timings in her head hadn't changed. She still reckoned she had no more than half an hour.

She checked her watch. It was 5.27 am. She had to be out of the house by six.

It took her a couple of minutes to have a quick scan of every downstairs room. Other than the study, there was nothing that surprised her. If you'd have asked her to describe an empty, out-of-season holiday home, it would have been the villa.

She'd dwelt on the 'month at a glance' calendar that hung on the wall in the kitchen. It was still open at August. And the entries were all written in Hungarian Latin alphabet. She couldn't decipher them. She took out her phone and snapped a photo.

The study.

The first thing she did was check the mug. It was quarter full. Black coffee. No mould. That made it reasonably fresh. Someone had been in here in the last couple of days.

Sam looked around.

Computer first. Tower; monitor; mouse; and keyboard.

It was turned off. She found the power button on the tower and pressed it. The little men inside started their merry dance. She turned around and left them to it.

A bookshelf. It was now just light enough to pick out the titles. They were all in Hungarian apart from one. She pulled it off the shelf.

Revolutions and Dictatorships: Essays in Contemporary History. Hans Kohn.

She recognised it immediately.

It was essential reading during her SIS case officer training. Kohn was a moderate American Jew who, in the first half of the last century, wrote extensively about nationalism, both good and bad. It was an important, but minor work. She put the book back and was about to pick out another, to see if she could decipher its title, when a blue hue lit the spines of books not shadowed by her back. The computer was awake.

She turned.

Bugger.

The screen was asking for a username and password.

She sat at the desk without a glimmer of hope.

She tried 'Viktor Molnar' and 'password'.

Nothing.

She tried 'viktormolnar' and 'password'.

Nothing.

And then ...

... her hand shot forward and found the monitor's power switch and turned it off.

There was movement outside?

Something. Like someone passing the window.

Light!?

She turned and stood in one movement. And blinked.

Her eyes were taken by surprise. The overhead light was on and, *shit*, there was a man, might be a boy, in the doorway.

A man, might be a boy - with a shotgun.

How did you ...? He must have moved really fast to get from the window to the study door as quick as that.

Gareth was bricking himself. He had no idea what he was doing. It was dark. And cold. Like something from a thriller movie. Giorgio had told him to come to the villa as soon as he could - and call him once he got there. He'd let him in. They had a lot to discuss. He hadn't wanted to talk about it over the phone. Face to face was better.

Gareth had pressed him. Why was he in trouble? Was he OK now? Why hadn't he got in touch with him sooner? The answer to all of those questions had been, 'Not on the phone. We'll talk. I'll tell you everything when I see you. Please come quickly. We don't have much time.'

Gareth had started to ask a hundred supplementary questions, but Giorgio had cut him short. Pleaded with him. 'No more questions. Please. Not on the phone. Face to face. Come as quick as you can.'

So he had done as Giorgio had instructed. He'd caught a train to Amantea and then a taxi had brought him the remainder of the way. It had cost him a fortune but he didn't care. Giorgio sounded desperate. And Gareth wanted nothing more than to be at his side.

He'd phoned Giorgio at the bottom of the drive. His phone had rung and rung, eventually diverting to an answer machine. He traipsed up the drive to be met by an imposing sliding metal gate with spikes and barbed wire. At that point he'd phoned Giorgio again. His phone had again gone to answer machine.

Gareth gave the gate a shake. He pulled it to one side and then to the other. It didn't move.

What next?

The villa was about 30 metres away. It looked ominous. Dark and empty ... and unwelcoming. But Giorgio had been explicit. This was the place.

He'd tried Giorgio's number for the third time. Again, no reply.

Sod it.

He grabbed hold of the side of one of the gate pillars with one hand and a spike on the gate with the other, and, after a huge effort and a shuffle, managed to pull a knee up onto the top of the gate, his free leg hanging. He wobbled. He then lifted his hand and placed it on a small fraction of plinth on top of the pillar that wasn't swarming with barbed wire.

Push. And up.

He now had a foot on the top of the gate, crouching between two of the spikes, his other hand holding a third. He was stuck between falling back onto the gravel, or launching himself over.

Here goes.

Launch.

Shit!

He was a pile of body parts on the gravel on the villa-side of the gate. He held his shoulder, which screamed at him. His eyes were open, but they weren't focusing on anything useful. His ears rang as though someone had slammed a pair of cymbals together beside his head … which thumped and thumped … and hurt and hurt.

He was a mess. Tears formed in his eyes. He shouldn't have left the hospital. The doctors had told him he wasn't ready. That concussion would dog him for a couple of days. And if he did leave he was to rest. And not do anything stupid.

Like vaulting a spiky gate and falling six feet to the floor.

He was panting; waiting on all fours for his senses to calm. For the *thud, thud, thud* of the blood pulsating around his already swollen brain to calm down.

He waited.

The villa came into focus. It was still darkish, but to his right the sky had turned from black to orangey-black. Dawn was on its way.

He stood; and swayed. He reached back for the gate to steady himself. And then he tentatively walked towards the villa, with *thud, thud, thud* still an unwelcome guest in his head.

The front door was an ornate double, under a small porch which extended around the front of the house. The door had big, round brass-type handles. There didn't appear to be a bell.

Should I knock?

No. *Why?* He didn't know.

He tried the door. Slowly. Nothing.

What now?

He picked his phone out of his pocket. He speed-dialled Giorgio again; it went to answer machine.

Shit.

He'd come this far.

Gareth decided he'd walk round the outside of the villa. It seemed a sensible thing to do. And then, if there was still no sign of life, he'd find somewhere to sit, nurse his wounds and wait until the sun was properly up. In daylight surely things wouldn't seem so weird? Maybe then Giorgio would pick up his phone?

He walked round to the left, staying under the porch,

It was eerily dark. And eerily quiet.

Whoa!

There was a light on, of sorts. In the corner room round the back. It was blue - from a computer. As if someone had left it on.

He carefully stuck his head round the window frame and peered in.

It was hopeless. He couldn't see anything; the angle was too oblique and the curtains half-closed.

He jogged past the window just in case there was someone there.

And ... a back door. It was open. There was glass on the floor.

Should I go in?

Should he go in?

He dithered.

Then something changed his mind.

A voice. Inside the villa.

He tentatively took a couple of steps into a small hallway, avoiding the glass.

It wasn't any voice.

It was Giorgio's.

He was sure. And he was talking loudly. Like he was shouting at someone. He sounded confident, but scared. It was a strange combination. And there was a light now, where there hadn't been a second before. It was a beacon: light and noise; pulling him in.

Gareth shuffled forward. And shuffled some more. Giorgio's voice was louder. He was barking Italian, nervously.

'Tu chi sei? Cosa stai facendo qui?'

Gareth put his head round the door.

What the ...?

There was a woman. She was mid-sized, standing nonchalantly, her hands on her hips - but favouring one leg. A rip in her jeans - blood. *An intruder?* Giorgio was standing between him and her. He was ... *he has a gun!* And he was pointing it at the woman.

None of this made any sense.

Giorgio with a gun?

'*Rispondimi, dannazione!*'

Giorgio's shoulders shook. The long barrel of the gun rose and fell with his remonstrations.

Gareth's head hurt. His shoulder hurt. His brain was doing nineteen to the dozen.

And then the woman moved her head slightly, as if she had noticed him ... and she nodded in his direction. A signal.

Giorgio followed the sign, turning. The gun followed, remaining horizontal.

Gareth flinched, rearing backwards just before Giorgio pulled the trigger on the shotgun. The noise in such a small space was the loudest thing he'd ever heard. It easily drowned out his cry of, 'Giorgio!'.

Is he trying to kill me? Is this why he's brought me here? And the woman?

His thoughts were accompanied by a peppering of pain down his left side.

This isn't good.

He fell. Another pile of body parts on the floor.

Sam had been about to launch herself in the direction of the Italian man, could be a boy, when the arrival of a second man in the study doorway had made her choices much simpler. After the incomprehensible shouting the man, could be a boy, turned and the shotgun had gone off - thankfully not in her direction. A second earlier she'd motioned to the man, could be a boy, that they were not alone. Sensing the same thing, he'd clearly panicked, spun and pulled the trigger without thinking through the consequences - like, someone might actually get killed. The look in the man in the doorway's face had been a mixture of surprise, horror and, *what was it*, affection? Sam thought he knew the man, could be a boy. Indeed, she picked out a shouted name (*Giorgio?*) as he'd pulled away from the shot, taking what looked like a hit in the shoulder and arm.

The man, could be a boy's, panic levels had then broke through the roof. He'd dropped the shotgun and fell to his knees, next to the body on the floor. The Italian that followed was a foreign language to her, but the tone was loud and clear: it was tender, remorseful - and hysterical. The man, could be a boy, definitely knew the man on the floor. And cared very deeply for him. The kissing and blubbing painted the picture.

She knew the man on the floor wasn't dead, although he'd taken some pellets which would definitely leave a scar. And he would need those extracted before they went septic. And he would need a stiff drink, as would his attacker, who was wiping the man on the floor's brow, kissing him on the cheeks and then mopping his brow again. The man on the floor was awake and … offering consoling words in broken Italian. It was all very curious.

Sam picked up the shotgun, checked the safety catch and moved away from the two men. She slung the weapon under her arm. And waited.

There was more Italian between the two men. Then they both seemed to remember that, when all this had kicked off, they hadn't been alone. And that situation hadn't altered much.

The man, could be a boy, stood, turned to Sam and carefully raised his hands, shoulder height.

The man on the floor was more stoic. He lay on his back, his torso raised by his elbows and he stared in Sam's direction.

'*Chi è la ragazza?*'

Sam thought she got that, but couldn't answer.

'English please. I can't do Italian.' Sam replied.

'Who are you?' The man, could be a boy, then asked.

Sam was reassessing the Italian who originally had the shotgun. He wasn't a boy. He was probably mid-20s, slim, but athletically built and *very* attractive - in a young *Clint Mauro* way. Of course, for her he lost all of that attractiveness the moment he broke down in tears, but that was Sam's view. Some people found men who blubber a lot pressed all their buttons.

Now that he had both hands up and was surrendering, she found him less attractive still. But, there was no doubt that he'd look good on a catwalk.

Sam raised the barrel in the direction of the Italian model.

'I have the shotgun. I ask the questions. Who are you?'

He looked confused.

'I am Giorgio Placido.' The Italian model sniffed.

She pointed the gun at the man on the floor and nodded.

'And you?'

'Gareth. Gareth Jones. Are you going to hurt us?' He was nursing his arm.

'Don't touch the wound. You'll make it worse. You two know each other?'

The two men looked at each other. They nodded.

'Lovers?'

They looked again. And nodded again.

She pointed the gun at the model.

'You're the guard?'

'Yes. You have broken the door.' His English wasn't that bad.

'Who do you work for?'

The man on the floor made an attempt to get up. Sam swung the barrel faster than he was moving and raised it to her shoulder so he could see she was clearly taking aim.

'Let's not do anything rash, Gareth.'

Whilst pointing the gun at Gareth, she nodded to Giorgio. 'Answer the question.'

He looked to Gareth for support. Gareth nodded.

'My father.' Giorgio replied.

'Who is your father?'

There was a pause.

'I'd like to know that as well, please, Giorgio.' Gareth added.

The three of them remained still. The room was a mixture of silence and expended cordite. This was clearly a big question.

'Come on. I need to know.' Gareth asked again.

'Andrea Placido.'

'And he employs you to guard this house?' Sam added.

'Yes.'

'But a week ago you were a waiter?' Gareth asked.

Giorgio didn't know which way to turn. Whom to answer first.

'He's with the Mafia. He's very high up ...'

Sam was a question ahead of both of them.

'Which Mafia?'

Sam could see that Giorgio was at a crossroads. And she wasn't the only one urging him to choose the right road. Gareth was hung on every syllable; his face scrunched up in pain.

Giorgio's shoulders went first; they began to rock gently. His hands fell to his side, and then he started to blub - again.

Gareth ignored the trained weapon and struggled to his feet, pain writ large across his face. He took

Giorgio by the shoulders and turned him so that they were face to face. He then pulled him close.

Sam let the tragedy unfold.

The next half an hour was one of those extraordinary stories that you couldn't write in a book. Without disclosing anything about herself and keeping a firm hold on the shotgun, Sam moved the two lovers to the kitchen. Gareth had defrocked - he wasn't bad looking himself - and Giorgio had taken a pair of tweezers to the fifteen shot holes that had punctured Gareth's arm and shoulder. There was some TCP under the sink, along with plasters and bandages. Giorgio was tender. And Gareth was brave.

Gareth told his story of trying to investigate his third-year arts dissertation whilst being terrorised and then beaten by, 'Your Dad's lot?'.

'They weren't stopping you from your studies.' Giorgio stopped dabbing for a second. 'They were stopping you from seeing me.'

Sam had got there before Giorgio had made the comment - but it was easy to make that leap in hindsight.

Giorgio had been a waiter, but his Dad had pulled him out of Naples, away from Gareth. He'd been given the simplest of tasks: guard the villa.

And then there was a bombshell.

Giorgio was now behind Gareth, wrapping a bandage around his shoulder.

'I am to marry tomorrow. In my village. Serrastretta.' He whispered.

'You can't!' Gareth turned in his chair. 'To a woman? You don't want to. It's not right. You … love me!' Gareth was furious. He'd obviously forgotten about the pain in his shoulder. He stood, the bandage unravelling to the floor. He put his hands on either side of Giorgio's head; their faces no more than a few inches apart.

'I have to.' More tears. 'But I don't want to. My father will kill me if I don't. Really. Kill me. The girl is from a very important family. He knows that I am not straight … and he thinks this will cure me. He wants *bambinos*. Lots of them. And he's never wanted a gay son.'

At that point the soap opera had run to too many episodes for Sam. She had things to do. And her own leg to bathe and dress.

'Stop!' She shouted. Both men shut up. Gareth turned to face Sam.

'Giorgio, put the kettle back on. I'll finish the dressing. And Gareth, sit down. You can get dressed when I've finished what Giorgio started. And then I've got things to do.'

Giorgio looked confused. Gareth translated. Giorgio did as he was told and headed across the kitchen for the kettle.

And then a second bombshell.

'You never fully answered my original question, Giorgio.' Sam had put the shotgun down within easy reach and had a pin in her mouth. She was winding the dressing around Gareth's arm. 'Which Mafia does your father work for?'

Giorgio paused, kettle in hand.

'I don't want to have to shoot you ...' She nodded to the gun.

'The 'Ndràngheta.'

Sam immediately stopped nursing.

Shit!

Frank had said the 'Ndràngheta ran Gioia Touro.

The container port.

It's all connected. The men from Eritrea, their route to the UK. The ferry hijacking. The Hungarian prime minister - with the oddest of change of hearts. He gets a free holiday home, with Mafia guards.

Are the 'Ndràngheta the orchestrators of NT?

It all makes sense?

'What are you thinking?' Gareth asked; he'd reached to the floor and found his peppered shirt.

She ignored him. 'Do you have a car?' Sam's question was directed at Giorgio.

He nodded. 'In the garage.'

'I need to dress my own wound. And then we're all going to Serrastretta. You ...', she nodded at Giorgio, '... are going to tell your bully of a father that you're not going to marry a woman. You ...', she nodded at Gareth, '... are coming along to provide moral support. And I'm going to meet your father, Giorgio. And we're going to have a heart-to-heart.'

'What? About the wedding?'

'No. About something even more serious.'

Chapter 13

Roseberry Gardens, Orpington, London, UK

The polyphonic sound of Status Quo's *Rocking All Over The World* cut through Frank's sleep. It took him a couple of seconds to compute it was his phone. Half-awake he tried to grab it, knocked it off his bedside table, reached down and picked it up, and then, bleary-eyed, swiped the green phone icon to the right. He hadn't registered who it was.

'Frank?'

It was Sam.

Frank pulled the phone away from his ear and checked the time on the top-right corner of the screen. It was 5.15 am.

Sam didn't make a habit of phoning at unearthly hours, so this was probably important. But, then again, Sam didn't do time. She did awake and asleep; this might, therefore, not be a call about the end of the world.

'Yes, Sam. Do you know what time it is?'

Frank shuffled around in his single bed until he was half-sitting up. The room was dark, save for a frame of streetlight-yellow that backlit the bedroom window behind the curtains.

'Yes. But it's not that early. You're an hour behind?'

'Yes. That still makes it a quarter past five. That's early in my country.'

'Oh. Sorry. Look, I've made a bit of a breakthrough here. I think. I need you to get someone in Babylon to do some translation for me. I've just pinged you a photo of Viktor Molnár's August calendar. It's in Hungarian and I can't make head nor tail of it.'

Frank was awake now.

'Where did you get it from?'

'In his kitchen. His Italian villa's kitchen.

What?

'Hang on, Sam.' He was whispering now. He had no idea why. 'Did you break into the villa?'

'Yes. But don't worry. I've befriended the guard. It's a very long story, but all you need to know at the moment is the guard is the son of the 2IC of the 'Ndràngheta Mafia.' Sam paused, probably waiting for that point to sink in.

Frank made the connection instantly. His brain was catching up.

'So, this could be about the Mafia? They've bought Viktor Molnár? Literally? Given him a villa? And they provided the conduit for Abir al-Rasheed and the rest of the ferry team to get onto mainland Europe? They run the port of entry?'

'Exactly. But … that's nowhere near enough to declare that we've solved the problem. It's all pretty circumstantial. But it should give you something to work on. The problem will be getting a handle on the 'Ndràngheta. If they could be dissected the Italian anti-corruption police would have done that long ago. Even with this sort of lead, getting in among them is going to be tricky, if not impossible.'

'That's because the anti-corruption police are corrupt.' Frank added.

And then something struck him - a random but penetrating thought. All of a sudden he was absolutely convinced that this was Mafia related.

'Sam?'

'Yes, Frank.'

'Hold the phone for a second. I'm going to send you a couple of animations that one of the team knocked up for Jane. Let me know when you've looked at them.'

Frank reduced the phone screen and dabbed at the SIS's secure drive. He found Jane's presentation, accessed a drop-down box, pressed the 'declassify' button and downloaded it. He then sent it to Sam.

'I declassified it - I have that authority, it was only marked "Confidential" in the first place. Let me know what you think.'

'OK.'

Frank put Sam on loudspeaker. He left the phone on his bedside table, got out of bed and put the light on. He then slipped on his woollen dressing gown, found his slippers, picked up his phone and went downstairs.

Tea.

'Italy.' The phoned squeaked from the small kitchen table where Frank had placed it. Sam's voice could only just be heard above the boiling kettle.

Frank shouted across the small kitchen.

'I need more than that.'

'Eritrea and Libya are ex-Italian colonies. They've not had a terrorist attack in the past nine months. That in itself may not be unusual. But neither has Italy, when nearly all other countries in Europe have suffered multiple attacks. The Mafia are looking after their own?'

'That's what hit me just now. Anywhere with Italian connections has been avoided by NT. But neither Switzerland nor Sweden have been hit?' Frank added. He was pouring boiling water into a Roger Daltrey mug.

There was a pause.

'Neutral countries?' Came the squeal from the phone.

Frank fished a tea bag out of the mug with a spoon.

'So was Ireland. But that's been hit twice. The Cork waterfront shooting and the Dublin bar bomb. Seven neutral Irishmen are dead.'

'Maybe they've been ignored so we can't see the pattern? To put us off the scent that someone in Italy is making this happen, whilst the only safe place to be is in Italy or one of its ex-colonies.'

Frank took two steps to the fridge.

'Don't know.' He replied.

'No. Looking at Jane's work, there is something very particular about the way this has been organised. Very detailed. Sweden and Switzerland have been left untouched for a reason. But, I do think the Italian connection is decent intelligence. It all adds up. You've got to talk to Jane about it. Oh, and get that calendar translated.'

'OK, boss.' Frank had his backside against the worktop and a cup of tea in hand. 'And what are you doing now?'

'The 2IC of the 'Ndràngheta Mafia's son is taking me to say hello to his dad.'

Frank coughed a mouthful of hot tea over the top of his mug and onto to the floor.

'Are you mad? We'll never see you again?'

'That's why I'm phoning you now, Frank. The three of us ...'

The three of you?

'... are heading to his dad's house now. His name's Andrea Placido. We're going to stop for breakfast and I need a shower and a change of clothes. And then we have to think through the best way to pull this off. I'll keep you in the picture. But if you could let Jane know. Oh, and the team in Rome, that would help.'

'The three of you?'

'That's the bit of the story I've not told you about.'

Café Noir, Catanzaro, Calabria, Italy

Gareth played with his empty espresso cup.

What an unlikely trio they were. Giorgio, his gorgeous and ever-so gay lover, who had taken a pot shot at him but had now regained his composure. Sam (no surname elicited), who claimed she worked for the Department of International Trade and was trying to meet with someone senior in the 'Ndràngheta Mafia because there were potential conflicts of interest in the exportation of olive oil. He didn't believe that for a moment. Nobody from the British government breaks into an Italian villa unless they were a spy or an undercover policeman. She wasn't working for the government. His guess was she was involved in industrial espionage. But there was no elaborating on her cover. Every time he pressed her, she changed the subject.

And him, a love-struck lunatic chasing across Italy in the vain hope he'd rescue his darling from the clutches of an unworthy woman.

First, though, they'd have to deal with an evil dad. And Gareth didn't know what he thought about that.

Giorgio's first reaction to Sam's idea that they confront the issue head-on, was one of panic.

'I can't! I can't! He'll kill me!'

Sam, who Gareth was already beginning to like even though she was as non-committal as a priest in a betting shop, had made Giorgio a cup of coffee whilst keeping the shotgun within arm's reach.

'I met a Romanian truck driver yesterday.' She'd said. 'He was an unassuming man with a pivotal message. "Face your demons. Fight them. It is the only way. And God will judge you kindly on that." And that's what I'm doing. And you, Giorgio, unless you deal with this now, it will dog you all of your life. You have to make a stand.'

Gareth had had to translate some the message. It didn't lose much: Giorgio got it. He sniffed. And then accepted Sam's coffee.

'You two talk this over whilst you clear up any of the mess you can.' She'd tipped her head towards the hall which led to the study. 'I need half an hour to phone a pal and deal with this.' She was pointing at her leg. 'We leave at six-thirty. Giorgio, you can drive as I guess, like me, Gareth's not slept much.'

The two of them had stared at each other for a couple of seconds. Gareth was trying to work out why, other than the fact that the woman had the shotgun, she was naturally in charge.

'Come on, fellas. Get a move on.'

And they had done.

That was six and a half hours ago. Giorgio had driven all the way to the major town in the area, Catanzaro. Sam had sat in the front of the ancient Fiat with the shotgun resting between her legs - and slept. He had napped in the back. They made the town for shop opening time and parked in the first carpark they could find.

'Do you need a shower?' She'd asked, looking over her shoulder.

Gareth definitely needed a shower.

'Yes. Why?'

She turned her shoulders so that she was facing both of them.

'Look, you could run away together and I wouldn't come looking for you. I now know where

Giorgio's father lives, which I guess is a closely held secret. So I don't need the pair of you to do what I need to do - although it would probably be easier to get to Giorgio's dad with him present. Leave if you want to. But, if you're unsure, we can figure this all out together. I can get a room in a local hotel. I can shop - eat something. You can sort yourselves out. I'll then have a shower and we can sit down over a cup of coffee and work out a game plan. What do you think?'

He'd had a brief conversation with Giorgio in Italian, who'd agreed that he needed the biggest posse available to help him confront his dad. His view was they should stick with the strange British woman.

'We're with you. Which hotel?'

Sam had got her phone out.

'Hotel Altavilla. It's the priciest, which means it's the most likely to be open out of season.'

She'd then given Giorgio instructions as he drove and they were outside the hotel ten minutes later. They'd booked in (Lord knows what the woman at the front desk had thought) - Sam had paid in cash. After eating, showering, a short exertion with Giorgio when Sam was out shopping - *mmm!* - they'd left the hotel and headed for a coffee shop Sam had found earlier.

'So what's the plan?' Gareth asked when their coffees and patisseries had arrived.

Sam, who was carrying a new backpack and wearing pretty much exactly the same clothes that she'd worn first thing, except newer and without a rip in the jeans, answered the question with a question.

'How did you get over the fence? Did Giorgio let you in?'

Gareth finished his pastry.

'I vaulted over the gate. Banged my shoulder and my head, which isn't in the best shape, as you know.'

'Good drills. Well done. Are you OK now?'

'Sore, but fine. You? Your leg looked really cut up.'

'I bought a needle and thread. I stitched it up after my shower. It should hold.' She took a sip of her coffee. 'Who are you meant to be marrying, Giorgio?'

'A girl from the village. She's nice, but she doesn't want to marry me. It's not fair.'

'Does she know you're gay?' Gareth asked.

Giorgio laughed.

'Look at me.' He used both hands to point to himself. 'Everyone knows I'm gay. That the marriage is a sham.' Giorgio shook his head, hiding more tears.

Gareth felt the lump in his throat grow. If it grew any bigger he wouldn't be able to breathe.

This is shit.

He placed a hand on Giorgio's cheek and wiped a forming tear from his eye.

'OK. Enough. The plan.' The strange woman was back on message. She was obviously embarrassed when people showed their emotions.

Sam turned to Giorgio.

'How does the wedding work?'

Giorgio outlined the celebrations. There was a family get together tonight. He was expected. And then the church service was at 11.00 am tomorrow in the villa's chapel with a reception for over 150 guests in the garden straight after.

Your dad's place has its own chapel?

'It sounds like a big place?'

Giorgio smiled.

'About five times as big as the Villa Feradina. It has large gardens. We have a massive tent and lots of flowers. It's a yellow and white wedding.'

'Will it be easy to get into the grounds?' Sam continued.

'Yes, providing I am there. You can come as my guests. Come for tonight's meal?'

'Won't your mum and dad be surprised when we turn up unexpectedly?' Gareth asked.

'No. Papa may be worried about security, but there are all sorts of people in and around the house at the moment. Nobody messes with Papa. He wouldn't expect anyone would try and get into his house. And there is always room for two more mouths. This is Italy. There will be food for a thousand. Mama will be very pleased.'

'Won't they recognise Gareth? They've hunted him down twice already.' Sam asked.

Giorgio looked back at Gareth, he smiled and touched his leg playfully.

'We should cut and dye your hair. Maybe dress you a little different?'

'We don't have time for any of that.' Sam cut through the bonhomie. Gareth sensed irritation in Sam's voice.

That stopped the conversation. Giorgio looked at his coffee cup. Gareth tried to wrap his head round the enormity of what Sam was suggesting they do.

'Maybe I shouldn't come, or if I do, I come incognito. The swelling in the back of my skull is telling me this is not a great idea.'

Sam didn't reply. She played with her empty coffee cup.

Eventually she asked, 'What time is tonight's supper, Giorgio.'

'After seven, some time.'

'We should all go. And you, Giorgio, must talk to your father. Tonight. It's only fair you have that conversation with him today, so that they can call off the wedding as soon as possible.'

The blood seem to run from Giorgio's cheeks as Sam carried on with her instructions.

'It's ...', she checked her watch, '... two-fifteen. That gives us, three hours? I reckon it's no more than an hour to your dad's place from here. Is that right, Giorgio?'

Giorgio nodded. It seemed that words were failing him at the moment.

'Let's aim to get there for 6.00 pm. And let's do as you suggested, Giorgio. You have two hours to find some dye and colour Gareth's hair. I need to go and get a posh frock and I'll find Gareth some different clothes - something less fashionable, more conventional. We'll assume your father has been leaving his minions to do his dirty work, and maybe hasn't seen a photo of Gareth.

Even if he has, you're going to need him close by when you have that difficult conversation with your father. There's no point pretending he doesn't exist.'

Giorgio put his hand on top of Gareth's and squeezed. He smiled a thin smile.

'Giorgio?' Sam wanted his attention. Giorgio hadn't reacted, he was staring intently into Gareth's eyes.

'Giorgio!' Sam barked. Giorgio's head snapped in Sam's direction.

'Phone your mother. Tell her she's got an additional two mouths to feed this evening. If she asks who we are, say we're a couple you met … I don't know where, make it up. I guess not in Naples as your father might put two and two together. Anyhow, phone her. It's only polite.'

La Poste, Passage Bruyas, Montpellier, France

Jeanne pushed on the pedal of her yellow *La Poste* electric bike. The little motor kicked in immediately. The power was set at its lowest level but it still gave the wheels a boost. When they got their bikes a couple of months ago all of the *facteurs* had been asked to attend a lecture about how to use them. From what she could tell, they were to ride them as normal and only use the power when there was a hill, when it was windy or when they were tired at the end of a shift. It was all to do with wearing the battery out. Apparently it only had so many charges before it needed replacing. And at over 200 Euros each the bosses couldn't afford to replace them too frequently.

'*Dans quel but?*' Pierre, her friend had whispered to her. '*Nous pourrions aussi bien marcher*!'

Jeanne wasn't sure. She liked her new bike. And she certainly liked it more than walking. Pierre was old school. He didn't like change and he always thought management was out to get them, eroding this, taking that. Jeanne was more *Macron*. She knew that French working practices couldn't stay in the dark ages forever. There were only so many Euros to go round. She saw how the workforce cut corners. How they snuck in extended lunch breaks, took too many days off. The bikes were meant to make them more productive. New houses were being built everywhere in Montpellier. Old school reckoned this meant more jobs for the boys. But she knew she could reach maybe ten more streets on her round if she tried. Maybe 15 with an electric bike. She saw the point of it. Even if Pierre didn't.

Yes, she loved her new bike.

First off was a set of businesses in Rue Baudin. She knew her route like the back of her hand. And she knew most of the shopkeepers and a lot of the residents in the apartments off the main drag. She always looked out for the older folk, even though their post boxes were in the atria on the bottom floors of the blocks.

First was Fraysinne, a specialist watch shop. Mr Bardonne. He had big eyebrows and wandering hands. But he was harmless enough.

She hopped off her bike and reached into the first of three waterproof bags that were behind her saddle.

Four letters. Two were brown - bills. A third was a colourful circular. And the fourth was a plain white envelope with a typed address sticker and - and she didn't know why she checked - a stamp franked from Lyon. There were no other markings. No return address. There was nothing official about the envelop. In fact the sticker had been put on at a slight angle, almost carelessly.

Tant pis.

Mr Bardonne was behind the counter. He was serving an elderly lady who was immaculately dressed and was carrying a fluffy white dog, the size of a small handbag.

'*Post, Monsieur Bardonne.*' She placed the letters on the counter next to the elderly woman. Mr Bardonne reached for her hand, but she moved before he had time to caress it.

'*Merci, mademoiselle.*' Mr Bardonne's eyebrows did that thing when they were excited.

'*Au revoir.*' Jeanne made her escape.

By the time Jeanne finished her first round she'd been out for two and a half hours. It had been, like it was most days, uneventful but energetic. She loved her job. She loved being outside. She enjoyed meeting people, even if one or two of the older male shopkeepers hadn't yet got the #*metoo* message. That wasn't really fair and none of them had ever made a pass at her … and she never felt uncomfortable. They were a different generation, when

French men had mistresses and that was the way it was. Thankfully, though, times were changing.

As she walked her three empty bags back to the sorting room she reminded herself it hadn't been a completely uneventful day.

Those envelopes?

The first one to Mr Bardonne. And then six others. Same plain envelope. Same typed sticker, carelessly stuck on, as if in a rush. And all of them with a stamp franked in Lyon. Six seemingly random addresses.

Maybe they're from a political party?

She didn't know.

I wonder if I'll get any more on my second round?

Villa San Francesco, Serrastretta, Calabria, Italy

Sam worked her toothbrush hard. Her mum had told her to always count to 100; only then could her teeth be anyway near clean enough. She was at 87 and white froth was escaping her bottom lip and abseiling into the sink.

95, 96, 97, 98, 99 ... 100.

All done.

At least she'd managed to successfully complete one job tonight. Other than that it had been an abject failure.

They'd arrived just before seven to be met by a smothering of hugs from Giorgio's mum, and open arms from his dad. If he suspected anything, he was either the coolest man in southern Italy, or had the arrogance of ten men. They'd been shown to their rooms. Her's was perfect. Double-windowed, ornate but not fussy antique furniture, a huge bed with white cotton linen, an *en suite* larger than any family bathroom she'd ever been in, and views over the marquee and the pool. Everywhere was decorated beautifully with yellow and white flowers, dark green foliage and matching two-tone ribbons. The colours were further enhanced with the odd pair of bright red roses. It was achingly beautiful and someone had spent a lot of money and a lot of time making the place 'just so'.

Dinner was much later than she expected, but that was so Italian. They ate outside with half of Giorgio's family who had descended on the house earlier in the day. The food was a mountain of fabulous 'chicken and lime' pasta served with a tomato salad. The accompanying dressing stole the show. For afters there were more puds than there were guests. And the wine flowed a little too freely.

All of which gnawed at her.

She knew she was being lavished on the back of other people's misfortunes. That tonight's company, whilst welcoming and intelligent, were all soiled by their association with the Mafia. The 'Ndràngheta were ruthless and unforgiving. Even if they weren't involved in the NT attacks, which Sam was sure they were, they had a history of brutal violence and intimidation. Whilst Giorgio had been dyeing Gareth's hair (he hadn't done a bad job; Gareth now looked more ginger-Irish than jet-black Welsh, and Giorgio had cut and styled his hair so that by the time he'd finished he really didn't look at all like Gareth) she'd asked Frank for anything he could get on the 'Ndràngheta. The read-out painted a blacker picture than Sam had imagined.

Whilst it was commonly assumed that the 'Ndràngheta had close links to the Sicilian Mafia, which was no more than three klicks across the Straits of Medina, it was a wholly separate organisation and now the largest crime syndicate in Italy. They excelled in drug trafficking, extortion and money laundering; the latest figures showed that in 2016 they accounted for at least three percent of Italy's GDP. A Europol report detailed them 'among the richest and most powerful organised crime groups at a global level'.

No wonder the wine was so good.

And the bathrooms so luxuriant.

Sam poked at her eye. The swelling had gone down. All that was left was a yellow tinge as the bruise said its last hurrah.

She sighed.

They hadn't got very far.

For a start, Giorgio hadn't confronted his dad.

'Why on earth not?' Sam had asked.

The three of them had gone for a walk in the grounds after supper; out of earshot. She needed to find the house's perimeter just in case she had to escape without using the front entrance. Gareth wobbled as they walked. He'd clearly had too much Dutch courage. She couldn't blame him. The last time he was this close to a member of the 'Ndràngheta, they'd been carrying a baseball bat and had used his skull as the ball.

Giorgio had stammered. 'I just ... it was ... I don't know.'

He looked deflated.

Gareth had tried to put his arm round Giorgio at that point, but Sam had stopped him.

'Not here.' She rasped.

They carried on walking, over the edge of an immaculately cut lawn into ankle-high grass. It was difficult to tell in the dark but she reckoned there was a tree line about a hundred metres ahead. She hoped that was the boundary. They'd get to there, turn round, and head back.

'I can't help you, Giorgio. Unless you want to live a lie and marry a woman who doesn't love you, and probably never will, you're going to have to talk to him.'

'I know, I know. It's just ...'

'It's just, what?' Gareth asked kindly.

The three of them stopped. They were still short of the treeline. A half-moon was out; it cast a mild blue light on Giorgio's face. He was crying again.

'I'm scared. My father has never touched me. He has always been kind. But I have heard him shout at other men ... in his study. On the lawn. There is a, how do you say, viciousness in him? It is something he has never used on me. This ... me, not wanting to get married ... will be huge.' Giorgio turned and faced back towards the house. 'The tent. The flowers. The guests. He will not want to lose face. It will bring shame on my family.'

It was Sam's turn to put her arm round Giorgio. Giving physical comfort wasn't something she was good at, or was comfortable with, but it felt like the right thing to do. She was a couple of inches shorter than him, but that didn't stop him resting his head on her shoulder. She awkwardly tapped his arm gently with her fingers.

'If he really loves you, Giorgio, he will understand.' She knew as soon as she said it, she didn't believe it. Andrea Placido was almost certainly a ruthless murderer. Every member of the Mafia, no matter how good their breeding, had to learn the ropes. Giorgio had started by guarding a villa. For which he was given a shotgun and was expected to use it.

Giorgio pulled back. He looked at Gareth and then back at Sam.

'You don't mean that. It's different here. He can love me, but still make me marry. It has never been said, but he knows that I am gay. If he loves me like you say, he wouldn't have planned the wedding - at all. But that's not possible here. *Questa è l'Italia. La Mafia.*' He threw his arms up to strengthen his Italian.

Looking in Giorgio's damp eyes Sam knew he was right.

Why am I bothered?

What part of this story was she actually involved in? She was herding two grown men as though she were *Oprah Winfrey*. Why did she feel the need to step up to the plate?

Who did she think she was?

That question again.

And, frankly, she had much more important things to be getting on with.

She broke Giorgio's imploring gaze and looked across at the tree line. There'd be a fence there. It would be rigged with all sorts of security paraphernalia. This wasn't a small villa used once a year by a politician. This was the domestic empire of an Italian demigod. A man one branch down from Mafia sainthood. Yes, there was more warmth here than she'd ever experienced at first invite. But that warmth was borne from a confidence that only money and power can pay for. It was a charade. Thicker than veneer, but not as thick as a prison wall. They all deserved to be behind bars. The lot of them. And if they were behind the NT attacks, they deserved much worse.

She hated them. All of them. And just then she didn't have a great deal of sympathy for the weepy Mafioso's son.

That's better.

She loathed people who abused power. Big bullying small. Rich stamping all over the poor.

Bullies seeking out and attacking the weak.

As a kid she'd been picked on when she first went to secondary school; called all manner of names, mostly to do with the fact she always looked uncomfortable around other kids. 'Zombie bitch' was a favourite. She was pushed up and down the school's unforgiving concrete and brick corridors - and had her locker broken into, and her books ripped apart. She was relentlessly called names both to her face and in graffiti on the toilet walls. Her first year had been a waking hell.

And then, at the beginning of Year 8, she found the solution.

Fight them.

Bullies bully because they can. Because it's easy. If they come across an immovable object, they steer round it and pick on someone else.

It was a Tuesday breaktime. She had been walking on her own across the playground to a favourite spot of hers in the far corner. Almost there she'd been pushed from behind. A push became a shove, which turned into a fight. Normally she'd have run away, but this time she was stuck. She had been forced into a corner by a girl two years older than her, and ten centimetres taller. She was caged. Locked in. There was nowhere to go.

Fingernails scratched exposed flesh; knees were raised; forearms bitten. There was spitting, yanking of hair and, eventually, a punch: her fist to Julie Barne's chest.

And the red mist had come down for the first time. One minute she was fighting for her life, the next she was all focus.

There were other kids in the corner of the playground and, just before she'd punched the girl, she caught a glimpse of a teacher jogging across the tarmac. But they were peripheral. A blur. Julie Barne was coming in for the kill. She held a fist up high. Snot dripping from her nose, her lips apart making a sound like an air-raid siren, her eyes full of destruction.

Sam's energy, which spiked like something she'd never experienced before, coalesced. Whilst the girl was all arms, winding up her fists, Sam had perfect clarity.

She jabbed violently with a straight arm, sensing speed was everything. She learnt later in a physics lesson that the velocity of impact is vastly more important than the weight of the moving object. That's how rounds from a rifle pick you up and hurl you backwards when they hit you in the chest.

And she was fast. *Very fast.*

She hit Julie Barne just to the left of her sternum, nipple height. The girl was 14 and had proper boobs. So Sam found some flesh before smacking her rib cage. The speed of the punch was exacerbated by the fact Julie Barne was coming forward, and it helped that Sam had her back against the wall and could use it to lever more power.

There was a *crunch.*

And a cry.

And the world stopped.

Julie Barne collapsed in a pile, her heart stopping as her eyes opened wide with disbelief. She pulled her hands to her chest and began to pant. Sam, who had broken two fingers, held her scream. Everyone else stood stock still, apart from the teacher who'd arrived too late to stop the punch and whose attention was immediately focused on the coughing and gasping child, writhing on the floor.

Sam's red mist dissipated as quickly as it had arrived. Ignoring the teacher's shouts, she stepped over the girl on the tarmac and walked home.

Julie Barne's heart had only stopped temporarily and, other than a broken rib and severe bruising, she fixed quick enough; she was given an afternoon detention for taking part in a fight. Sam had her fingers bandaged together at the local hospital and when she returned to school the next day was suspended for a week for throwing a punch.

She'd thought that that was tough. But didn't complain. It was behind her and she moved on.

But she didn't forget the lesson. Julie Barne and her cronies never touched her again. In fact they walked on the other side of the corridor whenever she was around. Sam didn't take any particular pleasure from that, but, in a way, she was glad the girl had taught her a life lesson. *Fight or flight.* If you can't run away from it, you have to fight it. And since that day in the playground, she knew the red mist was a friend of hers.

Mostly.

But she wasn't Giorgio. This was his fight. He'd need to deal with it his own way and in his own time. Giorgio had got her into the Mafia's compound. He'd done his bit. The wedding of the year wasn't her war.

'You're right, Giorgio. I shouldn't be encouraging you. You and Gareth must do what you think is right. I've said my piece. Now, do you mind if we walk to the perimeter? I'd like to see how big your dad's place really is.'

They'd made it to the line of trees. And she'd been right. The fence was state-of-the-art, with movement sensors and cameras on tall masts. With watchers looking on she tried not to pay too much interest, but she needn't have bothered. Gareth had sobered up a bit and was taking more interest in the fence than she was.

'Wow. This is something else, Giorgio. You dad likes to keep people out.'

Giorgio was caressing the fence. With his hand gripping the mesh he looked back from where they'd come. Sam followed his gaze. The house and marquee looked small from this distance.

'You are right, Sam. I must do something about this. I must.' He still had a hand on the fence

Sam touched his arm.

'Sleep on it, Giorgio. You should never make a decision late at night. Have a chat with Gareth in the morning. And then speak to your dad if you still feel that way inclined.'

Gareth reached for Giorgio's hand.

'That's good advice, Giorgio. And I'm with you whatever you decide.'

And that had been that. The deed had been put off until tomorrow.

Likewise, Sam. There really hadn't been an appropriate time for her to confront Andrea Placido. To press him and gauge his reaction. He'd always been talking to someone. And she'd been distracted. The timing just hadn't seemed right.

She knew she would face up to the bully. Tomorrow. At the wedding. When there were more people about, other than just family.

She had managed to scout out the house. She'd snuck into many of the downstairs rooms and three or four upstairs. There were two studies. Sam assumed a his and a hers. The more masculine one, with red wallpaper and a boar's head on the wall, was full of opulent hardwood furniture and some very fine pictures. An ornate desk carried a couple of computer screens and there were two antique filing cabinets.

But that was all for tomorrow.

What she needed to do now was catch up on anything Frank had sent her, and then get some sleep.

She wiped the toothpaste from the corner of her mouth, had a pee and then, with her phone in her hand, plonked herself on the centre of the bed.

There was one new email. From Frank. It included an attachment; the translation of Viktor Molnár's August calendar. Sam read it. Most of it concerned excursions to the beach and trips to the local towns. Frank had highlighted two entries which were less ordinary.

The first was: 15 August. 7.15. Supper with AP and FD.

AP? Andrea Placido? Could be? But who was FD?

The second was a three-day block, the appointment framed between two arrows: 19 to 21 August.

Viktor. Trip to CH.

Where did Viktor Molnár go between 19 and 21 August?

CH?

CH could be any forename and surname.

Or Chiaravelle, a beautiful mountain town they'd driven through this morning? Maybe Viktor and his wife had left the children home alone and taken a car to a hotel in Chiaravelle?

Or …

CH, as in Switzerland?

Libya, Eritrea, Italy, *Switzerland* and Sweden.

Five countries that had yet to be subject to an NT terror attack. Libya and Eritrea had Italian history. Switzerland and Sweden, whilst neutral by nature, were not. If Viktor Molnár, and by association Andrea Placido, had business in Switzerland, why not make them a special case? Leave them clear of carnage?

And Sweden?

Sam thought she was clutching at straws.

Nonetheless.

She pressed 'Reply' to Frank's email.

Hi Frank.

Thanks. Can you check the movement of Viktor Molnár from any southern Italian airport to any airport in Switzerland over the period 19 - 21 August. And, if he did travel, could you see if you could piece together an itinerary?

S xxx

She pressed 'Send'. And then absently stared at the wall in front of her. Green striped wallpaper. Velvet and satin. *Tasteful.* In the middle of the wall there was a picture of a sunset over a sea - oil or acrylic. In the distance on the horizon was a pair of islands, volcano shaped. Sam reckoned they were the Aeolian islands, which included the charismatic Stromboli - still an active volcano; a cone of cold magma sticking out of the sea. She'd spent a long weekend in Sicily after she'd finished recruit training. Most of the platoon had buggered off to Ibiza and Benidorm for a week of sunshine and Sangria. She and a pal had flown to Palermo and spent the week hiking along the north Sicilian coast. They'd camped one night high on a cliff. They'd spent ages with a pair binos and a rubbish map trying to work out if the speck in the distance was Stromboli. They'd been none the wiser in the morning when the sun and haze had obscured any distant views.

She reckoned the person who had painted the canvas on the far wall had taken liberties with their artistic licence.

But it was a lovely picture of ...

... *an active volcano.*

How appropriate.

She needed to get some sleep.

Something told her tomorrow was going to be a bit of a day.

Chapter 14

Headquarters SIS, Vauxhall, London

The lift door to the fifth floor opened. Ahead of her was the familiar set of three wooden commemoration boards set side by side. They were ornately framed, with the title carved on the first board, inlaid with gold leaf: *To The Memory Of Those Members of The Secret Service Bureau Who Gave Their Lives In Service Of Their Country.*

Jane had stopped by the boards every morning since she started working on the fifth floor. There were 137 names on the three boards. The first was recorded in 1915, six years after the formation of SIS's founding parent - the Secret Service Bureau - which was set up by the Admiralty to collect intelligence primarily on the expansion of the Imperial German Government. Most of the names were concentrated between 1939 and 1945 when the Special Operations Executive (SOE) sent officers abroad to spy on German units and link with the French Resistance. In that period 12 of those killed were women. The last entry on the third board was dated 2017. A case officer killed by a rogue Afghan policeman who was meant to be providing security cover for a Provincial governor. The governor had been leaving a mosque in Jalalabad having completed consultations with the local Taliban. The case officer was killed along with the politician, a US Army officer and four others.

Even though it was still dark outside and had only just turned 6.00 am, Jane paused by the boards as was her ritual. She picked out a name. Jacob Naseby: killed on the 4th March 1966 in Oman. The board gave no other details, but Jane suspected Jacob Naseby was working alongside the British-supported Sultanate against the Dhofar Liberation Front (DLF), possibly running agents who worked within the DLF. From a recess in Jane's mind she remembered a little of the history. The DLF, who were funded and equipped by Russia, Iraq and China, attacked government positions and oil installations. Anyone in those locations would have been, for them, a legitimate target. It was a classic 'hit and run' insurgency, and effective up to a point. The civil war had lasted 14 years and Jacob Naseby was one of 1,500 people, from both sides of the conflict, who had been killed.

Jane had been under fire herself, three times. The first was in Iraq in 2006. She was working in a multi-agency team in Basra, supporting Operation SINBAD, the UK military's purge of the militia from the city. She was running three agents, all of whom had links to the militia: a shopkeeper, a teacher and a cleric. She had arranged to meet the cleric after prayers and was being escorted to a drop-off point short of the mosque when the Army patrol was attacked. The lead vehicle had been hit by a rocket-propelled grenade. Her vehicle, a Land Rover Snatch fitted with outdated armour and with a soldier on 'top-cover', his head and torso sticking out of the roof, had been sprayed with machine gun fire. The vehicle's armour had stopped and slowed some of the bullets. She and the two soldiers sitting in the back had been lucky; none of them were hit. Unfortunately the soldier on top-cover took two rounds to the head.

He'd fallen into the back of the vehicle, his face, which was no longer recognisable, landed on her lap.

She knew immediately he was dead.

The commander of the patrol had acted quickly and effectively. The soldiers had exited the vehicles, returned fire and the enemy had been 'suppressed'. Air support was in the sky within minutes. And a second patrol with medical backup arrived a few minutes later, whisking her and her blood-drenched cotton trousers back to the relative safety of the camp.

She'd never got the blood out of her slacks. And she had never thrown them away. They still hung on the right hand hanger in her wardrobe, fawn with brown patches above the knees, covered in one of those opaque plastic suit covers. Protected. Safe. Out of sight.

But never far from her consciousness.

She'd finished her tour and come home. Jacob Naseby hadn't. Nor had their top-cover soldier.

She touched the gold-leafed name and said a quick prayer to a God who was unknown to her. And then made her way to her office.

The open-plan main office was awake. She did a head count. There were seven of them in. Eight more and she'd have a full team. She needed them. All of them. Because, after a two day hiatus, someone had pressed the play button. And the result was more chaos than she thought was possible.

She pushed her door open and the lights came on by themselves. She was de-coated and sitting at her desk a few seconds later, her fingers working the keyboard. As her machine skipped its way through the various security protocols, she reached for the TV remote and turned on the BBC news channel. Unsurprisingly it led with the latest 'neo-terrorism' attacks.

Ricin.

It started yesterday afternoon in France. The numbers weren't clear yet, but the *Gendarmerie* were currently investigating 171 separate cases of the delivery of ricin, or a ricin lookalike substance, to random addresses across France. All of the envelopes were the same: off-white and personal letter-sized, addressed with a typed sticker. Apart from a first-class stamp, franked from one of five different towns and cities in the country's southeast corner, the envelopes were unmarked. Inside each envelope was a single sheet of A4 paper, folded on itself three times. On the paper was a childlike drawing of a hangman, with the word '*Huer!*' scribbled next to the drawing.

Contained within the folds of the sheet was a white powder weighing about 100 milligrams, although, like the addressing and the drawing, there didn't seem to be any rigour in measuring the amount of powder. Current thinking was whoever had sent the letters had done it in a rush.

So far the *Gendarmerie* had only confirmed five positive cases of ricin. The rest tested had all been common flour. But that didn't matter. The effect was the same as if all 171 envelopes had contained the poison. The country was in meltdown within three hours. Social media had worked at lightning speed, and was far quicker than conventional TV and radio. The symptoms of ricin poisoning were all that people were talking about. The questions, endless. Do you have to swallow it? Can it enter your bloodstream through your eyes? How much of the substance is fatal?

Soon everyone was a ricin expert.

It comes from ground castor beans. It's a toxin that attacks your ability to make a certain protein. It causes haemorrhaging, vomiting and diarrhoea; fever, difficulty in breathing and rashes. It can lay dormant for days. You only need to inhale a quarter of a teaspoonful for it to kill you.

There was no antidote.

And *Huer!* translates to 'Boo!'.

The spread of fear was exacerbated by the fact there didn't seem to be any pattern to those targeted. This wasn't a major political statement, or an attack on any one stratum or segment of society. Shopkeepers, grandparents and teenage girls were addressees; Catholics, Muslims and atheists.

If Michelle from down the road had been sent an envelope, then I might be next. And, if not an envelope full of deadly ricin, then what? Arson of a tower block? Poison in a reservoir? A bomb in a football stadium? Machine guns in the market square?

Where would the terrorists strike next?

The answer to that question was: the UK.

Jane had left the office at half-past-midnight last night. She'd got to bed an hour later, having had two pieces of toast and Marmite for supper. She'd been woken by the duty officer three hours later. Bristol's main sorting office had picked up a similar pattern to that in France. This time it was light-brown manila envelopes. They had 47 of them, all similarly addressed. The night-time manager had pulled the sorting staff off the floor and called the police. Within an hour Birmingham had done the same. The Post Office couldn't confirm if other regional sorting offices had been quite so vigilant.

It wasn't just the UK. Unfortunately Bielefeld's *Deutsche Post* main sorting centre had not been alive to a cross-continent threat. There was already one report of a ricin-type letter having been opened in a small village in the *Teutoburg Wald*. Similar incidences were being reported in Spain and Norway. And nobody yet knew whether or not the threat was restricted to Europe.

Whilst this chaos was the first reason Jane had been called in, there had been a second major alert. Two hours ago The Service had uncovered a threat against 'a major public figure'. The threat was: Gold; Imminent, which meant the source was immutable and the timing within the next seven days. The least clear piece of intelligence was who the 'major public figure' might be. The term had no official definition. It could be a member of the Royal Family, a politician or a celebrity. The cast list was one of thousands.

SIS was always interested in threats to major public figures, even though it may look like a domestic issue. Public figures travelled. The two young princes and their wives were always representing The Queen abroad. Other than a few days a year, there was always a member of the Cabinet overseas. And, to pick one of hundreds, Daniel Craig was filming the latest 007 movie in the Caribbean. Once abroad, it was SIS's responsibility, along with their traveling CPOs (close protection officers) and bodyguards, to make sure the great and the good were tucked safely in their beds at night.

The threat was: Gold; Imminent. The target was a major public figure. And the location was worldwide.

Jane had work to do.

She was just about to open the email tab when her phone rang. It was Langley. The Deputy Director.

What?

She picked up the receiver.

'Linden? How did you know I was in?'

'It was a stab in the dark - no pun intended. I guess the streetlights are still on where you are?'

Jane looked unnecessarily to the window. It was still as dark as night. Even though dawn was on its way, it was being stalled by a thick duvet of cloud.

'Yes. It must be dark with you too? Shouldn't you be at home?'

'Ordinarily I'd be dead to the world. A couple of beers short of a hangover after the Redskins match.'

'Did they win?'

'Nope. But that didn't stop a couple of us celebrating anyway.'

The Deputy Director, Linden Rickenbacker, had that wonderful East Coast accent; soft and lyrical, but strong. He always sounded intelligent and thoughtful.

That's because he was.

Enough.

'Have there been any ricin attacks yet in your neck of the woods?' She asked.

'I'm sorry to say, yes. West Coast. California and Washington State. Five cases. We have no idea what the size of the problem is, yet. The FBI are expecting a deluge. It's all over the news. People are going crazy here.'

Likewise.

But she guessed that's probably not why he phoned. There was something else.

'But that's not why you phoned?'

'No. We have intel pointing to a possible assassination attempt on our VP.'

Jane didn't reply immediately. The Vice President was visiting the UK later today to discuss the President's abandonment of the 1987 INF Nuclear Weapons Treaty with the Prime Minister. Was the DD's intelligence and The Service's threat assessment one of the same thing?

It's possible?

'The VP's coming here today.'

'Correct.'

'Does your intelligence point to an attack on foreign soil?'

'Not explicitly. Nor does it necessarily point to the VP. But the indications are strong.'

'We have a Gold; Imminent; major public figure, threat from MI5. It could be one of the same?'

The Deputy Director didn't reply straight away.

'That's odd,' he said after a couple of seconds.

'It is. But why do you say that?' Jane asked.

'Isn't it just a bit too obvious? Both of us getting the same intel at the same time.'

Jane's concentration was momentarily broken. Claire had come into the office carrying a mug of coffee. Jane smiled and nodded her approval.

'Wait, Linden, please.' Jane took the phone away from her face.

'Thanks, Claire. Can you get the whole team together as soon as they are in, please? And then come and get me?'

Claire placed the mug on Jane's desk.

'Sure.' And then she was off.

Jane re-engaged Linden.

'Since the ferry attack, and after the brief hiatus, everything seems to have been a bit of a rush. The ricin letters seem loosely organised and haphazard. And you can't pull off a successful attack on a senior political target without a great deal of planning.'

'No. And the VP's visit is pretty impromptu. The President only announced his plan to drop the treaty three days ago. There can't have been enough time to plan anything?'

'What are they playing at?'

'I don't know, Jane. I really don't.'

Villa San Francesco, Serrastretta, Calabria, Italy

Sam's plan was straightforward and not without risk. Assuming Giorgio went ahead with the wedding, and she was reasonably sure that would happen no matter what he'd said last night, she would stay away from the chapel during the service and see if she could find something incriminating in Andrea Placido's study. If nothing came from that, and supposing she hadn't been smothered by a couple of Italian thugs and thrown in the cellar, she'd confront Giorgio's father. Face to face. Have it out.

Light the blue touch paper ...

It was, as were most of her plans, ambitious and designed without a great deal of rigour. But she reckoned that the last thing Andrea Placido would want to do on his son's wedding day was make a huge scene. So she'd ask a few questions, like, 'Why did you sell Viktor Molnár a villa for one euro? And what have you asked for in return?', and, 'What do you know about four Eritrean terrorists entering Italy from Tunis via Gioia Tauro, a container port you run, albeit illicitly?'.

That should be enough to get a reaction ... and for her to get thrown off the premises. Or worse.

The ceremony was planned for 11.00 am; about an hour and a half's time. She'd not seen either Gareth or Giorgio at breakfast - they were clearly late risers - and so she'd taken herself outside into the beautiful grounds that were being gently bathed in late autumn, Italian sunshine.

The preparations for the wedding had taken on a whole new dimension since last night. Florists and caterers mingled with family and newly arriving guests. Suits were the order of the day and some of the wives/girlfriends looked gorgeous in their pastel dresses and matching hats. The marquee, which she hadn't been able to appreciate in the dark last night, was something out of the early pages of *Hello* magazine. She didn't know if she were breaking protocol as she wandered in and around the marquee, popping into the other smaller tents and poking around the cocktail bar and ice cream stand at the swimming pool - 'soaking up the indulgence'. Sam thought there were a lot of flowers inside the house. Outside there was a nursery's worth.

The marquee poles were wrapped in gold and pine-green ribbon and further decorated with hanging baskets of yellow and cream. Each table (Sam had counted: there was seating for 180 guests) had its own floral table centre, heavy solid silver cutlery, and white porcelain china. In remembrance of her mum she lifted a plate and checked the label: Villeroy & Boch; gold and green rimmed with a small bowl of fruit motif in the centre of each plate. Perfect for an autumn reception.

At one end of the marquee was a dance floor, a 'top-table', which was even more lavishly decorated than those in the not quite so expensive seats, and a five-tiered wedding cake that must have taken a shortening of pastry chefs to bake. Sam wasn't sure if that was the right collective noun, but it work for her.

She stopped by one of the tables and picked up a programme. The white card was tastefully decorated, the letters proclaiming the marriage of Giorgio Placido to Sofia Pacelli embossed in gold. Inside was in Italian; much of what she scanned was a guess. There was a page dedicated to a nine-course menu - the word *pasta* required no translation, a programme of events, and, at the back, a list of … she ran her eyes over three pages … 177 names. She found hers: *Miss Green*, in English.

How?

Reprinting the programmes overnight with her name included must have cost a shed-load of cash and given the printers palpitations. Unless they were psychic?

She put the programme on the table and straightened her back. Her stomach was niggling, she guessed after the fall from the branch in Villa Feradina. And the make-do stitching in her leg was pulling with an associated pain. But at least her face was no longer telling her off. The bruising wasn't completely gone so she did look a little like she'd come off the set of *Halloween*. But, thankfully, the pain was negligible providing she didn't poke it.

In daylight the outside of house looked as fabulous as the inside; red and purple bougainvillea contrasting with the white render. It was a fairy tale setting, made more colourful by the guests who were continuing to arrive. The last wedding Sam had attended was Uncle Pete's daughter's. She and her fiancé were married in the local registry office and they all celebrated with a slap up meal at the local Toby Carvery. Sam fondly remembered the oversized Yorkshire puddings.

Money wasn't an issue here. This wedding was almost certainly being unobligingly financed by Calabria's shopkeepers, and most of Italy's addicts. Uncle Pete's kid and her bloke paid for their meagre reception on his mechanic's and her teaching assistant's salary.

Chalk and cheese.

Off to one side, close to the house, was a long, white-cloth covered table. It was attended by a couple of attractive female *baristas*. They were all in black and white with blouses that could do with a button fastened. They all had great teeth and were all armed with a smile as wide as their ears. And they were serving coffee and pastries, which, having finished breakfast a couple of hours ago, seemed to Sam like a remarkably good idea.

There was a small queue, which she joined. The guests were typically Italian, tanned and immaculately dressed, with pleat-edges and trouser creases that would cut your hand. She was taller than most of them, both the men and the women. They were of a mould ...

... except one.

At the end of the long table was a paler, tall man wearing an expensive cream suit complemented by tan and cream brogues; peeking out from the suit's top pocket was a pink and white polka dot silk hanky. He wore a girl-pink shirt, with the collar cut back and double cuffs that stuck out of the suit's sleeves by just the right amount. She couldn't make out the cufflinks from this distance. To finish off, he wore a red, green and cream paisley tie. If he hadn't been attending a lavish wedding in Calabria he would not have looked out of place at a classy restaurant in Havana, or wandering down the boardwalk along Ocean Drive.

Sam reckoned he was northern European; possibly British. He had Sting's angular features and wispy, blonde hair. She reckoned he was six-two and was a slight, maybe 80 kilogrammes. And early forties.

Rich, well dressed and *attractive.*

All in all, a bit of a catch. She glanced down at her recent red dress purchase and removed a speck of imaginary dust from just above her left boob - and she ran her tongue over her teeth.

Stop it.

Not wholly for childbearing reasons, she couldn't keep her eyes off ... *Charlie.* That was a good name for him, if he were English. Charlie Faversham.

He was ... different.

What was it?

He was confident, for sure; it oozed out of him as he stood by the pastries - completely at ease with the opulence of his surroundings.

Particular?

Yes.

It was the way he was going about choosing whether or not to take a small, delicate pain au chocolat, or a cream-filled puff pastry delight that was decorated with a tantalising touch of red conserve - which was screaming to be licked. Coffee in one hand, he used his other to point delicately at his choices.

Very particular.

He wasn't picking up each pastry and checking it, but he was studying them, head on one side. To Sam, it looked like quite a complex decision-making process.

Then he said something to himself, and smiled ... another worldly, sardonic smile? As though he'd selected a villain from a police line-up. He chose the puff pastry, lifting it to his mouth before stopping short of taking a bite. The movement was almost theatrical.

He'd noticed something.

What?

Next to the array of cakes were a stack of small plates, a line of cake forks and napkins. He moved to his left a touch so that he was standing directly in front of the cutlery. He looked quizzically at the forks, and then his bottom lip protruded slightly.

Sam's view was momentarily blocked by an Italian couple. She was so entranced by Charlie she'd stepped out of line so she could watch the scene unfold.

He'd put his coffee down and, with his now free hand, was moving the handles of a couple of forks so that they were perfectly in line. He stood back and checked his handy work. No, that wasn't good enough. He moved another. But then his whole world was sent into a spiral as another guest helped himself to a plate and a fork, knocking a couple of others out of place. Sam sensed Charlie's body tense as the forks were nudged by the man. He grimaced, shook his head in small movements, snatched his coffee and briskly walked off.

'*Signora, del caffè?*'

Sam's concentration was broken. She smiled at the young woman with the cleavage, who was holding a silver coffee pot.

'*Sì, grazie*'.

As she waited for it to be poured, she checked on Charlie. He was now standing by a dinner table. He had the programme in his hand and was reading it intently.

Sam helped herself to a pain au chocolat and quickly pulled herself away from the forks for fear that she might spend the next half an hour finishing the job Charlie had started.

Enough.

The pain au chocolat was gone in a single mouthful and, with coffee in hand, she made her way across a short piece of lawn, between a gap in a flower bed and onto the gravel path that surrounded the house. Her new black flatties, which were already rubbing, scrunched on the small pebbles all the way to the last window of the bottom floor.

The man's study.

Sam nonchalantly stared out across the spectacle that was the wedding, sipping her coffee. And just as nonchalantly she turned her head towards the study window.

What the ...?

The study was busy. And it wasn't a nice busy.

Giorgio and his father were having a very animated conversation across the massive desk that dominated the room. The windows were well insulated - she couldn't hear a word - but it was clear Giorgio's father was not happy. There was pointing and banging on the table. Giorgio was shaking his head, he turned, and then turned back again. He said something that looked like a shout, and that stopped his father in his tracks.

His father regained his composure, stood to full height and then …

'Sam, Sam!'

It was Gareth's voice off to her right, getting louder as he galloped towards her.

And to his *right, looking on?*

Charlie. With an open wedding programme in hand. And an intense expression.

She dismissed him.

'What?'

Gareth was on her now, slightly out of breath.

'Giorgio's in with his dad. The door's slightly ajar. There's a helluva argument. I'm really worried. You've got to come!'

Gareth had taken Sam's hand and was dragging her towards the doors in the centre of the house. Sam spilt her coffee, it missed her dress but splashed her shoes.

Shit.

The pair of them dodged Charlie, who had his mouth open in a scowl as if he were about to say something, but they had passed him before he had chance.

Sam was now jogging to keep up with Gareth.

Left and left again. Into the house. It flashed by. Wooden parquet flooring, with a red woollen runner. A semi-circular walnut table with its diameter lying flat against the wall - adorned with silver picture frames. A beautiful impressionist painting. It looked old; could well be early last century. Original. Expensive.

Then the study door. Which was, as Gareth had promised, slightly ajar.

Two men screaming. An old and a young voice. It was another language to Sam.

Gareth poked his head round the door; a lover anxious for his love.

This wasn't her fight. Sam felt like a carrot in a fruit salad.

His head was back out now; red faced.

'He's just slapped him! His dad's gone mad! I'm going in!' A shout delivered as a whisper.

Sam tried to stop him, but it was half-hearted. The cavalry had charged. Tunics and lances. It was probably for the best. He was in, the door still half-closed.

It was her turn to listen. She moved to the gap, but didn't enter the fray.

'Chi è questo?' The older voice.

'Il mio amante, Gareth, lui è Inglese.' The younger voice.

'Tu! ... Te l'avevo detto!' Older, again - a shout.

Then quiet – the stillness laced with anticipation. Anger and desperation seeped out through the gap between the door and frame. There was shuffling, a drawer opening, and then absolute silence. Broken by ...

'No, padre!' A scream. Giorgio - despair now, not anger.

Nothing.

Sam felt the tension. Sensed the heartbeats.

'*Per favore, per favore, padre!*' The plea was almost impossible to hear. Giorgio's words mixing with tears.

She'd had enough. An adult was needed in the room.

Sam pushed the door wide open with her foot just as Giorgio's father pulled the trigger of the M9A3 Beretta. This noise of the 9mm round leaving the grey barrel was deadened by a silver silencer; but the noise was still as loud as someone dropping a tray of rocks onto the wooden floor. Sam had always thought that 'silencer' definitely broke the trades' description act.

Gareth's body, which was half-turning away from the shot, arched backwards as the round hit him in the rib cage, the back of his suit jacket flicking high as the exiting bullet tore a hole through the material. His feet briefly lifted off the ground before his body collapsed to the floor. Both she and Giorgio screamed at the same time. Giorgio's was a high-pitched wail of unknown origin; Sam's an extended, 'Nooo!'.

She was about to rush forward into the melee to do something that had yet to form as an idea in her brain, when she was stopped abruptly by a grabbing hand.

Caught off balance, she turned her head.

You!?

It was Charlie. He had hold of her arm and was pulling her away from the door.

'You don't want to go in there, Sam. It's not your business, is it?'

What? Who the …?

She looked back to the room. Gareth was a crumpled suit on the floor. Giorgio had his head in his hands, caught between screaming out his grief and dropping to his knees.

Andrea Placido was stood pistol in hand. His red face scrunched in anger, his eyes betraying his guilt.

A second later Sam was now a metre from the study door and being dragged back towards the exit to the garden.

But they didn't make it that far. Charlie opened a new door on the left. He launched her into the room, but held her arm tight - she lost her footing and was about to fall when he stopped her from toppling over. She caught a glance at those immaculate pink cuffs - emerging from the cream suit. Cufflinks. Gold with enamel inlay. A multi-petalled white flower, with a yellow centre. Almost too small to make out.

Who is this man?

She knew nothing. *Nothing!* Other than he was remarkably strong for his frame.

They were in a sitting room of sorts. Sofas, chairs, a drinks cabinet … a crazy man in a cream suit.

'So.' It was him again. 'You're. Sam. Green. *The* Sam Green? I think so. Don't you?'

His face was animated. It was like watching a cartoon character. His voice rose and fell - pausing for effect. It was Saturday night amdram.

Her brain spun. Gareth was dead. Probably. *How does that happen?* She was in the clutches of a stranger who thought he knew who she was.

None of this makes sense.

'Who are you?' She was fed up with not knowing with whom she was dealing.

'Me? Ahh. Well. That's a bit of a puzzle. Isn't it?' That face again. That tone. Like a primary school teacher speaking to a child who's about to be sent to the naughty corner.

Then a smile. Sardonic. *Definitely.* Crazy. *For sure.*

All of a sudden, Sam didn't feel so good. The man had control. Complete control. Outside of that tight perimeter she was in the Mafia's den. Surrounded by the enemy, And no good was going to come of it.

There was movement outside in the corridor. Heavy shoes on the carpet. Male voices. Then a female one, raised. In anger. Now the voice was screaming.

A slap across her face.

Oi! What the ... !

'I'm here, Sam.' The crazy man, Charlie. But not Charlie. *Definitely not a Charlie.* Not now. 'Don't worry about what's going on out there. This is about you ...' He still had the programme in his spare hand. He tapped it on her forehead. More theatrics. '... and me.' That smile again. Perfect teeth.

No, it's not.

The red mist came on cue. Focus was all she had. She raised her knee with a ferocity that surprised even her. As her knee connected with his groin, not-Charlie lost his smile, his mouth puckering, his eyes opening wide.

As he crumpled, letting go of Sam's arm, she clenched a fist and jabbed upwards towards his chin. It was another Julie Barne. She was back in the playground, escaping the bully.

There was a connection. Bone on bone.

Fuck, that hurt.

Crazy man not-Charlie fell backwards, his arms out wide. Sam turned.

Then she momentarily stopped. He was on the floor. Writhing and groaning. She reached for the guest list in his hand. And was out of the door a second later.

She looked right. There were men. Not guests. Too casually dressed. And then there was a woman. She had just come out of the study, her arms clinging to Giorgio. Behind them was Andrea Placido. The pistol was gone.

Giorgio, whose face was a waterfall of tears, caught Sam's gaze.

'Go! Go!' There was no noise accompanying the shout; just a shaking of his head. A soundless warning. A secret exchange between him and her.

Go! Go!

There was nothing she could do. If Gareth wasn't dead, he would be soon. The Mafia would see to that. His body in a concrete block, or at the bottom of the ocean with dumbbells around his ankles. Giorgio was being consoled by his mother. He was broken. It was over. Sam imagined him being sorted, spruced and still making the ceremony. His father would say his tears were ones of joy.

The door opened behind her.

It was the crazy man. Blood - and a grin. He wiped his mouth on his sleeve, which was now cream and smeared red. Not a bad colour combination.

The chase was on.

Sam knew her way round the house. And she was quick. Quicker than crazy man, not-Charlie. She played for time. Doubled back. Hid. Ran. Just a couple of minutes or so. But enough to give her a head start on the final dash.

The entrance hall.

It was big. Squash court sized. There were guests. And staff. Drinks. Champagne. And a butler - Italian style. He was taking bags and the odd over-jacket. It may be warm to a Brit, but it was autumn to the locals. Vests and jackets.

There was a door leading to a ... cloakroom? Sam saw a chance.

The butler was some feet from the door. He was helping an Italian couple with their wedding presents. There was a table festooned with them across the hall.

Sam waited. He was heading that way, overburdened with gifts.

She darted into the cloakroom.

Jackets. Male ones. Pockets.

Keys.

The first set was a huge bunch. House keys and everything. No good.

Next. Two keys and a leather fob, with a badge.

Piaggio.

Scooter.

Perfect.

The butler burst in.

'*Che cazzo?!*'

Sam didn't need to translate.

She pushed past him.

'*Scusa.*'

And she was out. Quickly, through the guests and onto the gravel courtyard.

Stop.

There were cars everywhere. She spotted five Maseratis.

And, no …

Wait.

There was a bike, scooter. *Over there.*

Two. And one to her left. They were an odd choice for a wedding reception? How Italian.

And there.

A back box above the rear wheel with the Piaggio motif. Thirty metres away, under the trees.

She ran, stuffing the programme down her bra as she did.

Shit. It was a three wheeler; an MP3. Two small wheels at the front. She'd seen commuters use them in London. They were all the rage.

Think.

She put the key in, turned it, releasing the handlebar lock. She tried to push it off its kickstand. It wouldn't move. She tried again. Nothing.

Sam glanced behind.

Shit.

Crazy man, not-Charlie, in the cream and red suit. On the steps. Looking.

Think!

There was a silver handle sticking out from the body of the front of the bike, between where her legs should be.

What's that?

A handbrake?

She forced it down - it fitted into a recess in the coachwork. She pushed the bike forward, it rocked, dropped, and it was free.

On it.

She glanced behind. He'd seen her. He was running.

Think. She'd driven a moped illegally in Spain as a 15 year old kid. Borrowed from a Spanish lad who had been trying to get in her knickers.

To start.

Brake on the handlebars!

Pull that, and press the start button.

Which is ...?

Shit! Where is it?

There!

The MP3 turned over as not-Charlie put his hand on her shoulder. She twisted the grip and the 300cc engine shot forward ... but she remained still, pivoting sideward and backwards off the bike, which twisted and fell to the floor, its motor still running.

She was on the floor; not-Charlie was standing over her. A foot on her left shoulder - the one that pops out of its joint unnecessarily and makes her pass out.

'Hello again, Sam Green. Are you in a rush somewhere?' That look on his face again. Distorted. A touch of blood. But happy. A smile.

Crazy.

Who are you?

A car pulled up. A big Audi.

Avant. A6. All Road. 440 bhp. She couldn't stop herself.

Not-Charlie noticed; his face a smudge of blood and flesh. His immaculate suit no longer ready for the party. He'd have to get it changed. He couldn't go to the wedding like that.

A male guest got out of the car.

'*Cosa sta succedendo qui?*'

She had no idea.

'*Solo qualche problema locale.*' Not-Charlie replied.

Still no idea.

The guest looks confused. This wasn't right. It was an Italian thing. A woman being held down, attacked, by a man with a bloody face. That's not what we do. Not here.

'Help me. Please. *Signore. Per favore*' Sam pleads. And then she moaned. '*Signore. Per favore.*' She moaned some more. Tears came from nowhere.

'*Lasciala da sola!*' The Italian guest was stocky - and now indignant. His wife, wearing a pale hat with some feathers, came to join him. Sam sensed not-Charlie was confused. *He's used to being in control. Never questioned? It's his exacting way, or nothing. Not anyone else's'.*

The forks. Perfectly placed.

And then he lost it.

'Fuck off, Mussolini. This is my problem - and I'm dealing with it. Now ... *va via!*' Not-Charlie waved the Italian off with a hand, and then looked at Sam. 'These locals, you know ...'

He stopped mid-sentence.

What?

'*Lascia andare la ragazza.*'

Mussolini hadn't gone anywhere. He was right beside not-Charlie; he'd be breathing down his neck if he were tall enough. Sam moved her head to get a better view, but she couldn't see much, save the Italian with his hand and something metal on the small not-Charlies' back.

A weapon? Guests are obliged to come armed?

Not-Charlie lifted his hands to shoulder height. *Definitely a weapon.* Sam noticed the rattle of the MP3's engine still running a few feet from her.

'*Togliti il piede.*'

Nope. *Still no idea.*

Not-Charlie lifted his foot from Sam's shoulder. He backed off a little. The Italian man with the gun had the upper hand.

She didn't wait for any further conversation. She got up on her feet and ... *God this is heavy* ... lifted the MP3 into the upright.

And then she was off.

There's something about riding a bike without a helmet, and Sam wasn't sure she enjoyed the feeling. The MP3 was quick, and having two wheels at the front didn't stop it from leaning into the corners. She had no experience of riding a 300cc motorbike, but she'd watched them do it in the films.

Lean left. The bike turns left.

Up ... and lean right. The bike turns right.

Good.

She was five or six klicks from the house now - and she needed a plan. She should ride for half an hour and then ...

Shit!

Behind her. A matt black Bentley Continental GT.

And crazy man not-Charlie. There'd be blood on the leather seats. He wouldn't like that. Doubtless he'd have someone to clean it up.

He was right behind her!

She accelerated hard, the MP3 eager.

But so was the Bentley.

It was a huge car. Black, menacing - and quick.

She twisted, leant, turned, accelerated and leant some more. The Bentley was a match for her. On the short straights it came so close to her rear number plate, she had to shimmy the bike for it not to knock her off.

And then ...

A village!

Brake! Turn, Accelerate. The back end of the bike was trying its best to overtake the front; she had to put a foot down to stop it from falling over and throwing her onto the road..

A narrow passage.

The Bentley braked and spun in turn, a shower of small stones pelting a cat which hissed and leapt behind a bush.

Sam accelerated between two walls that were narrower than the width of the Bentley. She missed a set of stone steps, washing baskets and two small boys playing football in a tiny courtyard.

A junction.

She braked hard and put her feet down.

Breathe.

Ahead was another passage too small for the Bentley. It led to another road. To her left, the same; it also led to a road. To her right. A set of stone steps leading up to a low sandstone wall ... and a church.

Movement.

She glanced to her left again.

The end of the passage was now Bentley driver's door shaped. She couldn't make out the expression on not-Charlies' face. But she could make one up.

Crazy.

She looked right, turned the handlebars in the same direction and twisted the accelerator.

It looked easy in the films. She dropped the bike twice. And there were only 35 steps. But she got to the top in one piece and put her feet down in a small patio in front of the church. The views were far reaching - over the village and across to the hills on the other side of the valley.

And then she heard the unmistakable growl of a Bentley in a car park off to her left. He had followed her up on the road.

Sam looked around. The church was the end of a road. There were only two ways down. The steps - which would be the death of her - or through the car park, and a face-off with the crazy man in the Bentley.

Wait.

There was a gap in the wall to her right. A footpath into a vineyard. The gap between the vines big enough for a man.

She'd make it big enough for a woman on a trike.

Sam knew she closed her eyes as she accelerated through the gap in the wall, the fibreglass footplate of the scooter scraping against rock, a piece of faring being ripped off. And she knew she hardly had her eyes open as she navigated the vines, the odd thin branch slashing at her face and drawing blood from her arms.

But she kept the bike going. She knew the Bentley couldn't come this way, but not-Charlie was a resourceful adversary and crazy enough to try anything.

She pushed on …gently climbing all the way.

Slap! *Ouch.* Slap, slap! *Shit. Ouch.*

And then there was a break. And a stone wall. And a wooden gate.

She was over a kilometre from the church by now. She must be in the clear?

Stop.

Sam pulled the trike up to the wall, which was higher than its handlebars, stepped off and pulled it back onto its kickstand. She switched it off.

And collapsed in a heap on the grass next to the wall.

Breathe.

She was out of sight. There was a road on the other side of the wall. She had found some space ...

... for her mind to spin.

Gareth was dead. She'd brought him here.

Hadn't she?

To his death.

It was her idea ...

Breathe.

Why did this always happen? People close to her?

She was a plague. A menace.

Breathe.

But ...!

Breathe. Concentrate.

She took out the programme from the front of her dress and opened it up at the guest list. She scanned it.

Signor Bianchi, Signore Bianchi, ...

There were 174 guests prefixed with *Signor* and *Signore*. The 175th was a doctor: *Dottor Romano*.

And there were three with English titles. Miss S Green. Mr D Cassidy - Gareth had chosen a pseudonym and went for his grandmother's favourite singer.

And a Mr F Derwent.

With a cream suit, two-tone brogues and a pink shirt, sleeves sticking out the regulation length from the jacket.

The crazy man.

F?

F.

F for …?

Shit.

Sam shut her eyes as her world pressed in and started to disintegrate around her. Gareth was dead. Probably. Giorgio was now likely married to a woman he never wanted to wed.

And she had just come face to face with the man who persecuted her in her dreams?

She was sure of it.

F was for …

She couldn't finish the sentence.

But …

… she had to push through. To think positively. To overcome. There was too much at stake.

But …

... she was tired. Emotionally spent. And the man in her dreams now had a face. He would be there. Every night. Without fail.

But ...

... she knew what he looked like. She could paint a pixel-perfect photofit. And she had the Swiss registration of his matt black Bentley Continental GT.

Grave

Chapter 15

Martin took a final slurp of his coke, put the covered cup on the table, had a flash of conscience about plastic straws - which he disregarded almost immediately - and reached for the last of the fries he'd put in the top of the Quarter Pounder box. They were only warm to the touch, which irritated him. One of the problems with thin chips was they lost their heat quickly. It was a surface area thing. That's how radiators in cars worked. Lots of fins to dissipate the heat.

'We should get a move on.' He chirped. 'We don't want to miss the show.'

He was talking to his mate, Simon, who was absently stuffing the remains of a Big Mac into his mouth, whilst staring at a girl's arse as she made her way with a tray full of rubbish to the bin.

'Yeah, whatever.' Simon replied, still gawping at the girl's backside whilst chewing mindlessly.

Martin didn't quite get why he'd befriended a man with an insatiable appetite for fast food and even faster women. He guessed there was a gravitational pull between the two physics majors which had something to do with the fact that they both liked board games, real ale and classic cars. And they were both in the same halls of residence at Warwick University. His pal also liked women. A lot. There was nothing he wouldn't sleep with. Nothing. Martin wasn't so keen on that side of his pal.

Simon had driven them to London in his orange MGB; chrome bumpers and wire wheels, *please*. Nobody in their right mind drove the later version with rubber bumpers - MG having sold their soul to meet the US market's safety requirements - and Rostyle wheels. They both agreed with that.

He stood, put his and Simon's packaging on his tray and walked over to the bin. Simon was left finishing his own coke.

'Come on. We need to be outside the Foreign Office in 20 minutes. I want to see the whites of his eyes and hurl abuse so loud he can hear me above everyone else.'

The arrival of the US Vice President and a clear day in both of their lecture schedules had been a fluke. It was too good an opportunity to miss. A day off, a trip to the big smoke and a chance to shout loudly at a man who was half of an administration that was driving a Greyhound bus through the future of the planet. They'd have preferred an opportunity to throw eggs at the top man, but the Vice President was the next best thing.

Simon caught up with him as he squeezed past scores of tourists all queuing up for their lunch. A few seconds later they were out on Whitehall, a couple of hundred metres from King Charles Street, He had no idea how many protesters would be at the Foreign Office. All he did know was they'd be at least two.

'Hey!' Martin shouted. A man had hold of his arm; firmly but not so it hurt.

'Hi. Sorry I don't mean …', the man started to say something.

'Leave my friend alone. Got it!' Simon was in the man's face like a shot. He had his finger close to the man's nose. There was real intent in his eyes. It was a side to his pal Martin had not seen before.

As the man let go of Martin's arm, he noticed that, in his other hand the man was holding a banner of sorts: two tall wooden poles wrapped in a white plastic sheet.

'Sorry. I meant no harm. Look. Would you like to earn a little bit of cash?'

Never talk to strange men …

Martin was 20 years old, but his mother's maxim still rattled around his head.

'No. Thanks. Come on Simon, let's leave the weirdo behind.'

'Wait.' The man continued. As Martin had turned, the man had stayed on his shoulder, Simon's finger still close to the man's face. 'I couldn't help noticing that you're wearing anti-US badges. Are you going to the protest? The VP - coming in a few minutes?' The man was well spoken.

For some reason that stopped Martin.

'Yes? Why?'

Simon had dropped his finger and was looking quizzically at the man with the banner.

'I need you to do me a favour and I'm willing to pay handsomely for it.'

Martin was caught between sense and intrigue. Sense won. He turned again.

'Let's go, Simon.'

'Five grand. Cash.' The man blurted it out. 'All I need you to do is hold up this banner so the cameras get a look.'

'Five grand? Cash?' Simon had stopped. If Martin wasn't interested, he was.

'Yes. This is the banner. It says nothing illegal. Nothing inflammatory. In fact, you won't understand what it means, without some context. But those watching will.'

A red double-decker drove past. Martin caught sight of the latest advert running along the side. It read: *#enoughisenough - vote them out!*

'What's on the banner?' Martin was interested now.

Headquarters SIS, Vauxhall, London

The phone rang in his ear with the 'long tone' of an overseas mobile. Three times. Four. Five. Frank was starting to get worried.

'What?! What?' The speaker barked.

He wasn't worried anymore.

'Hi, Sam. Have you got five minutes?'

There was a noise Frank didn't recognise. It could have been a word. Or a grunt. He wasn't sure.

'Give me two minutes. I need a pee. I'll call you back.'

The phone went dead.

He had fifteen minutes of updates for Sam. He hoped she had something for him from the wedding. The Mafia/Italy link was the one he was pressing hardest with Jane and he wasn't sure he was getting very far. She hadn't been convinced by the connection. That both Viktor Molnár and the leader of the FFO had spookily used the exact same words; the first on a major TV speech, the second, in passing, to Sam acting as a Reuters journalist in the Caucasus mountains. Or Sam's link of the Hungarian PM to the 'Ndràngheta, via a holiday villa in Calabria. Or the conduit for the four terrorists from Eritrea via Gioia Touro.

He'd raised it at this morning's cabal. The focus of the meeting had been the threat against 'a major public figure', with eyes on the US VP's visit to meet with the Foreign Secretary in … he checked his screen … ten minutes time.

What had Jane said in reply?

'Check it out, Frank. Speak to Rome and Budapest and paint a better picture. Where did this come from?'

He'd replied, 'Sam'. To which there was the slightest of groans from around the room. There was no doubt (*was there?*) she was well respected in the building. But the events of two years ago, when she'd gone after the oligarch Sokolov having been explicitly instructed not to by all the senior hoods in the building, tainted that reputation. She was seen as a competent maverick. Very good at her job. But not to be trusted fully.

Frank trusted her. With his life.

The phone rang.

He connected.

'What have you got, Frank?'

She sounded tired. No, that wasn't right. *Wired.*

'You OK, Sam?'

There was a pause.

'No.'

Frank didn't know what to say. Sam was always under the cosh. There was always an issue, but she never said so in so many words. She always grinned and bore it.

The pause was uncomfortable.

'I need to get into the Embassy in Rome.' Frank heard an exhalation of breath bordering on a sigh. Then she continued. 'I've got some photofitting to do.' Sam was quiet, and slow. It was as though she was concentrating on every word.

'Where are you? And have you got transport?' Frank asked.

There was another pause.

'This is … bigger than the Mafia, Frank.'

Sensing what was coming was key he dabbed at his middle screen and Cynthia started recording their conversation.

'I left the wedding, although I'm not sure there was going to be one, a couple of hours ago. I was …', she coughed, 'I was chased off Andrea Placido's villa by an Englishman. His name, according to the wedding guest list, is ...' Her voice broke towards the end of the sentence.

She stopped.

'Are you all right, Sam?'

'F Derwent.' It was a whisper. He hardly picked it up.

Frank hated hearing her like this. She was tough - for sure. And always calm. Focused. He'd only heard her lose it twice. Both of those were associated with the deaths of people she cared for. Her uncle Tony in the plane crash. And Ginny, last year. The girl she'd got close to in Miami. On both those occasions she'd flipped. Anger and single-mindedness had merged into one. There had been outpouring ... and everyone got a bit.

This was different. Her mood seemed reclusive. As though she were on the edge of a breakdown. And it hurt like hell.

'Sorry.' A sniff. 'You talk for a bit. I'll come back to all this.'

'OK.' He stiffened himself. 'Viktor Molnár caught an Alitalia flight from Reggio Calabria to Zurich on 19 August. He returned two days later. He hired a car at Zurich. As you know we don't have a station in Switzerland so I'm currently struggling to work out where he travelled to. Does this add any colour to the picture?'

There was a further sniff.

'Sam?'

'Yeah. That makes sense. Go on.'

'The calendar. I've nothing other than the marker for his time away and the two initials: FD. I've run those through Interpol and Europol and came up with a couple of would-be thugs, but no one in Switzerland, and nobody you might think worth dragging the Hungarian PM away from his family vacation for.'

He paused. Waited.

'Fuck this.' It was a soft *fuck*.

'What, Sam?'

'FD. F Derwent. How did I not see that?' It was more mumbling. To herself.

The phone went quiet again. Frank could hear the sound of a bird in the background. And tears? He sensed Sam had pulled the handset away from her face. He imagined her standing in a garden or park somewhere, sobbing uncontrollably with the phone held to her chest.

He listened for a heartbeat.

And waited.

Nothing. Another sniff. A noise as though someone was wiping their nose with a hand. Then more nothing.

'Let me know when you want to continue, Sam.'

As he waited he opened up Cynthia's database and typed in F Derwent. There were no entries.

He looked around the room. The place was packed. Leave had been cancelled. Everyone was busy. On a big screen in the corner of the room the BBC was showing the latest from the VP's visit. According to the red and white headline the VP would be arriving at the

FCO in three minutes. The crowd waiting for him had been corralled across from the FCO's offices on Parliament Street. There were maybe a thousand people held back by police tape and a thin blue line of bobbies. The crowd wasn't there to welcome the statesman; their placards and signs made that clear.

Hey?!

Among the, *You're not welcome here!*, and, *VP go home*, was a large two-man banner: big, red, professionally stencilled letters on a white background.

Not the right man, Jane. Try again.

Shit!

Frank took the phone from his ear and pressed it against his shoulder. He was on his feet.

'Claire!'

Jane's PA had her the desk as close to Jane's door as was possible. She looked up - confused.

'Get Jane onto BBC News. Now! If she hasn't seen the last 30 seconds of the crowd outside the FCO, get it on catch up.' Claire wasn't reacting fast enough for him.

'It's important, Claire. Now! Please!'

She was on her feet and in Jane's office a second later.

'Frank!' It was a squeak from his shoulder. He quickly brought the phone back to his ear.

'Sorry, Sam. It's a flipping madhouse here at the moment. Sorry.' He sat down and tried to refocus.

There was a long, loud exhalation of air all the way from Italy. And then she started.

Sam told him about Gareth and Giorgio. About their affair. And then about the shooting in Giorgio's father's study.

'We need to get Rome onto the *Carabinieri* as soon as possible. The chances of the body still being in the grounds is unlikely, but they have just cause.' Another sniff. 'If nothing else, it's a good reason to start an interrogation of Andrea Placido. I'm absolutely convinced the 'Ndràngheta are running the operation.' Sam's voice was more steady.

'Jane's not convinced. Not enough to take it upstairs. Not yet.'

'She's wrong.'

A thought caught him. According to Sam the murder was at about 10.30 this morning. It was now past 2.00 pm. Why had it taken Sam so long to get in touch?

'I tend to agree with you.' He took a breath. 'Just a thought, Sam. Why have you waited until now to phone me with the details of Gareth's murder?'

There was that pause again.

'I crashed.' A sniff. 'A couple of hours ago. More of that in a second. Let me finish what I have. It might all make sense by then.'

'OK.' He glanced up. Jane was out of the office. She was heading his way.

'I was attacked just as Gareth was murdered. Recognised by ... by a man.'

Jane was at his side. He didn't turn away from his screen. Instead he put a hand up to shush her, and then touched his keypad. Sam was now on speaker. It was a combination of words, sniffs and pauses.

'He was English. Drove a Bentley Continental … are you recording?'

'Yes. Jane's here. Carry on.' He glanced up at Jane. She had a look which spelt, 'Have we really got time for this now?'. He ignored it.

Sam read out the Bentley's Swiss number plate.

'According to the guest list his name is …' *Did she just gulp?* 'A Mr F … F Derwent. He knew who I was. He called me "*The* Sam Green", as though I was really well known to him.' Sam sniffed. 'He would have done me harm. But, with the help of some Italian good manners, I got away.'

There was another pause. Frank looked at Jane, who shrugged her shoulders.

'Got that Sam. But, sorry, you still haven't told me why the delay.'

'Don't you sodding get it!?' A scream of frustration.

Whoa.

Jane put a hand on his shoulder.

'No, sorry, Sam. There's a lot going on here …'

'F. Fucking F. *Fucking F* for *Fucking Freddie*. There, I said his name out loud. It was him. I'm sure it was.'

Frank looked around. A couple of colleagues sitting at adjacent desks were looking his way.

Freddie?

'She means Freddie, from Croatia. The one who got away from Samostan monastery, last year. The one nobody can find any trace of.' Jane added.

'What does this mean, Sam?' Jane asked.

There was another pause and another long exhale.

'It means my life has just crashed around me. Look, I got away on a scooter. He chased me in his Bentley.' A sniff. A further pause. 'He almost caught me. I ended up in a vineyard. Hidden. And then the enormity of it all hit me. I'd been running from Ralph Bell for four years. And then he's replaced by a man without a face. Haunting me. And then I saw that face … at the wedding … and I crashed.'

'You mean, off your bike? Are you OK?' Frank spoke quickly. He was really concerned now.

A kind snort from the other end. Not a demeaning one.

'No, Frank. My brain shut down. Tiredness. Adrenalin. Fear. You woke me where I dropped. In the vineyard. If you hadn't phoned, I'm pretty sure I'd be flat out now.' Another pause. 'I'm not sure I can cope with this anymore. Where is he now? Is he …?' She stopped talking. Frank imagined Sam looking around. Searching …

Frank waited. Nothing.

'Sam?' Jane this time.

'I'm here. Just.'

'Are you in Calabria?'

'Yes.'

'Can you get to Rome?'

A pause.

'Yes. I think. I need to get out of my best frock. And lose the bike. But I should be able to get there by late evening.'

'Good. I'll give the head of station a call. They'll be expecting you. Are you still convinced this is Mafia based?'

'Yes. How FD, F Derwent, fucking … Freddie fits in, I'm not sure. But he's pulled the big strings before. We know that. And maybe he was the one Molnár went to see in Switzerland? He could well be using the 'Ndràngheta to make this happen. They have the reach, the cover and the acumen.'

'Mmm. Let's see.' Jane paused in thought. 'I'm sure Frank has told you we have a lot on here. The ferry, the global ricin attacks and now an indeterminate threat against a major public figure, whatever that means. And the same threat has been issued in the US, China and Australia. None of it makes any sense. And we have a global population on the verge of uprising. If we, the CIA, whoever, don't come up with something soon, governments will fall.'

'It's about money.' Sam said. 'This is not ideological. The 'Ndràngheta haven't got a Catholic bone in their bodies. It's about cash. I'm convinced. So we need to find out who and how that works. We should start with the Mafia and Viktor Molnár's trip to Switzerland. And F …', she stalled again, '… Derwent, if that's his name. I can photofit him. And two thugs who chased me out of a service station in northern Italy. That may help.'

Sam still sounded flat. Frank was really worried about her. Something pulled at him, like a dog at his shoe laces.

'Are you feeling better?' Frank asked.

'No, Frank. I feel like shit. I know if my mind pauses for a second it will melt quicker than an ice cube in a microwave. It's irrational. And it's bloody scary. I know I shut down when I'm knackered, but I can mostly second-guess when that's going to be.' There was pause. Frank thought he could here Sam's bottom lip quivering. 'This is different. What worries me now is if I stop thinking and start imagining, it'll all be over and I'll end up as a gibbering wreck.'

Jane squeezed Frank's shoulder.

She replied. 'You can't afford that. Nor can we. I have a team here, Sam, who are chasing every lead we have. Yours makes sense. It does. But we need more. Get to Rome, now. I'll have the station there give you a desk and a buddy. You can work together.'

There was a pause and then Sam's reply was heartfelt, almost a plea.

'I need Frank?'

Jane didn't say anything. Frank tensed. Jane must have felt it through his shoulder.

Rome? Me?

The one and only time he'd been in the field, he'd ended up in the basement of a Munich mansion that had been set on fire by a couple of rockets. He'd got out. Just.

The question hung over them like wet towel. Jane didn't say anything for a second. She was looking across at the TV in the distance. Someone in the team had replayed the shot of the two men and the banner. They'd paused it.

'OK. Good idea. Frank?'

He was lost for words.

Rome?

Whatever.

Vineyard, near Tiriolo, Calabria, Italy

Sam put her hands, her mobile held loosely in one of them, on her lap. She leant back, relaxing her head against the hard, limestone wall. She moved her neck until the back of her head found a gap between pointed rocks. Any energy she had left after the phone call with Jane and Frank trickled out of her, leaching into the wall and the soil beneath her.

Rest. Just a bit longer.

Her leaden eyelids closed of their own accord.

Darkness came.

She woke with a start.

Shit!

Dusk would be on its way soon. The temperature was already dropping. Her joints ached.

What time is it?

She checked her phone. It was 5.30 pm. She had lost another three hours. Just gone. Stolen from her by a thief. He'd taken her time and left her with aches in places she didn't know she had bones. And he'd poisoned her dreams. Freddie, all angular faced and salivating ... white flowers with yellow centres turning red with blood ...

Nope.

She didn't want to think about that.

Action was needed.

Come on.

Frank was probably on his way to Rome and she was about 500 klicks behind him. As always she had her essentials with her in a bum bag, but she was still ridiculously dressed in a red frock and inappropriate shoes. Nothing warm. The shops would all be closed and she had to get to Rome tonight.

First, a plan ...

Think.

No. Her brain was fog. Her limbs weak. And something inside wouldn't let her press for action. She wanted to stand. To get on. But somewhere in her frontal lobes was an immovable object. It wasn't adding to the conversation, it was preventing any. Like an over-sized dumpling in a small bowl of stew.

She closed her eyes. Darkness descended.

And then she opened them again.

Don't do that.

She couldn't sleep. With open skies and the stars beginning to wink at her, she knew soon any residual heat she owned would be bought for next to nothing by the surrounding countryside. Robbed again.

She looked at her phone. The battery was half-full. She looked across at the trike. It was still there. At least she had transport. If she could be bothered to get on it.

Monster tiredness assaulted her and she let her chin drop, her phone falling from her hand.

Her eyes closed.

And Freddie came.

No!

She woke - too scared to sleep.

But that's what her body was telling her to do.

Come on, love. You need to get some rest. They'll deal with it all. A soft voice. Calming. Closing.

You're not worth it. You think too much of yourself. The soft voice now laced with menace. *They'll do a better job without you. You just complicate matters.*

The voice's tone was changing all the time. And Sam knew whose it was: mocking and degrading.

No. She couldn't allow this.

She prised open her eyes - and blinked a couple of times. She picked up her phone. She'd lost another 25 minutes.

It was getting dark now. Everything still ached … and she knew she had to move.

Hand to the floor. *Push.*

Nothing.

Shit.

She tried again. No. Her body was dead weight. Fat and bone in a human-shaped sack.

What to do? She was no longer fighting the Mafia and Mr F *fucking* Derwent. She was exchanging fisticuffs with an unseen enemy. A hooligan inside of her.

She'd felt this way before. Post injuries in Afghanistan. A mortar shredding her stomach. And killing the man she loved. The doctors had patched her up in Bastion. They'd done a fab job. But they could do nothing about her anxiety. She slept. And slept. And when the nurses had tried to get her out of bed, her body wouldn't respond. And the fog that permeated every corner of her brain told her not to give a shit. What did she have to live for? What was the point?

It took them a week to get her mobile. Up on her sticks. She hobbled here. Then rested. And she hobbled back again. The soldiers' best friend, black humour, deserted her. A couple of lads from the local Regiment who were both in with amputations, took the piss out of her in a kind, military way you would have thought would have done the trick. But she turned them away, sour-faced and miserable.

In her bed on the front line she knew she had to take back control. She had to beat the fog; and the lump in the front of her head that was stopping any sensible, cognitive thought.

She had to do something.

So she did.

There were plenty of hospital sharps about. She stole a scalpel and, late one night when the ward was being serenaded by far-off gun fire and manly snores, she cut the top of her thigh.

Inside.

The pain was instant and overwhelming.

The blood relentless.

She had cut too deep. But what did she expect? She was hardly an expert.

In panic she scrambled around for something to press against the wound to stop the flow. She remembered there was a box of tissues on the bedside table. In the part-darkness she reached for them, inadvertently pushing the table away from her, the castor wheels squeaking as they helped the box make its escape. Sam was angry now. With one wet, red hand pushing against the wound she quickly she slipped her legs off the bed and took a step to the table. She ripped out a dozen or so tissues and pressed them hard against the cut. In the darkness she looked for seeping blood. The tissue turned red directly above the wound. She reached for some more. And applied them to the makeshift dressing.

'Are you OK, Sam?'

The voice was from the next door bed. A soldier. REME. He was in with shrapnel wounds from a rocket attack against a vehicle he'd been travelling in.

'Piss off, Ginger.'

That was his nickname. And, of course, he was ginger.

She ignored him and, with her back to him, checked the dressing. It was holding. She must have looked a sight. Half-light, hunched and staring at her crotch.

'Have you lost something? You know. Like a cherry?'

That stopped her. She closed her eyes. And smiled to herself.

She turned, with her hand still between her legs.

'Is that how your mother taught you to sweet talk a girl, Ginger? Now, piss off and get some beauty sleep. Dream of being blonde, brunette ... or even bald. Anything's better than the excuse growing out of your head at the moment.'

She smiled a forced smile and, without turning her back on the soldier, she checked the wound. No blood.

'Are you sure you're OK? Can I get you something?' He was on his side now, his head propped up by a hand. Even in the poor light Sam could see genuine concern.

She smiled again.

'I'm fine, thanks. I cut myself shaving.'

'Well, it's really good to see you on your feet and sparky.'

That stopped her as well.

'Thanks, Ginge. Mean it.' And with her hand still pressing against the wound, she hopped back into bed.

'Now, piss off and get some sleep.'

The memories washed over her.

The cutting hadn't cured the anxiety, but it had allowed her to take back some control. She remembered cutting herself three more times in as many weeks, at the end of which she was able to banish any oncoming anxiety with exercise. Lots of it.

Sam pulled her bum bag round from behind her. She unzipped it. Inside was a passport, a small wallet, a toothbrush, some pocket tissues and a penknife. She took the penknife and tissues out and pulled up her dress, exposing her inner thigh.

She remembered how to cut - and more importantly, how not to cut. She had the open penknife in one hand and a still-folded paper tissue between her teeth.

It was dark now. But she didn't need any light.

She pulled the skin apart so it was tight between two old wounds with her free hand.

And cut.

Slowly.

One ... two ... three.

She reckoned the line of blood was about five centimetres long. She couldn't see it, but she imagined it bubbling up from the open wound, gathering itself together and then allowing gravity to take it by the hand, down the length of the cut, onto pristine flesh and then track to that point when the weight of blood was heavier than the meniscus force holding it to the skin. In Sam's head the trail fell, like wax from an upturned candle, hitting the ground, turning the brown earth black.

The pain shot up through her crotch, across her chest and made her heart briefly palpitate at a million beats a minute.

Shit, that hurts!

She let go of the wound, reached for the tissue and pressed it hard against the red line, counting to twenty.

... nineteen ... twenty.

That was enough. Enough time. Enough blood. And enough pain.

She removed the tissue and replaced it with a fresh one. It wouldn't hold, but it would do for now. In any case, her dress was red. It would be difficult to tell.

She checked for aching limbs.

A little ... here and there. But better.

Let's go.

She stood unsteadily. Took a couple of deep breaths, and staggered over to the trike.

Sam had memorised the route from Google Maps. It was 505 kilometres. With a couple of fuel and pee stops she reckoned she'd be in Rome just after two in the morning. She'd SMS'd Frank. His reply had been immediate. He would be in Rome by ten. He'd have the kettle on.

She had decided to keep the trike. Mostly because she didn't think she had the time to find a hire car, and even if she did it was likely her name would be marked and if she used a debit card, two thugs would appear from somewhere - and she couldn't cope with that.

It did leave the issue of the stolen nature of the MP3 which may well have an 'all-stations' call out on it.

And that's when she'd been lucky.

As she drove off the hill, winding her way down to the motorway and beginning to freeze in the cold temperatures which were lashing her at up to 60 kilometres per hour, she spotted a small farmhouse off to one side. It had some barns and a yard full of cars and a motorbike. It looked like there was a party going on, which had moved inside to escape the cold.

She left the trike on the road and jogged into the yard, her thigh protesting every time her foot hit the floor.

Bike first.

Hiding in the shade of a pickup truck, she used her penknife to remove the plate from the back of the bike.

Next, the barns. There were two of them. Both open.

She pushed on the door of one. It creaked. It was dark inside. She slipped in and switched on her phone's torch. She shone it around the darkness.

The barn was split into bays by wooden fences, and there was a hay loft. No cattle.

She looked around.

Shit!

There was noise from up top. Giggles and 'shushes'.

Just my luck.

A female head and naked chest, blinking in the glare of the torch. It ducked down. More giggles.

Assuming that she wasn't going to be ratted on by a couple having fun in the hay, she continued her search.

You can do anything once. Although, here, she shouldn't hang about.

There.

Coveralls. And some wellies. Big wellies. Ordinarily too big for her.

Over there. A wax jacket.

Perfect.

She left more giggling behind, pulled the door to and headed back to the trike. Five minutes later, dressed as a Somerset pig farmer's assistant, she was on the same, but different MP3. And now warmed and more protected from the cold, she was on her way to Rome.

Via a couple of fuel and pee stops ...

Headquarters SIS, Vauxhall, London

Jane paused outside her door, her foot keeping it ajar. She looked across the main office's empty desks to the windows. The night sky was heavy with low clouds which reflected London's ambient light, giving them a mauvy tinge. Rain was coming. Buckets of it. The forecasters reckoned they'd have a month's worth in the next couple of days. The farmers and reservoirs needed it after the long dry summer. And the capital needed it too. Rain dampened enthusiasm for marches. People were less inclined to come out onto the streets and make a noise if they were going to get drenched in the process.

The Met reckoned tomorrow's march would be the largest in London's history, with over one and a half million protesters planning to invade the city. If they were right that would be double the 2003 'Stop the War' march, which in itself dwarfed all of the city's previous marches. The problem was coincident protests were being held in nine cities across the UK. The police were at breaking point. If any of the marches turned violent, there was no backup. Riots would lead to looting. Looting would lead to more crime. The Met Commissioner's brief earlier today spoke of possible vigilantism post any looting, which could mean further societal breakdown. The PM was standing by to take the unprecedented step of imposing a curfew in areas where the police might lose control. And, across the country, the Army were practising crowd control in the quiet corners of their barracks.

It had all happened so quickly. The ferry disaster. And the ricin attacks. After almost a year of sporadic terror people had had enough. They were at their wit's end; she felt it too. She travelled to work most days on the tube and she'd noticed two things. First, the carriages were less full. People were avoiding enclosed spaces. Second, everyone was jumpy. She could sense it on the trains. They were quiet; fearful. There was a palpable sense of desperation everywhere.

Closer to home a small group of activists had camped outside Babylon's main entrance. A couple of hours ago Jane had popped out to get a sandwich and some fresh air. On the way back in one of the protesters had thrown an egg at her. It was ridiculous.

And now the bloody VP's visit.

How did they know my name?

OK, so the names of senior staff in SIS weren't a national-level secret, but you'd have to work quite hard to uncover the details.

It was clear to everyone in the building she was the Jane on the banner. The CT police had picked up the two lads almost immediately, but the trail had gone cold within an hour. It was another low-energy, but clever and confounding act. As at nine o'clock this evening ten nations were chasing their tails on what would, ordinarily, be very solid intelligence of an attack against a 'major public figure'. All of them had been fed the threat by bona fide agents. In isolation every state had to assume the threat was real. And yet, surely, the neo-terrorists couldn't have that much stretch? Not ten separate targets in ten separate countries?

The CIA and they had worked tirelessly for 12 hours. The VP as a target was a sound, intelligence-consolidated, choice.

And yet they had been played. His visit had gone off without a hitch.

They'd been sent off elsewhere, whilst the real threat would pop up where they least expected it. And if recent history was anything to go by, they were looking at something which would terrorise great swathes of population. She was convinced this wasn't about incisor-sharp, political assassinations. Certainly not the US Vice President on an impromptu visit to the UK.

No. It was about mass terror. It was about bringing the world to the boil. If NT were to murder a public figure - or figures - they would be ones whose death would cataclysmically undermine public confidence. Whoever they were.

And, if she listened to Sam Green, it was all about money. The whole thing.

Sam, and Frank, were convinced the 'Ndràngheta were coordinating the attacks. They certainly had the reach. And they had the cellular structure to keep the thing tight and secure.

But were they really the power behind this?

Jane couldn't see it. They had no history of fermenting chaos. Their MO was extortion; medium and low level business interference, for which they were paid well. Drugs, now thought to be Europe-wide, with fingers in the US and Canada. And subverting power with bought influence; but only so they could keep doing the drugs and extortion with impunity.

Whilst they could probably pull it off, a terror racket on the world stage wouldn't be on their agenda.

Surely?

Just before she left the office Carla had dropped a report on her desk. It was the current state of play concerning the Brit billionaire. The front page summary had some new news. AfH International Bank, Geneva, the largest of the 296 overseas accounts that likely laundered the man's money, had been subject to GCHQ scrutiny. AfH held 14 separate accounts the Doughnut attributed to a shell company based in Jersey: Lakeland Industries. Lakeland Industries held four accounts in The Cayman Islands, two of which linked back to the yet-to-be-named British man. They'd managed to uncover the signatory of one of the Cayman accounts. His name was Mr Helvellyn. Wires connected to other wires, connected to others. Which joined the circuit back at the beginning. It was a labyrinth. Carla reckoned they'd have a matrix of links of all of the accounts by size and geography within 48 hours.

That wasn't quick enough for Jane. She was attending the JIC tomorrow morning where they would press her on 'money' being a driver for the terror. She really could do with more. She'd dropped Carla an email asking her to pop in first thing.

Still standing in the doorway, and still staring out into the gloom, Jane checked her watch. The JIC was in eight hours' time.

Go home. And try to avoid another egg shampoo.

Her phone pinged. It was a secure email from the Asmara team in Eritrea. They were working late. It was addressed to Frank, cc'd to her. Frank would be in Rome by now. Hopefully with Sam. She opened the mail and scanned it. And then read it in detail.

A few seconds later she pulled her door open fully and headed back to her desk.

Sam was right?

The Eritrean team's agent had delivered a copy of the contract behind the new-build waterfront fishing warehouses in Mersa Fatma. The government signatory was a known, bent politician - which was neither a surprise, nor the key piece of intelligence. What was, was the company contracted to build the warehouses was Italian: *Astal Generali*, which the team had investigated.

It was another shell. Based in the town of Scilla … in Calabria.

Mafia central.

Jane took off her coat whilst speed-dialling Frank on her mobile.

Were they at last making progress?

Chapter 16

Frank was struggling to stay awake. He'd spent the last two hours pulling together all of the threads of Operation Peacock. Op Peacock was the new, unimaginatively named title for the intelligence gathering effort to piece together the Italian/Mafia/Swiss/British NT conglomerate on which the UK and now the CIA were focusing their efforts. In parallel, they were also chasing down the latest extant threat to a major public figure. The latter was also now exercising the minds of the intelligence agencies of 12 other nations, including the recent additions of Brazil and Japan. Someone back at Babylon had done some sums. The total number of 'major public figures' distributed among the 12 countries stood at 14,357. Frank was sure if there were such a threat, and he and Jane thought it was now a red herring, the target would likely be the 14,358th - and not on the list.

He was clear. The key now was breaking into the 'Ndràngheta Mafia.

And that was a problem.

The Station's chief, R1 (Rome, 1), had pulled together a three-man team to assist Frank. All of them were case officers. As such, all of them outranked him, and that wasn't just in actual rank. Frank wasn't a field officer, so he couldn't pass stereotypical judgements on every serving-overseas member of SIS, but he reckoned the station where you were based influenced how you were dressed. In Rome's case it was all sharp grey suits, single-colour all-cotton shirts and, as it was most places today, no tie. One of the three wore sunglasses in the office, which Frank thought was overkill as the station had been relegated to the Embassy's basement.

Out of sight, out of mind.

In terms of fashion then, they also outranked him.

In his defence, today was a travel day. That meant timeworn fading black jeans, a Greenpeace - *Put Earth First* - t-shirt, and a heavy woollen cardigan which either his Mum had knitted, or he'd bought from a charity shop. He couldn't remember which. Oh, and red with white banding, old-style, long-lace basketball sneakers. The ones with flat, beige tread that was good at stopping you in the gym, but hopeless on wet pavement. It had been raining in Rome when he got off the plane and he'd almost fell on his backside twice on the short route from the taxi to the tradesman's entrance of the Embassy.

But, he was directing effort - and the team were lapping it up. Significantly Op Peacock now had its own op code, with a budget large enough to organise a successful coup in a West African country.

First was getting an 'in' on the 'Ndràngheta Mafia. His new friends told him they had no agents in its ranks. If you believed AISE, they didn't either. The mafia grouping had been torn apart a couple of years ago by a governmental anti-corruption effort. It had rounded up a good number of players just at the point where the 'Ndràngheta had become rather bourgeoisie and complacent. The purge had made them rethink their structure and MOs, and the outcome was a much leaner, more efficient, and pretty impenetrable organisation. It didn't help that Rome Station believed the 'Ndràngheta had a number of senior policemen and intelligence operatives on their payroll. The bottom line was that SIS could and would push AISE for support, but movement would be slow. Certainly slower than what everyone needed right now.

The next approach was to press the *Carabinieri* on the murder of Gareth Jones. One of Frank's team had put this in motion within half an hour of them all getting together. They were waiting for an outcome on that.

In the meantime, and whilst Frank waited for Sam to arrive, him and one of the team who had not yet gone home, had put together a couple of white boards detailing the sum of everything they knew.

He was staring at it now.

Frank had purposefully placed Freddie Derwent at the centre of the main board. Something told him that is what Sam would want. The spokes from the centre of the wheel led to the 'Ndràngheta Mafia, Andrea Placido (annotated '2IC of the 'Ndràngheta'), Viktor Molnár - with a link to Andrea Placido above which Frank had scribed Villa Feradina, and the FFO and Hasan Kutnetsov - with a link back to Viktor Molnár, on which was scribbled, 'same words'. There was a link from Andrea Placido to Astal Generali, the Italian warehouse company, with a further link leading to Abir al-Rasheed and the other three terrorists from Mersa Fatma, although no one yet knew if the woman in the team was from the village -

CT police had still not managed to get anything from them. Various other links tied together Lakeland Industries and AfH International Bank, the Cayman Islands, a Mr Helvellyn, the G7 and G20 countries. The 12 countries currently chasing down potential assassination attacks on their 'major public figures' had been written in a different colour, and those countries which had suffered ricin attacks a different colour again. Some of the countries' names were overwritten in two colours as they were investigating a potential assassination of a public figure, and had also been subject to a ricin attack.

There were five separate goose eggs which had to be penned on the second board because he'd run out of room: Italy, Sweden, Switzerland (which had lines leading to Freddie Derwent and AfH International Bank), Eritrea and Libya.

It was a mess.

And whichever way you looked at it, it made no sense at all.

With Jane's authorisation Frank had refocused GCHQ. Without AISE support they were targeting Andrea Placido and other 'Ndràngheta players known to Rome Station. Via the SIS team in Budapest, they were also working harder on Viktor Molnár's internet presence. In conjunction with the fraud section at The Treasury, GCHQ had a team working flat out to unpick the 296 business and account links which Frank now, on a hunch, had associated with Freddie Derwent. And SIS's Asmara team were pushing every contact to expose more potential dealings between the Eritrean government and the Calabrian shell company, Astal Generali.

Jane, who was still concerned they might be placing all their eggs in one basket, was working a series of external links, including liaising with the CIA. Unbeknown to the Eritrean government (and currently even the British Embassy in Asmara) tomorrow night the Special Reconnaissance Regiment were dropping an eight-man overwatch team a tabable distance from Mersa Fatma. They would sit a couple of kilometres back from the village in two separate locations and report anything suspicious. The CIA, who were behind the curve and not wholly sold on the Italian connection, had a team in Tunis who were, via a couple of well-placed agents, interrogating the container port where the Eritrean hijackers were known to have embarked.

And Jane had held various late-night calls with oppos around the globe, giving them most of the British intelligence's view of how and where NT were operating. She'd asked for support and advice ... would they please get back to her.

That's where they were.

Frank had fallen out the final member of the team, had made himself a cup of mint tea, had his feet up on his desk and was running the names on the boards around in his head. It was like looking at the scribblings of a three year old. Meatballs and spaghetti. Nodes and connections. And there was no sense to be made of it.

He was shattered. He checked the time. It was 02.45. He wasn't a natural traveller and certainly wasn't a night owl.

Sam had SMS'd him three-quarters of an hour ago. She had stopped for some fuel - and coffee - which she would gulp down once she'd leaked out the previous cups that had, according to her, 'passed straight through me'. She'd be with him soon.

'How soon?' He'd tried very hard not to sound in desperate need of sleep.

'An hour. Depends whether or not I fall asleep … or succumb to the cold.'

He sighed. And stared at the board, The words and lines became one jumble of multi-coloured, dry-board marker. His eyes itched. His lids flickered.

'Sir?'

Frank's drifting off was stopped in its tracks.

It was the on-duty Embassy security man. Frank had met him earlier. He was huge - probably ex-Army. He had called Frank from a far-off doorway.

Frank turned his head and smiled.

'Yes, John? And Frank. Please.'

'OK. I think the woman visitor you told me about has arrived. She's at the back door.'

'Thanks, John, I'm on my way.'

Frank stood, stretched and followed John down the hallway, up a flight of stairs and into a small atrium. At the far end of the atrium was a ceiling-height, metaled fence with a single entrance: a 'machine-that-goes-ping' security gate.

On the other side of the gate Frank thought he recognised Sam, although it was difficult to tell. The apparition was Sam's height and the face under the makeshift scarf looked like Sam. But all other comparisons stopped there.

Wellies, coveralls, a wax jacket and ...

Sam's knees buckled under her and she fell to the floor, missing one of the metal prongs of a three-pronged rotating arm by a whisper.

'Quick, John! Get her in here.'

John pressed a button and pushed open a, previously unseen to Frank, gate that emerged from the fence. He had Sam in his arms in a second, swung the gate to with his foot and headed for the stairs.

'She's shivering and delirious. Do you know the details of the Embassy's quack?', John asked.

'No.' Frank was chasing after him down the stairs, taking two at a time, his tiredness gone. 'But I know where the duty officer is. He'll have a number, I'm sure.

Ten minutes later, with Sam lying awkwardly on the largest chair in the office and John trying to force-feed her warm tea, Frank came back from the duty officer's bunk.

The sight of her lying in a heap, semi-conscious, made his own knees go weak.

'How is she?' He asked.

'Not making much sense. And shivering like a jelly on a waterbed. What did the doc say?'

'As described, he's really worried about her. From here to Calabria on a bike in this weather, wearing inappropriate clothing ... he's pretty sure she could have hypothermia, which is no surprise. If we don't get her warm quick, he can't guarantee what will happen next. He's on his way in, but it might take him half an hour. He said stick her in a warm bath or shower. Plenty of hot drinks. And sugar. Check for dilated pupils and try and keep her awake, even if she continues to be incoherent.' He paused, touching Sam's forehead. *She's very cold.* 'Do we have a bath - or a shower?'

'In the gym. A couple of showers. Just down the hall. Are you going to do it?'

A million things ran round Frank's head at the same time. The duty officer was a man. John was, well, a big man. Frank was a man.

Sam wasn't.

Oh, sod it.

'Can you carry her to the shower please, John.'

John didn't blink.

Definitely ex-Army or Marine. He knew the score. Apply heat to cold.

Frank was on his tail. They were in the shower room in seconds. John held her tight and kept talking to her. He stopped in the middle of the room.

He doesn't want to put her on the cold floor?

'Turn the shower on, sir. Hot, but not burning.'

Frank did as he was asked.

'What now?' Frank had become follower.

'Turn the other one on. And the taps in the sink. Let's make this place steam. We'll wait for a few seconds for the room to heat up.'

Frank rushed round turning on taps.

Thirty seconds later they were in a sauna. Frank hadn't originally noticed, but John had brought the cup of tea with him. The liquid had been lost in transit, but he was now catching hot water from the shower, opening Sam's mouth gently by pressing on her cheeks, and dripping in warm water. Between sips he was reassuring her. Sam made some noises that didn't make any sense.

'I'm going to take her in the shower. And keep feeding her warm water. We need to be careful. If she gets too hot too quickly her core will try to leach more heat and she could well close down. Do you have any spare clothes?'

What? Eh ...

'Oh, yeah. In my suitcase. In the office.'

'Anything warm?'

'Some stuff.' Frank replied, trying to work out what would fit Sam - actually most of his stuff would work.

'Wait. Take off her coat and wellies.'

Between them they managed that, whilst John kept Sam as close to him as he could. Frank noticed his forearms were as thick as Sam's neck.

Then, fully clothed, and with a, 'It's OK, Sam, we're just going to try and get you warm.', John walked into the shower. He turned, moved his giant frame to one side, and let the hot water pour over Sam. Within seconds they were both soaking. Sam made a noise. Then another. And then fell silent under the torrent of hot water.

John filled his cup and did his thing again with Sam's mouth. She glugged it down.

'I've got a Buffalo jacket in the security post.' He explained where it was. 'Go and get everything you can, including something to dry her with. Then make sure the aircon in the basement is turned up warm. There's a control box by the far doorway. Get back here as soon as you can.'

Frank looked at the man who had taken control. It was a sight that would take forever to leave him. A giant of a man standing steadfastly and incongruously in the shower, holding onto what, in his arms, was a slip of a woman.

A woman in danger - but who was in safe hands.

A woman ... who I love?

He dismissed the thought with a violent shake of his head. And then he was off. His orders clear.

It took Frank ten minutes to sort everything he needed to. As he re-entered the shower room it was as he had left it. A large, fully-clothed man holding a wretch of a woman ... in a steaming shower. He was still feeding her hot water. And still talking to her.

He looked up.

'Good, sir. We need to undress your friend now. I didn't want to do it without you here. I think we both need to look after her, if you know what I mean - and ourselves. I'm going to hold her, and you're going to take off her clothes. OK?'

Frank blew a raspberry. He looked at John, and then at Sam.

'Shall we tell her what we're doing?' Frank asked.

'Good idea, sir. You talk to her.'

'OK.' Frank placed Sam's new clothes and towel he had brought onto a white polyprop chair. He then quickly took off his shoes and socks and stepped into the line of fire.

He paused.

'Hi, Sam. It's Frank. How are you doing?'

She grunted.

'You got very cold on the drive here. You're ...', he thought about what to say next, '... getting warm at the moment. John is holding you. He's a good guy. I'm going to get you undressed ...'

He waited for a reaction. There was another grunt.

'Then we'll get you dry, get you dressed and feed you so much tea you'll be dying for a wee.'

He waited again. His shirt and trousers were soaking. As he spoke, water sprayed from his mouth.

'I'm taking off your very fetching coveralls now, Sam.'

A grunt.

Between them they carefully undressed Sam. As Frank took off her undies he noticed a recent scar on her leg. It was originally covered with blooded tissues, but, once damp, that fell onto the shower floor creating a splodge of red. The blood from the tissues snaked to the back of the pan and into the plughole.

The cut started to bleed.

'Shit.'

'What?' John asked. Water dripped from his eyelids, and off his cheeks. He glanced down.

'She's got a wound on her inner thigh. It will need steristripping at the very least.' Frank said, water spraying from his lips with every word.

'There's a first aid kit in the security post. I'm a bit uncomfortable about being in here on my own ...'

Frank didn't wait for John to finish his sentence. He shouted, 'Don't be!', as he dashed out of the door.

It took the pair of them 15 minutes to dress Sam's wound, dry her ('dabbing, not rubbing', according to John from previous first aid training. It was about not forcing more blood to the surface), overdress her in Frank and John's stuff, and then carry her to the basement office - which was now getting nicely warm. As they left the shower, Frank leading - still wet through, and John carrying Sam at arm's length so he didn't get her dry clothes wet, she opened her eyes.

'Who's the big fella?'

It was a whisper. Frank stopped in his tracks and turned. John shuddered to a halt.

Sam, who now had colour in her cheeks, raised her eyes upwards to show that she was talking about John.

Frank could have cried.

But not in front of the Army.

'His name's John. he's just rescued you from hypothermia - we think.'

Sam closed her eyes.

'Thanks, John.' Another whisper.

'All in a day's work.' He replied.

Probably not, John.

Sam woke. Slowly. That was a new experience for her. Things came at her in a dribble.

I'm hot.

I've seen this room before.

There's Frank, asleep on a chair opposite.

Why are there a load of chocolate bar wrappers on the table next to me?

Then quicker.

What am I wearing?

I recognise the words on those boards.

Last night ...

It all came back to her, her dreams finding their place in her wakefulness.

Her shoulders dropped. Tiredness enveloped her. She closed her eyes. And she couldn't stop herself from crying. Small, female bleats. A sniff; she was careful not to wipe away the mucus with, she guessed, Frank's clothes.

My cut?

It was sore. She felt for it.

That's strange.

It had been closed with some steristrips.

Frank must have done that. *And ... what's his ... John?* That's it. He was the big man carrying her.

They had cared for her. Looked after her. Maybe saved her from ...?

More tears came. She had to use something to wipe away the tears. She looked around. Nothing. Sod it, the Buffalo she was wearing (*surely not Frank's?*) would have to do. It did.

She sniffed. Frank stirred, but didn't wake.

She looked across at the board. In her state it was a mumble of words and lines, the wetness in her eyes distorting her middle-distance vision. She wiped the tears away again, the olive green of the Buffalo turning dark green in widening ovals.

She looked again.

No. She couldn't focus.

Come on.

Again.

OK. She had it now. It was titled Op Peacock. *Who on earth thought of that name?*

And it made sense. Frank, she assumed it was Frank, had done a good job.

She studied it. Played it over in her head. Ran along the lines. Joined a couple more.

F Derwent. She could handle 'F'. On its own. Just the initial. Not the complete word; not the whole name.

But his surname wasn't Derwent. She was sure of it,. The board made that point. It shouted at her.

'Frank.' She was hoarse. It came out like a strangled croak.

'Frank!' Louder this time. If he didn't wake she'd have to get up and give him a kick. She didn't think she had the energy for that.

He moved. And moaned.

'Frank!'

'What? What!' He was up now. Awake but not alive. His eyes were open but they weren't sending messages to his brain. She waited. He blinked. And yawned. And settled for some more sleep.

Sam checked her watch for the first time. It was 6.45 am. The office was empty. There were maybe ten desks. As many screens. There were three windows, but they were at ceiling height. She snorted. The Embassy loved Rome Station so much they'd banished it to the cellar. SIS were the unruly cousins. A cardamom pod in a mild curry. Necessary but unpalatable.

'Frank. Wake up.' Softer this time. But firmer.

'What?' Grunt. His eyes opened; focusing. 'Sam! Goodness, you're here. And awake. And talking! How are you?' He was sat on the edge of his chair now; excited - like a puppy. That almost made Sam choke again.

'It's not Derwent.' Sam was hungry now. She craved sugar. Next to the pile of wrappers were two Mars Bars and a Bounty. She hadn't noticed them earlier. She reached for the Mars, ripped off the end and bit off a big chunk. She wouldn't be able to talk for a few seconds.

Frank was on his feet.

'What do you mean? Did you discover something on the way here?' He was up by the board, a marker in his hand ready to scribe.

Sam tried to say something, but the words came out all caramel. She chewed and swallowed.

Then, 'Look at the names on the board: F Derwent and Lakeland Industries. What's the connection?'

Frank looked at the board. He stepped back and looked again. He shook his head.

'Sorry. Can't see it.'

'Cumbria, Frank. Derwent water. Lakeland Industries. They both have Lake District associations. And Helvellyn. It's a mountain in the Lakes.'

'Is it a code?'

Sam had the rest of the Mars Bar in her mouth and was reaching for the Bounty. She chewed. And chewed. And then gulped.

'Can we get some tea. Like, with lots of sugar?'

Frank looked confused. 'Yeah, sure. It's ...' He went to point and then headed dutifully to the corner of the office.

Sam was on her feet and staggered, wavered, and then sat back down again.

'Sorry. I didn't mean ...' Sam had started to apologise to Frank.

'Don't worry. Tell me the connection.' It was Frank's turn to interrupt. He shouted over his shoulder as he reached the kettle.

'It's not a code. It's … the man from Switzerland. He's making up names by some form of geographical association. And he's chosen The Lakes.'

'Why?'

Sam heard the chinking of mugs.

'Lots of sugar please, Frank. Because. I don't know. Because the Lakes are important to him? He comes from there? He went to school in Cumbria?'

Frank didn't reply. She heard the kettle boil and saw steam rising. A few seconds later Frank was back. He was carrying two mugs in one hand and his phone in the other.

'Sam?'

'What?'

'I've had an alert from the duty officer.' He paused and looked at her. This wasn't going to be good news. He looked back at his phone. 'The *Carabinieri* have discovered a body in Taranto. The body was carrying Gareth Jones's passport. He's the man you described to me. The report says he'd been shot and mugged - last night.' Frank stood awkwardly. The two mugs were in danger of spilling.

She looked at him. He was wearing his genuinely sorry face.

'Sorry,' he whispered.

Sam's brain hit a juncture. It wavered. One avenue took her back to desperation. To blackness. Where curtains closed. The other way was madness. Shutters open. Hair on fire. A bath full of energy draining

461

at a rate that couldn't be filled. Who knew where it would end?

'He kept his passport and his money together. In a Mulberry man-bag. He was gay, for Christ's sake.' Sam whispered. She had clarity, even though her brain fizzed. Decision made. Path chosen. 'I need to do the photofit of ... Brit-Swiss-man ... F Derwent. And then we need to get it to the UK police, the DVLA, all the schools in Cumbria, Carlisle University. Anywhere where someone might remember his face. We have to find his real name.'

She was on her feet. She took an offered mug from Frank whilst reaching down for the second small bar of the Bounty. She stuck the whole thing in her mouth.

'Sure. I'll boot up Cynthia's photofit.'

'Good.' *Chomp.* 'And, as you do that ...', *chew, gulp, '...* explain the rest of this to me.'

Frank did both things. His explanation was clear and succinct.

'So. We have Brit-Swiss-man using the 'Ndràngheta Mafia to coordinate the attacks?' She confirmed.

'Seems so. Although Jane is unconvinced.'

Sam ignored the comment.

'And he's funding this through 296 accounts split between in The Caymans, Jersey and Geneva - to varying degrees?'

Frank nodded from behind the desk. 'Yup.' Sam glanced his way. His screen was black with a green grid. He pressed a key. The outline of a blank face emerged.

She paused in thought.

'I saw something at the wedding. Brit-Swiss-man. He was moving plates and cutlery around on a table. It was all very OCD.'

'Hmm?' Frank was both questioning and agreeing with her, whilst working the screen.

Sam now had the marker pen in one hand, and mug in the other. She wrote *MONEY* next to the title.

'He only works in straight lines. Clear boundaries. He's accurate. Very particular. You said something about the ricin attacks being haphazard?'

Frank stopped and spun in his chair.

'Yeah. Jane commented on that. She thought it was a bit rushed. Not quite the previous MOs.'

Sam chewed at the end of the pen.

'And the latest threat. The intelligence is clear, concise? But yet to manifest itself in an attack?'

'Yeah. What, you think the latest stuff isn't him?'

'Possibly. Or, after the ferry … which was huge and disproportionate in comparison to all of the other attacks, he expected that to be the finale?'

'But it wasn't? Something went wrong? And now he's making it up as he goes along?'

Sam took the pen from her mouth. She underlined *MONEY*.

'Maybe.' She glanced across at Frank's screen. She really didn't want to do the photofit thing. Describing and then seeing his face was going to send her into spasms of something.

'Wait.'

Frank waited.

Sam turned and reached for the final Mars Bar. She opened it.

'It's about money, Frank.'

Frank didn't say anything.

Someone shouted from a recess in her mind.

'Boot up the London FTSE index. Find its value a year ago. And now.'

Frank worked the keyboard deftly. Sam took a bite of Mars Bar.

'7,210 then. 4,592 now. That's a 34% fall in a year. That's massive.' He looked at her. Their eyes met. 'What are you thinking?'

She closed her eyes. She squeezed them tight.

'I've no idea. Except, how do you make money when the world goes batshit?'

Frank didn't reply immediately. Then, 'Gold.'

Sam opened her eyes.

'That's it!'

'What?'

'Get the price of gold up. Now - and a year ago.' She barked.

'Which country?'

'London.'

Frank tapped and tapped.

'£1,004,21 per ounce a year ago, £1,451.07 now.'

Sam span round. She screwed her face up in disgust.

'Shit, that's not it.'

'What, Sam?'

She was pacing now. Short steps up and down the aisle between the desks.

'He's about lines. Exactness. I was hoping there'd be a link. You know. Sell shares and buy gold early. Send the world into a spin. Shares plummet. Gold rises. And then, at some predetermined point ... some line in the sand, drawn by a man where precision counts more than anything, the line gets crossed. Then you stop the chaos just before everything melts. There's a pause as everyone takes a breath. And bingo! You sell gold and buy shares. People forget about the chaos. The market rebounds - because, as we know, the economic numbers are all good ...'

'And you make a killing?' Frank finished Sam's sentence.

'Exactly!' She blurted the word with a little too much enthusiasm. Out loud her explanation didn't make as much sense at it did in her head.

Frank didn't answer. He was working the screen.

'It's not gold per ounce, the usual US/UK scale.' He spoke quietly, with a sense of incredulity.

'What? What do you mean?' She asked.

'As at last night, the FTSE 100 stood at 4,659 points. Gold was retailing at £41.12 *per gram*.' Sam was at his shoulder looking at the numbers. Frank worked the screens like a 12 year old on a PlayStation. Fifteen seconds later he had the price of gold per gram and the FTSE 100 graphs on the same grid, stretching back over the past 12 months; the FTSE's vertical, y-axis in 'points' on the left of the graph, the price of gold in '£s per gram' on the right. Time ran along the bottom. The FTSE was in freefall left to right; the price of gold the opposite.

Frank had constructed a horizontal line through 4,500 points and £45. Both graphs were very close to crossing that line. One upwards; one downwards. The biggest jump and fall was four days ago, after the ferry attack. But it hadn't been enough to make the lines cross.

That's the cause of the impromptu ricin attacks? Keep the momentum going?

Sam stood up, stretching her arms to the ceiling. Frank pushed back in his chair.

'It makes sense to me?' But it was a question from Frank, not a statement.

'No. No it doesn't. It's a fluke, that's all. Do you know why?' Sam asked.

Frank was staring at the screen, hoping for inspiration.

'Nope. Sorry.'

'Because the markets won't recover. Not quickly. Not for a long while. Without a line drawn under the series of NT attacks, nobody will think it's over. Not for certain. Unless someone's in jail, there will be talk of a pause. People will still want answers. And if NT just closes down, the world will not go back to the way it was. There will still be unease. Continuing disquiet. People will be waiting for something deadly to happen. There needs to be an almighty closure. Arrests. Publicity. Success! *Death.* I just can't see how that will happen. You don't plan this and then get caught in order to bounce the markets.' She chewed on the end of the pen again. 'No. It's a fluke. We were looking for something. And we found something. But it's not the right something. Sorry, Frank.'

There was quiet for a moment. Sam felt the burden back in her shoulders. She looked at Frank. He was staring at his shoes. He had the demeanour of a man who needed a decent night's sleep.

It was rubbish.

An open hand and a bunch of straws. One wasn't even close to clutching at the other. They were miles away.

Come on.

A quiet voice. A nudge. From within. She wasn't done yet. The bath was still full.

'Tea, Frank? And then the photofit?' He looked up at her.

She continued. 'And then, I don't know, a road trip to Switzerland?'

Headquarters SIS, Vauxhall, London

'I should be back at about lunchtime, Claire. Can you get me a flight to Rome? Say, early evening. Unless something positive comes out of the JIC, I'm heading out there. C's orders. Is that OK?'

Jane was standing at Claire's desk. She wore a long, light-blue Mammut waterproof jacket over her work clothes, she'd changed her brown slip-ons for a pair of ageing walking shoes and she had a floppy, blue-waxed,

467

brimmed hat in her hand ready to stick on her head the moment she braved Westminster Bridge. She knew she would look like either Bill or Ben, but needs must. She'd chosen to walk because, according to the Met's secure link which she had open on her machine, there were already 300,000 people in and around Trafalgar Square, with 50,000 arriving every hour, most of them using the tube. They'd suggested to the PM's office they close one or two of the mainline routes - maybe a fake terrorist attack at Reading - to blunt the influx, but that had been immediately dismissed. Twenty minutes ago the latest post on the Met's link predicted a march of close to two million people. It was going to break the capital.

'Sure. Rome's nice this time of year?' Claire grinned. Jane had checked the weather there a few minutes ago. The west coast of Italy had been suffering from major flooding and the rain wasn't due to let up any time soon.

'Possibly not.' Jane forced a smile back.

'I'll put an Op Peacock pack together for you. Do you need anything else?'

Jane thought for a second.

'Carla's out until mid-morning, I think. Make sure the latest update from Frank has been passed around the team. And once Carla is back, get her to look over the Cayman accounts again in light of Sam and Frank's madcap gold and share price theory. But it's not to divert her efforts from finding an address for this Freddie chap. And, key, I want to know as soon as we have anything on Sam's photofit Frank just sent through. Oh …' Jane stopped and looked at Claire. She was writing all of her instructions on a pad in shorthand, whilst looking intently at her.

What would I do without you?

'Go on.' Claire prompted. Her pen wavering above the pad.

'And I need to know as soon as we have anything on the Bentley, other than its number plate.'

Claire was still looking at her. Jane's instruction was written down before she'd finished the sentence.

'And?'

Jane didn't say anything. Instead, she theatrically stuck her hat on her head with each hand on opposite sides of the brim; the room immediately grew darker.

'Keep your head up. We wouldn't want you bumping into 'His Handsomeness', would we? Not looking like that.' Claire quipped.

'I think you'll find, Claire, that beauty is both in the eyes of the beholder and only skin deep.'

'Sorry. Of course. I forgot that. But keep your head up anyway.'

'Just sort the blooming flights out ...'

Claire smiled.

And Jane waved.

Crowd dependent, it would take her 20 minutes of brisk walking to get to Whitehall. She'd come back to the office and pick up her overnight case, unless something between now and her flight forced her to stay in the UK.

Frank and Sam's argument - that Freddie (unknown surname) was masterminding the NT attacks using the 'Ndràngheta Mafia - was even more persuasive this morning. There was nothing particularly new in terms of evidence, other than Sam identifying that many of the case's components were linked by name association to the Lake District. But the underlying, Italian organised-crime connection was too strong to ignore. And, frankly, there were no other substantive leads.

Frank's brief, which he'd emailed through an hour ago, concluded with a conjectural thought. Sam and he had run a scenario where the attacks were purposefully driving the price of gold up, and share prices down. And that at some predetermined point, the gains and losses would be big enough to warrant selling piles of gold and buying undervalued shares. She had read the words, agreed it was a fanciful theory, but stuck it in Carla's brief anyway.

It wouldn't, however, be in this morning's briefing to the JIC. Most of her slides focused on the Italian connection and the 'Ndràngheta Mafia. She had included a slide on the mysterious Freddie, and a couple of slides on where other nations had been making some progress. France's DGSI were now certain their ricin and fake-ricin letters had been pulled together over the border in Turin, Italy. She'd had a telephone one-to-one with DGSI's deputy first thing. The French had tracked down an apartment in Turin's Santa Rita district from where they believed all of the letters had originated; they currently had an obs team in place, and taps on appropriate phones. Interestingly they hadn't included AISE in the op for fear of leaks. It was highly unusual for EU countries to work in this manner, but these were highly unusual times.

The one notable success was from the US. Last night the FBI had arrested two men in Baltimore; the Bureau were convinced the men had links to last week's Seattle bombing. The men were 'explosive experts', although the 'experts' bit was tongue-in-cheek. Both men had worked in a quarry and had access to half-decent plastic and detonators. It was crude stuff, but the pipe bomb used in the attack was crude. What was interesting to her was that the arrested men were immigrants from Libya. It was an afterthought at the end of this morning's update from Linden Rickenbacker on the continuing threat to a 'high profile individual'.

'Libya?' She'd asked.

'Yes, why?' Linden had replied.

'It's the Italian connection again.'

'Sorry?'

'Well, it's the fact that, as well as two other nations, Italy, Libya and Eritrea have not been targeted by NT. Libya and Eritrea are both ex-Italian colonies. Your bomb makers are from Libya. Bingo. Is that too much of a coincidence?'

'This is your 'Ndràngheta Mafia connection. I read your latest brief an hour ago.' Linden added.

'Correct. Currently it's our only viable line of enquiry. In fact, I'm heading to Rome later today. The Chief wants me to personally press AISE's director to rip the 'Ndràngheta apart. He reckons that's best done face to face.'

Linden hadn't replied immediately.

Then, 'I'll join you. I've not been to our Rome office since I took over this job. And we have nothing better here.'

That'll be nice.

Linden continued. 'And you're still after that Freddie Derwent chap. The Brit billionaire mischief-maker? That line doesn't do well here.'

'Yes. And I can see why you are struggling with the connection. Again, it's the best we have.'

'OK. I'll get Christy to send my travel details to your Claire. Meet you by the Trevi Fountain. I'll be the one wearing the Redskins cap.'

'Aren't spies meant to be incognito?'

'You're right. It'll be a Crimson Tide cap.'

'Sorry?'

'Alabama. They're a lesser known team.'

And that's where they'd left it.

So, unless someone at the JIC came up with something more substantial, and having read the initial reports that seemed unlikely, she'd be spending an evening with Linden Rickenbacker, the Deputy Director of the CIA. Thankfully she'd packed at least one thing less frumpy than a green woollen suit and a cream blouse.

Chapter 17

Sam glanced at her watch.

27.35. Keep going. She was less than three minutes out from the Embassy. Turn right at the end of the road, and then right again.

She was sweating. The rain had stopped first thing and the sun was out. It wasn't particularly warm, but she was working hard. Her breathing was linked to her strides. Four strides; one breath - two strides in, two strides out. Four strides - another breath. Someone had once told her to run at six strides per breath. She had tried that for a couple of weeks before recognising dizzy spells mid-run probably wasn't a good sign. So she'd stuck to four.

This morning she was concentrating on working her body hard; watching where her feet landed and keeping an eye out for further obstructions. But that didn't stop her mind from unpicking the last couple of hours.

Getting the photofit right had been a struggle. She'd walked away three times. Each time Frank had been incredibly patient. Each time she'd sat back down again and, with her hand on her wound, she'd squeezed: a finger and a thumb. The pain was sharp and disturbing. But it provided just about enough focus.

She only hoped Frank hadn't noticed.

By the end the 3-D image was perfect. And she was washed out. Her lethargy was debilitating; it felt almost insurmountable. She looked at the comfy chair she'd slept in last night and felt its gravitational pull. She was just about to ask Frank for ten minutes when his trio of case-worker helpers came into the office. There had been brief introductions, followed by the bizarrest of conversations.

'You're Sam Green? *The* Sam Green?' It was the tallest and eldest of the three: two piece Italian suit, black leather belt with a Gucci buckle, a pink, cotton shirt with a collar that was so cut back it was almost non-existent, and regulatory sunglasses in his suit's breast pocket.

Sam hadn't known what to say. So she didn't say anything.

'You are, aren't you?'

Do I have to?

Really? Now?

'I guess so.' It was a tired but honest answer.

'You're the case officer who tracked down the North African with the dirty bomb. In a campervan. Here in Rome?'

'Wow.' The third of the three, the youngest; same attire but with permanent sunglasses.

'I thought the files were closed? Orange markers and all that.' Sam was convinced her whole op-file had been shut away in the bottom of a secure filing cabinet somewhere. The key melted in acid. Her checkered history buried and forgotten.

'Not anymore. I've just come back from Fort Monkton. I was an instructor there. Your history is now essential reading for all trainee case officers.'

What?

'I'm surprised.' She was.

'Yes. I hope you don't mind?' The man had an open face. He obviously wanted to talk some more.

Sam shook her head. This was going to be very dull.

'Yes. We study your methods - how to use initiative. MOs for operating as a singleton. We spend a couple of days looking at The Church of the White Cross timeline. From Berlin through to Venezuela, over a three year period. Studying independent thought and tenacity.'

'Wow.' The youngster with sunglasses again. Sam couldn't tell if he were taking the mickey, or was genuinely in awe of her. The shades made it difficult to say.

'I'm betting it's not all good news?' She asked.

'Uh, no. We spend an afternoon looking at ethics, responsibility and trust.'

How appropriate.

'You mean, blindly following orders? Or not?' Sam's response would have been tarter if she'd had the energy.

'Yes. We look at that as a case study. We encourage our students not to take matters into their own hands. That SIS protocols should be followed. Etcetera.'

'Wow.' The young lad was gently shaking his head.

Great.

'Great.'

'I have to say, I think saving the German Chancellor's life by working out who the assassin was was an act of genius.' The first man was obviously impressed.

Sam was stuck again - lost for words.

'Does any of the material mention Frank, here.' Sam pointed.

The first man looked confused.

'No. I don't recall it does.'

'Well you should all know Frank was as much involved in Berlin, Moscow, Rome, Munich, The Bahamas and Venezuela as I was. He was central to gathering the necessary intelligence. I followed his lead and, by chance, I just happened to be in the right place at the right time.'

'Wow.' A deeper *wow* this time. Real respect from the man in the sunglasses.

He's irritating me now.

Frank moved about in his seat, obviously uncomfortable with the accolades.

'Well …', the first man stuck out his hand, '… it's great to meet the legend.'

Sam sighed inwardly.

If I must.

She offered her hand and they shook.

The third man offered his hand. Sam ignored him.

'Well, now you're here, and other than Frank's lists of tasks from last night, is there anything in particular that we can do for you?' The first man had completed his adulation. It was time for action.

Sam thought for a second.

She looked at the third man.

'Do you mind taking your sunglasses off?' She was as polite as she could be.

'Sure. Sure.' He whipped them off and put them in his breast pocket.

'I need some running kit. Now. Size six shoes. Male or female. Don't care. I need a top, a t-shirt will do. Shorts and a pair of socks.' She had her bum bag open.

'Are you sure? After last night?' Frank interrupted her personal shopping order.

Bless him.

She was completely sure. It was either a beasting on pavement or a sharp knife. The first would be much better for her.

She put a soft hand up in Frank's direction and, with her other hand, fished out a one-hundred Euro note. She offered it to the third man.

'Well, OK. Like, wow.'

He took the money, but didn't move.

'Now. Please.'

'Oh, sure. Like. I'm going.'

And he did.

Whilst the puppy went off to get her running kit, Frank updated the two remaining case officers on where they were and what he and Sam had planned to do. The *Carabinieri* were due upstairs at 10.00 am to take a statement from Sam about the incident in Villa Feradina, and Gareth Jones's murder. After that they were heading off to Switzerland. Exactly where in Switzerland was not yet clear, but they hoped to get further direction from Babylon during the day.

Frank reiterated his instructions to the team. They were to continue to press every button and break as many protocols as they needed to either get the Italian intelligence infrastructure to break into the Mafia and/or specifically target Andrea Placido. Or do it themselves via on-the-books agents. They were to identify phone numbers, cars, number plates, villas - anything that might add some structure to how the 'Ndràngheta were coordinating the NT attacks. This included their control of Gioia Touro.

And Frank had given the eldest case officer a new instruction.

In one of the breaks during the tortuous photofitting experience, Sam had mentioned to Frank about the Brit-Swiss-man's cufflinks.

After she'd described them, Frank had said, 'You mean a daisy?'

'No, not a blooming daisy.' Just then she had been feeling particularly tired and irritable. 'I know a sodding daisy when I see one.'

'What about a sunflower?'

'I'm not a complete idiot!'

'A cornflower?'

'I don't know. What's a cornflower look like? Aren't they blue? If it's white-petalled with a yellow centre, then maybe?'

Frank didn't answer. Instead he worked his magic with his keyboard. A few seconds later the screen was a bloom of white and yellow flowers - all similar, but all different.

Sam put her hand on his shoulder and leant forward.

'Scroll down.'

Oops. Not so sharp, Sam.

'Please.'

The images moved upwards.

'There. That's it. What's that?' Sam pointed at a flower that looked like a small, but complicated daisy.

Frank enlarged it.

'It's an edelweiss.' Frank said.

'What? As in *The Sound of Music*?'

'Yes. You know the Alps … Switzerland. That would make sense under the circumstances?' Frank replied.

'To split hairs *The Sound of Music* was based in Austria. Although I think Julie Andrews did a reverse-Hannibal and took the kids into Switzerland at the end.' Sam added.

'Why edelweiss?' Frank asked.

'Beats me.' Sam let go of Frank's shoulder and took a pace back. 'It's obviously an alpine flower, so the

Swiss connection is a good one. It could be decorative.'
She paused. 'Maybe.' She thought some more. 'I tell you
what. We should do a complete Cynthia search on
edelweiss. See if there's anything in her records. And get
one of your team to check all of the 296 companies and
accounts to see if they have edelweiss as their logo. In
fact, let's find any industrial or company linkage to the
flower, anywhere in the world. Just in case.'

And that was the additional instruction Frank had
given to the first case officer. Find any associative
connection between Op Peacock and edelweiss -
anywhere.

Sam turned the last corner. She could pick out the
Embassy a couple of blocks down.

She lengthened her stride.

Three hundred metres.

She pushed some more, slowing only to slip
between a couple of parked cars and cross a side street.

One hundred metres.

Shit!

She half-skidded, half-stumbled to a halt. And
then threw herself into an arched doorway of some
Roman mansion.

She was breathing through her ears as well as her
mouth - anything to get her breath back. She kept herself
pressed against the side of the arch closest to the Embassy
- out of sight of the main entrance.

Out of sight of the silver BMW 530 that had just
pulled up to enter through the main gate.

Her breathing was more regular now. But her heart rate was over 100 - she had to get that down.

She dropped to one knee. If they'd spotted her they'd be searching at head height. It was a simple military camouflage technique.

She leant forward.

The Beemer was still there; its driver and passenger facing forward. The security guard was walking around the car with a mirror on a stick, looking under the sills for IEDs.

She studied the driver. No change from her initial glance.

The man from the service station in Ferrara. For sure.

She couldn't see, but she'd bet a day's wages the passenger was the woman who had chased her through the service station's kitchen.

Who are *you?*

She pulled back into the archway, picked out her phone from her bum bag and speed-dialled Frank ...

... who picked up straight away.

'Are you all right, Sam?'

She took a breath. She hadn't recovered as quickly as she thought she had.

'There's a silver BMW 5-series just coming into the compound. A man and probably a woman. I need you to find out who they are. Now.'

'Where are you, Sam?'

'Outside the Embassy. I'm not coming in until I know who they are.' She cut Frank off before she got any more supplementaries. She needed him to act now.

She popped her head out again. The car was through security and was parking up. It took a couple of attempts; space in the Embassy grounds was tight. Both doors opened.

Gotcha.

The man *and* the woman. *Déjà vu.*

Her phone rang. It was Frank.

'What have you got?'

'They're AISE. Two officers. They're coming here. Just as you left the building for your run we got a call from the *Carabinieri*. The AISE have pulled rank. They want to interview you about Gareth's murder.'

Sam thought for a second.

'Did they say anything about taking me to the Ministry of Defence? Maybe to use their facilities?'

'Wait. I didn't take the call.'

Sam waited. In the pause she put a finger to her neck to check her pulse. It was now at about 85. That was good.

The phone chirped.

'Yes. That's what they want to do. And, sorry, I didn't know that. We won't allow it.'

Sam slumped onto the cold floor of the steps and put the phone on her shoulder. She closed her eyes.

'Sam?' A squawk from Frank.

She didn't move.

Come on. That voice again. From somewhere in a recess.

She put the phone to her ear.

'OK, Frank. Here's what I want you to do. Get your team to welcome them. Get all of their details. Every last thing. Then they need to spin a yarn. Give them coffee. Move rooms. Move back again. Blah, blah. Make it slow. Get them to make excuses. And get the puppy ...'

'The what?' Frank interrupted.

'Sorry. The young lad in the team. Permanent sunglasses. Get him to let a tyre down in the Beemer. Maybe two. Right down. So the car won't move. In the meantime, get all of your and my stuff, and any surveillance kit you can carry, and stick it in whatever inconspicuous Embassy car you can find. And get out of there as soon as you can.'

'What? Why, Sam?'

'There's no time to explain, Frank. But it's imperative that you leave the building before the AISE thugs do.'

A1 Autostrade, 50 kilometres north of Rome, Italy

Sam pressed one of the many buttons on the central consul of the Range Rover. The LED screen above the heating vents changed from a satnav map to a rear view camera. She pressed it again. The screen now showed the front right bit of road zooming along at 115 kilometres per hour. It made her feel dizzy. She pressed it again. The aspect changed, but the motion-sickness factor didn't.

She ignored the button and felt the faux-leather covering on the front dash. It was of the highest quality. She then pressed her electric window button. The glass descended with a grace that wouldn't be amiss in a ballet class. Frank's hair blew about in the newly introduced cold wind. She touched the button again; the window stopped. She nudged it upwards. The window closed. No squeaks. No judders.

It was a beautiful car.

'Do you want to drive?' Frank's question bordered on exasperation. To counterbalance his tone, he looked across at her and smiled.

She forced a smile back.

'No. Thanks.' She leant forward and turned the radio on. It was set to 102.5 FM. They were playing *Up Town Funk* with Mark Ronson and Bruno Mars. The latter was doing his, *take a sip, sign a check ... Julio, get the stretch.*

She studied the scrolling information that came with the RDS signal. It read: *Very Normal People.*

The station's strapline clearly didn't include her, but she tapped her feet anyway.

'I didn't see you as a Bruno Mars fan?' Frank quipped.

Sam snorted. But she still kept tapping her feet, her right knee rising in time to the music.

I'm too hot ... hot damn.
Called a po-lice, and a fi-re-man.

'Is this the best you could do against the very clear instructions to get an inconspicuous car?' Sam asked.

Girls hit your hallelujah - whoo.

Frank was tapping the steering wheel now. Sam glanced at him. He was mouthing the words.

'It's all they had. The Ambassador's out of the country. Everything else was taken.'

'Cause uptown funk gon' give it to you.

Sam stared straight ahead. The damn song was playing with her rhythm bone.

'Cause uptown funk gon' give it to you.

Frank was now singing it, quietly. He obviously wanted to belt it out, but was too embarrassed to do so. It was a chink of joy in an armour of misery. She smiled.

The brass section were now doing their bit. It was *so* catchy.

And it was loud.

Frank must have turned the radio up using the steering controls. She let the music engulf her.

Well it's Saturday night and we in the spot.

Don't believe me just watch ... come on!

'Do, do, doh ... do, do, doh.' Frank was in the groove.

She shook her head and smiled again.

The song ran its course and once it was finished Frank turned the radio down.

'How are you doing?' Frank asked.

'Fine.' She replied much too quickly.

There was quiet for a bit. The Range Rover's soundproofing was exceptional. They were in their own private jet, flying above the autostrade at a million miles an hour.

'John and I dressed the wound on your leg last night.'

Sam said nothing. She fixed a stare out of the side window and watched the world fly by.

'Do you want to talk about it?' His voice was soft and full of concern.

No.

She concentrated on the crash barrier. It was a blur. Like everything at the moment.

'Did Derwent do it to you?'

That was it.

Enough!

She tried to stop the tears, but she couldn't. She didn't break down. She didn't blubber. Her tears came in a trickle, as though someone had gently turned on a tap. Like you would if you wanted to add water to your Scotch, but were concerned about drowning it.

She turned away as far as she could without looking behind.

Why?

Why was she crying? How could she go from the high of desperately wanting to sing slightly out of tune with Bruno Mars, to running along the bottom of a seabed gasping for air?

Frank was a darling. He always had been. He was, without doubt, the nicest person she knew. He had never let her down. When she had needed him, he had always been there. And he had never questioned her actions or her motives. And now, when she so wanted to talk to someone about how she really felt, he was inadvertently offering her a way out.

That's it. Brit-Swiss-man had done it.

But she couldn't lie. She couldn't.

The crash barrier was a silver-grey smudge. Life rushed passed.

Frank's phone pinged.

She had been saved by the bell.

Sam quickly wiped her tears with the sleeves of the Buffalo Andy had now leant her on 'long-term loan', and picked up Frank's phone. It showed a secure email from GCHQ.

'It's from the Doughnut. Are you happy I open it?'

'Sure.' Frank gave Sam his passcode. She unlocked his phone.

The email was titled: *Hungarian PM's Swiss itinerary*. It took Sam a few seconds to read it. She then found the button she'd played with earlier - and repeatedly pressed it until the satnav came back onto the central screen. She reached forward and pressed the 'Where To?' icon.

'What's it say?' Frank asked.

'GCHQ have pieced together Viktor Molnár's summer travel from his trip to Switzerland.'

'And?'

'He bought a train ticket at Geneva airport to Visp.' Sam was typing the Swiss town's name into the Range Rover's sat nav.

'Visp?'

'It's in a Swiss valley; mid-south.'

'Have you been there before?'

'Once.' She'd finished. The little men in the Range Rover's computer were working out how best to get to the pretty town in southern Switzerland.

'Go on.' Frank pressed.

'It's the Swiss mainline station where you hop off and catch a connecting train to Zermatt.'

'Am I supposed to know where Zermatt is?'

'It's the car-free town at the bottom of the Matterhorn.'

'Oh.' Frank didn't seem much the wiser.

'You know, the Toblerone mountain. Shaped like a pyramid.'

'Oh.'

Bless him.

Mamma Angela, Via Palestro, Rome, Italy

Jane checked her reflection in the glass door to the restaurant. She had an errant, dangly strand of hair falling from her forehead. She used a finger to stick it behind an ear. She pursed her lips and then squeezed them together, rolling the top over the bottom, then pursed them again.

Her reflection was more tonight's menu, which was being elegantly displayed in a silver frame on the warmer side of the door, than Jane's face, but it was enough to get a picture. She knew she looked travelled and exhausted. No amount of thinly applied make up could disguise that.

Life was tough and then you die; as her father always used to say.

She pushed open the door, looked to the ornate bar on the left wall of the restaurant and spotted Linden. He was wearing, unnecessarily as she'd met him dozens of times before, a baseball cap. She smiled to herself - and then overtly as he turned, caught her eye, stood and raised a welcoming hand.

Linden was Jane's favourite. He was around six-foot, attractive in a preppy way, always wore tasteful, but not expensive clothes, and had a shallow east-coast accent that resonated an Ivy League education and a decent middle-class upbringing. He'd sadly lost his wife to cancer ten years ago and had two late-teenage children. She'd seen a photo of them on his desk. They looked well-behaved and washed-behind-the-ears. And - not forgetting - he was the Deputy Director of the CIA at 48, having originally spent eight years as a Marine.

He outranked her by at least one rank, and by a factor of ten if you considered the size of the CIA against the number of staff who worked for SIS. But he never once let that show. He'd always treated her as an equal, even when they'd first met and she was just a senior case officer standing in for David Jennings, her previous boss.

And now, here in a city steeped in romance, he had worn a Crimson Tide cap as he quipped he would. He must have made a special effort to make that happen - unless he had a box of hats covering all of the NFL teams in a drawer in his office. Maybe he did this for all the girls?

Who was she kidding? They were both professionals. They were both up to their shoulders in an Orwellian, global crisis that could bring down governments - his and hers included - and he had followed through on a joke he'd made to a foreign colleague a few hours earlier. She'd have done the same.

But that didn't stop her stomach from fluttering as they cheek-kissed.

He offered her the stool next to his. She took it.

'Drink?' He asked, the accent was raspberry ripple and chocolate sauce.

Large gin and tonic - without the tonic. No ice.

'Coke, please.'

Linden, who had taken off the cap and placed it on the bar, ordered her drink.

'How's London?'

Good question.

She'd checked with Claire before she'd left her hotel. The genuine, well-behaved 1.8 million protesters in London had made their point and most of them had headed home, causing all sorts of travel disruption. However, there had been a full-scale riot in The Strand, led by a mixture of antifascista and a couple of hundred indeterminate thugs who had come for the violence …

and the spills of the looting. It had taken the police a couple of hours to disperse the crowd; they hadn't moved on easily. The police had had to use horses and teargas. She'd seen some video. It was something out of the Troubles in Northern Ireland from the `70s.

That seemed to have sparked off smaller, but just as violent skirmishes in five of the poorer London districts. The worst was in Lambeth where an orchestrated crowd of around 500 had ambushed the riot police. To begin with they had attacked the police with Molotov cocktails; a couple of policemen had needed treatment for burns. Then the crowd had pulled back into a high-rise estate. Naively the police's shield-line had followed them, with the less well-protected, but much more mobile 'snatch and arrest' teams sheltering behind the line. As one of the arrest teams skirted around the shield-line to grab a ring-leader, pre-positioned rioters had dropped breeze blocks from a fifth-floor balcony. One of the policemen had taken a direct hit and had been killed instantly. Seconds later the crowd had dispersed, reformed in a local high street, this time as a group of looters, and had taken the shops apart until police reinforcements had arrived 20 minutes later.

Although the death of the police officer had yet to hit the mainstream media, it hadn't stopped the news reverberating around the Met's frontline staff. As a result, and against very clear orders from above, the police had become heavy-handed. An hour ago Guy's hospital in central London had reported an influx of civilian casualties, many with breaks allegedly caused by baton swipes. If the rioting and looting didn't run its course in the next couple of hours, Jane feared for what the city would look like in the morning.

There were similar reports of violence in Liverpool and Glasgow.

And Paris. And Munich. The list kept growing.

In Warsaw, alt-right supporters, with red flares and carrying red and white Polish flags, had set fire to a block of flats in a city suburb where there were known to be a preponderance of Syrian and Afghan immigrants. The number of casualties was, as yet, unknown.

London was bad. But so was everywhere else.

'Not good, Linden. I'm afraid. It's the Brixton riots all over again, but this time it's not a race thing. It's frustration - which is understandable - being exploited by anyone with a grievance and a desire to smash a window. I have to say we're maybe two hours away from calling in the Army.

'Sorry. We have the National Guard stood by in 15 states. But we don't feel so bad about deploying them as you Limeys do. I think we'll be able to keep a lid on it.'

Jane's drink arrived. She took a sip. And then continued.

'Unless we find out who's behind the NT attacks, it's just going to get worse. As you know, our government is surviving with a tiny minority and the PM's leadership is constantly being challenged. I go to bed most nights not knowing who will be in charge when I wake up.'

She took another sip and then noticed Linden had his suitcase with him.

'Have you not been to your Embassy?'

'No. Straight off the plane. I wanted to have a face to face with you. See what you've got and agree tomorrow's approach with AISE and the 'Ndràngheta. We need to press them hard. If your case officer's reports are accurate, then, if nothing else, they've murdered a British citizen. And, if we follow your lead about the source of the NT attacks, then we've got to bust the 'Ndràngheta right open - as soon as we can. Even if you're wrong, and I no longer think you are, that can't be a bad thing?'

'Have you any corroboration, other than the FBI's call that the Seattle pipe bomber originated from Libya?'

The bartender was back. The conversation stopped. He pointed to a table across the room.

'*Il tuo tavolo è pronto.*'

'*Grazie.*' Linden replied. He waited for the man to move away. 'Our team in Tunis have established a link between your four ferry terrorists and a Tunisian. His name is Karim Beji. He's a local hood with fingers in a number of pies. They pulled him in a couple of hours ago. He's very jumpy. At the same time we sent in a team to his apartment. They found drugs, money - euros and dollars - and a second passport.' He stopped, opened his hands and nodded. He was suggesting she completed the briefing.

'It's Italian?'

'Yes.'

'That's pretty unusual. Tunisia is an ex-French colony.'

'Correct. Anyhow, Langley have matched the passport to movement. He travelled to Gioia Touro - on the same container ship as your team.'

'Goodness. So he's the movement kingpin between Tunisia and Italy.' Jane took a sip of her drink.

'Correct again. We have two of his phones. The SIMs have been opened. We expect the home team to have phone records, etcetera, in the next 12 hours. I'm guessing we'll be able to find a link to the 'Ndràngheta, or a link to someone who has a link to the 'Ndràngheta, real soon. No. I'm with you Jane. This has the Italian Mafia's sticky fingers all over it.'

Linden stood, and offered a hand in the direction of the table.

Jane was about to get up when her phone rang.

She took it from her handbag. The screen displayed a single name: *Sam.*

'Excuse me.'

Linden nodded.

'Hi, Sam. Kinda busy. Can we talk later?'

'Put the news on.'

'What?'

'Whatever you're doing, put the news on. And then cancel all of our rush-hour trains.'

'What are you talking about?'

'There's been a train crash in Melbourne. And a second, an hour later in Shanghai. Both were passenger trains. They've hacked into the signalling infrastructure, I'm sure of it.'

Jane put her hand on the mouthpiece.

'Linden. Can you get your phone out and bring up CNN. Or something?' She put the phone back to her ear.

'Sam, we can't just stop the trains. There's enough chaos as it is?'

There was silence from her phone.

Then, 'Look, Frank and I are into something here. We can't do any more than we are. Stop the bloody trains!'

'Jane?' It was Linden.

'Yes?' She was caught between two conversations.

'There have been three train crashes. Melbourne, Shanghai and, just now, Mumbai. They're working their way across the globe. It seems the sun rises and the trains fail. Commuter stuff. Am I wrong?'

No, Linden. I don't think you are.

46°00'23.8" N; 7°43'13.1" E, Matterhorn, Switzerland

Frank was breathless. He wasn't overweight, but he wasn't fit. He kept himself in shape by eating the right things and walking everywhere. But the air felt thin; as though someone had sucked out a lot of the oxygen and replaced it with something much less useful, like nitrogen - or carbon dioxide. And Sam's pace was relentless. She was ahead of him and slightly higher, on a track that snaked its way up the valley. He could pick out her silhouette against the side of the mountain and, with the moon as bright as an overhead lamp, her shadow danced on top of the freshly fallen snow. They had emerged from the treeline about ten minutes ago. A couple of minutes before Sam had let him catch up.

'How are you doing?' She'd asked.

'Just great.' He lied.

'Not far now. I reckon about 800 metres, maybe a klick. No more. And it's path all the way.' She had tried to sound positive.

'It's fine.' He lied again.

She'd nodded and sprinted off into the distance.

Having taken the train up to Zermatt, which turned out to be like Mayfair in the mountains, they'd stopped in a bar, had a couple of beers and ordered raclette. The bill would have fed a family of four for a week in Slough. He would have been happy to put the tab on Op Peacock's expenses, but Sam had insisted on paying.

They were just about to find a hotel when Carla had phoned. She was excited. In the space of five minutes she'd had two notable intelligence successes. First, Freddie Derwent's Bentley had been found. That is, a parking permit bearing its number plate had come to light. It was in a secure, underground garage in Staldenried, just short of the train station to Zermatt. The fact that they'd managed to find anything had been a surprise to Carla. SIS had no operatives in Switzerland -

the country forbade it. And it took any violation of that rule extremely seriously. The country's 'neutrality', strict obedience to rules and regulations, and somewhat secretive administration made it unnecessary and unattractive for any non-Swiss intelligence force to warrant a presence in the country. Carla's success was, therefore, a bonus.

Second, and the reason why he and Sam were tabbing up the mountainside, was a live mobile signal had been intercepted by GCHQ. Originally they had been tasked by Carla to look for any signal intercept on any of the Op Peacock accounts in the Cayman Islands. That instruction had been much too broad to expect success. After Frank had narrowed that down to any account with a Cumbrian association, they had picked up a Swiss mobile number that, over the last day and half, had been passing data instructions to one of the accounts. The transactions had been all low-level - thousands of dollars, not millions - but the signal was live and the Doughnut had triangulated its position to a small corner of Switzerland: 1500 metres south of Zermatt, in the valley leading to the base of the Matterhorn.

Whilst Frank had been dealing with Carla, Sam had been watching the TV in the bar. They were covering a Champion's league match. Engrossed in his conversation and taking notes on a small pad, he'd paid little attention to the football until Sam had grabbed him by the elbow and pointed to the screen. The footy was no longer being shown. Instead the Swiss channel was showing footage of two train crashes. One in Australia, the other in China. As he finished his conversation with

Carla, Sam had got on the phone to Jane. He overheard Sam say, 'Stop the bloody trains!' before she'd hung up.

What is happening?

He briefed Sam on Carla's int and, after a quick conflab, Sam had dashed across the street - with him in pursuit - to a late-opening mountain equipment shop. In ten minutes she'd spent an eye-watering sum of money on some gear that was better suited to a hike in the mountains than his jeans and her new running shoes. He'd bought a hat and a pair of gloves. And kept the bill. He couldn't afford not to put the exorbitant sum against the op code.

Then they were off. Sam striding ahead with her phone's GPS providing the directions.

That was 40 minutes ago.

'Shhh! Get down!'

Sam had stopped about ten metres ahead. She'd gone down on one knee. He found a boulder on the side of the track and knelt beside it, his lungs and legs thankful for the rest.

Up ahead on a ledge was a mountain hut, no bigger than a small garage. The moon picked out its shape, lighting up one side of the chalet-style roof, the snow on it reflecting moon-blue back to an enveloping graphite sky. There was a small chimney, but no smoke. The hut had a door, a small, deep window on the front aspect - which glowed a dark amber - and a snow-covered bench out front. The mountain rose sharply behind. Any trekking from here would have to be left to the experts.

Sam was beckoning him forward.

Keeping low, he made his way to her side.

'There's a light. There could be someone in there. Have you got a mobile signal?' Sam was whispering. He had no idea why he hadn't considered it before, but all of a sudden he felt uncomfortably nervous. His stomach did a little turn.

He took his mobile out of his jacket. He had five bars of 4G. *How Swiss.*

'All good.' He whispered, showing Sam his phone.

'OK. If Carla's not in, get Babylon's duty officer on the phone. Tell them what we're up to and keep the phone live. If anything happens they'll be able to pick it up.'

That sounded like a good idea. So, as Sam crawled ahead, he phoned Carla. She picked up and he whispered what they were up to. She replied that she'd put the phone on speaker and, not to worry, there were eight of them in the office and they'd be round her phone like wasps on an open can of coke in no time.

He wasn't sure if that made him feel any better.

Sam was at the hut. She didn't try the door. She was looking inside the window. She paused there for a few seconds, before disappearing around the back.

He waited.

Nothing.

'What's happening, Frank?' A high-pitched question all the way from London.

'Nothing. Shhh.'

He kept looking to the hut, but it was getting more difficult to see. The moon had disappeared behind a cloud. He squinted his eyes, hoping to get a clearer view.

Not a dicky bird.

I can't stay here.

With his phone in one hand and his other pushing off rocks so he could stay low, he shuffled his way to the hut. Once there, he stood and put his back to the horizontal logs that made up the front wall of the hut.

His heart was pumping away.

He should have stayed down by the rocks. *No, I should have stayed in London.*

He listened. He strained his eyes.

No sign of Sam.

Other than the pitiful light from the hut's front window, the world had turned black since the moon had slid behind the cloud. The heavy green of the pine forests below were now darker than coal. The mountains rising out of the valley, a sooty grey. The sky was a mixture of heavy blue and school-shoe black. The only other light in the valley was the far-off, wealthy glow of Zermatt.

Sod it.

He took a deep breath … and slid his head round the corner of the timber wall, peering into the small recess which housed the window.

It was what it looked like it would be. A one-room, simply-furnished, wooden chalet. A single, low-watt bulb hanging by a long wire lit up a bench, an old pine table and a shelf under a second window which was on the back wall. On the shelf was an unused gas stove and ... he stuck his head into the recess so he could see more of the room.

Inside the hut was a mixture of barely-lit, dense-brown, ageing pine and impenetrable dark shadows.

Until then.

What the hell is that?

A spark of light.

Frank thought he saw cans. *Jerry cans*? And a box and some wires. A mobile - possibly an antennae?

His eyes lost all focus as, instantaneously, there was more light than the midday sun. It was a small ball at first, but that was maybe for no more than a millisecond. And then it was huge. Massive. Like a fireball.

Yellows. And reds.

But mostly white.

And heat.

Oh, God.

Heat. And light.

Fire.

He'd been here before. In a cellar in Munich.

Yellow. White. Burning. More heat than he could bear. And Wolfgang. Like a statue.

And death. And pain.

And ...

The incendiary device burnt quicker than his mind could compute. The fuel was contained in cans, which exploded under pressure. The walls of the chalet were tree trunk-thick, and as strong as concrete. So the fireball escaped where it could.

Frank's primeval reactions, his eyelids closing and his head turning without cognisant instruction, saved his eyesight.

Sam saved the rest of him.

Somehow she had known what was coming and had dashed around the front of the cabin just as the device went off. She launched herself at him, catching him around the chest and forcing him away from the window just before it became a flamethrower.

As the wind was taken from him and he toppled sideward, Frank knew he was on fire. He could smell the plastic in his jacket burning. His bobble hat felt oddly liquid as it contracted to meet the contours of his head. And, for a second, he thought this time it was all over for him.

Oddly he quickly sensed cold. Everywhere. And a thud of pain. And more cold. He was turning and twisting. And then, with his back on the floor and an arm out straight, he was being dragged downwards - bumping.

BANG!

A noise like a champagne cork, but hundreds of times louder. He opened his eyes and swore he saw the door of the hut fly through the air above him.

More bumps. A bit more pain, but nothing a good bath wouldn't sort.

And then more cold. Snow. On his face. Over his arms. His hat was off. And now there was snow on his head.

Shit, that's cold.

But it was no longer cold.

Because, from where he had just come was the warmest fire he'd felt since round his auntie's house last Christmas. He couldn't miss the orange glow from the burning chalet; feel the strength of a thousand bar fires.

'Frank!'

It was Sam.

He should have known it was her who was dragging him through the snow. Dealing with his burning clothes. Pulling him to safety.

He sat up and focused. She was kneeling in front of him, her face lit orange by the glow of the burning chalet.

Orange.

Like an angel.

She was smiling.

'Are you OK?' She asked.

Like an angel.

He looked at her now, in more detail. Her clothes were charred. She had been burnt.

'I think so. Are you?'

'Yeah. That was close.'

'Frank? Sam?' The squeak came from Frank's hand. He was still holding his mobile.

'I'd better get this.'

Sam nodded.

'Good idea, Batman.'

Chapter 18

*46°00'55.9" N; 7°44'34.5" E, South of Zermatt,
Switzerland*

Sam was working Frank as hard as she could, without breaking him. He didn't seem to be badly burnt, and he may have a few bumps and bruises from the fall and the drag, but she reckoned he'd be OK. His face, probably like hers, would look like they'd spent a week in the sun without any sunscreen. But other than that ...

They were halfway to the outskirts of the town. She'd feel safer once they were lost in the crowds. When she glanced over her shoulder, she could easily pick out the fire against the backdrop of the cold, dark mountain. Doubtless the Swiss *police municipale* would be on the scene shortly. They couldn't afford to get picked up by the police. In their grips no amount of Embassy leverage would prise them out of their clutches. They *had* to make the town.

She thought she knew what had happened at the mountain hut and was angry with herself for being so gullible. It was obviously a recently set trap. The mobile signal GCHQ had intercepted was new; and it was designed to lure somebody - probably anyone close to the case - to the cabin and then kill them. Sam guessed all of the poking about into the Cayman Island accounts had set off an alarm somewhere. And that alarm had prompted

Brit-Swiss-man (she still couldn't think his name out loud) to bait a trap. Which had almost worked.

It was genius. GCHQ had triangulated the location. Normal accuracy from them was a 15 by 15 metre square, which wasn't always helpful in a built up area, but worked perfectly on a lonely hillside where there was only one hut. The lure consisted of an incendiary device linked to a short timer which was set off remotely via an electronic signal. That signal came from a laptop outside of the chalet, which she had been investigating when she'd spotted Frank at the opposite window.

The laptop was connected to a standard microwave repeater on the rear eave of the building, which would be linked to another repeater down the valley - in line of sight. That repeater would be connected to the GSM mobile network.

The linking of 'repeaters' was common practice in remote areas. It's how people in far-off places got their Wi-Fi and mobile data. In this case she was convinced the laptop broke into the repeater station at the chalet and listened for pings from local mobiles - maybe even specific numbers, like hers or Frank's. Once those mobiles were within a couple of metres of the repeater at the chalet, the laptop sprung the timer. She'd found all of this gubbings in a waterproof box at the back of chalet - which was being kept charged by a 12-volt vehicle battery.

Get close. And say bye-bye.

Sam reckoned she had set off the fuse and Frank had caught the brunt by being next to the window when it went off. The booby-trapper had probably planned for them being inside the building when it blew.

She'd tried to explain this to Frank on the way down, but all she got was a lot of 'ohs' in response. She'd held his hand for most of the way as, when they'd started, he'd fallen a couple of times. He clearly wasn't well enough for another trek - not at the pace she was demanding.

But they had to get off the mountain.

She'd taken Frank's phone from him just before they'd left the chalet. He wasn't making much sense and so she'd explained to Carla they were both OK and Carla was to phone the Embassy in Bern and give them a heads up. And, as soon as she had done that, she was to look again at the phone signal and see if she could find any pattern that might give them another lead. Sam remained convinced Brit-Swiss-man had met Viktor Molnár in Zermatt, just as she was convinced he had a place in the town. The Bentley's long-term parking permit told that story. And the lure to the cabin only added to her feeling that Zermatt was his playground.

Sam still had Frank's phone to her ear as they started their descent - Carla had some more news for them.

'The Cayman accounts are definitely being used to launder money.' Carla was excited. Sam was already breathing hard.

'Most of the transactions have been cash to gold purchases, which was fairly normal practice when it came to washing someone else's illicit funds. Have a guess how much money has passed through the accounts and turned into gold?'

Sam wasn't up for a quiz, especially as Frank had just tripped and almost pulled her over.

'Hit me.' She said.

'$1.9 billion. And that figure is likely to grow. A lot.'

That didn't surprise Sam. It fitted the model which she and Frank had dismissed earlier: sell shares and buy gold now; sell gold and buy shares later.

She didn't reply for a couple of seconds as she carefully led Frank down a rocky bit of path, Frank's hand still in hers.

'What's the closing level of the FTSE today, Carla?'

If Carla had been surprised by the request, she didn't say anything.

There was a pause.

'4,611. Down 40 points.'

'And gold? Per gram?'

Frank had toppled over at that point. Sam helped him up, turning his head gently to the direction of the blaze to check his pupils. They were OK. He must be emotionally shattered and there was probably some shock there. Key now, after the snow immersion to deal with the burns, was to make sure he didn't get cold and allow any shock to take control. They needed a pub and a couple of large *chocolats chaud.*

'£44.41, up 32 pence today.'

So still no crossing of the lines. Maybe the train wrecks would do the trick?

She dismissed the thought. It still didn't make its way round the elephant in the room: once the imaginary line was breeched, how do you convince the world the threat of NT has been dealt with so shares can become rocket-assisted?

'Thanks, Carla. We'll call you once we're clear of any police.'

There was noise ahead. And some lights.

Sounds like quad bikes.

'Come on, fella.'

She pulled Frank into the woods off to the side of the track. He followed easily.

They lay low.

One bike. Two policemen.

Another bike. Two more.

Nothing else following.

'Come on.'

They were off again.

It took them another ten minutes to hit the first ski chalet, an opulent three-storey structure with a full-height, picture window looking up at the Matterhorn; there were no blinds. Inside were a couple of well-to-dos sitting on a huge sofa drinking something expensive, whilst warming their feet on a fire which sat obliquely in the main room. It was surrounded by a bum warmer; the flue's huge silver-chimney rising to the ceiling. The pair had ringside seats to the unfolding arson/fire mystery. If it wasn't already, no doubt tomorrow it would be a huge story in the achingly affluent and very well behaved Zermatt.

They were in a crowded bar 15 minutes after that. And ten minutes later, sat in a dark corner away from fidgeting eyes, they were two hot chocolates to the better. Frank, red cheeked and with a charred jacket looking every bit an arsonist, was faring well. Sam had checked all of his cognisant functions (how old are you?; what's your mother's maiden name?; what's the name of the lead guitarist in Status Quo?) whilst nonchalantly looking for any wounds.

'Let's pretend to be lovers, Frank,' as she ran her hands all over his body studying his face for grimaces. No, he was fine; giggling as she caught a tickle-spot.

They discussed what had happened. And had a brief chat about a way ahead. Trains left Zermatt every hour to Täsch, where they'd left the Ambassador's Range Rover. But Sam was worried that if they tried to leave now the trains would be empty and they'd be easily compromised. If they stayed the night and tidied themselves up, they'd be better prepared for tomorrow and, hopefully, get lost in the crowd.

'Sorry, Sam. But I'd go for option two. I'm dead to the world. And, frankly, I'm going to be a bit of a burden to you until I've had some sleep.'

Frank was right on that count. And they had no plan. A night under the watchful eye of the Matterhorn would do them both good. And, who knows, by the morning someone might have found out where Brit-Swiss-man's Zermatt lodgings were? If they did, they'd be best placed to investigate.

She ordered a couple of pricey beers.

Why not?

British Embassy, Via Venti Settembre, Rome, Italy

Jane, Linden and Stewart Hall - R1, the head of Rome Station - were all sitting around Stewart's chic glass and metal conference table. Their flask of coffee had just been refilled, which had arrived with a tray of sandwiches and a plate of biscuits. Jane didn't need any more food. And she certainly couldn't manage another coffee without a trip to the loo. So, when Stewart offered she declined.

'Is there anything else we can do tonight?' Linden asked.

Tonight was a loose term under the circumstances. It was nearing 3 am. Dawn would be next and who knew what that would bring. London was literally burning, as were many cities in Europe.

Jane and Linden had both been onto their respective governments about 'stopping the trains'. Since Mumbai, there had been two other incidents in two other countries, but, thankfully, no lives had been lost. It appeared NT had targeted countries where the signalling system was centrally coordinated via computer systems, but with some regional autonomy - which allowed different parts of different networks to make best use of the track they had available. These were the preferred systems of countries or regions with modern infrastructure. Hence attacks in Australia, Japan and eastern India. They were still establishing what happened, but initial thoughts were hackers had exploited whatever weaknesses they could find, turned systems on and off, corrupting code and generally caused merry hell. It was all low-key, agricultural cyber warfare. But it had been effective.

The UK's rail network was reasonably sophisticated. The head of Network Rail had been hoofed out of bed a couple of hours ago and appraised of the situation. Having checked with his Chief Operations Officer, a hastily-assembled, secure-video-linked COBRA had been given a number of options. They ranged between 'close down the whole network', to 'do nothing at all'. Network Rail were confident their cyber-security infrastructure was so good it couldn't be hacked. In the end it was the PM who made the decision (which Jane thought was a particularly brave one): keep the wagons rolling.

It was more complicated in the US as their system wasn't wholly centrally controlled. In the end the White House delegated the decision-making down to state level. So far 14 out of 53 states had closed all rail links down, even though it was nowhere near their morning rush hour. It was out of his hands, but Linden reckoned closing down the railways wasn't the best call.

'Your PM has made the right decision. If you close the system, then the folk will tick it off as another 'neo-terrorism' triumph. More of the government losing control. Sure, if there's an accident then he might regret it, but I think that's a risk worth taking.'

For the last hour the three of them had been discussing how to approach tomorrow's meeting with the director of AISE.

'What have you got on him?' Linden had asked Stewart.

'A fairly full file, actually. He looks clean. For a start he's from the northern Po Valley, where there is little Mafia reach. And his records show a steady, but smooth rise through the ranks. He was an intelligence officer in Beijing in the early 90s, held various positions in Rome thereafter, before becoming head of station in Addis Ababa. That was his last job before this one.'

'Hang on.' The words came out of Jane's mouth before she'd had time to really think through Stewart's last sentence. 'Does that post cover the whole of the Horn of Africa?'

'Yes, I believe it does.'

Jane looked at Linden, who raised his eyebrows.

She continued. 'How many of the central briefing notes have you been keeping abreast of?'

It was a rhetorical question, but Jane let it hang anyway.

'Well, we keep up to date here.'

Maybe not as much as you think, Stewart.

'You knew you had a member of my team fly in here last night. And a seconded, ex-case officer, joined him in the early hours?'

'Yes. My deputy dealt with that. We assigned your chap three case officers. We did the right thing?' Stewart replied, a touch defensively.

'Yes, yes.' Jane paused for breath. 'We know, for sure, that three of the four terrorists who took down the Pride of Eastbourne were from Eritrea. And they'd only left the country about three weeks ago, transiting through Tunis.'

'Eritrea. Horn of Africa, Eritrea?'

'Exactly. And, this morning my two staff were literally chased off your premises by two AISE staff.'

Stewart looked confused. As did Linden.

'The seconded case officer originally entered Italy from Hungary. She was tailed and she thinks pursued by two AISE staff. She didn't know they were Italian secret service until the pair of them pulled up at the Embassy this morning. AISE had usurped the *Carabinieri* and were keen to take my officer "back to the Ministry of Defence" for questioning about the death of a UK national in Calabria. Thankfully both of my team got clean away and lost any potential tail.'

'You're saying AISE were tailing with, maybe, malice, Sam and Frank?' Linden asked. Jane had managed to brief Linden on much of Sam's recent travails, but not all of it.

'And you're also saying that senior staff, and maybe the head of AISE, are on the 'Ndràngheta's books?' Disbelief laced Stewart's question.

'It's not impossible.' Jane replied. 'We know - you know, Stewart - 'Ndràngheta have reach into both the *Carabinieri* and AISE. Otherwise it would have been taken apart long ago. With the origin of the ferry terrorists and the director's East African links, we can't dismiss the possibility that he's in their employ.'

Jane's final statement seemed to stop the conversation in its tracks.

'So, what do we do?' Stewart eventually asked.

There was no obvious answer. But the question couldn't be ignored. The 'Ndràngheta needed to be broken into.

'We'll do it. We'll blow them apart.' As soon as Linden uttered his statement he sat back in his chair. Jane studied his face. It was one of resignation, not of smugness. He wasn't happy with his own suggestion and it showed.

'How?' Jane asked. Under huge scrutiny and only with the highest possible sanction could the UK think of carrying out an operation of the kind she thought Linden was suggesting. It would have to be Special Forces led, and would require much more intelligence than they had now. Who were the targets? Were they to be killed - or captured? Was the risk worth the international and, particularly now, domestic repercussions? It wouldn't swim. No, worse than that. It would sink without trace. The JIC wouldn't consider it.

The US, on the other hand …

'We could put a recon team together in the next 24 hours and have an attack team ready 24 hours later. Under the closest of holds we would need to pool all of our intelligence resources in order to target the right HVTs (high value targets), and we'd need to know exactly where they were. It's possible we could be in and out before the Italian government knew of the attack, although I guess POTUS would phone his opposite number as soon as the attack teams were on the ground. And, afterwards, I'm pretty certain we could mop this up.'

'Isn't there a line in your Constitution somewhere?' Jane asked.

'Maybe. But if we consider the 'Ndràngheta as a threat to our national security, then no. And if the Italians had formally asked for our help, then it wouldn't be a problem at all.'

'But they won't have.' Stewart stated the obvious.

'Not to begin with. But that would be one reason why POTUS would make the call. He can be very persuasive.'

'And the UN?' Jane asked.

'If we can get the Italians to say they'd asked for our support, then the UN will have nothing to shout about.'

Sounds like a plan.

Jane leant forward and poured herself a coffee which she didn't want and didn't have the bladder for.

But if Linden was as good as his word, the next couple of days were going to be very sleep deprived. And caffeine was the answer. She offered the jug to the two men. They both nodded.

'My secondee, Sam Green, spent almost 24 hours at Andrea Placido's villa in Calabria, the night before last - it's a long story. She has a photographic memory for faces and places. I'm sure she'd be able to give you chapter and verse on the villa's security arrangements. Also, and I know we have a copy on file, she has a list of 180 or so names of guests at Andrea Placido son's wedding. If we can match any of those names to any detail you have here or at Langley, that might help.'

'Thanks, Jane.' Linden said. He had his phone out and was tapping at it. 'I'm confident our local CIA office will have a myriad of intel, and I know we have a small team working out of Palermo, Sicily. They've been looking at links between the Sicilian Mafia and organised crime in Chicago. We'll tap into them. Hang on …'

Linden's phone was ringing. He raised it to his ear.

'Jim? It's Linden. Get the whole office in now. No excuses. I'll be with you in under an hour. And get a video link up with General Franks.' There was a pause. 'No, I don't care what time it is. Not his deputy. No. The general. And, he'll need the Joint Chiefs and POTUS ready for an emergency briefing at, say, 10.00 pm EST. Got it?'

Linden put the phone in his pocket. Jane and Robin were both looking at him. She realised her mouth was slightly ajar. She closed it.

'This is going to be something to tell the grandkids.' Linden said.

Café Sérac, Triftweg, Zermatt, Switzerland

Sam and Frank had circled the chalet twice. There was a sharp uphill road running alongside its boundary, a contouring footpath a couple of chalets above it, a further road which led back down towards the town and another level path below the house that led back to the road where they'd started. Between them they'd given the chalet a detailed once over. Sam was trained to recce a site, both from her early army days and as a case office at SIS's training ground at Fort Monkton. Frank was clumsier, but effective enough. Once Sam thought they'd seen enough, they'd left the chalet and walked the short distance downhill to a local cafe. They were lucky, the cafe was strategically placed. Sam was able to use the pair of binos they'd bought at one of the shops earlier (*ouch*) and given the chalet a further once-over, whilst seemingly focusing on a distant object.

The coffee was good, but unacceptably expensive. The service perfunctory. The cafe ambience nowhere near as 'chocolate box' as similar ones in Austria. *Never mind.* It was all serving a purpose.

They'd been woken just after six, which, looking across at Frank as he fumbled with his phone, was eight hours too soon for him. Frank had mumbled, 'Morning, Eithan', in between yawning. Eithan was the eldest of three case officers in Rome.

Sam was convinced that Frank was hearing Eithan, but not listening, so she jumped out of her single bed and unceremoniously took the handset from him.

'Eithan? It's Sam. the sharp-tongued woman with Frank. Wassupppp?'

'Oh, hello, Sam.' He sounded surprised. 'Have the pair of you not found somewhere to get your heads down?'

Sorry?

'Yes. You woke us up.'

'Oh.'

I get it.

'We're sharing a room. Two single beds. The Queen can't afford two rooms in Zermatt. Not without selling a tiara or two. Anyhow, what's new?'

'Oh. OK. I've got some edelweiss news which I thought you'd want to hear about. It's a bit of a story. Do you want the short or the long version?' Eithan was managing to sound excited and shattered at the same time. It didn't sound as though he'd had much sleep.

Sam sat on her bed, her feet on the floor.

Phoneless, Frank had made it to the bathroom. He hadn't closed the door and there was the sound of water swashing about. He came back in with a wet face. He mouthed, 'That's better,' to Sam.

'Whatever, Eithan. If there's too much I'll hurry you along. I'm putting you on speaker.' Sam put the phone down on the bedside table and pressed the loudspeaker icon.

'OK.' Eithan was loud and clear. 'The edelweiss search was inspired, I have to say. I've got a couple of industrial connections, but key is a Special Reconnaissance Regiment report from 18 months ago. They conducted a three-month observation insertion in central Belize. The team had eyes-on a compound owned by a Xavier Turner, a Belize national with British roots. He was thought to be one of the major players in the export of opium from seven or eight rainforest locations in the centre of the country. At the time the business was said to be worth over £500 million a year. April before last, the SRR team clocked a well-dressed Caucasian man arriving in a hired Toyota Landcruiser. The man stayed overnight and left the next day. The team believe Xavier was in the compound for the meeting. As you know, the SRR report and photograph, they don't follow up - we do that ...'

Yes, I know.

'Get to the point, Eithan.' Sam's stomach was rumbling.

'What was interesting was whilst the photos of the visiting man were pretty inconclusive, in that he always wore shades and a panama, there is a clear image of his cufflinks sticking out of a cotton jacket.'

'Edelweiss.' Sam knew what was coming. She'd seen the cufflinks two days ago.

519

'Correct. I've looked at all the photos. I'm putting 65% certainty on the man being the same one you photofitted. But I'm attributing 90% certainty on the cufflinks. They are exactly as you described.'

'That's great Eithan, and what was the SIS follow up?'

Whilst Eithan had been talking Frank had made them both a cup of coffee. He put them on the bedside table next to the phone. Sam nodded her thanks.

Eithan continued. 'The hire car was rented to an F Cleaton.'

Sam racked her brain.

'Cleaton Moor.' She had it.

'Correct. That's the west corner of the Lake District. It fits the pattern you described yesterday. The SIS analyst working with the obs team here at Babylon had interrogated Cleaton's route in and out of the country. He flew via Miami to Brussels, at which point the trail goes cold. Although I am on that now.'

'Good, Eithan. Good work. Anything else?'

Frank was sitting on his bed. He was wearing peejays, with a button-up front shirt and cotton tie around the waist of his loose-fitting trousers. Sam had been too tired to bother last night, but after a couple of hours sleep she was more attuned to his nightwear; red, with white dinosaurs. She shot him a frown.

'I didn't know I'd be sharing a room!' He whispered loudly.

'Yes. Some good stuff.' The phone was talking to them again. 'I've checked out Xavier Turner. He's still in business and still subject to our interests - his file is live. It's not clear why we've not reined him in.'

'Go on.' Sam pressed.

'He has a number of overseas accounts; one in the Cayman Islands. It is managed under the umbrella of Lakeland Industries, the one Freddie, whatever his real name is, has been managing.' Sam winced at the name. Eithan wasn't with the programme. 'A week after Freddie's visit there were a dozen major transactions through The Caymans.'

'Gold.' Sam interjected.

'Correct. $162 million dollars' worth.'

'Wow.' Frank joined the conversation for the first time. 'You were right Sam. This is all about gold.'

Sam got to her feet, picked up her coffee and walked to the bedroom window. She pulled back the curtains slightly and peeked out. It was still dark. And it looked very cold.

'That's good work, Eithan. Anything else?' She shouted from across the room.

'No, that's it for now. I'll interrogate Xavier some more this morning.'

'Have you slept?' Frank interjected.

'No, not yet.'

'Get your head down for a bit. And then get back on task. I don't think this is going to come to a conclusion anytime soon. We all need to stay as sharp as we can for as long as we can.' Frank sounded very managerial. If it wasn't for his horrendous pyjamas, Sam would have been impressed.

'OK, Frank, will do. Keep safe.'

The phone went dead.

Sam let the curtains go. They were making progress. Baby steps. NT was about money. And Brit-Swiss-man was the man making it, probably for a lot of people. But they were no closer to finding him.

'We should get dressed, Frank. And eat something. Let's have a look at your face?'

Frank turned the side that had been closest to the fireball towards her. It was red, but not blistering. He was going to be OK.

As Frank made his way back to the bathroom, she picked up her own phone. There was a missed message. It was from Jane, sent at 03.15 this morning. It read:

> *Come back to Rome asp. We have an anti-Mafia op going down and need your support here. Give us a call when you're on your way. J xx.*

Sam swiped at the phone and the message disappeared. She wasn't ready to give up on Switzerland just yet. London may be able to dismantle the 'Ndràngheta, but until Brit-Swiss-man was behind bars the job would never be done.

Twenty minutes later, having avoided a couple of embarrassing semi-naked moments, they were both showered and were just about to head downstairs to breakfast when Frank's phone rang again. It was Carla. Frank stuck it straight on loudspeaker and placed the phone on his bed.

'Go ahead, Carla. You've got both of us.' Frank said.

'Hi, you two. I now know who our mystery man is! And I might know where he lives!'

Sam, who had been absently staring out the window looking at the orange sun slowly raise her veil on the beautiful mountains, left the window and shot back to the gap between the two beds. Frank was already on his, knees to chest.

'Brilliant, Carla. Let's hear it.' He said.

'Yesterday we sent a JPEG mugshot of Sam's photofit to every educational establishment in Cumbria. We followed it up with phone calls, with the edict we'd take any return call at any time, night or day, should a name be found. National security and all that. About an hour ago, would you believe, I had a Mrs Julia Lefton on the phone, apologising for calling me at an unearthly hour. Anyway, she's a matron at St Bees College, which is a private school on the Cumbrian coast. She'd been working at the school for over 25 years in various administrative capacities. The school secretary had sent the photo to all staff and, as a poor sleeper, she'd opened her emails in the middle of the night. She recognised the face immediately, even though it was a long time ago. She convinced the photo is Freddie Forester. He was expelled from the sixth form for attempting to set fire to the school chapel, among other misdemeanours. Have you got this so far?'

'Yes.' They both replied in unison.

'Good. With that name I've found a lot of useful background stuff, like parents and place of birth - and I will follow all that up later. But I know you've been pushing for a current domicile and I've had a stroke of luck.' Carla paused for the big finale. Frank looked at Sam. She looked back, betraying no emotion. 'Mr Forester has a minimal police record here in the UK; a shoplifting caution in 1990. After that there is no record of him anywhere in Britain - on any database. No NHS number, no National Insurance number. Nothing. So I checked Europol and Interpol. Nothing there. Thinking outside the box, I called an estate agent pal of mine in Basel. As a Brit if Forester wanted to buy a property in Switzerland, he'd need a G-permit, which is a cross-border work visa. And to get one of those he'd have to prove his nationality. In Switzerland they need to see a passport *and* a birth certificate. That led to a full house - bingo!'

'And Forester got himself a G-permit? Using his original name?' Frank asked.

'Seems so. My pal tells me he's own a chalet in Zermatt. He bought a plot of land with an old chalet on it 20 years ago and had it revamped in the last five. I guess when he acquired the plot he was less worried about his identity being discovered and linked to a strip of land in Zermatt?'

Sam had as much as she needed.

'What's the address, Carla.'

Carla read it out.

'Anything else?' Sam asked.

'Nope. That's it. I'm pressing on here with untying the knots that are the many accounts owned and overseen by Forester. Jane has asked me to press The Treasury to prepare to block all movement in and out of the accounts.'

Sam thought for a second.

'Just be careful, Carla. The more the accounts transact, the more we'll be able to track those Forester has been dealing with. We are widening the net - we don't want to drag it in just yet.'

'Got it.'

'And will you keep an eye on the price of gold and value of the FTSE and let me know if they cross?'

'Sure. I've got an alert on that. I'll let you know.'

Sam finished the call.

Since then they'd had a continental breakfast, recced the chalet and were now a couple of cups of coffee to the better in a downtown cafe, with eyes-on Forester's home ...

... which they had to break into.

Frank finished his coffee.

'Have another, Frank.' Sam suggested.

'What about you?'

'I'm going up to the chalet.'

'But all the shutters are closed.'

Sam was on her feet. 'Not all. On the top floor balcony, at the back, one of the shutters isn't completely down. I'm going to see if I can get in. If nothing else, peer in.'

'Don't you want me ...'

Sam put up a hand.

'No, Frank. I want you to stay here and watch both of the roads up to the chalet. As soon as it looks like anyone in authority is heading my way, call me. But only if we've been compromised. OK? No other circumstances.'

Sam smiled at him. He smiled weakly back and nodded at the same time, the wrinkles on the burnt side of his face showing up dark red.

'OK.'

And then she was off.

Frank grew more and more impatient as time went on. He alternated between using his binos and then his naked eye. Sam had disappeared around the back of the chalet ten minutes ago and there was no sign of her. He reckoned the building, which was chalet style but a mixture of grey-painted wood, white render and brushed metal - *very chic*, would have security devices up the yin yang. The shutters alone looked impenetrable. He hadn't seen one partially closed as Sam had described, but then again Sam had that knack of spotting things others hadn't.

Wait.

A police car. No light or sirens. It had come from the town centre and had turned up the road towards the chalet. It would be there in a minute. He fumbled for his phone. And dialled.

It rang. And rang. And then went to answer machine.

Come on, Sam.

He dialled again.

The police car had stopped short of the entrance to the chalet. Two uniformed men got out. They were carrying sidearms.

The call went to answer machine. He checked the number.

The policemen were studying the chalet. One tried the gate. It opened. He walked up the tarmac path towards the building.

The number Frank was phoning was the right one. He dialled it again.

The policeman was at the front door. It looked like he pressed a doorbell on a pillar beside the heavy, grey wooden door. He stood back.

The phone went to answer machine.

Shit.

The policeman by the car was using his mobile. The one by the chalet was walking around the back. He'd be out of sight in less than a minute.

No sign of Sam.

Shit.

The policeman by the car stayed on the phone. He was still looking at the chalet. There was no sign of the policeman who had gone round the back.

And no sign of Sam.

The man round the back reappeared. In a rush. He was gesticulating to the second policeman. And ...

He's got a pistol in his hand!

Frank called Sam's line again.

The second policeman was rushing to the house; he had drawn his pistol as well. Seconds later they were both round the back of the chalet.

It rang. And rang. The ringtone got louder. And louder still.

Uh?

'Thanks, Frank.'

He turned sharply, almost falling off his chair.

'What? How?'

Sam looked hot. And a bit sweaty.

'You called me. I got out of the place. And then ran wide, down to the village, and then back down the main street.'

She sat down. The waiter spotted her straight away. He headed over.

'*Chocolat chaud, s'il-vous-plait.*' She turned back to Frank. 'We should get out of here.'

'Sure. I'm ready when you are. Did you get anything?'

'I'm not sure. I managed two rooms. I had to break the window of the one with the open shutter. That took me ages. It was a bedroom. Next to it was a study of sorts. There were some photos and stuff, and then you called. So I took a quick video of the place and got out. I won't know what we have until we look over the video. We may have something, maybe not.'

The waiter arrived with the hot chocolate. Sam paid him straight away.

As she took a sip from her cup, Frank looked at her. She was still wearing the jacket she'd worn up the mountain. It was charred on her left shoulder. Her beanie was placed at an odd angle and her now damp auburn curls, darkened due to sweat, stuck out from the hat haphazardly. One or two strands were glued to her forehead. She also had red patches of skin from the fire but, unlike him, it made her cheeks glow. He knew she wasn't well inside, but externally she looked in great shape, if a little beaten up. She wore a distance stare - of someone who was with you, but also somewhere else. He daren't ask her where that was.

She caught him looking at her.

'What?'

I want to make things right. Make you feel better.

'Nothing. Just … nothing.'

She took a final swig of her hot chocolate.

'Come on. We've got a video to look at - and a municipal police force to evade.'

She stood before he had chance to reply.

From that point to the *Gotthard Bahnhof* he was always three steps behind her.

Chapter 19

'The Glacier Express', between Zermatt and Täsch, Switzerland

Sam stared out of the window of the train. Green, brown, off-white and grey trundled past. The train, a 20 minute journey and the only way in and out of 'car-free' Zermatt unless you took a taxi - or helicopter - snaked its way through the steep valley of pines and scree and narrow pastures. The sun was playing hide and seek behind tall mountains and towering trees which seemed to brush the train as it sped past. Without the sun's radiance the recent snow was pale grey. Close to the train it was speckled with the black and dark brown of grime and dirt. It was a miserable outlook. Cold and closed. Restricting and regretful.

The video from Forester's chalet (she could call him that, just not the other 'F' word) had been a washout. The bedroom gave no clues at all. The study was immaculately tidy, as she would have expected. The walls were all painted white. Everything else, the furniture, the floor, doors, door frames, were all a classy, matured pine. There was a computer screen and keyboard on top of a glass-covered, ornately-carved pine desk; an expensive office chair and a full-length mirror. In one corner was a wood burner, possibly filled with fake coal and gas-fired. The only non-functional accoutrement was a large, wonderfully-detailed painting of the Matterhorn, the mountain piercing a cloudless blue sky; unlike today. She'd managed a glance up the valley as they'd circled the chalet first thing. The apex of the mountain had been smuggled away by thick cloud.

The video told them nothing they didn't already know. Forester was very rich. And very tidy.

And he wasn't at home.

He was probably still with his Mafia friends? Or perhaps he was visiting another equatorial drug dealer; eliciting cash or plotting and planning his next conspiracy?

What a waste of time. They'd been lured and ambushed, and almost killed. And, with a smallest of opportunities - a couple of minutes in the monster's lair, Sam had managed to glean nothing of import. And she was shattered. What little sleep she'd had recently had been cram-packed full of things she didn't want to think about. She was firing on a single cylinder. Her energy bath was running dry.

Anxiety and lethargy stalked her like a jilted ex.

They should have spoken to Jane, that's what they should have done. Got the Embassy involved. With help of the Swiss police they'd have been able to organise a full search of the property.

Probably.

Possibly.

In a week's time.

Next month sometime.

More greens and browns; and greys and off-whites. The scenery wasn't changing. It was still a tunnel of misery.

They had no choice but to come off the mountain. They'd have to obey Jane's original request. Pick up the Range Rover and head back to Rome. Sam had no idea what SIS was up to under the banner of 'an operation' Jane had mentioned, but she couldn't see what her involvement might be. If Jane was in such desperate need to see her they could have spoken via secure video on Frank's phone.

She hadn't the energy for it. She hadn't the energy for anything.

She caught Frank's reflection in the window. He was sitting opposite her, a table between them. They'd had a brief chat about the video as soon as they'd sat down. Like her, he couldn't pick anything from it. However he had insisted they forward it to Carla to run it through Cynthia's image sharpening programme and ask her to have another look at it on a large screen. Once the email had been sent, Frank had sat back in his chair and almost immediately fallen asleep. His head was leant back, his Adam's apple doing its own Matterhorn impression, and his mouth currently open for business.

She imperceptibly moved her head and altered the focus of her eyes so that she lost Frank in the glass and was presented with the greens and the browns of the passing valley.

She didn't know what she felt about Frank. She thought maybe he had a soft spot for her? If that were the case it was too bad. It could never be reciprocated. *Never?* He was neither man nor woman enough for her. It wasn't that she was attracted by physically big people, she just needed someone who would take charge every so often - allow her ... no, *tell her* ... to shut up, sit down and switch off. Frank wouldn't do that.

He was too kind. *Too nice.*

Even dissecting her feelings made her innards shrivel. Self-loathing wasn't an unfamiliar sensation, but, just now, it was more powerful than those it was competing with. Anxiety was a close second, followed by an unnatural fear of failing. Failing to find Forester. Failing to meet him again. To have a confrontation. For one of them to come away elated; the other defeated. Either outcome would do for her. At least then she wouldn't have to skulk about the place forever worried he might be watching.

Waiting.

Toying.

She closed her eyes. The dull, rushing colours turned to black. The lyrical *clatter-clatter* of the train rolling along the track burrowed into her.

Her anxiety grew. She became more and more tense. Her heart rate quickened. Her hands clasped together and she felt her short nails pressing into the flesh on the opposite hands. She was beginning to panic.

What had her last therapist told her?

Think nice thoughts. Bright, bold colours.

Her happy, positive image.

A beach. The first light of dawn. Her VW camper, Bertie. The sliding side door pulled back. The low, but warming sun drenching the furniture inside the van. A seabird. The splash of low-energy waves rippling along the shore …

Frank's phone broke the illusion. It took him a few seconds to wake, find his mobile deep in a pocket, and answer.

The whole slow waking thing was another reason why he didn't stir anything in her other than the closest of friendships. It was frustrating - which she knew was her problem. And it didn't push any of her endearing buttons.

'Hi, Jane.'

Sam only got one side of the conversation.

'No, we're in Switzerland. Just coming away from Zermatt.'

There was a long pause from Frank whilst his face forged a serious look.

'You better speak to Sam.' He passed the phone across the table.

She put it to her ear, but didn't say anything. A steady *ping* that told her she was on a secure line was an irritation. Words were going to be difficult.

'Sam?'

She grunted in return.

'You should almost be in Rome by now. Why are you still in Switzerland?' Jane was frustrated.

Ping.

Sam looked out of the window. The valley was widening out. They'd be in Täsch in a couple of minutes.

The sun was brightening the hillside off to her left. The rest of the valley was still a pallet of muted colours.

'Sam!'

She took a deep breath.

Ping.

'Yes.'

'I asked you to get back here. We, that is the US with our intelligence support, have got an anti-Mafia op going down in the next 24 hours. They need everything you have on Feradina villa. And they need it now!'

Ping.

The last thing Sam needed *now* was a bollocking. Yes, she deserved one. She would have felt the same as Jane if she were in her position. More so. But Jane didn't have all the facts. And Jane wasn't Sam. She wasn't being stalked by the devil.

'We had a lead.' Sam's tone was flat. Unremarkable.

'What lead?'

Her response was short; a couple of sentences to explain the burning chalet and, although she knew she'd get another bollocking, to talk through her entry into Forester's chalet - and the video.

Ping.

Jane was initially stuck for words. Her reply was soft, but not conciliatory.

'If you had come to me this morning we may have been able to get the Swiss police on side and *maybe* they'd have done a better job?'

Sam knew that was the textbook answer. But she also believed that Jane was wrong.

'The Swiss wouldn't have cooperated. Not without a referendum. And there's no SIS in the country apart from us. You would have done the same as me.'

Jane hesitated.

Ping.

'And ...', Sam continued, '... I have already produced a detailed 3-D map of Andrea Placido's villa. It's on Cynthia. Eithan will know where to find it. I can talk through any ambiguities on the phone. Who's going in? The Unit? Avoiding any connection with AISE until the job is done?'

'The Unit' was the colloquial term for Delta Force, the US Army's special mission organisation. It operated very much like SAS, but there was often more civilian cross-over. Sam had personal experience of them. They'd pulled her off a flat roof of a satellite control station in Venezuela just over a year ago. That was after they strafed the whole place with a thousand, half-inch rounds. She was lucky not to end up looking like the local Swiss cheese.

'We don't know yet. But, yes. The Americans want to bring this thing to a conclusion and are doing as you suggest. It's "need to know", so, well, you know, just you. Anyway. I need you to come back here. If nothing else we can pool resources.'

Sam stared out of the window again. The train was slowing. The snow hadn't made it this far down the valley. Now it was just greens and browns and greys.

Could she leave Switzerland without knowing that Forester wasn't in the country? Would she really be of any use in Rome alongside Jane? Was Jane calling her back just so she could keep an eye on her?

Frank's phone buzzed in her hand. She glanced at the screen. It was an email from Carla. The title was: *Look at this*.

'Jane - do you know we have all of the Swiss-bloke's details? Carla found his surname, birth certificate, where he went to school … and other stuff. We're *so* close to getting him.'

Sam had another quick glance at the phone. It was a pointless gesture. Nothing had changed. There was still an unopened email from Carla. And it was still titled: *Look at this*.

'That's all good stuff, Sam. But it's the Mafia who are making this happen. You put us on to this. You know. Once they're broken the attacks will stop.'

I really want to look at this email.

She glanced at Frank. He was looking at her impassively. Sam pointed to the phone and mouthed, 'Email from Carla.'

He perked up a bit.

'OK, Jane. Got it. We'll head back now. Got to go.'

Sam pressed the red telephone icon. The line went dead.

Jane didn't get it. Forester was everything. Yes, the 'Ndràngheta might be coordinating the attacks, but the intellectual property was with Forester. He was the centre of the wheel. He couldn't be allowed to walk free.

Feeling just slightly more alive, she tapped Frank's phone and opened the email. It read:

Frank/Sam. Better vid attached. Doesn't help much but look at 21.5 secs. What is the paper/photo under the glass of the desk? Cynthia has done all she can. We're working on it now.

'Look here, Frank.'

Sam put the phone on the table so they could both see it, and pressed play.

Carla was right. The video was much sharper, but just as dull. That was until about 18 seconds: Sam's slowmo of the desk. Forward-right of the keyboard, under the glass which covered the whole of the desktop, was a rectangular piece of paper - in portrait. It looked like an invitation, or a business card, turned on its end. The top of the card was a headshot of man?; underneath was some writing. Sam thought she recognised letters and numbers. The angle of the card and the resolution was making it difficult. She paused the clip.

Without asking, Frank picked up the phone. He brought it to his face at eye level and then laid the phone almost flat.

He's changing the perspective. Clever.

Keeping the phone almost horizontal he twisted it left and right and then passed it back to Sam at the same oblique angle.

She looked at it, hunching her shoulders so her eyeline and the screen were one. She raised the far end, so the phone came to the vertical. And then lowered it again. It was definitely a man. Balding. Slightly tinted glasses. A red and yellow top, of unknown description.

I have no idea.

She had no idea who it was.

'Sorry.' She said to Frank as she passed the handset back.

He took it and prodded and pressed the screen.

A few seconds later he handed it back to Sam.

The screen showed the blue and white of a *Twitter* profile page. The profile picture was the same man as the oblique one on Forester's desk. But on *Twitter* the resolution was much better; much clearer. And instantly recognisable.

'Why the bloody hell has Forester got a card on his desk with the Dalai Lama's mugshot on it?' Sam asked.

Frank had his eyes closed. It was a thinking Frank.

He opened them.

'I don't know. But I can tell you something. Along with the Pope, the Dalai Lama's *Twitter* account has gone ballistic over the past month. He now has over 240 million followers, that's up from a baseline of 20 million just six weeks ago.'

Sam thought for a second.

'Are you on *Twitter*?' She asked.

'Yes.' Frank replied. 'Although you can't find me unless you really look for me.'

'Go on.' Sam knew he wanted to share his secret.'

'My profile name is @GaryGygaxRocks.'

Sam shook her head in bewilderment.

'He's one of the founders of Dungeons and Dragons.' He smiled sheepishly. 'I play a bit.'

'A bit?'

'Well, anyway. This may or may not be important, but I was looking over some social media research a couple of days ago. Since NT got out of control, all major public figures, politicians etc, have lost massive numbers of followers on *Twitter, Instagram* and *Facebook*. People don't trust them, so they don't follow them. Now, it seems, people are getting their direction from celebrities they feel they *can* trust. People who seem to empathise with them. Who they resonate with. The Pope and the Dalai Lama are currently in vogue.'

'Are the followers worldwide?'

'I think so. Certainly the Dalai Lama's attraction doesn't appear to be limited by ideology; it seems to be based on global reach and trust.'

'Does he travel?' Sam was piecing together something she really didn't want to contemplate.

'Dunno.' Frank put his hand out, asking for his phone. She gave it him back. He tapped and pressed. 'Appears so.' He passed the phone back to Sam.

The page open was His Holiness The 14th Dalai Lama of Tibet's web page. There was a photo of him planting a tree somewhere in India.

Sam scrolled down. And a bit more. She stopped.

Shit.

There it was. Yelling at her.

She looked up at Frank.

'I don't think Forester has left Switzerland.'

British Embassy, Via Venti Settembre, Rome, Italy

Jane and Eithan were huddled around Stewart's desk. They were looking over a paper copy of a draft US instruction titled Operation CAPONE. It had been couriered to the Embassy half an hour ago from the CIA's Rome office. Whilst the US could guarantee their national e-security between Rome, Washington and Fort Bragg, they couldn't trust their links with SIS. Not when the operation was as sensitive as this.

The paper was short on detail. With SIS help the CIA had identified 15 HVTs in Calabria and Sicily, and six locations. A number of the targets and locations had been under GCHQ scrutiny over the last five days and the collective view was if the operation managed to capture and arrest at least 10 of the HVTs and destroy the six locations, then the 'Ndràngheta would be deemed ineffective. Those arrested would be extradited immediately, which was a euphemism for sticking a bag over their heads, throwing them in the back of a Black Hawk and dropping them on one of the US Navy's Sixth Fleet's Arleigh Burke Class Destroyers in the Med. Further immediate interrogation might well identify some additional HVTs. Phase Two of the op was a second wave of arrests asap after the first.

There was no footnote to amplify on what the paper meant by 'destroy the location', but Jane read it to mean anything vaguely associated with any illicit activity would either be dismantled on site, or taken, interrogated, in the case of laptops and hard drives, and destroyed later.

Timings were very keen and she was impressed by how quickly the US thought they could pull an operation such as this together. Ten Delta Force recce teams were flying in undercover tonight. Assuming they were able to provide sound intelligence, the arrest and destroy teams would fly tomorrow night. The operation was due to go 'noisy' at 00.45 hours the day after tomorrow and be closed 90 minutes later.

'Nothing like this has ever happened before. Not on this scale.' Jane commented.

'If you remember, we carried out a much smaller insertion in 1984.' Stewart replied. He was older than Jane and had spent nearly all of his time as a case officer in the field. If SIS had 'invaded' an ally without their permission, he'd probably know about it. 'There was a German spy grouping working on a UK base in Rheindahlen. Over the period of three weeks MI6, as it was then, with the help of the SAS, took the ring apart. We flew the spies to Cyprus. I think, eventually, one was re-inserted as a double agent and the other four sent to Angola with very clear instructions not to leave the country. I think we informed Bonn once it was all over. It didn't go down well.'

'How do you think the Italian government will react?' Eithan asked to no one in particular.

Jane deferred to Stewart.

'It depends how noisy the operation is. It will hit the press, for sure. If it's a success and the Italian PM feels he can take the accolades then, whilst he won't be happy, he'll tell everyone it was his idea. He'll need to work hard to get his party onside. The rest of the opposition will be horrified, even though they'll know it was the only viable way to bring down the 'Ndràngheta. They will make political hay and there's a real chance the government will fall.'

'But, that happens a lot here. Italian governments rarely last longer than a year. Two tops.' Jane added.

If she were honest she didn't really care if the Italian government fell. Around the world governments of every description were struggling to stay in power. After last night there was talk of a vote of no confidence in London. The current coalition was as fragile as order was on the streets. This morning's news had both the opposition and a good slab of the government's members of parliament demanding the prime minister's resignation. The leader of the opposition had also tabled a motion to bring all of the security and intelligence services under new, centralised control. He'd coined it 'TISA': The Intelligence and Security Agency. SIS, The Service, GCHQ, Special Forces and the police's Counter Intelligence apparatus would be brought together and overseen by a committee of MPs and civil servants. Worryingly the agency would be not necessarily be led by a former member of one of the branches, but might be an ex-businessman or similar.

'TISA would be a not-for-profit, non-partisan organisation, managed by someone with proven leadership ability. The agency would be accountable to a new, standing intelligence and security committee of cross-party MPs, which would re-evaluate threats and needs, attributing funds where appropriate. It would be agile and focused. Not, as the disparate groups are today, self-serving and secretive.' The leader of the opposition's statement had flashed its way across all intelligence officers' desks as soon as the words had left his mouth.

It was a horrifying thought. Jane didn't think, between them, they could work any smarter. Very few operations at home or abroad were conducted without cross-agency support. They shared everything. There was no partisanship; no secrecy.

But she could see why someone might think it sensible to throw the whole security apparatus in the air and catch it in one big bucket. The country was on the brink. And it was her organisation - and its sisters - which had, so far, let the country down.

Maybe, only until now.

She was pretty confident that in less than 48 hours NT would be finished.

And whilst she heard Sam, that Freddie Forester was the man in the middle, they would find him in their own time. Once 'Ndràngheta were down and the terror stopped.

'What do you want me and the team to do now, Jane?' Eithan asked.

'What have you got outstanding from Frank and Sam?'

'We're pursuing a Xavier Turner, a Belizean drug dealer. We think he's one of Forester's investors. In addition, along with Carla, we're putting together a list of account holders in the Cayman Islands. It looks very likely Forester has persuaded a number of investors, including Xavier Turner, to sell stock and buy gold. Sam reckons that there's a trigger when the price of stock and price of gold hit a certain level. At that point he will sell the gold and reinvest in the markets. Carla reckons return-on-investment could be close to 400%.' Eithan paused, perhaps waiting for a question. Jane didn't have one. She knew of Sam's gold and stocks equation. She still wasn't convinced.

Eithan continued. 'Other than that, we're in touch with Carla. She's working hard on fleshing out Forester's background.'

Jane nodded. 'OK. Good, Eithan. I'm hoping Sam and Frank are back here later today. In the meantime, Stewart, do you have anything for Eithan?'

'No. I've got some non-NT business to deal with.'

Jane put the Op CAPONE folio back in a pink folder which was marked, TOP SECRET UK EYES A.

'Eithan, do you have any contacts in Switzerland?' Jane asked.

Eithan thought for a second.

'Yes. One. Why?'

'If you haven't got it already, get hold of Forester's Swiss address from Carla. The one Sam had a look at this morning. Then speak to any contacts you have, keeping the Bern Embassy in the loop. See if you can persuade the Swiss police to raid the chalet. It would be good if we could get a Brit involved on the ground. If that means one of the three of you legging up there, then so be it. Happy?'

'Sure.' Eithan stood to go.

'Are you staying here, or heading over to join the US's Rome team for the op?' Stewart asked Jane.

She was heading over to join Linden. She'd already spoken to the Chief. He wanted one of his team in the CIA's hub in Rome throughout and she was the obvious choice. She did, however, want to check on Sam and Frank first. Hopefully they'd be back in a couple of hours. After a quick debrief she'd pop to her hotel for a brush up, and head to the CIA's house before the recce teams went in.

It was going to be another long night.

Burger King, Outskirts of Davos, Switzerland

Frank ate his burger because he was hungry, not because he was enjoying it. He'd lost his enthusiasm. The excitement of last night's fireball and this morning's overwatch of the chalet - his heart in his mouth as the Swiss police had gone in with Sam still in the building - had taken a lot from him. And following another of Sam's hunches from one end of Switzerland to another, when they should have been back at the Embassy in Rome, was poking a needle into his nerves.

He always did as he was told; he always had done. At school, at work, at home. Disobeying Jane's direct order - twice - was not something he was in any way comfortable with.

But he found himself torn.

He loved Sam. He'd admitted that to himself as she dragged him off the mountain. And it was a passionate love, not a sisterly one. He loved everything about her. Everything. The way she looked. The way she acted. The way she did the right thing. The way she looked out for everyone, but rarely for herself. The way she ate her fries, two at a time, all the same length. He even loved the way she was direct; blunt. To him, and everyone else.

He loved her.

But I always do as I'm told.

And that juxtaposition between doing what he'd been told - following Jane's order, against chasing Sam, the woman he loved, around the country - jarred. And he hated that was how he felt.

Right now he wanted to walk out into the carpark and shout, 'Sod you, world!'. He wanted to remove his institutional shackles, grab Sam by the hand and head off into the hills for an eternity.

Yes, he had his small rebellions: what he wore; the way he spoke; the board games he played. But you didn't need to scratch too deep to discover the truth. He wasn't a risk taker. He wasn't a maverick. He was a good lad. Reliable. Dependable.

Institutionalised.

Sam was the opposite. She knew no boundaries. She had wings. She lived by her own rules: good rules; the right rules.

Her own rules.

'Not hungry?' She asked, slurping her coke through a straw.

'Sort of. It's, well …'

'What, Frank?'

He stared at her. Her round face, pointed nose and uncontrollably curly hair. She was nibbling two fries like a gerbil, small piece by small piece until they were gone. He loved that too.

'We should be in Rome, Sam.'

Sam's hand stopped in mid-air. A new couple of equal-length fries suspended inches from her mouth. They stayed there for a second. And then met the same fate as the previous two, munch after munch.

She finished her mouthful and wiped her lips with a paper napkin.

'Jane doesn't need us in Rome. It's her way of keeping control. Their focus is Calabria. We are a diversion and she worries we will, somehow, light a fuse which might interfere with the US operation.'

'Might we?' Frank hadn't really made that connection. Could they do something that might upset the US's assault on the 'Ndràngheta?

Sam was staring out of the window. It was snowing again, the street lights turning the white flakes grey as they passed, only to allow them back to a yellowy-white as they muzzled into the ground. It wasn't dark yet, but it would be in another hour.

Davos wasn't quite as high as Zermatt, but they were well into the mountains. The *Kongresszentrum* was 1500 metres away, in the centre of the town. Tomorrow the Dalai Lama was due to give a lecture to a multinational audience. The title of the talk was, 'Globalism in a Prayer'. This evening he was to be guest of honour at a dinner at the Hilton Garden Inn, a hotel opposite the congress hall. From what Frank could find on the internet, the guests were prominent business people, high-ranking politicians and notable environmentalists from across Europe.

Sam was convinced assassinating the Dalai Lama, especially in front of a large audience, was the final act in the NT terror cycle. He was the 'high profile individual' so many nations were pressing their security services to protect. But she reckoned that they had all missed the point.

Forester hadn't; he was well ahead of them. He knew people no longer cared about their politicians, celebrities, or even their royal families. Joe Public had lost faith in everything - and everybody. They were running out of options and had turned to people they thought they could trust. People without agendas. People of faith. People who, for as long as anyone could remember, were selfless; unencumbered by greed and power.

The Dalai Lama was such a person. The epitome of their needs. He was a rock-like figure in a river of uncertainty and terror. A steadfastness in a world spinning out of control.

Forester knew his assassination would destroy the final pillar of what was good, kind and right.

'Forester didn't cut me.' Sam's reply was quiet. Almost ghostly. She was still staring out of the window.

It took Frank's brain a short while to catch up.

'Then, how did you get the cut?' He asked.

She didn't answer to begin with. She just stared and stared. Frank saw her eyes moving slowly down and then quickly lift up again. She was following individual snowflakes.

'I did it myself.'

He was about to pick up his last piece of burger. But didn't. His appetite had completely left him.

He didn't say anything. He didn't know what to say.

Sam turned and looked him in the eye, impassively.

'I had an episode. After Forester had attacked me at the wedding. I needed to get to Rome to meet you. But I couldn't. All I could do was sleep. But I *had* to get to Rome.'

He studied her face. She had her hands on the table. He wanted to reach for them. To hold them. But he was too shy, too embarrassed to do so.

What if she pulled away?

Then he chastised himself for making the situation about him.

'I'd cut myself before. I found it helps to break an impasse, between what I wasn't doing and what I should be doing. It's like a jolt. It helps me take back control from forces I don't understand.'

'This is all about Forester? That is … your relationship with him?' Frank had found his tongue.

Sam nodded. She then turned to face the snow again, raising one hand and placing a single finger on the pane of glass.

'Originally it was Ralph Bell. And when he died and we couldn't find Forester, it became him. They are with me all the time.'

Sam's face was so close to the glass her breath was condensing on it. She drew small circles in the condensation. And then a tear appeared. Just one. It took a while to form and then it trickled down her cheek.

He wanted to hold her. To never let her go. To tell her things were going to be OK. That he'd be there for her. Forever.

But he couldn't do or say anything. His fear of rejection was greater than the strength of his feelings.

How can that be?

'We should get going, then.' He said. It wasn't what he wanted to say, but he felt he had to say something.

She didn't reply.

'Sam?'

'Mmm?' She hadn't been listening. She was still watching the snowflakes.

'We should go. See if we can find Forester. Maybe spot his Bentley in a car park. See if we can work out where the Dalai Lama is staying. Work out his movements. Try and establish how we would assassinate him, and then plan to stop ourselves. That's how you military work, hey?'

Sam pulled away from the window and turned again to face Frank. She hadn't bothered to wipe away her tear.

'I can't afford for you to get hurt, Frank.'

Huh?

'What do you mean?'

'Forester is a monster. He's deranged. And he wants to be here. To see this through. But, if there's a trigger to pull, I don't think he's going to pull it. He won't put himself in harm's way. Not here. So he won't be alone. We're up against a team of professionals. Could be one. Might be a number.' She stopped and reached for his hands. She held them. His legs turned to jelly.

'I don't think I have the capacity for love, Frank. Any notion like that was stolen from me in Afghanistan, all those years ago. I can't change who I am. I'm sorry. But, you are very precious to me. I can't lose you.' Sam's tone was flat; distant. 'We'll find a hotel room. You can work the net, I'll go out on my feet. We'll operate like that.' She placed a very small smile at the end of her sentence.

Frank gently pulled his hands away. Sam did the same.

He didn't know what to feel. There was too much happening at a time when he was too tired to rationalise it all. He needed some space, but the walls of their situation were too close. He had so much to say, but he knew much of it would be lost on this very lovely, but very functional woman. And she was right. She was incapable of love. He sensed that. Perhaps he'd always known that.

But that didn't dent his feelings. Nothing would.

He coughed.

Now?

'I love you.' He watched the expression on her face. It betrayed nothing. He continued quickly. 'But, that's OK, Sam. I get it. I get you. I think I always have.'

They stared at each other for what seemed like an age.

'We should go and find Forester. Let's put these demons of yours to bed.' He added.

Sam dropped her gaze. She then brought her uneaten food and packaging together onto the red tray.

She stood as he did. She reached out for a hand. He offered one.

'Sorry, Frank.'

'It's OK, Sam. I'll be a dungeon master next year, and won't have any time for a grown up relationship.'

She smiled a big smile that showed a glimpse her teeth.

That's better, Sam.

Chapter 20

To start with they'd decided to take a couple of hotels each. Sam was in the underground garage of the Hilton. She'd then check the *Steigenberger Grandhotel* followed by the *Waldhotel*. Frank was currently in the carpark of the *Ameron*, whereafter he'd try the *Edelweiss* and then the Chalet *Züriberg*. Until they'd looked they had no idea there was a hotel in Davos named Edelweiss. Whilst it was an obvious choice for Forester, it was only 2-star and Sam was convinced that would be beneath him. Once they'd searched the car parks/garages of the hotels closest to the *Kongresszentrum,* they'd move onto ones a further distance away. Google reckoned there were 23 hotels in Davos and they only had two hours before the gala dinner. Sam knew that, unless they were lucky and found the Bentley, they didn't have enough time.

They'd booked a twin in the Hilton. It was where the evening's dinner was being held. Having slipped the concierge a 100 euro note he'd looked at the current guest list and it seemed 'unlikely' they had the Dalai Lama staying as a guest, and, no, he'd not heard of a Mr Forester. Sam ran off a couple of other Lake District surnames. The concierge had shaken his head at every offer.

They'd then walked into the hotel's *Seehorn* conference room which was being laid out for the evening's event. It was smaller than Sam was expecting, with places for about 100 guests. The picture windows gave spectacular early evening views of the town's lights twinkling up the mountainside. Before they were shooed out of the room by a very stressed, dark-suited and yellow-tied 'man-who-does', Sam had the layout clear in her mind.

The room was rectangular, about the size of two tennis courts. The large, ceiling-height windows filled one long wall. On one of the short walls was a double door leading back into the hotel lobby, from where they had just come. Opposite was a swing-door which Sam thought probably led to the kitchen and service area. The other long wall was unbroken. It was decorated with large black and white photos of famous politicians and business people who had attended previous World Economic Forums at the *Kongresszentrum* - for which Davos had world renown. Sam recognised a few before she was frogmarched back into the main atrium.

If the Dalai Lama were to be assassinated at this evening's event, there were numerous possibilities, but in her mind only two provided an assassin with an escape route. And, according to Sam's logic, only one was guaranteed.

She had discounted an attack by someone at the same reception. It would be audacious and, provided the assassin could get close enough, pretty failsafe. But the chances of escape seemed unlikely. Whilst Davos wasn't in a closed valley like Zermatt, there were only two routes in and out - up and down the valley - and if your face was known, those routes could be closed by the *police municipal* in minutes and the face found.

Poisoning was an option. It was an ancient and effective art. Although Sam guessed the Dalai Lama wasn't a big eater or drinker, all that was needed was access to tonight's menu or his drink. The problem for her was poisoning wasn't dramatic enough. Other than a nerve agent, like VX - which was the Russian SVR's current murder weapon of choice and can kill in minutes, botulism was the world's most lethal and effective poison. In the right dose against a healthy, average-sized human, the poison would kill with certainty ... but it takes time. Anyone ingesting the poison would become ill over many hours; they certainly wouldn't drop dead in their soup. Which Forester would want.

A nerve agent attack was a possibility.

The right dose on the skin - some spilt wine from a waiter - would react in seconds. Within a minute the victim would be frothing at the mouth and convulsing as if they were an epileptic. A minute later they would be dead.

It would certainly be dramatic.

But VX and similar nerve agents were weapons of states, not criminal gangs and terrorists. They were incredibly difficult to manufacture both because they require really tricky science and because they were so dangerous. They have to be made in special labs, with protective suits and face masks. They were kept in very secure facilities and whilst, like the recent attack in the UK, can be transported in scent bottles, getting the stuff in the first place is almost impossible unless you work for a special branch of a government. In her previous life she'd read somewhere that it would be easier and cheaper to procure a kilogram of plutonium than a millilitre of VX.

Five countries held the VX stockpile: the US, the UK, Israel, Russia and North Korea. And all of them hold onto their stock as if their lives depended upon it. Because in the hands of terrorists, many of their lives might.

For Sam, poisoning was out.

That left a long-range shot. Although it may have to be two shots.

The picture windows were the main reason people chose the *Seehorn* conference room for their events. And unless she could do something about it, the blinds would be left drawn for the duration of the dinner. The Dalai Lama would sit at the top table against the back wall. He was wholly recognisable and, other than maybe a Buddhist entourage, he would be the only man not in black tie. A sniper in any one of scores of vantage points outside the hotel would be able to secure a shot.

But, and it was a big but, most of them would need to take two. And that presented a problem and, she reckoned, ruled out all but a handful of positions.

Sniping wasn't like the movies. Much.

The bullet of choice was a 0.5-inch, which in a decent rifle lost velocity and started to be affected by weather and atmospherics after 800 metres. That's if it had had an uninterrupted path; which, in the case at the

Hilton, it wouldn't. Sam had checked. The hotel windows were triple-glazed. For a 0.5-inch round travelling at 1200 metres per second this would not be an issue if the bullet hits the window early on and dead straight. The round, which before impact would be spinning to retain accuracy, would tumble and start to lose accuracy when it smashed the first pane of glass; more again a second sheet; much more a third. But if the shooter was close, say 200 metres, the effect would be minimal. If the distances were longer, and the panes of glass more oblique to the trajectory, then the round would have to travel through more glass, and the impact on the flight would be greater.

It didn't matter how good the shooter was. Sam reckoned any oblique shot would smash the glass and probably hit someone, but possibly not the intended target. A second shot would be needed to guarantee a kill, but after the first everyone would be taking cover … and movement is not a sniper's friend. And, unless the sniper had already practiced, they'd have no idea how the glass would react. It might craze. Or shatter completely - falling glass obscuring the sniper's field of view for a split second.

It was a single shot, then.

Or failure.

Just before she and Frank had parted company to look for Forester's Bentley she'd got onto Google Earth and checked where she would place the bipod of a sniper rifle.

There was only one option.

The *Kongresszentrum*. It was directly opposite the hotel, about 75 metres away. Until she had chance to look outside any number of front aspect windows were possibilities. As was the roof.

If they hadn't found the Bentley in an hour that's where she'd go next.

As she walked rapidly up and down the lanes in the cellar garage she phoned Carla.

'Sam?'

'Carla. We're made it to Davos.'

'Yes. How can I help?'

'Have you spoken to Jane? Or the Embassy in Bern? Any chance of calling off tonight's dinner?'

'I've tried. Jane's furious. She's Calabria-focused and is fretting that yours is a sideshow and is going to undermine everything. And the duty officer at the Embassy in Bern just laughed at me. He said he'd phone someone, but the whole thing sounded too incredulous to sell - especially to a Swiss.'

Sam was still walking. And still looking. She'd found a Bentley, but it was two-tone red and mauve.

Not the right car.

She didn't want to hear that Jane was angry. Or that chasing down Forester was potentially a mistake. The Americans would pull their operation off: bigger the problem, bigger the hammer. And they had some bloody big hammers. No, her tinkering with a long screwdriver in Switzerland wouldn't unhinge the multi-billion dollar tool kit of the US's Special Operations Detachment - a whole country away. She'd been at the wrong end of a Delta

Force chain gun when all she'd had was a couple of pistols. They would do what they had to do. Nobody would get in their way, least of all her.

And she had to do this.

The world couldn't have Forester on the loose. *She* couldn't have Forester on the loose. And just talking to Carla about him made her legs weaken and she almost tripped over her own feet.

Get a grip.

'Listen.' Sam was edgy, but not angry. 'The dinner is being held in the *Seehorn* conference room in the Hilton Garden Inn.' Sam paused to ensure Carla had the details.

'Yes.'

'Do what you can to continue to alert the authorities. But, and if nothing else, try and get them to close the blinds on the windows.'

A further pause.

'You think there may be a sniper on the loose?'

Good girl.

'Possibly. But I could be wrong. Best answer is still for the event not to happen; for it to be cancelled. Second best is to close the blinds. Got it?'

'Sure. I'll try everything and everybody.'

There was a further pause.

'Sam?' Carla had a supplementary.

Sam was distracted now. Carla had a job to do. So did she. There were no Bentleys in the car park. She checked her watch. It was 6.27 pm. The dinner was due to start at 7.30 pm. If she were right the sniper would be close by. She reckoned on a shot during the Dalai Lama's after-dinner speech, say between 9.30 and 10.00 pm. He'd be standing. Everyone else sitting. Biggest target. Most attention.

Bang.

Dead Dalai Lama.

Greatest effect.

If she found Forester, would he lead her to the sniper? If she found the sniper, would he know where Forester was?

Who was more important?

There were two answers to that question. And that depended upon who you asked: herself, or the rest of the world.

'Sam!'

'Yes? Sorry Carla. Look …'

'It's a mess back here.' Carla interrupted. 'There are currently riots in three London boroughs. The police are using tear gas. The mayor's looking at declaring martial law in those areas. This afternoon the Army moved 1,000 extra soldiers into Wellington Barracks. The PM's facing a vote of no confidence in the House at 9.30 pm. It's crazy. And that's being replicated all over the world. Get him, Sam. We both know the US will dismantle the Mafia. But Forester is key. If he's on the loose this thing may never end.'

Sam was heading up a ramp into the cold of the night.

Where was Forester?

Should she abandon him? Stake out the *Kongresszentrum* and hope she was right about a sniper?

The cold hit her like opening a walk-in freezer. She pulled her beanie over her ears with her free hand.

She turned left, heading for the *Steigenberger*. Another hotel, another car park.

Where was Forester?

He's here.

He has to be.

It makes sense. How else could he be sure the job would be done?

And he had to know; he had to see it happen.

He was particular. Exact.

It was obvious.

He'd be at the dinner. He was a high-powered and very wealthy businessman. Getting a ticket for the Dalai Lama's dinner would be a cinch.

But that still left her on the horns of a bison-sized dilemma.

The *Kongresszentrum* or the *Seehorn* conference room?

Sniper? Forester?

And what about Frank?

'I'll do what I can, Carla. And you get the blinds in the conference room closed. Ack?'

'Ack.'

Kongresszentrum, *Davos, Switzerland*

Ergorov was stiff. And cold. The janitor's cupboard was big enough for him to stand up in, but it was hardly a gymnasium. With a gloved hand he twisted the door handle and pushed it open; slightly. And waited. It was dark in the corridor, but lighter than the cupboard. He listened. He looked for subtle changes in the shaft of grey that exposed the cupboard shelves' cleaning equipment, brooms and other janitorial gear with which he'd shared his last three hours.

Nothing.

There was no sound. And no flickering.

The world was still.

He pushed the door open further. And waited.

Nothing.

He lifted his rifle case onto his shoulder and stepped out into the corridor.

And waited.

Nothing.

He knew his route. He knew the internal alarm system. He knew the room. He knew his window. He knew what equipment was available to set up a steady firing platform, one big enough for a 1.79 centimetre, 92 kilogram man to lie down in the prone position with an *Accuracy International* AS50. He knew exactly where the platform would be positioned and he knew, once set up, he would have line of sight to the target.

He knew this because he'd visited the *Kongresszentrum* twice before, had blueprints of the building and had arrived today at 2.30 pm - on the janitor's day off.

It was an interesting target, for sure. He'd not met his paymaster. His instructions, as always, had been sent and received by encrypted messaging on a series of other people's phones. His protocols were completely secure. He was offered contracts via only three intermediaries, all of whom he trusted completely. All of whom shared his fee. They were old men. Russian men, with bad livers and red, vodka-addled noses. He didn't think they had long left. And when they were gone, it would be over for him. A well-deserved and restful retirement. Then, the only shooting he'd be doing would be in the forest, away from his cabin.

It was an interesting target. And, in the dark of the cupboard he'd amused himself as to who the paymaster might be.

The Chinese?

The next in line to the throne, if that's how you thought of it?

Did it matter?

Not really.

He had a target. And a reason - he always needed a reason. It was his way of squaring the circle of what he did. It might be an errant husband, or a politician on the take. A threat to national security? He'd done one of those a couple of years ago, taking out an oligarch on the back of a huge yacht.

Today?

Preventing the reordering of the world.

Ergorov was a simple man. He was a soldier; a long time ago. He followed orders. Saw things through. But he'd always liked to know why. Preventing the reordering of the world seemed like a grand notion. He didn't really understand what it meant, but he could say it out loud. And he didn't want the world to be reordered. He liked it just the way it was. And if the man from Tibet was preventing that from happening, then he was happy with his target.

He walked cautiously along the corridor, his slippered feet making no noise. He came to a double door that led to a stairwell. He pushed it ajar - slightly. No noise from the door. No noise from the stairwell. He pushed the door fully open. And waited.

Nothing.

He climbed the stairs two at a time until he'd reached the first floor. He made his way out of the stairwell, following the same 'push and wait' procedure. Three rooms down on the left were the female toilets. Four rooms down was a classroom.

He pushed the door of the toilets open and listened.

Nothing.

He placed his gun case on the vinyl floor so it propped it open. He waited. The door didn't move. He then moved to the classroom, always following the same essential procedure. Push, listen and wait.

Inside the classroom were 43 student desks, with 41 separate polyprop chairs. He needed three tables. He knew they stacked and he knew he could lift them. He used the table closest to the door to hold it open and then chose the three next closest, stacked them and carried them into the toilet. He then retraced his steps, moved the tables and chairs around so anyone entering the room wouldn't suspect anything had been removed.

He left the classroom, closing the door behind him and moved into the women's toilet. He lifted his rifle case from the floor and helped the door to. Slowly.

Silently.

And then he set to work making a platform, dim light from the three opaque windows providing enough to work with. After a recce of the hotel's conference suite and an illicit trip to the women's toilets on his first trip, he'd chosen the middle window. The window was opposite the basins which were set back far enough to allow three student tables, one behind the other, to provide a rectangular platform perpendicular to the wall. The window was tall and narrow, its ledge at knee height. With the first table close to the outside wall and the barrel of rifle forward of the edge of the table, but not puncturing the outside space, he knew he would get a good field of view. And he would be comfortable. A prerequisite for any sniper.

With the tables in place he opened up his rifle bag and pulled out an inflating roll mat. He laid it out on the tables, pulled the air-stopper out and blew in four breaths; the exact amount to ensure the mat provided a comfortable lying surface, but not so inflated it encouraged movement.

Leaving his weapon in the bag, and with the window still closed, he lifted himself onto the platform and lay down on his stomach, his right knee pulled up and away from his body, creating a triangle of two lower limbs and a torso: the perfectly secure and balanced firing position.

He took aim with an imaginary rifle. Adjusted his position.

Like an actor before a performance he went through his ritual of tensing and then relaxing every muscle in his body. He started with his feet. Then his legs. All the way through his arms and then his face which he scrunched up and relaxed.

He re-adjusted his position.

And breathed. In. And out. Slowly. Listening for his heart beat. Forcing it to moderate.

In. And Out. Shallow breaths.

Fifty-two beats per minute. He knew. He didn't need a watch.

In. And out. Forty-eight beats per minute.

Nee-naw, nee-naw.

A siren. Outside. It broke his concentration. His body tensed.

He listened.

Nee-naw, nee-naw. It had changed pitch. The doppler effect. A higher pitch coming towards you. And, good news for him; a lower pitch moving away.

The police weren't busy in Switzerland. It was a surprise to hear a siren.

He listened. The siren disappeared into the distance, to his right.

Fifty-eight beats per minute.

He'd have to go through the routine again to be sure. And then assemble, clean, oil and check his weapon and magazine.

He looked at his watch. It was 7.16 pm.

He had plenty of time. Ergorov wouldn't open the window until fifteen minutes before his shot. At around 9.10 pm. He'd watched six videos of the target giving after-dinner speeches, so he knew how long he spoke for. And he'd researched gala dinners. The number of courses. Average length of a course. Every detail he could get.

Not that it mattered. Once he was happy that everything was ready at the platform end, he'd check both his escape routes and then position himself at the back of the classroom. At the end of the working day, and before he'd moved into the janitor's cupboard, he'd made sure the blinds in the classroom had been left open. From the professor's desk, and hidden well into the shadows of the room, he'd have a ringside seat of the dinner. It would take him two minutes and forty-five seconds to be in a position to shoot. His target had never spoken for less than seven minutes.

He'd be ready.

Chalet Züriberg, Davos, Switzerland

Frank was jogging alongside the last ten cars in the car park when he heard the siren. It wasn't the same sound as a British police car, the wailing was much more grating. He reached the last car, a Passat estate, and stopped. The siren was coming quickly from his right. He waited.

There it was. And it wasn't a police car. The bodywork was bright red with white flashes, and had red and white top-lights spinning like a crazed ballet dancer. It looked more like a fire chief's car. As the car slowed to turn up the hill behind him, he picked out the ubiquitous white cross on a red background - the Swiss flag. And the word '*Reha*' - white letters on a red again, on its left flank. It wasn't fire or police. Or an ambulance. He thought maybe it was some form of mountain rescue; but the car didn't look big enough to squeeze in a St Bernard.

And then another noise. He turned to his right, tuning his ears. A far-off, heavy *clump-clump-clump*, from down the valley.

A helicopter.

The unmistakable beat of its rotating wings grew louder as the siren on the red car softened. The red and white flashing lights of the car became stationary, up on the hillside above him, maybe 50 metres away.

The helicopter was still moving. It was now just short of the town and slowing. Frank couldn't make it out, other than a bright white spotlight, presumably on its underbelly, and a couple of other flashing lights picking out the aircraft's extremities. It was over his right shoulder now, high but not distant, and slowing further. Then, a black object against a dark grey mountainside, it turned - moving closer. Now it was hovering above the red and white flashing lights of the '*Reha*' car, freshly fallen snow re-joining the air, whisked away and then settling on a different planet.

A helicopter-landing site?

A VIP landing.

The Dalai Lama?

Frank took off. It wasn't in Sam's brief - when he'd finished here he was meant to move onto another car park - but he felt oddly drawn to the meeting of the red and white car and the helicopter.

He was walking quickly; as fast as he could against the gradient. He was sweating. And breathing hard.

His phone rang. It was Sam. In less than an instant his brain replayed the scene in the Burger King.

I don't have the capacity for love, Frank.

'Frank?'

The image was lost.

'Yes, sorry. How's it going?' Frank was struggling to get the words out between breaths.

'Have you finished your last hotel?'

'Yes. You?' He was 20 metres short of the helicopter. It was above him, on a ledge.

'Yes. Did you hear the helicopter?'

'Yes. I'm just short of it now. I'm guessing it's the guest of honour arriving?'

'Oh … good. Good plan. Have a quick recce. Could be the Dalai Lama. Look, I'm going into the *Kongresszentrum*. I'm still working on a sniper, and that's his most likely vantage point. I reckon Forester is going to the dinner. I should be able to pick him out with the binos. Once you've finished with what you're doing, head down to the Hilton. Try and find someone in authority. Show them your SIS ID and get them to close the blinds in the *Seehorn* conference room. Make up any story you like. Tell them the truth, if necessary. But get the blinds closed. And then keep your eyes out for anything suspicious.' The words in the speaker stuttered. 'And, Frank …'

'Yes, Sam?'

He was glad for another break. Words were difficult when your lungs were recycling as much freezing air as they could.

'Be careful. Please.'

Frank thought he felt his cheeks warming as he instinctively dropped down to one knee and his mind emptied. He was still on the road, but his head was now above the parapet. He could see the helicopter, which turned out to be in the same livery as the car with the roof lights: red, with white flashes, a Swiss flag and the '*Reha*' logo.

The helicopter's blades were slowing to a halt. A man from the car had run forward to the main door in the fuselage. It was open. There was a single passenger. He was getting out.

It wasn't the Dalai Lama.

'Sam?'

'What?' Her tone was terser. She'd finished one job and was onto another. She didn't like interruptions.

'It's not the Dalai Lama.'

There was a pause.

'Who is it?'

'Forester. He's getting VIP treatment. And he's definitely going to the dinner.'

Frank felt Sam tense across the airways.

'Why do you say that, Frank?' There was a quiver in her voice.

'He's in a tux. He'll be at the Hilton in no time. He'll be blue-lighted down in a red car with a '*Reha*' logo on it.' Frank stopped. He was expecting Sam to ask him to spell '*Reha*'. But she didn't.

Because the phone had gone dead.

Outside the Kongresszentrum, Davos, Switzerland

Sam stood still. A solitary snowflake meandered its way past her nose and then dropped to the grey tarmac and vanished. Then another. And another. She stared into the distance, at the vertical planks that covered much of the *Kongresszentrum*. It was a curvy building, with large sections of glass interrupting a wooden exterior. Her distant focus lost the ever increasing snowfall as she worked hard to nail her mind onto something tangible. Like a building.

The temperature had dropped. But she hadn't felt it. Soon the snow was falling in such quantity the grass surrounding the building had turned from green-black to light grey - yellow where the warm-LED car park lights ventured off the tarmac. It was going to be a cold night. The dampness on the roads would freeze and the snow would find a home there as well.

It would be beautiful.

Christmassy.

She should ski tomorrow. She hadn't been this winter. And she so loved to ski. And then go home. Find another menial job. Get a boyfriend - or girlfriend. Tony the tills would do. Watch TV. Walk in the park. Have nights in, and pub meals out. Have rubbish sex, but appear grateful. Get a cheap car. Avoid the pills. Drink less.

Get old. And die.

That's what she would do.

Her new plan. It was better than every alternative she could think of.

If she could get her body to move. If the sodding thing would listen to her.

Nee-naw.

The noise cut through her like an east wind. It destroyed her wistful imagineering. Her new life shattered into a million pieces, and scattered - and frozen - onto the snow accumulating around her feet.

She turned. And looked.

There it was. Red and white flashing lights, heading down the hill high to her right. It would be down in the town in no time.

Sam was a minute from the *Kongresszentrum*. It was in front of her. She was in the shadows of another building, but had an uninterrupted view. Wood interspersed with glass. A massive, decorative overhang protected and proclaimed the entrance. Then, to the side of the entrance and one floor up, a series of windows facing the main road - and the Hilton. Seven useful ones, if you were a sniper. Four medium to large sets of panes. Three dusty ones; long - almost floor to ceiling. Dusty meant light, but no see. They could be loos. Or a small laboratory, where those inside didn't want prying eyes.

The shooter would be behind one of the seven. The angles were right. The distance perfect. She'd know which one when they opened the window. They would have to do that for observation, and also to prevent early deviation to the round. The sniper would be half a metre back from the opening to offer himself some cover whilst giving the best field of view. If the window at the firing end were shut, even a millimetre displacement caused by the round cutting through the early glass would deflect the bullet 15 centimetres at the target's end - and that's before the round shattered the triple glazing of the conference room. The round would miss. Someone might die. But not the intended target.

The sniper would open a window. She was sure of it. And she would know.

What to do?

It was a minute before Forester arrived at the hotel.

A minute from the *Kongresszentrum*.

There was a fight in her head. But it didn't last long.

Any serving member of SIS would have broken into the *Kongresszentrum*. Make a detailed but sharp search of the premises with the aim of spooking an assassin. They'd go in armed if possible. If not, they would find a makeshift weapon from somewhere. They would enter quietly and look behind the doors that shielded the seven windows. They may not be able to disarm the shooter, but they would stop him.

Professional assassins were never ideological. They do a job and they do it secretly. And every contract has a get-out clause. If someone interrupts their shoot, they bail out. Ready for the next job.

She should break into the *Kongresszentrum*. Stop the sniper. She should do that.

I should.

But she didn't. The siren was enchanting; mystical - like a siren should be. It pulled at her. Dragged her to an abyss. It fought protocol and common sense. It was overwhelming.

She walked.

The siren got louder.

She was 100 metres from the Hilton. She could see the front door. A smartly-dressed porter held open a gold-handled door for guests dressed for a banquet. Tuxes and cocktail dresses. Furs and beautifully tailored, long woollen coats. Black ties and big jewels.

Eighty metres now. It was a trance-like approach. Iron filings to a magnet. Her brain was fluff. She had no plan. She had no weapon - not even her wit. She was heading for a fight there was no way she could win.

Nee-naw.

The red car, as Frank had described. It was decelerating as it neared the entrance to the Hilton. Heading in her direction as she crossed the road and joined the pavement that ran alongside the front of the hotel.

Sixty metres.

She should run?

No. She couldn't.

The siren had stopped, but the flashing lights continued. The car was at the entrance to the hotel. The porter hesitantly opened the kerbside door of the car.

Sam stopped.

Waited.

It took a few seconds for the man to unfurl himself from the back seat of the red car with white flashes.

He stood.

Forester stood.

It was him.

A small crowd, who had previously been trying to get into the hotel, had paused. Forester greeted them. There was bonhomie. And smiles.

Sam tried to shout something. She didn't know what. But nothing came out.

She tried to move. But nothing worked.

And then they were gone. Inside the hotel. Into the warmth. Away from the cold. And the snow.

Sam hadn't realised there was an accumulation of snowflakes on her eyelashes. Her shoulders were white, as was her beanie. If she stood still much longer she would be covered. Someone would put some lumps of coal down her front and a carrot where her nose was.

Her brain gave no instructions.

She stood. Fixed. An immovable object; a depository for snow.

And then she saw Frank. He was jogging past the red car. He hadn't been in her earlier dreams of tomorrow's new life. The one with the nights in and pub meals out. She'd excluded him from the equation. He was too good for her. She would bring him down. He deserved better.

Maybe Tony did too?

She hated herself then. She hated herself for thinking Tony would want her regardless of the fact she was a freak.

'Sam!'

Frank was beside her. She looked at him. He was red-faced and out of breath, his back bent slightly, his hands on his thighs.

'I thought you were going to the *Kongresszentrum*?'

Poor Frank. He loved her, and she couldn't love him back. She had too much else going on upstairs. Her mind was locked in a duel. There was no room for company.

'Sam!'

He'd raised his voice. Her eyes moved. Looked him up and down. Trying to take in her new world. The one where she was here and now - but not quite. She had form, but no control. It was an inner body experience.

'Sam. It's Frank. Come on, we've got things to do. You wanted me to get the blinds closed in the conference suite. I need to do that. You need to get to the *Kongresszentrum* and disrupt any potential shooters.'

She stared at him.

He lifted his hand and waved it in front of her eyes.

She saw that. And had heard every word. But there was a disconnect. The words were for somebody else's ears.

Smack!

Frank slapped her across the face. It wasn't a gentle slap, like waking a drunk from the couch. It was a full-strength, angry smack.

And it stung like hell.

Stars. Connections.

'What the hell are you playing at, Frank?'

She was back. She didn't know for how long. But everything was connected again. She instantly raised her hand to hit him back. He dipped his head and raised his own hands in submission.

'Sorry, you … just … well …' A whimper from Frank.

The tension fell away. She lowered her hand. She moved her jaw to lessen the pain in her cheek.

Her mind raced.

'Me too. Sorry.'

Think.

'Go and do as I asked. You create a diversion, close the blinds - do something. I'll deal with Forester and the shooter. I reckon I can do one before I do the other. We've maybe got an hour.'

'How come. They'll be in the conference room any moment now.'

'The sniper will wait for the speeches. I'm pretty sure of it. And we're looking for one of those seven windows on the *Kongresszentrum* to open, the ones up and to the right of the main entrance.' Sam was pointing. 'As soon as one does you've got no more than three minutes. Now go!'

Chapter 21

Sam gave Frank a 15 second head start whilst she came up with a plan - which didn't transpire. With no obvious option materialising she applied her 'sod it' principle and followed him through the main entrance. Forester had a couple of minutes on them. He'd be at the bar, or in an adjoining reception room where the guests would be up to their collars in cocktails and canapes.

She needed to find him. She wanted him to know she was here. That would be enough for her for now. He couldn't touch her in public. But she could unnerve him. Let him know he was not alone. That his plan was unravelling. Maybe then he'd do something rash which would make him easier to find next time.

The porter opened the door for her and as soon as she was in the warm she took off her beanie and jacket. Underneath she was wearing a black roll-neck, a green and red chequered fleece gilet and blue, heavy-cotton trekking trousers. And walking shoes. She was hardly dressed for a party.

It would have to do.

The *Seehorn* conference suite was up a short flight of steps to her right. A second set of doors to its left led to another, smaller room on which poshly-dressed guests were converging. Through the melee Sam spotted an elaborate candelabra and small circles of people oozing confidence - and money.

Movement to her left.

There!

The Dalai Lama. As per his *Twitter* profile. Orange, red and yellow robes. Round glasses. Big eyebrows. Sandaled feet. A genuine smile that would turn the devil.

And ...

... Forester. She hadn't spotted him before. He must have been hidden behind a pillar.

The Dalai Lama was heading for the smaller room. Forester was on intercept.

Sam moved. Quickly.

There were three other monks with the main man. She dodged them, only to the extent that one reached for her and grabbed her by the arm. She let her arm go to its full extent, dragging behind her ... but it didn't stop her getting to the Dalai Lama's side.

He noticed her immediately. And stopped. And smiled.

Sam bowed, a reverential nod.

'Your Holiness.' She held out her hand. She'd heard The Queen didn't like to be touched and to do so would land you in the Tower. She had no idea if the same rules applied here.

She felt the warm touch of an immense but gentle human being, and immediately sensed a surge of goodness flowing through her. The minder monk let go of her arm.

'Yes, child. How may I help you?' Perfect English.

Sam's mind went into overdrive. In a few seconds he had done so much already. But there was still more to be done.

'I think, your Holiness, I might ask this woman to leave you in peace.'

It was Forester. He was in the circle now. All sharp creases, starched shirt and patent leather shoes. Sam glanced at him. She could do no more.

'Not at all ... mister?' The Dalai Lama replied.

Forester didn't answer.

With me here he's having to work through his aliases.

'His name is Freddie Forester, your Holiness.' Sam filled the void.

She'd said it. Out loud. The 'F' word. The Dalai Lama had given her renewed strength.

'And he's ...' She was being lifted from her feet. A hand under each armpit. Two beefy, Hilton security guards were on her. They dragged her away. '... planning to have you assassinated!' She shouted the final words over her shoulder, her eyes keeping contact with the Dalai Lama's. His look was one of bewilderment. But not fear.

And then he was gone. Taken into the second room by his monk entourage, followed closely by Forester, who didn't look back.

They literally threw her into a small office. She pivoted off a desk and managed to find a seat to collapse into.

One of the security men entered with her. The other closed the door from the outside.

'Who are you?' The man's English was good, with a German clip.

Who am I now?

Her mind raced for the right answer. She went for something close to the truth.

'Sam Green. I'm working with the British Special Intelligence Service. I don't have a card, but if you let me use my phone ...' She reached for her pocket.

'Don't even think about it!' He grabbed her wrist. And squeezed it - hard.

'Shit! Stop that, for Christ's sake. I'm a British citizen. You can't hold me here. Let me go!'

The security guard released her hand and stood to his full height. Sam reckoned he was 1.90 cm and weighed the same as an elephant seal. His clothes didn't quite fit. They probably didn't make them big enough. The buttons on his shirt were close to needing a license.

'We've called the police. I'm holding you here until they arrive.'

Great.

'How long's that?'

He shrugged his shoulders.

Sam looked around the room: desk; no window; coat stand; two chairs - she was sitting on one. The desk had an old fashioned in-tray, a computer monitor, keyboard and mouse. And a stapler.

A stapler.

It wasn't lined up with the side of the desk, which irked her.

'They're going to assassinate the Dalai Lama. There's a sniper in the *Kongresszentrum*. I've been sent here to stop it. I was warning His Holiness when you stopped me. If he dies it will be on your head.'

He snorted.

'I do as I am told. That is all. Orders.'

Sam didn't think that would have held up well at Nuremberg.

'I need the loo.'

The elephant seal stood firm.

'The toilet. *Toilette.*' She raised her voice.

Nothing from the elephant seal.

She closed her eyes.

And yelled.

'HELP! HELP! HELP!' She kept on yelling.

It took the big man five seconds to realise he had a problem on his hands. When Sam lifted up her roll neck and pulled a boob from her bra and started yelling, 'RAPE! RAPE! RAPE!', he was completely at sea.

He dithered. Turned to the door, and then turned back. And turned again.

Which was a mistake.

Sam grabbed the stapler and, holding it in a flat hand, smashed it on the back of the big man's head.

It was about speed. Mass multiplied by velocity equals momentum. Small mass; quick velocity. Lots of momentum. It was going to hurt.

She thought she'd broken a bone in her hand, but didn't have time to worry about it The man the size of an elephant seal probably thought he had a broken bone in his head and whilst his brain didn't shut down, the pain was so bad he fell to his knees and brought his hands to the back of his head to protect himself from further attack.

He may be big, but he's no soldier.

Sam seized the opportunity. She slipped round the elephant seal with the bleeding head, and shot out of the door into the corridor.

Where she ran into a woman.

A receptionist?

Sam realised she was still in a state of undress, did some work with her midriff to cover herself up, and said, 'The man in there. He was trying to rape me. I've got away, but I think I hurt him. Sorry.' And then she was off.

Sam made the atrium a second later. It looked like the final guests were entering the conference room. The elephant seal's buddy was standing by the door, arms folded. The main door was a no-go.

Think.

What about the other door, the one that lead to the kitchen? On the opposite side of the room?

Or the *Kongresszentrum*?

The choice was made for her.

'*Halt!*' The shout came from behind. She looked. The elephant seal, one hand on the back of his head, was lumbering her way.

Three seconds later she was out in the cold.

Shit.

She'd left her coat and beanie in the pretend-rape room. Her phone was in her coat. She was out of touch with the world. With Frank. And Carla.

She was on her own.

Shit!

The hotel door was forced open. The elephant seal was still in pursuit.

Sam legged it. Hard right. Then right again, away from the *Kongresszentrum*, and then left. Past a bank. A backlit yellow sign telling everyone what make the bank was. A couple, walking casually in the snow. She must have looked like an idiot. Running. Near naked. Freezing temperatures and a skip load of snow.

Left. Down to a jog. Then a brisk walk. She was back out onto the main road now, the one that ran back towards the hotel. The *Kongresszentrum* was off to her right, slightly elevated. She thought as she walked. The snow would present a bit of a problem for the shooter. It wouldn't affect the trajectory of the round, but acquiring the target would be like taking a shot at an old-fashioned TV picture which was suffering from interference. Maybe the Gods were keeping an eye on His Holiness?

She'd have to make sure.

Sam looked back to the hotel. The porter was still there, stamping his feet to aid circulation. Watching him made her shiver involuntarily. No sign of the elephant seal.

Go.

She jogged from shadow to shadow, trying her best to keep out of sight of both the entrance to the hotel and the seven marksman windows. It took her a couple of minutes to make it to the rear of the *Kongresszentrum*.

The back of the building was unsculptured. More vertical planks of wood. Fewer windows. A shed-like extension, with gates and bins. She jogged along the wall until she came to a door. It was grey metal. She knew straight away it would be impossible to open, but she tried it anyway, the metal handle cold enough to invite her skin to stay for a while.

She jogged along some more.

The large bin shed. She could scale one of the gates, but on inspection into its interior it looked like it was a covered space to keep the bins tidy and the elements out - nothing else. There didn't appear to be any entrances to the main building inside the shed.

She jogged round the shed. The *Kongresszentrum* held few surprises. Another locked, ice-cold metal door.

Now the final side.

It was darker. There was no ambient light, and plenty of shade from a clump of close-to pine trees.

The side of the building was more wooden planks and ...

... an external fire escape? A zig-zag of grey metal steps surrounded by a wooden frame.

Perfect.

She jogged to the steps. There was a sturdy gate, over two metres tall. It was locked. She looked around, straining to take in as much light as possible. *There.* At the first landing. There was a key in a yellow 'break glass here' contraption. It was out of reach.

Sam stepped back. Could she scale the gate?

Possibly.

There was an almost Sam-sized gap between the top of the gate and a horizontal metal truss. It would have to do.

She found a foothold on the upright bars and put her hands on top of the gate. Her fingers gave a squeal of discontent as the cold of the surface leeched the remaining heat from her hands.

Up.

She put her head to one side and squeezed it through the gap. Then her right arm, which reached down and held a vertical metal bar at stomach level. Then she wriggled her shoulders.

And pushed.

And wriggled.

And put her left arm through.

Her shoulders were through.

Her boobs would protest, but they would get over it.

And then ...

'*Halt!*'

She recognised the voice straight away. It was the elephant seal.

And now they were in a race.

Sam needed to be on the right side of the gate. And he needed to be on the wrong side.

She had no idea how long she had. So she assumed she had none.

It was painful. And exhausting. And humiliating.

She wriggled.

And pulled.

And pushed.

...

And lost.

The elephant seal may not have known how to win a street fight in a small room with a girl, but he knew how to extract a female who was stuck in a metal fence.

Brute force. Which he had lots of.

He pulled her to the floor by her legs. Sam collapsed like her puppet strings had been severed.

She was bruised all over. She knew she had scrapes down her front, and along her shoulders. As the elephant seal pulled her from the grasps of the gate, she'd caught her chin on the top metal bar and she lost a chunk of flesh. There was a lots of blood, which made it look worse than it was, but it was still bloody sore.

And then the elephant seal lifted her from the ground, locked Sam's left arm behind her, pushed it high ... and it popped out of its socket.

The pain was instant and overwhelming. To which her brain said, 'sod this', and she passed out.

Forest Clearing, Davos, Switzerland

Sam woke and her senses kicked in immediately.

Cold. Ice. Snow on the ground - and still falling. There was little light. Trees. The sound of rushing water. A river. In spate. She could hear it, but couldn't see it.

Fuck, that's cold.

She lifted her cheek from the ground. The relief was worth the effort, although her shoulder screamed blue murder.

She was wet. She was in the same clothes she'd been wearing before the elephant seal had caught her. They clung to her as only damp fabric could. Her side resting on the ground was numb with cold. The rest of her hurt in spasms, like freezing fingers after a long snowball fight.

Her hands were bound behind her back with cable ties. As were her feet. Crude and extremely effective. She tried to move her legs. They protested. Against advice she raised her shoulders. An inch was possible.

Two?

Nope. Don't like that.

Her head flopped back onto ground. Her dislocated shoulder stopped yelling at her, but her cheek took over.

Where am I?

A forest, by a river.

She listened.

A torrent of water. Nothing else.

She was in a clearing, on gravelly ground. A car park in the woods? She had no idea.

Why have they trussed me and left me in the woods?

It didn't make sense.

A police cell made sense.

Force-fed alcohol and thrown deep in the forest, partially-dressed made sense.

Drunk British tourist gets lost in the woods and succumbs to the cold.

That would run for a day in *The Daily Mirror.*

Being kidnapped, cable-tied and dropped in a clearing in the trees to die from the cold presented far too many unanswered questions. It would be an international incident. The broadsheets would run with it for a week.

It didn't make any sense.

The noise from the water filled her ears. She felt she was facing the wrong way and with her hearing overwhelmed she had lost a vital sense. She needed to stand up and get out of here. She had some reserves of energy. She'd make an attempt to hop to a road. Or a house. Something. Somebody.

Lay on your back. And then sit up.

She tried that.

Twice.

Both times her shoulder jabbed at her as if a javelin was sticking out of the socket.

Stars and dizziness.

And an incomprehensible tiredness.

Reserves of energy?

Who was she kidding?

One more time.

Push. Twist. *Ouch, my hands.*

No.

Her shoulder's protests were deafening. She kept trying.

Got it.

She was there. On her back, her chin high, her head pushing into the ground, arching her back - finding room for her hands and arms.

Sit!

Sam was good at sit-ups. She'd do 50 after a run. Her feet held firm under an object, like a chest of drawers, and then 'hands behind her head', and sit. One, two, three … 48, 49, 50. The last ten were always a struggle, her stomach muscles sore, but she managed it.

All she had to do now was one … with her hands tied behind her back.

And her shoulder inconsolable.

She closed her eyes, as though that was going to help.

As though …

Come on.

Sit.

It was jerky and slow, and required two attempts, but she was up. Straight away her shoulder felt slightly better.

Good.

She opened her eyes and glanced around.

And immediately closed them again.

She'd heard fear can make a person wet themselves.

It was true.

Sam felt a trickle of warm urine soak through the crotch of her trousers. Whilst despair was already telling her not to bother, she pulled her pelvic floor muscles together and arrested the flow.

'Hello, Sam Green.'

She kept her eyes closed. She didn't want to look at the shadowy image that was sitting on a camping chair a couple of metres from her.

'You are tenacious, aren't you?' There was a lightness, a playfulness to his voice. It was theatrical. Almost comedic.

She kept her eyes closed. A void filled where there used to be thought. Her ears tightened. Every muscle in her body tensed. Her breathing shallowed - and quickened.

'Look, I have to congratulate you. Mmm?' An adult talking to a child. Which wasn't far from the truth. She was lost. He had found her. Like a disoriented kid in a supermarket now back in their parent's grasp.

'I know you were behind the Venezuelan fiasco. That was unfortunate. And then, popping up in Calabria? At the wedding, of all places? Well done you.' Bordering on sarcasm. 'And last night - in Zermatt? I was convinced you would try to find me - make some connection or other. Did you get burnt?'

She heard a crunch. She couldn't see; her eyes still closed.

Shoes on gravel. He was on his feet. Two steps. A pause. He had his hand under her bloody chin. He lifted it and turned her face from side to side. It all hurt. Everything hurt.

'Ahh. You did get a bit burnt, didn't you? You should be more careful.' That comic tone again.

He let go of her chin. There was more crunching of feet on gravel. He may have sat back down. Possibly not. She didn't know. Someone was telling her not to care.

'And now here, in Davos. My night with His Holiness. You almost spoiled it … in fact you have.' His tone had changed. The lightness gone. Menace had replaced it. 'Let's be clear about this.' He paused.

A footstep in my direction?

'I should be finishing my …'

Smack!

The new venom in his voice was accompanied by a blow to her face. She felt metal. And heard the crack of bone. She toppled. And tasted blood.

'… main …' A kick to her stomach. It was lost in the overmatching of pain which already flooded her senses. The dial was set at 'maximum', there was no room for it to go any higher.

'… course …'

He stamped on her ankle. Something may have broken. She didn't know.

She didn't care.

Sam sensed he was pacing. Frustrated. She didn't think he had sat down again.

She didn't think.

'Look at me, Green.'

Nope.

'Look. At. Me.' Anger bordering on madness.

Nope.

Nothing would make her open her eyes. She couldn't. It would be too awful. Any image would add form to the horror which was bad enough in the abstract.

He was close again now.

She felt it.

Her bladder relapsed. Much needed warmth spread between her legs.

She'd given in.

He was so close she could smell his breath. Still fresh. A touch of mint.

Jab.

Metal. In her face. On her cheek. She smelt it too.

And gun oil. And … spent cordite.

This is it.

This was it.

'Bye-bye, Sam Green.'

BANG!

Black.

Kongresszentrum, *Davos, Switzerland*

Ergorov was settled on the platform. This time he had his rifle with him. The front bipod was ten centimetres back from the edge of the table. The stock was in his shoulder and his cheek was resting on his right hand which was curled around the top of the stock, his index finger extended into the pistol grip.

He'd opened the window three minutes ago, twenty seconds after his target had stood up to make his after-dinner speech. He'd observed all of that from the back of the classroom, had walked briskly back to the toilet, opened the window and found his place.

Earlier he'd almost abandoned the mission. He had typed an 'Abort' message to send to his contact and was about to press 'Send' when the large man had appeared with the girl. He had her in an armlock and was pushing her in front of him, back towards the hotel. She seemed barely awake.

He'd watched the soap opera unfold over the past couple of hours, but was missing chunks of the plot.

It started with the girl and another shorter man outside the hotel; they'd both disappeared inside. Twenty minutes later she'd come out of the hotel in a fluster, and ran away from the entrance - left, into town. The large man had followed her out of the hotel, but hadn't pursued her down the road. Instead, looking frustrated, he'd gone back inside.

He'd lost the girl at that point and thought nothing more of it. Until the large man in a suit had jogged over from the hotel to the front of the *Kongresszentrum*. He then disappeared from view around the left hand side of the building. That's when Ergorov had set up to abort.

He had no idea what was happening. What was the large man doing at the *Kongresszentrum*? Was he trying to get in? It was all too close to home for comfort. Ergorov could leave by any door and was already working on which of those four would be the best option when the large man had appeared with the girl, round from his right. And they'd headed off to the hotel.

At that moment things had got really bizarre. A smart black Bentley had pulled up on the main road and the girl had been thrown in the back and the car had taken off. The large man had dusted himself off and gone back inside the hotel.

Was it a lovers' tiff? Was she a hooker? Was this part of some bizarre sex ritual?

Whatever.

He'd thought about it for a second and then decided not to abort. Failing a customer was always an option for him. His reputation was bigger than one missed opportunity. But it was always a last resort.

The excursion with the large man and the girl was an hour and a half ago. Now he was back on task. Doing what he did best.

To be certain he didn't lose the target he reckoned he had a maximum of five minutes to fire off the shot.

Plenty of time.

Get set.

He started his routine.

Tense. Untense. Feet. Legs. Torso. Neck. And face.

Relax.

He looked over the top of the sight. The target was still standing.

Breathe in. Hold.

Breathe out. Hold.

He brought his eye to the back of the scope. He adjusted the crosshairs with a small movement of his right hand.

Dead centre.

Breathe in. Hold.

Breathe out. Hold.

Nothing had moved. Everything was as it was.

As always his right eye looked through the scope whilst his left relaxed and took in a much wider field of view. It was an art, using both eyes to get two different perspectives. Not many snipers could manage it. It was natural to him.

Breathe in.

Hold.

Breathe out.

Hold.

He concentrated on his heart beat. It was slowing down.

Breathe in.

Hold.

Breathe out.

Hold.

Look.

Nothing had changed.

What?

His left eye was now telling a different story.

The blinds are closing from the sides!

How long did he have?

His pulse rate had stopped slowing; it had started to rise.

Five seconds maybe.

Breathe in. Hold. Breathe out. Hold.

This wasn't going to plan.

Hold.

Crosshairs on.

Gently squeeze the trigger.

Never force the pull. Let the shot surprise you.

Hold.

No!

The target had moved. He had dropped his head and shoulders, looking to his right. His head no longer in the crosshairs.

What should ...

The blinds answered the question for him. The target had disappeared behind them.

Epilogue

Anbu's Convenience Store, Orpington, London, UK

Five weeks later

Frank checked the list pegged to the front of the shopping trolley.

Lettuce, cucumber and radishes.

They'd be ... *over there.*

He wandered in the direction of the small fruit and vegetable stand. He looked at each item curiously before placing them in his basket. Next was ...

Oily fish.

That's something like mackerel. Pilchards?

He asked a woman who was on her knees packing shelves. She directed him a couple of aisles further down. On the way he spotted a bag of Brussel sprouts and some carrots. He'd have some of those.

Next: camomile tea. And sweeteners. Not ones with saccharin, which was linked to some cancers. Apparently.

Soya milk. Brown bread with lots of nuts and seeds. And oats for porridge.

It took Frank another 15 minutes to fill his trolley. He was beginning to get used to where these things were in the store. He'd have it under control in a week or so.

He paid the cashier, placed all his goods in his own 'bag in a bag' and headed out into the cold. It was *cold*. Bitterly so. He'd checked the weather before he'd left the office. The sun may have been out this afternoon and the temperature had nudged above zero but, as soon as it had disappeared behind Battersea Power Station the heat had chased after it. It was freezing now and the BBC reckoned it would touch minus three overnight. It would be another brisk walk and tube to work tomorrow, wrapped up well with many layers. He'd got his thermals out of the bottom drawer of his wardrobe last night. He couldn't see them going back there anytime soon.

It was ten minutes to his house, a Victorian two-up, two-down with a single bay window and a navy blue door with brass accoutrements - surrounded by an ornate white frame. It was big for a small house: a sitting-dining front room - with a fireplace, and a kitchen at the back looking over a long, thin back garden. The two were joined by a hallway and a loo under the stairs. Two large bedrooms and a 'family bathroom' completed the living space. The attic was huge and could be converted - his neighbour had led the way, Velux windows and everything.

He was very proud of his home. And it was his. Actually, it was mostly the bank's, but unless SIS cut posts willy-nilly he was well on top of the mortgage and he even managed some spare cash at the end of the month that made it into savings.

He crossed the street from between tightly parked cars. That was an issue in his street, but not for him. He didn't need a car in London.

Home.

He pulled a glove off with his teeth, fumbled for his keys and opened the door. Warm air rushed out to heat the rest of Orpington. He was inside as fast as he could, pushing the door closed with his bum.

'Ifs eee!' His words made no sense because his tongue had been usurped by the suede of a glove. But it was obviously a friendly call. Not one from an intruder.

The hall led to the kitchen and he passed the closed lounge door on his left. He put the bag of food on the pine kitchen table, reached behind and found the light switch, disrobed and put the kettle on - all in some sort of efficient sequence.

Two mugs later, one camomile with a non-carcinogenic sweetener, the other builders' - government standard - and he headed back into the hall. Before he opened the lounge door he turned on a small lamp that was on a hip-height table. The bulb lit a nicely-decorated space; the walls and cornices painted mute greens and greys. The black and reds of the polished diamond-tiled floor added depth and context. He'd recently bought a narrow green woollen runner from IKEA which kept delicate feet warm. He stopped and admired the view. Yes, he'd done a good job.

It was home. And he loved it.

He transferred a mug from one hand to another so he was carrying both in one hand. He squeezed and turned the round, brass handle with his free hand and the door into the sitting room opened.

It was semi-dark. The only light was from a distant, sharp-white streetlamp that apologetically slipped in through the bay window; although that was now mixed with the much warmer light from the hall.

He waited. And looked.

As far as he could tell nothing had changed. The cushions on the sofa and chair were unruffled and the TV's standby light was off – no one had turned it on. And the curtains were still drawn.

And she was there. Sitting on the window's bench seat. Knees to chest, her arms holding her legs tight, her mouth kissing the bottom of her thighs and her pointy nose resting on the patella of her left knee. She was staring out of the window – exactly as he'd left her this morning, her eyes fixed at some point in space.

'Hi, Sam.'

She lifted her head and slowly turned it towards him.

Was that a smile? It was difficult to tell in the dark.

'I got some oily fish. And the salad. We'll use the dressing from last night?'

A nod. Almost imperceptible. But it was there.

'How have you been?'

Another tiny smile. And then she turned her head back towards the street.

Avoiding the dark-wood coffee table, which was decorated with a small bunch of flowers in a simple glass vase, Frank turned on the modern, metal and glass standard lamp and then a Chinese-based lamp on a table in the far corner of the room.

Still carrying the two mugs he sat on the window seat next to Sam. He offered her her camomile tea. She took it and acknowledged the hot drink with another shallow smile. And then she refocused on whatever it was outside that had previously held her attention.

Frank studied her.

Had there been an improvement? Was she more communicative now than when she'd been released from hospital? He thought so. Yes, she still hadn't uttered a word since she'd been found in the forest in Davos. And whilst she was able to function normally - eat, sleep, ablute - everything was carried out at the pace of a snail. She was as lifeless as a person could be, without being in a coma. But there had been an improvement?

The doctors had given no prognosis. Violent shock on top of PTSD and an already overactive anxiety complex had taken Sam's mind into unknown territory. The psychiatrists hadn't added to Sam's already ambitious portfolio of complex conditions, but they'd agreed she was no threat to herself, or anyone else. However, unless she had somewhere to go where she could be monitored and, ideally looked after, they strongly suggested she was either sectioned or taken into adult care somewhere.

Frank couldn't accept either option. No way. He'd visited Sam every day in Tommie's and was sort of acting as next of kin; technically Sam didn't have one. Very quickly the doctors deferred to him as Sam had been unwilling to speak and very disinclined to communicate in any other way. The only instructions she'd given in four weeks in hospital were scribbled dietary ones. Early on, and when Frank was at her bedside, whenever the doctors or nurses had asked Sam a question, she looked to him with a blank expression. They'd followed her gaze and he'd answered on her behalf - initially hesitantly, and latterly with more confidence.

Much of the problem was the hospital staff didn't know the half of it. Nor the psychiatrists. There was an SIS 'red notice' on the events in Switzerland and only an agreed, short paragraph for external consumption. All the hospital had been told was Sam had been beaten up abroad. She'd arrived with a broken jaw, a smashed talus and abrasions over her chest and hips. Before she'd got to Tommie's the local medics had rescued her - again - from hypothermia. That was a footnote in the brief.

Frank had been the first Brit at the scene. He'd got the call from Carla who had been working the Swiss municipal police. With GCHQ help, she'd hacked into their radio frequency and had picked up that a woman - matching Sam's description - and a man had been found in a forest on the edge of Davos. The man was dead - gunshot wound to the back of the head. The woman was 'touch and go', having been badly beaten and left to die in the cold.

Immediately before Carla's call Frank had managed to get the blinds closed in the conference room. The police and the hotel staff were having none of it, no matter who he spoke to. Neither Carla nor the British Embassy had been able to force the issue via their external contacts. However, in a really decent hack, Carla had found the location of the control box for the blinds. It was in the conference room itself, to the right of the blinds. If all else failed ...

Which they had.

Whilst keeping an eye on the *Kongresszentrum* Frank spotted one of Sam's 'shooter's windows' open. He immediately knew what was about to unfold.

He'd had no choice. If the Swiss weren't prepared to save the Dalai Lama, then it was up to him.

He'd opened the conference room door and slipped in. The guest of honour was on his feet. He had started his speech and the room was a hush. Frank had a quick look at the picture windows, but couldn't see much because of the reflection from within.

He'd then taken a deep breath ... and with the confidence of ten men, which he didn't feel, he'd walked slowly down the side of the room. One or two guests gave him funny looks. One had to push their chair closer to their table so he could squeeze past. He found the control box within seconds, had a quick scan of the buttons and pressed the one marked, '*Schließen*' - another inspired pass from Carla.

To his surprise - and huge relief - the blinds whirred quietly towards the centre.

And then his phone rang.

Shit!

There was a murmur from the room. The Dalai Lama paused, looked across at Frank and smiled. Frank mouthed, 'Sorry'. The guest of honour smiled back and carried on talking. Frank muted his phone and was out of the room a few seconds after that, his phone to his ear.

Carla gave him the news from the police radio. And some directions.

The dead man and the freezing woman were about a mile away.

Frank ran. And ran.

He got the directions slightly wrong, but was quickly able to relocate when he saw the flashing lights deeper into the forest. On his final, punishing couple of hundred metres he jogged passed a matt black Bentley which was parked incongruously on a muddy track.

Ten metres later he was at the scene.

And he immediately threw up.

Lit by the red and blue strobe of a police car were the remnants of a man whom he assumed was Freddie Forester; it was difficult to tell. He was dressed in a severely ripped and blooded evening dress, his black bow tie still round his neck, but pushed off to one side. And he was pinned to a tree by three bloodied metal stakes. One was through his throat, a second sticking out of his chest, and a third piercing his groin. His faceless head fell forward onto his previously white, golf-ball indented dress shirt. Red and brown and cream gunge dripped from what was left of his chin.

Frank threw up again. Whitey-grey snow by his feet turned pizza.

Sam?!

She was there. In the front seat of the police car. She had her eyes open; unblinking. Her face was a mess.

She was staring through the same red, brown and cream mush that was falling from Forester's face. Frank stepped forward to check on her, but an unseen policeman, the only one on the scene, intercepted him.

'*Wer bist du*?!' He shouted.

The policeman, who looked younger than Frank, was gaunt and frightened.

'Friend. *Freund.*' He pointed towards Sam. 'Can I look at her?'

The policeman's car radio burst into life. The German was lost on Frank. He wasn't concentrating. He had to see Sam.

The policeman dithered, but the radio won. He left Frank and jogged round to the driver's side of the car, creating an opening.

Frank stepped forward and then knelt beside her, ignoring the ground's slushy mud. She was something from a horror story. Her face was covered in blood and goo, and she was shivering uncontrollably.

'Are you OK?'

Her face was misshapen. He sensed there was some of her own blood in among the mess, which he guessed was from the corpse. And one shoulder was unnaturally higher than the other.

'Get an ambulance!' He shouted.

There was more German from the policeman, and more in return from the radio.

'Are you OK, Sam?'

She continued to stare straight ahead. He followed her gaze.

She was looking at the dangling corpse. And her look was unwavering. Fixated.

Then, breaking his concentration, more lights flashed off to his left. Red and blue.

Hopefully it's an ambulance.

He took Sam's hands in his. Ice lollies into warm tea. She didn't flinch.

Less than a minute later there were more green vests with drips and blankets than were probably necessary. As two gentle male nurses helped Sam into the back of the ambulance, Frank noticed she was wearing a winter coat he'd not seen before. It was fawn coloured. Wool? And it had brown leather buttons on its front and at the end of its sleeves. It looked expensive.

It hadn't taken much to persuade the nurses to allow him to jump in the back of the ambulance. Twenty-five minutes later Sam was in the best possible hands, and a member of the British Embassy was *en route* from Bern.

A day later she was medevac-ed by the RAF to the UK, and blue-lighted into Tommie's. Frank had stayed with her every step of the way.

Without Sam's support - she remained insistently mute - it had taken him and Carla three days to piece together the story. Freddie Forester had caught Sam, taken her into the forest and, by the state of the marks on her hands and ankles, cable-tied her - and then beat her. Her body was badly lacerated and her cheek and an ankle bone were broken. The next assumption was that Freddie had put a gun to her head with the intent of murdering her. The police had found a pistol covered with Forester's prints next to his feet.

However, Forester had been shot in the back of the head with a 9 millimetre round, possibly a Beretta. At that point Forester's corpse had been nailed to a tree, and Sam wrapped in a *Gino Valentino* coat worth over 3,000 euros. A short time afterwards the Swiss municipal police had been called. They'd arrived at the scene ten minutes later. Frank, five minutes after that.

It was a start. But there was a vital piece of the puzzle missing: who had killed Forester?

A day later Frank had found the first piece of evidence that started to unlock that question.

He'd been looking through Sam's mobile's call and message log. At the end of a late night visit to Tommies, he'd asked her if she minded; she'd nodded her head.

None of the very recent traffic surprised him as he'd been with her most of that time. But there was a very odd text message sent 36 hours before Davos that needed unpicking.

She'd sent it to a 'G'. It read:

Tell your Dad that the smartly dressed Englishman at your wedding, Freddie Derwent, is going to rat on him and his Mafia pals. It's the only way to make the money work. Please. Sam xxx

Frank had drunk a lot of tea and spent at least an hour in the mood room until he had it. 'G' was Giorgio. And the message to his Mafia dad was that Freddie Forester (or Derwent as he was described in the wedding list) was going to provide evidence to 'the authorities' that the 'Ndràngheta were the organisation behind the 'neo-terrorism' attacks. Once The Mafia had been blown apart the world would calm down and the markets could rise quickly with confidence. Millions would become billions. Billions would become many billions. The world would have its terrorists. Freddie, and his investors, their money.

Frank was sure the Mafia had killed Forester because of Sam's text message.

But on its own the text message wasn't enough. It was supposition. What he and Carla needed was something more.

And she'd found it.

Whilst the US attack on the 'Ndràngheta had been extremely successful, if slightly over the top, Andrea Placido had not been arrested; The Unit couldn't find him. Nobody could. He wasn't at his villa or at any other of the known 'Ndràngheta locations. And he was still at large, even now.

And that's because when they had carried out their raids he was in a forest in Switzerland. With a 9mm Beretta.

Carla had become fixated with the coat Sam had been wearing when Frank had found her. As Frank had unpicked Sam's text message, Carla had scoured the internet and discovered where the coat had been bought, and who the customers might have been. Unsurprisingly, on the back of the mass media attention of the dismantling of the 'Ndràngheta, the CEO of *Gino Valentino* had opened his books to the British Embassy in Rome without protest. Sure enough, just over three years ago in Salerno an Andrea Placido had bought a coat matching the one worn by Sam in the forest. To be certain, Carla had painstakingly looked through all of the intelligence on Andrea Placido and every piece of Calabrian media that had his name tagged to it.

When she'd found a photo of Placido in the Italian paper, *Il Messaggero,* wearing *exactly* the same coat, she'd danced over to Frank's workstation singing, *Now That I've Found You,* by The Temptations.

It was all they needed. And it was a helluva story.

Without telling anyone and by way of some insurance, Sam had warned off the 'Ndràngheta that Forester was going to 'dob them in' - sometime soon. And, although she had no idea it would work out this way, her text had saved her life.

Andrea Placido knew where to find Freddie Forester. They were partners in crime. And he had travelled to Davos to kill him. Once that act was complete, and in Mafia tradition, he had turned the assassination into a statement: metal stakes 'n all.

And then, in typically southern Italian, patriarchal fashion, he'd found a woman in distress, untied her, wrapped her in a 3,000 euro coat and called the police.

As a result he'd saved Sam's life.

Again.

In some way Frank had a certain respect for Andrea Placido and was pleased he was still on the run.

Because that meant that Sam was still with them.

And now she was with him.

Sipping her tea.

And still staring out the window, which had attracted an oval of condensation from the steam rising from her mug.

'Shall I put the telly on?' He was never sure if she watched what was on, or just stared at the moving pictures.

Sam let her mug drop below the level of her kneecap.

She nodded, the shortest of nods.

'OK. And I'll go and make our tea?' A light question.

There was no answer. He didn't expect one.

He stood.

And then Sam surprised him. She held her mug by its rim with her left hand and reached out with her right. She gently touched his wrist. A small electrical pulse raced up to his arm and lit a small fire in his head.

She mouthed, 'Thank you'.

He smiled.

'You're welcome, Sam.'

Sam Green books by Roland Ladley:

Unsuspecting Hero

Sam Green's life is in danger of imploding. Suffering from post-traumatic stress disorder after horrific injuries and personal tragedy in Afghanistan, she escapes to the Isle of Mull hoping to convalesce. A chance find on the island's shores interrupts her rehabilitation and launches her on a journey to West Africa and on a collision course with forces and adversaries she cannot begin to comprehend.

Meanwhile in London, SIS/MI6 is facing down a biological threat that could kill thousands and inflame an already smouldering religious war. Time is not on anyone's side and Sam's determination to face her past and control her future, regardless of the risks, looks likely to end in disaster. Fate conspires to bring Sam into the centre of an international conspiracy where she alone has the power to influence world-changing events. Blind to her new-found role, is her military training and complete disregard for her own safety enough to prevent the imminent devastation?

Fuelling the Fire

Why are so many passenger planes falling from the sky? Why are two ex-CIA agents training terrorists in the Yemeni desert? Why is a religious cult transferring millions of dollars to unattributable bank accounts around the world? Are these events connected? If they are, is this the mother of all conspiracies?

MI6 analyst, Sam Green, desperately wants to establish why her only surviving relative died in the latest plane crash. But can she put aside her grief and make sense of it all? Or is the clock ticking just too quickly, even for her?

The Innocence of Trust

Sam Green's been promoted. She's now working out of Moscow as an SIS 'case officer' and hates it. She loathes her boss, feels out of place among SIS's elite and loses her only Russian informant to a bomb that also had her name on it.

On the verge of jacking it all in, Sam promises a beautiful stranger that she will find her boyfriend's murderer. That promise propels her into a web of top-level industrial crime and savage international terrorism. With reliable friends and colleagues in very short supply, Sam starts something she cannot stop. And this time, she's going to need more than an expert analyst's eye and a complete disregard for her own safety to prevent the most lethal terror plot since 9/11.

For Good Men To Do Nothing

Someone's messing with the Global Positioning System and no one knows who, or why. The CIA has intelligence of a major terror attack planned for the Middle East, but they have no idea of when and where. And the ultra right-wing Christian sect, The Church of the White Cross, is back doing what it does best: laying down carnage and inflaming anti-Muslim hatred.

Sam Green's been fired from SIS/MI6 for being a maverick operator and is trying to get her life back together. Skiing on a shoestring in Austria, she spots a face in the crowd. And it's a face that doesn't want to be recognised. But it knows she knows - and that can't be allowed.

Then someone lets slip the dogs of war.

Sam's back; this time without SIS support. Pursued from Europe to Venezuela, via The Bahamas and Miami, her enemies are seemingly one step ahead. With a single act of terror the world could be plunged into a religious war that would last for decades. With only the help of her old German hacking pal, Wolfgang, together can they prevent Armageddon?

+++++

Find Roland Ladley's books here:
https://www.amazon.co.uk/Roland-Ladley/e/B010MAOZOE

And keep in touch via his blog here:
https://thewanderlings2013.wordpress.com/

+++++++

Printed in Great Britain
by Amazon